Tales of the
Napoleonic Era: 1

Tales of the Napoleonic Era: 1

The Chouans, Juana,
An Episode Under the Terror &
The Napoleon of the People

Honoré de Balzac

LEONAUR

Tales of the Napoleonic Era: 1—The Chouans, Juana,
An Episode Under the Terror &The Napoleon of the People
by Honoré de Balzac

Leonaur is an imprint of Oakpast Ltd

ISBN: 978-0-85706-010-5 (hardcover)
ISBN: 978-0-85706-009-9 (softcover)

http://www.leonaur.com

Publisher's Notes

The views expressed in this book are not necessarily
those of the publisher.

Contents

The Chouans

Dedication

To Monsieur Theodore Dablin, merchant.
To my first friend, my first work.

De Balzac

1

An Ambuscade

Early in the year VIII., at the beginning of Vendemiaire, or, to con-
form to our own calendar, towards the close of September, 1799, a
hundred or so of peasants and a large number of citizens, who had left
Fougeres in the morning on their way to Mayenne, were going up the
little mountain of La Pelerine, half-way between Fougeres and Ernee,
a small town where travellers along that road are in the habit of resting. This company, divided into groups that were more or less numerous, presented a collection of such fantastic costumes and a mixture of
individuals belonging to so many and diverse localities and professions
that it will be well to describe their characteristic differences, in order
to give to this history the vivid local colouring to which so much
value is attached in these days,—though some critics do assert that it
injures the representation of sentiments.

Many of the peasants, in fact the greater number, were barefooted,
and wore no other garments than a large goatskin, which covered
them from the neck to the knees, and trousers of white and very
coarse linen, the ill-woven texture of which betrayed the slovenly in-
dustrial habits of the region. The straight locks of their long hair mingling with those of the goatskin hid their faces, which were bent on
the ground, so completely that the garment might have been thought
their own skin, and they themselves mistaken at first sight for a species of the animal which served them as clothing. But through this
tangle of hair their eyes were presently seen to shine like dew-drops
in a thicket, and their glances, full of human intelligence, caused fear
rather than pleasure to those who met them. Their heads were covered with a dirty head-gear of red flannel, not unlike the Phrygian cap
which the Republic had lately adopted as an emblem of liberty. Each
man carried over his shoulder a heavy stick of knotted oak, at the end
of which hung a linen bag with little in it. Some wore, over the red

cap, a coarse felt hat, with a broad brim adorned by a sort of woollen chenille of many colours which was fastened round it. Others were clothed entirely in the coarse linen of which the trousers and wallets of all were made, and showed nothing that was distinctive of the new order of civilization. Their long hair fell upon the collar of a round jacket with square pockets, which reached to the hips only, a garment peculiar to the peasantry of western France. Beneath this jacket, which was worn open, a waistcoat of the same linen with large buttons was visible. Some of the company marched in wooden shoes; others, by way of economy, carried them in their hand. This costume, soiled by long usage, blackened with sweat and dust, and less original than that of the other men, had the historic merit of serving as a transition between the goatskins and the brilliant, almost sumptuous, dress of a few individuals dispersed here and there among the groups, where they shone like flowers. In fact, the blue linen trousers of these last, and their red or yellow waistcoats, adorned with two parallel rows of brass buttons and not unlike breast-plates, stood out as vividly among the white linen and shaggy skins of their companions as the corn-flowers and poppies in a wheat-field. Some of them wore wooden shoes, which the peasants of Brittany make for themselves; but the greater number had heavy hobnailed boots, and coats of coarse cloth cut in the fashion of the old regime, the shape of which the peasants have religiously retained even to the present day. The collars of their shirts were held together by buttons in the shape of hearts or anchors. The wallets of these men seemed to be better than those of their companions, and several of them added to their marching outfit a flask, probably full of brandy, slung round their necks by a bit of twine. A few burgesses were to be seen in the midst of these semi-savages, as if to show the extremes of civilization in this region. Wearing round hats, or flapping brims or caps, high-topped boots, or shoes and gaiters, they exhibited as many and as remarkable differences in their costume as the peasants themselves. About a dozen of them wore the republican jacket known by the name of *la carmagnole*. Others, well-to-do mechanics, no doubt, were clothed from head to foot in one colour. Those who had most pretension to their dress wore swallow-tail coats or *surtouts* of blue or green cloth, more or less defaced. These last, evidently characters, marched in boots of various kinds, swinging heavy canes with the air and manner of those who take heart under misfortune. A few heads carefully powdered, and some queues tolerably well braided showed the sort of care which a beginning of education or prosperity inspires. A casual spectator observing these men, all surprised to find themselves in one another's company, would have thought them the inhabitants of a village driven out by a conflagration. But the period and the region in which they were gave an altogether different interest to this body of men. Any one initiated into the secrets of the civil discords which were then agitating the whole of France could easily have distinguished the few individuals on whose fidelity the Republic might count among these groups, almost entirely made up of men who four years earlier were at war with her.

One other and rather noticeable sign left no doubt upon the opinions which divided the detachment. The Republicans alone marched with an air of gaiety. As to the other individuals of the troop, if their clothes showed marked differences, their faces at least and their attitudes wore a uniform expression of ill-fortune. Citizens and peasantry, their faces all bore the imprint of deepest melancholy; their silence had something sullen in it; they all seemed crushed under the yoke of a single thought, terrible no doubt but carefully concealed, for their faces were impenetrable, the slowness of their gait alone betraying their inward communings. From time to time a few of them, noticeable for the rosaries hanging from their necks (dangerous as it was to carry that sign of a religion which was suppressed, rather than abolished) shook their long hair and raised their heads defiantly. They covertly examined the woods, and paths, and masses of rock which flanked the road, after the manner of a dog with his nose to the wind trying to scent his game; and then, hearing nothing but the monotonous tramp of the silent company, they lowered their heads once more with the old expression of despair, like criminals on their way to the galleys to live or die.

The march of this column upon Mayenne, the heterogeneous elements of which it was composed, and the divers sentiments which evidently pervaded it, will explain the presence of another troop which formed the head of the detachment. About a hundred and fifty soldiers, with arms and baggage, marched in the advance, commanded by the *chief of a half-brigade.* We may mention here, for the benefit of those who did not witness the drama of the Revolution, that this title was made to supersede that of colonel, proscribed by patriots as too aristocratic. These soldiers belonged to a demi-brigade of infantry quartered at Mayenne. During these troublous times the inhabitants of the west of France called all the soldiers of the Republic "Blues." This nickname came originally from their blue and red uniforms, the memory of which is still so fresh as to render a description superfluous. A detachment of the Blues was therefore on this occasion escorting a body of recruits, or rather conscripts, all displeased at being taken to Mayenne where military discipline was about to force upon them the uniformity of thought, clothing, and gait which they now lacked entirely.

This column was a contingent slowly and with difficulty raised in the district of Fougeres, from which it was due under the levy ordered by the executive Directory of the Republic on the preceding 10th Messidor. The government had asked for a hundred million of *francs* and a hundred thousand men as immediate reinforcements for the armies then fighting the Austrians in Italy, the Prussians in Germany, and menaced in Switzerland by the Russians, in whom Suwarow had inspired hopes of the conquest of France. The departments of the West, known under the name of La Vendee, Brittany, and a portion of Lower Normandy, which had been tranquil for the last three years (thanks to the action of General Hoche), after a struggle lasting nearly four, seemed to have seized this new occasion of danger to the nation to break out again. In presence of such aggressions the Republic recovered its pristine energy. It provided in the first place for the defence of the threatened departments by giving the responsibility to the loyal and patriotic portion of the inhabitants. In fact, the government in Paris, having neither troops nor money to send to the interior, evaded the difficulty by a parliamentary *gasconade*. Not being able to send material aid to the faithful citizens of the insurgent departments, it gave them its "confidence." Possibly the government hoped that this measure, by arming the insurgents against each other, would stifle the insurrection at its birth. This ordinance, the cause of future fatal reprisals, was thus worded: "Independent companies of troops shall be organized in the Western departments." This impolitic step drove the West as a body into so hostile an attitude that the Directory despaired of immediately subduing it. Consequently, it asked the Assemblies to pass certain special measures relating to the independent companies authorized by the ordinance. In response to this request a new law had been promulgated a few days before this history begins, organizing into regular legions the various weak and scattered companies. These legions were to bear the names of the departments,—Sarthe, Orne, Mayenne, Ille-et-Vilaine, Morbihan, Loire-Inferieure, and Maine-et-Loire. "These legions," said the law, "will be specially employed to fight the Chouans, and cannot, under any pretence, be sent to the frontier."

The foregoing irksome details will explain both the weakness of the Directory and the movement of this troop of men under escort of the Blues. It may not be superfluous to add that these finely patriotic Directorial decrees had no realization beyond their insertion among

12

the statutes. No longer restrained, as formerly, by great moral ideas, by patriotism, nor by terror, which enforced their execution, these later decrees of the Republic created millions and drafted soldiers without the slightest benefit accruing to its exchequer or its armies. The main-spring of the Revolution was worn-out by clumsy handling, and the application of the laws took the impress of circumstances instead of controlling them.

The departments of Mayenne and Ille-et-Vilaine were at this time under the command of an old officer who, judging on the spot of the measures that were most opportune to take, was anxious to wring from Brittany every one of her contingents, more especially that of Fougeres, which was known to be a hot-bed of *Chouannerie*. He hoped by this means to weaken its strength in these formidable districts. This devoted soldier made use of the illusory provisions of the new law to declare that he would equip and arm at once all recruits, and he announced that he held at their disposal the one month's advanced pay promised by the government to these exceptional levies. Though Brittany had hitherto refused all kinds of military service under the Republic, the levies were made under the new law on the faith of its promises, and with such promptness that even the commander was startled. But he was one of those wary old watch-dogs who are hard to catch napping. He no sooner saw the contingents arriving one after the other than he suspected some secret motive for such prompt action. Possibly he was right in ascribing it to the fact of getting arms. At any rate, no sooner were the Fougeres recruits obtained than, without delaying for laggards, he took immediate steps to fall back towards Alencon, so as to be near a loyal neighbourhood,—though the growing disaffection along the route made the success of this measure problematical. This old officer, who, under instruction of his superiors, kept secret the disasters of our armies in Italy and Germany and the disturbing news from La Vendee, was attempting on the morning when this history begins, to make a forced march on Mayenne, where he was resolved to execute the law according to his own good pleasure, and fill the half-empty companies of his own brigade with his Breton conscripts. The word "conscript" which later became so celebrated, had just now for the first time taken the place in the government decrees of the word *requisitionnaire* hitherto applied to all Republican recruits.

Before leaving Fougeres the chief secretly issued to his own men ample supplies of ammunition and sufficient rations of bread for the whole detachment, so as to conceal from the conscripts the length

13

of the march before them. He intended not to stop at Ernee (the last stage before Mayenne), where the men of the contingent might find a way of communicating with the Chouans who were no doubt hanging on his flanks. The dead silence which reigned among the recruits, surprised at the manoeuvring of the old republican, and their lagging march up the mountain excited to the very utmost the distrust and watchfulness of the chief—whose name was Hulot. All the striking points in the foregoing description had been to him matters of the keenest interest; he marched in silence, surrounded by five young officers, each of whom respected the evident preoccupation of their leader. But just as Hulot reached the summit of La Pelerine he turned his head, as if by instinct, to inspect the anxious faces of the recruits, and suddenly broke silence. The slow advance of the Bretons had put a distance of three or four hundred feet between themselves and their escort. Hulot's face contorted after a fashion peculiar to himself.

"What the devil are those dandies up to?" he exclaimed in a sonorous voice. "Creeping instead of marching, I call it."

At his first words the officers who accompanied him turned spasmodically, as if startled out of sleep by a sudden noise. The sergeants and corporals followed their example, and the whole company paused in its march without receiving the wished for "Halt!" Though the officers cast a first look at the detachment, which was creeping like an elongated tortoise up the mountain of La Pelerine, these young men, all dragged, like many others, from important studies to defend their country, and in whom war had not yet smothered the sentiment of art, were so much struck by the scene which lay spread before their eyes that they made no answer to their chief's remark, the real significance of which was unknown to them. Though they had come from Fougeres, where the scene which now presented itself to their eyes is also visible (but with certain differences caused by the change of perspective), they could not resist pausing to admire it again, like those *dilettanti* who enjoy all music the more when familiar with its construction.

From the summit of La Pelerine the traveller's eye can range over the great valley of Couesnon, at one of the farthest points of which, along the horizon, lay the town of Fougeres. From here the officers could see, to its full extent, the basin of this *intervale*, as remarkable for the fertility of its soil as for the variety of its aspects. Mountains of gneiss and slate rose on all sides, like an amphitheatre, hiding their ruddy flanks behind forests of oak, and forming on their declivities other and lesser valleys full of dewy freshness. These rocky heights made a vast enclosure, circular in form, in the centre of which a meadow lay softly stretched, like the lawn of an English garden. A number of evergreen hedges, defining irregular pieces of property which were planted with trees, gave to this carpet of verdure a character of its own, and one that is somewhat unusual among the landscapes of France; it held the teeming secrets of many beauties in its various contrasts, the effects of which were fine enough to arrest the eye of the most indifferent spectator.

At this particular moment the scene was brightened by the fleeting glow with which Nature delights at times in heightening the beauty of her imperishable creations. While the detachment was crossing the valley, the rising sun had slowly scattered the fleecy mists which float above the meadows of a September morning. As the soldiers turned to look back, an invisible hand seemed to lift from the landscape the last of these veils—a delicate vapour, like a diaphanous gauze through which the glow of precious jewels excites our curiosity. Not a cloud could be seen on the wide horizon to mark by its silvery whiteness that the vast blue arch was the firmament; it seemed, on the contrary, a dais of silk, held up by the summits of the mountains and placed in the atmosphere, to protect that beautiful assemblage of fields and meadows and groves and brooks.

The group of young officers paused to examine a scene so filled with natural beauties. The eyes of some roved among the copses, which the sterner tints of autumn were already enriching with their russet tones, contrasting the more with the emerald-green of the meadows in which they grew; others took note of a different contrast, made by the ruddy fields, where the buckwheat had been cut and tied in sheaves (like stands of arms around a bivouac), adjoining other fields of rich ploughed land, from which the rye was already harvested. Here and there were dark slate roofs above which puffs of white smoke were rising. The glittering silver threads of the winding brooks caught the eye, here and there, by one of those optic lures which render the soul—one knows not how or why—perplexed and dreamy. The fragrant freshness of the autumn breeze, the stronger odours of the forest, rose like a waft of incense to the admirers of this beautiful region, who noticed with delight its rare wild-flowers, its vigorous vegetation, and its verdure, worthy of England, the very word being common to the two languages. A few cattle gave life to the scene, already so dramatic. The birds sang, filling the valley with a sweet, vague melody that quivered in the air. If a quiet imagination will picture to itself these rich fluctuations of light and shade, the vaporous outline of the mountains, the mysterious perspectives which were seen where the trees gave an opening, or the streamlets ran, or some coquettish little glade fled away in the distance; if memory will colour, as it were, this sketch, as fleeting as the moment when it was taken, the persons for whom such pictures are not without charm will have an imperfect image of the magic scene which delighted the still impressionable souls of the young officers.

Thinking that the poor recruits must be leaving, with regret, their own country and their beloved customs, to die, perhaps, in foreign lands, they involuntarily excused a tardiness their feelings comprehended. Then, with the generosity natural to soldiers, they disguised their indulgence under an apparent desire to examine into the military position of the land. But Hulot, whom we shall henceforth call the commandant, to avoid giving him the inharmonious title of "chief of a half-brigade" was one of those soldiers who, in critical moments, cannot be caught by the charms of a landscape, were they even those of a terrestrial paradise. He shook his head with an impatient gesture and contracted the thick, black eyebrows which gave so stern an expression to his face.

"Why the devil don't they come up?" he said, for the second time, in a hoarse voice, roughened by the toils of war.

"You ask why?" replied a voice.

Hearing these words, which seemed to issue from a horn, such as the peasants of the western valleys use to call their flocks, the commandant turned sharply round, as if pricked by a sword, and beheld, close behind him, a personage even more fantastic in appearance than any of those who were now being escorted to Mayenne to serve the Republic. This unknown man, short and thick-set in figure and broad-shouldered, had a head like a bull, to which, in fact, he bore more than one resemblance. His nose seemed shorter than it was, on account of the thick nostrils. His full lips, drawn from the teeth which were white as snow, his large and round black eyes with their shaggy brows, his hanging ears and tawny hair,—seemed to belong far less to our fine Caucasian race than to a breed of herbivorous animals. The total absence of all the usual characteristics of the social man made that bare head still more remarkable. The face, bronzed by the sun (its angular outlines presenting a sort of vague likeness to the granite which forms the soil of the region), was the only visible portion of the body of this singular being. From the neck down he was wrapped in a *sarrau* or smock, a sort of russet linen blouse, coarser in texture than that of the trousers of the less fortunate conscripts. This *sarrau*, in which an antiquary would have recognized the *saye*, or the *sayon* of the Gauls, ended at his middle, where it was fastened to two leggings of goatskin by

16

slivers, or thongs of wood, roughly cut,—some of them still covered with their peel or bark. These hides of the nanny-goat (to give them the name by which they were known to the peasantry) covered his legs and thighs, and masked all appearance of human shape. Enormous sabots hid his feet. His long and shining hair fell straight, like the goat's hair, on either side of his face, being parted in the centre like the hair of certain statues of the Middle-Ages which are still to be seen in our cathedrals. In place of the knotty stick which the conscripts carried over their shoulders, this man held against his breast as though it were a musket, a heavy whip, the lash of which was closely braided and seemed to be twice as long as that of an ordinary whip. The sudden apparition of this strange being seemed easily explained. At first sight some of the officers took him for a recruit or conscript (the words were used indiscriminately) who had outstripped the column. But the commandant himself was singularly surprised by the man's presence; he showed no alarm, but his face grew thoughtful. After looking the intruder well over, he repeated, mechanically, as if preoccupied with anxious thought: "Yes, why don't they come on? do you know, you?"

"Because," said the gloomy apparition, with an accent which proved his difficulty in speaking French, "there Maine begins" (pointing with his huge, rough hand towards Ernee), "and Bretagne ends."

Then he struck the ground sharply with the handle of his heavy whip close to the commandant's feet. The impression produced on the spectators by the laconic harangue of the stranger was like that of a tom-tom in the midst of tender music. But the word "harangue" is insufficient to reproduce the hatred, the desires of vengeance expressed by the haughty gesture of the hand, the brevity of the speech, and the look of sullen and cool-blooded energy on the countenance of the speaker. The coarseness and roughness of the man,—chopped out, as it seemed by an axe, with his rough bark still left on him,—and the stupid ignorance of his features, made him seem, for the moment, like some half-savage demigod. He stood stock-still in a prophetic attitude, as though he were the Genius of Brittany rising from a slumber of three years, to renew a war in which victory could only be followed by twofold mourning.

"A pretty fellow this!" thought Hulot; "he looks to me like the emissary of men who mean to argue with their muskets."

Having growled these words between his teeth, the commandant cast his eyes in turn from the man to the valley, from the valley to the detachment, from the detachment to the steep acclivities on the right of the road, the ridges of which were covered with the broom and gorse of Brittany; then he suddenly turned them full on the stranger, whom he subjected to a mute interrogation, which he ended at last by roughly demanding, "Where do you come from?"

His eager, piercing eye strove to detect the secrets of that impenetrable face, which never changed from the vacant, torpid expression in which a peasant when doing nothing wraps himself.

"From the country of the *Gars*," replied the man, without showing any uneasiness.

"Your name?"

"Marche-a-Terre."

"Why do you call yourself by your Chouan name in defiance of the law?"

Marche-a-Terre, to use the name he gave to himself, looked at the commandant with so genuine an air of stupidity that the soldier believed the man had not understood him.

"Do you belong to the recruits from Fougeres?"

To this inquiry Marche-a-Terre replied by the bucolic "I don't know," the hopeless imbecility of which puts an end to all inquiry. He seated himself by the roadside, drew from his smock a few pieces of thin, black buckwheat-bread,—a national delicacy, the dismal delights of which none but a Breton can understand,—and began to eat with stolid indifference. There seemed such a total absence of all human intelligence about the man that the officers compared him in turn to the cattle browsing in the valley pastures, to the savages of America, or the aboriginal inhabitants of the Cape of Good Hope. Deceived by his behaviour, the commandant himself was about to turn a deaf ear to his own misgivings, when, casting a last prudence glance on the man whom he had taken for the herald of an approaching carnage, he suddenly noticed that the hair, the smock, and the goatskin leggings of the stranger were full of thorns, scraps of leaves, and bits of trees and bushes, as though this Chouan had lately made his way for a long distance through thickets and underbrush. Hulot looked significantly at his adjutant Gerard who stood beside him, pressed his hand firmly, and said in a low voice: "We came for wool, but we shall go back sheared."

The officers looked at each other silently in astonishment.

It is necessary here to make a digression, or the fears of the commandant will not be intelligible to those stay-at-home persons who are in the habit of doubting everything because they have seen nothing, and who might therefore deny the existence of Marche-a-Terre and the peasantry of the West, whose conduct, in the times we are speaking of, was often sublime.

The word *gars* pronounced *ga* is a relic of the Celtic language. It has passed from low Breton into French, and the word in our present speech has more ancient associations than any other. The *gais* was the principal weapon of the Gauls; *gaisde* meant armed; *gais* courage; *gas*, force. The word has an analogy with the Latin word *vir* man, the root of *virtus* strength, courage. The present dissertation is excusable as of national interest; besides, it may help to restore the use of such words as: *gars, garcon, garconette, garce, garcette*, now discarded from our speech as unseemly; whereas their origin is so warlike that we shall use them from time to time in the course of this history. "She is a famous *garce!*" was a compliment little understood by Madame de Stael when it was paid to her in a little village of La Vendee, where she spent a few days of her exile.

Brittany is the region in all France where the manners and customs of the Gauls have left their strongest imprint. That portion of the province where, even to our own times, the savage life and superstitious ideas of our rude ancestors still continue—if we may use the word— rampant, is called "the country of the *Gars*. When a canton (or district) is inhabited by a number of half-savages like the one who has just appeared upon the scene, the inhabitants call them "the *Gars* of such or such a parish." This classic name is a reward for the fidelity with which they struggle to preserve the traditions of the language and manners of their Gaelic ancestors; their lives show to this day many remarkable and deeply embedded vestiges of the beliefs and superstitious practices of those ancient times. Feudal customs are still maintained. Antiquaries find Druidic monuments still standing. The genius of modern civilization shrinks from forcing its way through those impenetrable primordial forests. An unheard-of ferociousness, a brutal obstinacy, but also a regard for the sanctity of an oath; a complete ignoring of our laws, our customs, our dress, our modern coins, our language, but withal a patriarchal simplicity and virtues that are heroic,—unite in keeping the inhabitants of this region more impoverished as to all intellectual knowledge than the Redskins, but also as proud, as crafty, and as enduring as they. The position which Brittany occupies in the centre of Europe makes it more interesting to observe than Canada. Surrounded by light whose beneficent warmth never reaches it, this region is like a frozen coal left black in the middle of a glowing fire. The efforts made by several noble minds to win this glorious part of France, so rich in neglected treasures, to social life and to prosperity have all, even when sustained by government, come to nought against the inflexibility of a population given over to the habits of immemorial routine. This unfortunate condition is partly accounted for by the nature of the land, broken by ravines, mountain torrents, lakes, and marshes, and bristling with hedges or earth-works which make a sort of citadel of every field; without roads, without canals, and at the mercy of prejudices which scorn our modern agriculture. These will further be shown with all their dangers in our present history.

The picturesque lay of the land and the superstitions of the inhabitants prevent the formation of communities and the benefits arising from the exchange and comparison of ideas. There are no villages. The rickety buildings which the people call homes are sparsely scattered through the wilderness. Each family lives as in a desert. The only meetings among them are on Sundays and feast-days in the parish church. These silent assemblies, under the eye of the rector (the only ruler of these rough minds) last some hours. After listening to the awful words of the priest they return to their noisome hovels for another week; they leave them only to work, they return to them only to sleep. No one ever visits them, unless it is the rector. Consequently, it was the voice of the priesthood which roused Brittany against the Republic, and sent thousands of men, five years before this history begins, to the support of the first *Chouannerie*. The brothers Cottereau, whose name was given to that first uprising, were bold smugglers, plying their perilous trade between Laval and Fougeres. The insurrections of Brittany had nothing fine or noble about them; and it may be truly said that if La Vendee turned its brigandage into a great war, Brittany turned war into a brigandage. The proscription of princes, the destruction of religion, far from inspiring great sacrifices, were to the Chouans pretexts for mere pillage; and the events of this intestine warfare had all the savage moroseness of their own natures. When the real defenders of the monarchy came to recruit men among these ignorant and violent people they vainly tried to give, for the honour of the white flag, some grandeur to the enterprises which had hitherto rendered the brigands odious; the Chouans remain in history as a memorable example of the danger of uprousing the uncivilized masses of the nation.

The sketch here made of a Breton valley and of the Breton men in the detachment of recruits, more especially that of the "*gars*" who so suddenly appeared on the summit of Mont Pelerine, gives a brief but faithful picture of the province and its inhabitants. A trained imagination can by the help of these details obtain some idea of the theatre of the war and of the men who were its instruments. The flowering hedges of the beautiful valleys concealed the combatants. Each field was a fortress, every tree an ambush; the hollow trunk of each old willow hid a stratagem. The place for a fight was everywhere. Sharp-shooters were lurking at every turn for the Blues, whom laughing young girls, unmindful of their perfidy, attracted within range,—for had they not made pilgrimages with their fathers and their brothers, imploring to be taught wiles, and receiving absolution from their wayside Virgin of rotten wood? Religion, or rather the fetishism of these ignorant creatures, absolved such murders of remorse.

Thus, when the struggle had once begun, every part of the country was dangerous,—in fact, all things were full of peril, sound as well as silence, attraction as well as fear, the family hearth or the open country. Treachery was everywhere, but it was treachery from conviction. The people were savages serving God and the King after the fashion of Red Indians. To make this sketch of the struggle exact and true at all points, the historian must add that the moment Hoche had signed his peace the whole country subsided into smiles and friendliness. Families who were rending each other to pieces over night, were supping together without danger the next day.

The very moment that Commandant Hulot became aware of the secret treachery betrayed by the hairy skins of Marche-a-Terre, he was convinced that this peace, due to the genius of Hoche, the stability of which he had always doubted, was at an end. The civil war, he felt, was about to be renewed,—doubtless more terrible than ever after a cessation of three years. The Revolution, mitigated by the events of the 9th Thermidor, would doubtless return to the old terrors which had made it odious to sound minds. English gold would, as formerly, assist in the national discords. The Republic, abandoned by young Bonaparte who had seemed to be its tutelary genius, was no longer in a condition to resist its enemies from without and from within,—the worst and most cruel of whom were the last to appear. The Civil War, already threatened by various partial uprisings, would assume a new and far more serious aspect if the Chouans were now to attack so strong an escort. Such were the reflections that filled the mind of the commander (though less succinctly formulated) as soon as he perceived, in the condition of Marche-a-Terre's clothing, the signs of an ambush carefully planned.

The silence which followed the prophetic remark of the commandant to Gerard gave Hulot time to recover his self-possession. The old soldier had been shaken. He could not hinder his brow from clouding as he felt himself surrounded by the horrors of a warfare the atrocities of which would have shamed even cannibals. Captain Merle and the adjutant Gerard could not explain to themselves the evident dread on the face of their leader as he looked at Marche-a-Terre eating his bread by the side of the road. But Hulot's face soon cleared; he began to rejoice in the opportunity to fight for the Republic, and he joyously vowed to escape being the dupe of the Chouans, and to fathom the wily and impenetrable being whom they had done him the honour to employ against him.

Before taking any resolution he set himself to study the position in which it was evident the enemy intended to surprise him. Observing that the road where the column had halted was about to pass through a sort of gorge, short to be sure, but flanked with woods from which several paths appeared to issue, he frowned heavily, and said to his two friends, in a low voice of some emotion:

"We're in a devil of a wasp's-nest."

"What do you fear?" asked Gerard.

"Fear? Yes, that's it, *fear*," returned the commandant. "I have always had a fear of being shot like a dog at the edge of a wood, without a chance of crying out 'Who goes there?'"

"Pooh!" said Merle, laughing, "'Who goes there' is all humbug."

"Are we in real danger?" asked Gerard, as much surprised by Hulot's coolness as he was by his evident alarm.

"Hush!" said the commandant, in a low voice. "We are in the jaws of the wolf; it is as dark as a pocket; and we must get some light. Luckily, we've got the upper end of the slope!"

So saying, he moved, with his two officers, in a way to surround Marche-a-Terre, who rose quickly, pretending to think himself in the way.

"Stay where you are, vagabond!" said Hulot, keeping his eye on the apparently indifferent face of the Breton, and giving him a push which threw him back on the place where he had been sitting.

"Friends," continued Hulot, in a low voice, speaking to the two officers. "It is time I should tell you that it is all up with the army in Paris. The Directory, in consequence of a disturbance in the Assembly, has made another clean sweep of our affairs. Those *pentarchs*,—puppets, I call them,—those directors have just lost a good blade; Bernadotte has abandoned them."

"Who will take his place?" asked Gerard, eagerly.

"Milet-Mureau, an old blockhead. A pretty time to choose to let fools sail the ship! English rockets from all the headlands, and those cursed Chouan cockchafers in the air! You may rely upon it that some one behind those puppets pulled the wire when they saw we were getting the worst of it."

"How getting the worst of it?"

"Our armies are beaten at all points," replied Hulot, sinking his voice still lower. "The Chouans have intercepted two couriers; I only received my despatches and last orders by a private messenger sent by Bernadotte just as he was leaving the ministry. Luckily, friends have written me confidentially about this crisis. Fouche has discovered that the tyrant Louis XVIII. has been advised by traitors in Paris to send a leader to his followers in La Vendee. It is thought that Barras is betraying the Republic. At any rate, Pitt and the princes have sent a man, a *ci-devant*, vigorous, daring, full of talent, who intends, by uniting the Chouans with the Vendeans, to pluck the cap of liberty from the head of the Republic. The fellow has lately landed in the Morbihan; I was the first to hear of it, and I sent the news to those knaves in Paris. 'The *Gars*' is the name he goes by. All those beasts," he added, pointing to Marche-a-Terre, "stick on names which would give a stomach-ache to honest patriots if they bore them. The *Gars* is now in this district. The presence of that fellow"—and again he signed to Marche-a-Terre—"as good as tells me he is on our back. But they can't teach an old monkey to make faces; and you've got to help me to get my birds safe into their cage, and as quick as a flash too. A pretty fool I should be if I allowed that *ci-devant*, who dares to come from London with his British gold, to trap me like a crow!"

On learning these secret circumstances, and being well aware that their leader was never unnecessarily alarmed, the two officers saw the dangers of the position. Gerard was about to ask some questions on the political state of Paris, some details of which Hulot had evidently passed over in silence, but a sign from his commander stopped him, and once more drew the eyes of all three to the Chouan. Marche-a-Terre gave no sign of disturbance at being watched. The curiosity of the two officers, who were new to this species of warfare, was greatly excited by this beginning of an affair which seemed to have an almost romantic interest, and they began to joke about it. But Hulot stopped them at once.

"God's thunder!" he cried. "Don't smoke upon the powder-cask; wasting courage for nothing is like carrying water in a basket. Gerard," he added, in the ear of his adjutant, "get nearer, by degrees, to that fellow, and watch him; at the first suspicious action put your sword through him. As for me, I must take measures to carry on the ball if our unseen adversaries choose to open it."

The Chouan paid no attention to the movements of the young officer, and continued to play with his whip, and fling out the lash of it as though he were fishing in the ditch.

Meantime the commandant was saying to Merle, in a low voice: "Give ten picked men to a sergeant, and post them yourself above us on the summit of this slope, just where the path widens to a ledge; there you ought to see the whole length of the route to Ernee. Choose a position where the road is not flanked by woods, and where the sergeant can overlook the country. Take Clef-des-Coeurs; he is very intelligent. This is no laughing matter; I wouldn't give a farthing for our skins if we don't turn the odds in our favour at once."

While Merle was executing this order with a rapidity of which he fully understood the importance, the commandant waved his right hand to enforce silence on the soldiers, who were standing at ease, and laughing and joking around him. With another gesture he ordered them to take up arms. When quiet was restored he turned his eyes from one end of the road to the other, listened with anxious attention as though he hoped to detect some stifled sound, some echo of weapons, or steps which might give warning of the expected attack. His black eye seemed to pierce the woods to an extraordinary depth. Perceiving no indications of danger, he next consulted, like a savage, the ground at his feet, to discover, if possible, the trail of the invisible enemies whose daring was well known to him. Desperate at seeing and hearing nothing to justify his fears, he turned aside from the road and ascended, not without difficulty, one or two hillocks. The other officers and the soldiers, observing the anxiety of a leader in whom they trusted and whose worth was known to them, knew that his extreme watchfulness meant danger; but not suspecting its imminence, they merely stood still and held their breaths by instinct. Like dogs endeavouring to guess the intentions of a huntsman, whose orders are incomprehensible to them though they faithfully obey him, the soldiers gazed in turn at the valley, at the woods by the roadside, at the stern face of their leader, endeavouring to read their fate. They questioned each other with their eyes, and more than one smile ran from lip to lip.

When Hulot returned to his men with an anxious look, Beau-Pied, a young sergeant who passed for the wit of his company, remarked in a low voice: "Where the deuce have we poked ourselves that an old trooper like Hulot should pull such a gloomy face? He's as solemn as a council of war."

Hulot gave the speaker a stern look, silence being ordered in the ranks. In the hush that ensued, the lagging steps of the conscripts on the creaking sand of the road produced a recurrent sound which added a sort of vague emotion to the general excitement. This indefinable feeling can be understood only by those who have felt their hearts

24

beat in the silence of the night from a painful expectation heightened by some noise, the monotonous recurrence of which seems to distil terror into their minds, drop by drop.

The thought of the commandant, as he returned to his men, was: "Can I be mistaken?" He glanced, with a concentrated anger which flashed like lightning from his eyes, at the stolid, immovable Chouan; a look of savage irony which he fancied he detected in the man's eyes, warned him not to relax in his precautions. Just then Captain Merle, having obeyed Hulot's orders, returned to his side.

"We did well, captain," said the commandant, "to put the few men whose patriotism we can count upon among those conscripts at the rear. Take a dozen more of our own bravest fellows, with sub-lieutenant Lebrun at their head, and make a rear-guard of them; they'll support the patriots who are there already, and help to shove on that flock of birds and close up the distance between us. I'll wait for you."

The captain disappeared. The commander's eye singled out four men on whose intelligence and quickness he knew he might rely, and he beckoned to them, silently, with the well-known friendly gesture of moving the right forefinger rapidly and repeatedly toward the nose. They came to him.

"You served with me under Hoche," he said, "when we brought to reason those brigands who call themselves 'Chasseurs du Roi'; you know how they hid themselves to swoop down on the Blues."

At this commendation of their intelligence the four soldiers nodded with significant grins. Their heroically martial faces wore that look of careless resignation to fate which evidenced the fact that since the struggle had begun between France and Europe, the ideas of the private soldiers had never passed beyond the cartridge-boxes on their backs or the bayonets in front of them. With their lips drawn together like a purse when the strings are tightened, they looked at their commander attentively with inquiring eyes.

"You know," continued Hulot, who possessed the art of speaking picturesquely as soldier to soldiers, "that it won't do for old hares like us to be caught napping by the Chouans,—of whom there are plenty all round us, or my name's not Hulot. You four are to march in advance and beat up both sides of this road. The detachment will hang fire here. Keep your eyes about you; don't get picked off; and bring me news of what you find—quick!"

So saying he waved his hand towards the suspected heights along the road. The four men, by way of thanks raised the backs of their hands to their battered old three-cornered hats, discoloured by rain and ragged with age, and bent their bodies double. One of them, named Larose, a corporal well-known to Hulot, remarked as he clicked his musket: "We'll play 'em a tune on the clarinet, commander."

They started, two to right and two to left of the road; and it was not without some excitement that their comrades watched them disappear. The commandant himself feared that he had sent them to their deaths, and an involuntary shudder seized him as he saw the last of them. Officers and soldiers listened to the gradually lessening sound of their footsteps, with feelings all the more acute because they were carefully hidden. There are occasions when the risk of four lives causes more excitement and alarm than all the slain at Jemmapes. The faces of those trained to war have such various and fugitive expressions that a painter who has to describe them is forced to appeal to the recollections of soldiers and to leave civilians to imagine these dramatic figures; for scenes so rich in detail cannot be rendered in writing, except at interminable length.

Just as the bayonets of the four men were finally lost to sight, Captain Merle returned, having executed the commandant's orders with rapidity. Hulot, with two or three sharp commands, put his troop in line of battle and ordered it to return to the summit of La Pelerine where his little advanced-guard were stationed; walking last himself and looking backward to note any changes that might occur in a scene which Nature had made so lovely, and man so terrible. As he reached the spot where he had left the Chouan, Marche-a-Terre, who had seen with apparent indifference the various movements of the commander, but who was now watching with extraordinary intelligence the two soldiers in the woods to the right, suddenly gave the shrill and piercing cry of the *chouette*, or screech-owl. The three famous smugglers already mentioned were in the habit of using the various intonations of this cry to warn each other of danger or of any event that might concern them. From this came the nickname of *Chuin* which means *chouette* or owl in the dialect of that region. This corrupted word came finally to mean the whole body of those who, in the first uprising, imitated the tactics and the signals of the smugglers.

When Hulot heard that suspicious sound he stopped short and examined the man intently; then he feigned to be taken in by his stupid air, wishing to keep him by him as a barometer which might indicate the movements of the enemy. He therefore checked Gerard, whose hand was on his sword to despatch him; but he placed two soldiers beside the man he now felt to be a spy, and ordered them in a loud, clear voice to shoot him at the next sound he made. In spite of his imminent danger Marche-a-Terre showed not the slightest emotion. The commandant, who was studying him, took note of this apparent insensibility, and remarked to Gerard: "That fool is not so clever as he means to be! It is far from easy to read the face of a Chouan, but the fellow betrays himself by his anxiety to show his nerve. Ha! ha! if he had only pretended fear I should have taken him for a stupid brute. He and I might have made a pair! I came very near falling into the trap. Yes, we shall undoubtedly be attacked; but let 'em come; I'm all ready now."

As he said these words in a low voice, rubbing his hands with an air of satisfaction, he looked at the Chouan with a jeering eye. Then he crossed his arms on his breast and stood in the road with his favourite officers beside him awaiting the result of his arrangements. Certain that a fight was at hand, he looked at his men composedly.

"There'll be a row," said Beau-Pied to his comrades in a low voice. "See, the commandant is rubbing his hands."

In critical situations like that in which the detachment and its commander were now placed, life is so clearly at stake that men of nerve make it a point of honour to show coolness and self-possession. These are the moments in which to judge men's souls. The commandant, better informed of the danger than his two officers, took pride in showing his tranquillity. With his eyes moving from Marche-a-Terre to the road and thence to the woods he stood expecting, not without dread, a general volley from the Chouans, whom he believed to be hidden like brigands all around him; but his face remained impassable. Knowing that the eyes of the soldiers were turned upon him, he wrinkled his brown cheeks pitted with the small-pox, screwed his upper lip, and winked his right eye, a grimace always taken for a smile by his men; then he tapped Gerard on the shoulder and said: "Now that things are quiet tell me what you wanted to say just now."

"I wanted to ask what this new crisis means, commandant?" was the reply.

"It is not new," said Hulot. "All Europe is against us, and this time she has got the whip hand. While those Directors are fighting together like horses in a stable without any oats, and letting the government go to bits, the armies are left without supplies or reinforcements. We are getting the worst of it in Italy; we've evacuated Mantua after a series of disasters on the Trebia, and Joubert has just lost a battle at Novi. I only hope Massena may be able to hold the Swiss passes against Suwarow. We're done for on the Rhine. The Directory have sent Moreau. The question is, Can he defend the frontier? I hope he may, but the Coalition will end by invading us, and the only general able to save the nation is, unluckily, down in that devilish Egypt; and how is he ever to get back, with England mistress of the Mediterranean?"

"Bonaparte's absence doesn't trouble me, commandant," said the young adjutant Gerard, whose intelligent mind had been developed by a fine education. "I am certain the Revolution cannot be brought to naught. Ha! we soldiers have a double mission,—not merely to defend French territory, but to preserve the national soul, the generous principles of liberty, independence, and rights of human reason awakened by our Assemblies and gaining strength, as I believe, from day to day. France is like a traveller bearing a light: he protects it with one hand, and defends himself with the other. If your news is true, we have never the last ten years been so surrounded with people trying to blow it out. Principles and nation are in danger of perishing together."

"Alas, yes," said Hulot, sighing. "Those clowns of Directors have managed to quarrel with all the men who could sail the ship. Bernadotte, Carnot, all of them, even Talleyrand, have deserted us. There's not a single good patriot left, except friend Fouche, who holds 'em through the police. There's a man for you! It was he who warned me of a coming insurrection; and here we are, sure enough, caught in a trap."

"If the army doesn't take things in hand and manage the government," said Gerard, "those lawyers in Paris will put us back just where we were before the Revolution. A parcel of ninnies! what do they know about governing?"

"I'm always afraid they'll treat with the Bourbons," said Hulot. "Thunder! if they did *that* a pretty pass we should be in, we soldiers!"

"No, no, commandant, it won't come to that," said Gerard. "The army, as you say, will raise its voice, and—provided it doesn't choose its words from Pichegru's vocabulary—I am persuaded we have not hacked ourselves to pieces for the last ten years merely to manure the flax and let others spin the thread."

"Well," interposed Captain Merle, "what we have to do now is to act as good patriots and prevent the Chouans from communicating with La Vendee; for, if they once come to an understanding and England gets her finger into the pie, I wouldn't answer for the cap of the Republic, one and invisible."

As he spoke the cry of an owl, heard at a distance, interrupted the conversation. Again the commander examined Marche-a-Terre, whose impassable face still gave no sign. The conscripts, their ranks closed up by an officer, now stood like a herd of cattle in the road, about a hundred feet distant from the escort, which was drawn up in line of battle. Behind them stood the rear-guard of soldiers and patriots, picked men, commanded by Lieutenant Lebrun. Hulot cast his eyes over this arrangement of his forces and looked again at the picket of men posted in advance upon the road. Satisfied with what he saw he was about to give the order to march, when the tricolour cockades of the two soldiers he had sent to beat the woods to the left caught his eye; he waited therefore till the two others, who had gone to the right, should reappear.

"Perhaps the ball will open over there," he said to his officers, pointing to the woods from which the two men did not emerge.

While the first two made their report Hulot's attention was distracted momentarily from Marche-a-Terre. The Chouan at once sent his owl's-cry to an apparently vast distance, and before the men who guarded him could raise their muskets and take aim he had struck them a blow with his whip which felled them, and rushed away. A terrible discharge of fire-arms from the woods just above the place where the Chouan had been sitting brought down six or eight soldiers. Marche-a-Terre, at whom several men had fired without touching him, vanished into the woods after climbing the slope with the agility of a wild-cat; as he did so his sabots rolled into the ditch and his feet were seen to be shod with the thick, hobnailed boots always worn by the Chouans.

At the first cries uttered by the Chouans, the conscripts sprang into the woods to the right like a flock of birds taking flight at the approach of a man.

"Fire on those scoundrels!" cried Hulot.

The company fired, but the conscripts knew well how to shelter themselves behind trees, and before the soldiers could reload they were out of sight.

"What's the use of *decreeing* levies in the departments?" said Hulot. "It is only such idiots as the Directory who would expect any good of a draft in this region. The Assembly had much better stop voting more shoes and money and ammunition, and see that we get what belongs to us."

At this moment the two skirmishers sent out on the right were seen returning with evident difficulty. The one that was least wounded supported his comrade, whose blood was moistening the earth. The two poor fellows were half-way down the slope when Marche-a-Terre showed his ugly face, and took so true an aim that both Blues fell together and rolled heavily into the ditch. The Chouan's monstrous head was no sooner seen than thirty muzzles were levelled at him, but, like a figure in a pantomime, he disappeared in a second among the

29

tufts of gorse. These events, which have taken so many words to tell, happened instantaneously, and in another moment the rear-guard of patriots and soldiers had joined the main body of the escort.

"Forward!" cried Hulot.

The company moved quickly to the higher and more open ground on which the picket guard was already stationed. There, the commander formed his troop once more into line of battle; but, as the Chouans made no further hostile demonstrations, he began to think that the deliverance of the conscripts might have been the sole object of the ambuscade.

"Their cries," he said to his two friends, "prove that they are not numerous. We'll advance at a quick step, and possibly we may be able to reach Ernee without getting them on our backs."

These words were overheard by one of the patriot conscripts, who stepped from the ranks, and said respectfully:—

"General, I have already fought the Chouans; may I be allowed a word?"

"A lawyer," whispered Hulot to Merle. "They always want to harangue. Argue away," he said to the young man.

"General, the Chouans have no doubt brought arms for those escaped recruits. Now, if we try to outmarch them, they will catch us in the woods and shoot every one of us before we can get to Ernee. We must argue, as you call it, with cartridges. During the skirmish, which will last more time than you think for, some of us ought to go back and fetch the National Guard and the militia from Fougeres."

"Then you think there are a good many Chouans?"

"Judge for yourself, citizen commander."

He led Hulot to a place where the sand had been stirred as with a rake; then he took him to the opening of a wood-path, where the leaves were scattered and trampled into the earth,—unmistakable signs of the passage of a large body of men.

"Those were the *gars* from Vitre," said the man, who came himself from Fougeres; "they are on their way to Lower Normandy."

"What is your name?" asked Hulot.

"Gudin, commander."

"Well, then, Gudin, I make you a corporal. You seem to me trustworthy. Select a man to send to Fougeres; but stay yourself with me. In the first place, however, take two or three of your comrades and bring in the muskets and ammunition of the poor fellows those brigands have rolled into the ditch. These Bretons," added Hulot to Gerard, "will make famous infantry if they take to rations."

30

Gudin's emissary started on a run to Fougeres by a wood-road to the left; the soldiers looked to their arms, and awaited an attack; the commandant passed along their line, smiling to them, and then placed himself with his officers, a little in front of it. Silence fell once more, but it was of short duration. Three hundred or more Chouans, their clothing identical with that of the late recruits, burst from the woods to the right with actual howls and planted themselves, without any semblance of order, on the road directly in front of the feeble detachment of the Blues. The commandant thereupon ranged his soldiers in two equal parts, each with a front of ten men. Between them, he placed the twelve recruits, to whom he hastily gave arms, putting himself at their head. This little centre was protected by the two wings, of twenty-five men each, which manoeuvred on either side of the road under the orders of Merle and Gerard; their object being to catch the Chouans on the flank and prevent them from posting themselves as sharp-shooters among the trees, where they could pick off the Blues without risk to themselves; for in these wars the Republican troops never knew where to look for an enemy.

These arrangements, hastily made, gave confidence to the soldiers, and they advanced in silence upon the Chouans. At the end of a few seconds each side fired, with the loss of several men. At this moment the two wings of the Republicans, to whom the Chouans had nothing to oppose, came upon their flanks, and, with a close, quick volley, sent death and disorder among the enemy. This manoeuvre very nearly equalized the numerical strength of the two parties. But the Chouan nature was so intrepid, their will so firm, that they did not give way; their losses scarcely staggered them; they simply closed up and attempted to surround the dark and well-formed little party of the Blues, which covered so little ground that it looked from a distance like a queen-bee surrounded by the swarm.

The Chouans might have carried the day at this moment if the two wings commanded by Merle and Gerard had not succeeded in getting in two volleys which took them diagonally on their rear. The Blues of the two wings ought to have remained in position and continued to pick off in this way their terrible enemies; but excited by the danger of their little main body, then completely surrounded by the Chouans, they flung themselves headlong into the road with fixed bayonets and made the battle even for a few moments. Both sides fought with a stubbornness intensified by the cruelty and fury of the partisan spirit which made this war exceptional. Each man, observant of danger, was silent. The scene was gloomy and cold as death itself. Nothing was heard through the clash of arms and the grinding of the sand under foot but the moans and exclamations of those who fell, either dead or badly wounded. The twelve loyal recruits in the republican main body protected the commandant (who was guiding his men and giving orders) with such courage that more than once several soldiers called out "Bravo, conscripts!"

Hulot, imperturbable and with an eye to everything, presently remarked among the Chouans a man who, like himself, was evidently surrounded by picked men, and was therefore, no doubt, the leader of the attacking party. He was eager to see this man distinctly, and he made many efforts to distinguish his features, but in vain; they were hidden by the red caps and broad-brimmed hats of those about him. Hulot did, however, see Marche-a-Terre beside this leader, repeating his orders in a hoarse voice, his own carbine, meanwhile, being far from inactive. The commandant grew impatient at being thus baffled. Waving his sword, he urged on the recruits and charged the centre of the Chouans with such fury that he broke through their line and came close to their chief, whose face, however, was still hidden by a broad-brimmed felt hat with a white cockade. But the invisible leader, surprised at so bold an attack, retreated a step or two and raised his hat abruptly, thus enabling Hulot to get a hasty idea of his appearance.

He was young,—Hulot thought him to be about twenty-five; he wore a hunting-jacket of green cloth, and a white belt containing pistols. His heavy shoes were hobnailed like those of the Chouans; leather leggings came to his knees covering the ends of his breeches of very coarse drilling, and completing a costume which showed off a slender and well-poised figure of medium height. Furious that the Blues should thus have approached him, he pulled his hat again over his face and sprang towards them. But he was instantly surrounded by Marche-a-Terre and several Chouans. Hulot thought he perceived between the heads which clustered about this young leader, a broad red ribbon worn across his chest. The eyes of the commandant, caught by this royal decoration (then almost forgotten by republicans), turned quickly to the young man's face, which, however, he soon lost sight of under the necessity of controlling and protecting his own little troop. Though he had barely time to notice a pair of brilliant eyes (the colour of which escaped him), fair hair and delicate features bronzed by the sun, he was much struck by the dazzling whiteness of the neck, relieved by a black cravat carelessly knotted. The fiery attitude of the young leader proved him to be a soldier of the stamp of those who bring a certain conventional poesy into battle. His well-gloved hand waved above his head a sword which gleamed in the sunlight. His whole person gave an impression both of elegance and strength. An air of passionate self-devotion, enhanced by the charms of youth and distinguished manners, made this *émigré* a graceful image of the French *noblesse*. He presented a strong contrast to Hulot, who, ten feet distant from him, was quite as vivid an image of the vigorous Republic for which the old soldier was fighting; his stern face, his well-worn blue uniform with its shabby red facings and its blackened epaulettes hanging back of his shoulders, being visible signs of its needs and character.

The graceful attitude and expression of the young man were not lost on the commandant, who exclaimed as he pressed towards him: "Come on, opera-dancer, come on, and let me crush you!"

The royalist leader, provoked by his momentary disadvantage, advanced with an angry movement, but at the same moment the men who were about him rushed forward and flung themselves with fury on the Blues. Suddenly a soft, clear voice was heard above the din of battle saying: "Here died Saint-Lescure! Shall we not avenge him?"

At the magic words the efforts of the Chouans became terrible, and the soldiers of the Republic had great difficulty in maintaining themselves without breaking their little line of battle.

"If he wasn't a young man," thought Hulot, as he retreated step by step, "we shouldn't have been attacked in this way. Who ever heard of the Chouans fighting an open battle? Well, all the better! they won't shoot us off like dogs along the road." Then, raising his voice till it echoed through the woods, he exclaimed, "Come on, my men! Shall we let ourselves be *fooled* by those brigands?"

The word here given is but a feeble equivalent of the one the brave commandant used; but every veteran can substitute the real one, which was far more soldierly in character.

"Gerard! Merle!" added Hulot, "call in your men, form them into a battalion, take the rear, fire upon those dogs, and let's make an end of this!"

The order was difficult to obey, for the young chief, hearing Hulot's voice, cried out: "By Saint Anne of Auray, don't let them get away! Spread out, spread out, my lads!" and each of the two wings of the Blues was followed by Chouans who were fully as obstinate and far superior in numbers. The Republicans were surrounded on all sides by the Goatskins uttering their savage cries, which were more like howls.

"Hold your tongues, gentlemen," cried Beau-Pied; "we can't hear ourselves be killed."

This jest revived the courage of the Blues. Instead of fighting only

33

at one point, the Republicans spread themselves to three different points on the table-land of La Pelerine, and the rattle of musketry woke all the echoes of the valleys, hitherto so peaceful beneath it. Victory might have remained doubtful for many hours, or the fight might have come to an end for want of combatants, for Blues and Chouans were equally brave and obstinate. Each side was growing more and more incensed, when the sound of a drum in the distance told that the body of men must be crossing the valley of Couesnon.

"There's the National Guard of Fougeres!" cried Gudin, in a loud voice; "my man has brought them."

The words reached the ears of the young leader of the Chouans and his ferocious *aide-de-camp*, and the royalists made a hasty retrograde movement, checked, however, by a brutal shout from Marche-a-Terre. After two or three orders given by the leader in a low voice, and transmitted by Marche-a-Terre in the Breton dialect, the Chouans made good their retreat with a cleverness which disconcerted the Republicans and even the commandant. At the first word of command they formed in line, presenting a good front, behind which the wounded retreated, and the others reloaded their guns. Then, suddenly, with the agility already shown by Marche-a-Terre, the wounded were taken over the brow of the eminence to the right of the road, while half the others followed them slowly to occupy the summit, where nothing could be seen of them by the Blues but their bold heads. There they made a rampart of the trees and pointed the muzzles of their guns on the Republicans, who were rapidly reformed under reiterated orders from Hulot and turned to face the remainder of the Chouans, who were still before them in the road. The latter retreated slowly, disputing the ground and wheeling so as to bring themselves under cover of their comrades' fire. When they reached the broad ditch which bordered the road, they scaled the high bank on the other side, braving the fire of the Republicans, which was sufficiently well-directed to fill the ditch with dead bodies. The Chouans already on the summit answered with a fire that was no less deadly. At that moment the National Guard of Fougeres reached the scene of action at a quick step, and its mere presence put an end to the affair. The Guard and some of the soldiers crossed the road and began to enter the woods, but the commandant called to them in his martial voice, "Do you want to be annihilated over there?"

The victory remained to the Republicans, though not without heavy loss. All the battered old hats were hung on the points of the bayonets and the muskets held aloft, while the soldiers shouted with

34

one voice: *"Vive la Republique!"* Even the wounded, sitting by the roadside, shared in the general enthusiasm; and Hulot, pressing Gerard's hand, exclaimed:—

"Ha, ha! those are what I call *veterans!*"

Merle was directed to bury the dead in a ravine; while another party of men attended to the removal of the wounded. The carts and horses of the neighbourhood were put into requisition, and the suffering men were carefully laid on the clothing of the dead. Before the little column started, the National Guard of Fougeres turned over to Hulot a Chouan, dangerously wounded, whom they had captured at the foot of the slope up which his comrades had escaped, and where he had fallen from weakness.

"Thanks for your help, citizens," said the commandant. "God's thunder! if it hadn't been for you, we should have had a pretty bad quarter of an hour. Take care of yourselves; the war has begun. *Adieu,* friends." Then, turning to the prisoner, he asked, "What's the name of your general?"

"The *Gars.*"

"Who? Marche-a-Terre?"

"No, the *Gars.*"

"Where does the *Gars* come from?"

To this question the prisoner, whose face was convulsed with suffering, made no reply; he took out his beads and began to say his prayers.

"The *Gars* is no doubt that young *ci-devant* with the black cravat,— sent by the tyrant and his allies Pitt and Coburg."

At that words the Chouan raised his head proudly and said: "Sent by God and the king!" He uttered the words with an energy which exhausted his strength. The commandant saw the difficulty of questioning a dying man, whose countenance expressed his gloomy fanaticism, and he turned away his head with a frown. Two soldiers, friends of those whom Marche-a-Terre had so brutally killed with the butt of his whip, stepped back a pace or two, took aim at the Chouan, whose fixed eyes did not blink at the muzzles of their guns, fired at short range, and brought him down. When they approached the dead body to strip it, the dying man found strength to cry out loudly, *"Vive le roi!"*

"Yes, yes, you canting hypocrite," cried Clef-des-Coeurs; "go and make your report to that Virgin of yours. Didn't he shout in our faces, *'Vive le roi!'* when we thought him cooked?"

"Here are his papers, commandant," said Beau-Pied.

"Ho! ho!" cried Clef-des-Coeurs. "Come, all of you, and see this minion of the good God with colours on his stomach!"

Hulot and several soldiers came round the body, now entirely naked, and saw upon its breast a blue tattooing in the form of a swollen heart. It was the sign of initiation into the brotherhood of the Sacred Heart. Above this sign were the words, "Marie Lambrequin," no doubt the man's name.

"Look at that, Clef-des-Coeurs," said Beau-Pied; "it would take you a hundred years to find out what that accoutrement is good for."

"What should I know about the Pope's uniform?" replied Clef-des-Coeurs, scornfully.

"You worthless bog-trotter, you'll never learn anything," retorted Beau-Pied. "Don't you see that they've promised that poor fool that he shall live again, and he has painted his gizzard in order to find himself?"

At this sally—which was not without some foundation—even Hulot joined in the general hilarity. At this moment Merle returned, and the burial of the dead being completed and the wounded placed more or less comfortably in two carts, the rest of the late escort formed into two lines round the improvised ambulances, and descended the slope of the mountain towards Maine, where the beautiful valley of La Pelerine, a rival to that of Couesnon lay before it.

Hulot with his two officers followed the troop slowly, hoping to get safely to Ernee where the wounded could be cared for. The fight we have just described, which was almost forgotten in the midst of the greater events which were soon to occur, was called by the name of the mountain on which it took place. It obtained some notice at the West, where the inhabitants, observant of this second uprising, noticed on this occasion a great change in the manner in which the Chouans now made war. In earlier days they would never have attacked so large a detachment. According to Hulot the young royalist whom he had seen was undoubtedly the *Gars*, the new general sent to France by the princes, who, following the example of the other royalist chiefs, concealed his real name and title under one of those pseudonyms called *noms de guerre*. This circumstance made the commandant quite as uneasy after his melancholy victory as he had been before it while expecting the attack. He turned several times to consider the table-land of La Pelerine which he was leaving behind him, across which he could still hear faintly at intervals the drums of the National Guard descending into the valley of Couesnon at the same time that the Blues were descending into that of La Pelerine.

"Can either of you," he said to his two friends, "guess the motives of that attack of the Chouans? To them, fighting is a matter of business, and I can't see what they expected to gain by this attack. They have

36

lost at least a hundred men, and we"—he added, screwing up his right cheek and winking by way of a smile, "have lost only sixty. God's thunder! I don't understand that sort of speculation. The scoundrels needn't have attacked us; we might just as well have been allowed to pass like letters through the post—No, I don't see what good it has done them to bullet-hole our men," he added, with a sad shake of his head toward the carts. "Perhaps they only intended to say good-day to us."

"But they carried off our recruits, commander," said Merle.

"The recruits could have skipped like frogs into the woods at any time, and we should never have gone after them, especially if those fellows had fired a single volley," returned Hulot. "No, no, there's something behind all this." Again he turned and looked at La Pelerine. "See!" he cried; "see there!"

Though they were now at a long distance from the fatal plateau, they could easily distinguish Marche-a-Terre and several Chouans who were again occupying it.

"Double-quick, march!" cried Hulot to his men, "open your compasses and trot the steeds faster than that! Are your legs frozen?"

These words drove the little troop into a rapid motion.

"There's a mystery, and it's hard to make out," continued Hulot, speaking to his friends. "God grant it isn't explained by muskets at Ernee. I'm very much afraid that we shall find the road to Mayenne cut off by the king's men."

****

The strategical problem which troubled the commandant was causing quite as much uneasiness to the persons whom he had just seen on the summit of Mont Pelerine. As soon as the drums of the National Guard were out of hearing and Marche-a-Terre had seen the Blues at the foot of the declivity, he gave the owl's cry joyously, and the Chouans reappeared, but their numbers were less. Some were no doubt busy in taking care of the wounded in the little village of La Pelerine, situated on the side of the mountain which looks toward the valley of Couesnon. Two or three chiefs of what were called the "Chasseurs du Roi" clustered about Marche-a-Terre. A few feet apart sat the young noble called The *Gars*, on a granite rock, absorbed in thoughts excited by the difficulties of his enterprise, which now began to show themselves. Marche-a-Terre screened his forehead with his hand from the rays of the sun, and looked gloomily at the road by which the Blues were crossing the valley of La Pelerine. His small black eyes could see what was happening on the hill-slopes on the other side of the valley.

"The Blues will intercept the messenger," said the angry voice of one of the leaders who stood near him.

"By Saint Anne of Auray!" exclaimed another. "Why did you make us fight? Was it to save your own skin from the Blues?"

Marche-a-Terre darted a venomous look at his questioner and struck the ground with his heavy carbine.

"Am I your leader?" he asked. Then after a pause he added, pointing to the remains of Hulot's detachment, "If you had all fought as I did, not one of those Blues would have escaped, and the coach could have got here safely."

"They'd never have thought of escorting it or holding it back if we had let them go by without a fight. No, you wanted to save your precious skin and get out of their hands—He has bled us for the sake of his own snout," continued the orator, "and made us lose twenty thousand *francs* in good coin."

"Snout yourself!" cried Marche-a-Terre, retreating three steps and aiming at his aggressor. "It isn't that you hate the Blues, but you love the gold. Die without confession and be damned, for you haven't taken the sacrament for a year."

This insult so incensed the Chouan that he turned pale and a low growl came from his chest as he aimed in turn at Marche-a-Terre. The young chief sprang between them and struck their weapons from their hands with the barrel of his own carbine; then he demanded an explanation of the dispute, for the conversation had been carried on in the Breton dialect, an idiom with which he was not familiar.

"Monsieur le marquis," said Marche-a-Terre, as he ended his account of the quarrel, "it is all the more unreasonable in them to find fault with me because I have left Pille-Miche behind me; he'll know how to save the coach for us."

"What!" exclaimed the young man, angrily, "are you waiting here, all of you, to pillage that coach?—a parcel of cowards who couldn't win a victory in the first fight to which I led you! But why should you win if that's your object? The defenders of God and the king are thieves, are they? By Saint Anne of Auray! I'd have you know, we are making war against the Republic, and not robbing travellers. Those who are guilty in future of such shameful actions shall not receive absolution, nor any of the favours reserved for the faithful servants of the king."

A murmur came from the group of Chouans, and it was easy to see that the authority of the new chief was about to be disputed. The young man, on whom this effect of his words was by no means lost, was thinking of the best means of maintaining the dignity of his command, when the trot of a horse was heard in the vicinity. All heads turned in the direction from which the sound came. A lady appeared, sitting astride of a little Breton horse, which she put at a gallop as soon as she saw the young leader, so as to reach the group of Chouans as quickly as possible.

"What is the matter?" she said, looking first at the Chouans and then at their chief.

"Could you believe it, *madame*? they are waiting to rob the diligence from Mayenne to Fougeres when we have just had a skirmish, in order to release the conscripts of Fougeres, which has cost us a great many men without defeating the Blues."

"Well, where's the harm of that?" asked the young lady, to whom the natural shrewdness of a woman explained the whole scene. "You have lost men, but there's no lack of others; the coach is bringing gold, and there's always a lack of that. We bury men, who go to heaven, and we take money, which goes into the pockets of heroes. I don't see the difficulty."

The Chouans approved of her speech by unanimous smiles.

"Do you see nothing in all that to make you blush?" said the young man, in a low voice. "Are you in such need of money that you must pillage on the high-road?"

"I am so eager for it, marquis, that I should put my heart in pawn if it were not already captured," she said, smiling coquettishly. "But where did you get the strange idea that you could manage Chouans without letting them rob a few Blues here and there? Don't you know the saying, 'Thieving as an owl'?—and that's a Chouan. Besides," she said, raising her voice to be heard by the men, "it is just; haven't the Blues seized the property of the Church, and our own?"

Another murmur, very different from the growl with which the Chouans had answered their leader, greeted these words. The young man's face grew darker; he took the young lady aside and said in the annoyed tone of a well-bred man, "Will those gentlemen be at La Vivetiere on the appointed day?"

"Yes," she replied, "all of them, the Claimant, Grand-Jacques, and perhaps Ferdinand."

"Then allow me to return there. I cannot sanction such robbery. Yes, *madame*, I call it robbery. There may be honour in being robbed, but—"

"Well, well," she said, interrupting him, "then I shall have your share of the booty, and I am much obliged to you for giving it up to me; the extra sum will be extremely useful, for my mother has delayed sending me money, so that I am almost destitute."

"*Adieu!*" cried the marquis.

He turned away, but the lady ran after him.

"Why won't you stay with me?" she said, giving him the look, half-despotic, half-caressing, with which women who have a right to a man's respect let him know their wishes.

"You are going to pillage that coach?"

"Pillage? what a word!" she said. "Let me explain to you—"

"Explain nothing," he said, taking her hand and kissing it with the superficial gallantry of a courtier. "Listen to me," he added after a short pause: "if I were to stay here while they capture that diligence our people would kill me, for I should certainly—"

"Not kill them," she said quickly, "for they would bind your hands, with all the respect that is due to your rank; then, having levied the necessary contribution for their equipment, subsistence, and munitions from our enemies, they would unbind you and obey you blindly."

"And you wish me to command such men under such circumstances? If my life is necessary to the cause which I defend allow me at any rate to save the honour of my position. If I withdraw now I can ignore this base act. I will return, in order to escort you."

So saying, he rapidly disappeared. The young lady listened to his receding steps with evident displeasure. When the sound on the dried leaves ceased, she stood for a moment as if confounded, then she hastily returned to the Chouans. With a gesture of contempt she said to Marche-a-Terre, who helped her to dismount, "That young man wants to make regular war on the Republic! Ah, well! he'll get over that in a few days. How he treated me!" she thought, presently.

She seated herself on the rock where the marquis had been sitting, and silently awaited the arrival of the coach. It was one of the phenomena of the times, and not the least of them, that this young and noble lady should be flung by violent partisanship into the struggle of monarchies against the spirit of the age, and be driven by the strength of her feelings into actions of which it may almost be said she was not conscious. In this she resembled others of her time who were led away by an enthusiasm which was often productive of noble deeds. Like her, many women played heroic or blameworthy parts in the fierce struggle. The royalist cause had no emissaries so devoted and so active as these women; but none of the heroines on that side paid for mistaken devotion or for actions forbidden to their sex, with a greater expiation than did this lady when, seated on that wayside rock, she was forced to admire the young leader's noble disdain and loyalty to principle. Insensibly she dropped into reverie. Bitter memories made her long for the innocence of her early years, and regret that she had escaped being a victim of the Revolution whose victorious march could no longer be arrested by feeble hands.

The coach, which, as we now see, had much to do with the attack of the Chouans, had started from the little town of Ernee a few moments before the skirmishing began. Nothing pictures a region so well as the state of its social material. From this point of view the coach deserves a mention. The Revolution itself was powerless to destroy it; in fact, it still rolls to this present day. When Turgot bought up the privileges of a company, obtained under Louis XIV., for the exclusive right of transporting travellers from one part of the kingdom to another, and instituted the lines of coaches called the *turgotines*, all the old vehicles of the former company flocked into the provinces. One of these shabby coaches was now plying between Mayenne and Fougeres. A few objectors called it the *turgotine*, partly to mimic Paris and partly to deride a minister who attempted innovations. This *turgotine* was a wretched cabriolet on two high wheels, in the depths of which two persons, if rather fat, could with difficulty have stowed themselves. The narrow quarters of this rickety machine not admitting of any crowding, and the box which formed the seat being kept exclusively for the postal service, the travellers who had any baggage were forced to keep it between their legs, already tortured by being squeezed into a sort of little box in shape like a bellows. The original colour of coach and running-gear was an insoluble enigma. Two leather curtains, very difficult to adjust in spite of their long service, were supposed to protect the occupants from cold and rain. The driver, perched on a plank seat like those of the worst Parisian *coucous*, shared in the conversation by reason of his position between his victims, biped and quadruped. The equipage presented various fantastic resemblances to decrepit old men who have gone through a goodly number of catarrhs and apoplexies and whom death respects; it moaned as it rolled, and squeaked spasmodically. Like a traveller overtaken by sleep, it rocked alternately forward and back, as though it tried to resist the violent action of two little Breton horses which dragged it along a road which was more than rough. This monument of a past era contained three travellers, who, on leaving Ernee, where they had changed horses, continued a conversation begun with the driver before reaching the little town.

"What makes you think the Chouans are hereabouts?" said the coachman. "The Ernee people tell me that Commandant Hulot has not yet started from Fougeres."

"Ho, ho, friend driver!" said the youngest of the travellers, "you

41

risk nothing but your own carcass! If you had a thousand *francs* about you, as I have, and were known to be a good patriot, you wouldn't take it so easy."

"You are pretty free with your tongue, any way," said the driver, shaking his head.

"Count your lambs, and the wolf will eat them," remarked another of the travellers.

This man, who was dressed in black, seemed to be about forty years old, and was, probably, the rector of some parish in the neighbourhood. His chin rested on a double fold of flesh, and his florid complexion indicated a priest. Though short and fat, he displayed some agility when required to get in or out of the vehicle.

"Perhaps you are both Chouans!" cried the man of the thousand *francs*, whose ample goatskin, covering trousers of good cloth and a clean waistcoat, bespoke a rich farmer. "By the soul of Saint Robespierre! I swear you shall be roughly handled."

He turned his grey eyes from the driver to his fellow-travellers and showed them a pistol in his belt.

"Bretons are not afraid of that," said the rector, disdainfully. "Besides, do we look like men who want your money?"

Every time the word "money" was mentioned the driver was silent, and the rector had wit enough to doubt whether the patriot had any at all, and to suspect that the driver was carrying a good deal.

"Are you well laden, Coupiau?" he asked.

"Oh, no, Monsieur Gudin," replied the coachman. "I'm carrying next to nothing."

The priest watched the faces of the patriot and Coupiau as the latter made this answer, and both were imperturbable.

"So much the better for you," remarked the patriot. "I can now take measures to save my property in case of danger."

Such despotic assumption nettled Coupiau, who answered gruffly: "I am the master of my own carriage, and so long as I drive you—"

"Are you a patriot, or are you a Chouan?" said the other, sharply interrupting him.

"Neither the one nor the other," replied Coupiau. "I'm a postilion, and, what is more, a Breton,—consequently, I fear neither Blues nor nobles."

"Noble thieves!" cried the patriot, ironically.

"They only take back what was stolen from them," said the rector, vehemently.

The two men looked at each other in the whites of their eyes, if we may use a phrase so colloquial. Sitting back in the vehicle was a third traveller who took no part in the discussion, and preserved a deep silence. The driver and the patriot and even Gudin paid no attention to this mute individual; he was, in truth, one of those uncomfortable, unsocial travellers who are found sometimes in a stage-coach, like a patient calf that is being carried, bound, to the nearest market. Such travellers begin by filling their legal space, and end by sleeping, without the smallest respect for their fellow-beings, on a neighbour's shoulder. The patriot, Gudin, and the driver had let him alone, thinking him asleep, after discovering that it was useless to talk to a man whose stolid face betrayed an existence spent in measuring yards of linen, and an intellect employed in selling them at a good percentage above cost. This fat little man, doubled-up in his corner, opened his porcelain-blue eyes every now and then, and looked at each speaker with a sort of terror. He appeared to be afraid of his fellow-travellers and to care very little about the Chouans. When he looked at the driver, however, they seemed to be a pair of free-masons. Just then the first volley of musketry was heard on La Pelerine. Coupiau, frightened, stopped the coach.

"Oh! oh!" said the priest, as if he had some means of judging, "it is a serious engagement; there are many men."

"The trouble for us, Monsieur Gudin," cried Coupiau, "is to know which side will win."

The faces of all became unanimously anxious.

"Let us put up the coach at that inn which I see over there," said the patriot; "we can hide it till we know the result of the fight."

The advice seemed so good that Coupiau followed it. The patriot helped him to conceal the coach behind a wood-pile; the *abbe* seized the occasion to pull Coupiau aside and say to him, in a low voice: "Has he really any money?"

"Hey, Monsieur Gudin, if it gets into the pockets of your Reverence, they won't be weighed down with it."

When the Blues marched by, after the encounter on La Pelerine, they were in such haste to reach Ernee that they passed the little inn without halting. At the sound of their hasty march, Gudin and the innkeeper, stirred by curiosity, went to the gate of the courtyard to watch them. Suddenly, the fat ecclesiastic rushed to a soldier who was lagging in the rear.

"Gudin!" he cried, "you wrong-headed fellow, have you joined the Blues? My lad, you are surely not in earnest?"

"Yes, uncle," answered the corporal. "I've sworn to defend France."

"Unhappy boy! you'll lose your soul," said the uncle, trying to rouse his nephew to the religious sentiments which are so powerful in the Breton breast.

"Uncle," said the young man, "if the king had placed himself at the head of his armies, I don't say but what—"

"Fool! who is talking to you about the king? Does your republic give abbeys? No, it has upset everything. How do you expect to get on in life? Stay with us; sooner or later we shall triumph and you'll be counsellor to some parliament."

"Parliaments!" said young Gudin, in a mocking tone. "Good-bye, uncle."

"You sha'n't have a penny at my death," cried his uncle, in a rage. "I'll disinherit you."

"Thank you, uncle," said the Republican, as they parted.

The fumes of the cider which the patriot copiously bestowed on Coupiau during the passage of the little troop had somewhat dimmed the driver's perceptions, but he roused himself joyously when the inn-keeper, having questioned the soldiers, came back to the inn and announced that the Blues were victorious. He at once brought out the coach and before long it was wending its way across the valley.

When the Blues reached an acclivity on the road from which the plateau of La Pelerine could again be seen in the distance, Hulot turned round to discover if the Chouans were still occupying it, and the sun, glinting on the muzzles of the guns, showed them to him, each like a dazzling spot. Giving a last glance to the valley of La Pelerine before turning into that of Ernee, he thought he saw Coupiau's vehicle on the road he had just traversed.

"Isn't that the Mayenne coach?" he said to his two officers.

They looked at the venerable *turgotine*, and easily recognized it.

"But," said Hulot, "how did we fail to meet it?"

Merle and Gerard looked at each other in silence.

"Another enigma!" cried the commandant. "But I begin to see the meaning of it all."

At the same moment Marche-a-Terre, who also knew the *turgotine*, called his comrades' attention to it, and the general shout of joy which they sent up roused the young lady from her reflections. She advanced a little distance and saw the coach, which was beginning the ascent of La Pelerine with fatal rapidity. The luckless vehicle soon reached the plateau. The Chouans, who had meantime hidden themselves, swooped on their prey with hungry celerity. The silent traveller slipped to the floor of the carriage, bundling himself up into the semblance of a bale.

44

"Well done!" cried Coupiau from his wooden perch, pointing to the man in the goatskin; "you must have scented this patriot who has lots of gold in his pouch—"

The Chouans greeted these words with roars of laughter, crying out: "Pille-Miche! hey, Pille-Miche! Pille-Miche!"

Amid the laughter, to which Pille-Miche responded like an echo, Coupiau came down from his seat quite crestfallen. When the famous Cibot, otherwise called Pille-Miche, helped his neighbour to get out of the coach, a respectful murmur was heard among the Chouans.

"It is the Abbe Gudin!" cried several voices. At this respected name every hat was off, and the men knelt down before the priest as they asked his blessing, which he gave solemnly.

"Pille-Miche here could trick Saint Peter and steal the keys of Paradise," said the rector, slapping that worthy on the shoulder. "If it hadn't been for him, the Blues would have intercepted us."

Then, noticing the lady, the *abbe* went to speak to her apart. Marche-a-Terre, who had meantime briskly opened the boot of the cabriolet, held up to his comrades, with savage joy, a bag, the shape of which betrayed its contents to be rolls of coin. It did not take long to divide the booty. Each Chouan received his share, so carefully apportioned that the division was made without the slightest dispute. Then Marche-a-Terre went to the lady and the priest, and offered them each about six thousand *francs*.

"Can I conscientiously accept this money, Monsieur Gudin?" said the lady, feeling a need of justification.

"Why not, *madame*? In former days the Church approved of the confiscation of the property of Protestants, and there's far more reason for confiscating that of these revolutionists, who deny God, destroy chapels, and persecute religion."

The *abbe* then joined example to precept by accepting, without the slightest scruple, the novel sort of tithe which Marche-a-Terre offered to him. "Besides," he added, "I can now devote all I possess to the service of God and the king; for my nephew has joined the Blues, and I disinherit him."

Coupiau was bemoaning himself and declaring that he was ruined.

"Join us," said Marche-a-Terre, "and you shall have your share."

"They'll say I let the coach be robbed on purpose if I return without signs of violence."

"Oh, is that all?" exclaimed Marche-a-Terre.

He gave a signal and a shower of bullets riddled the *turgotine*. At this unexpected volley the old vehicle gave forth such a lamentable cry that the Chouans, superstitious by nature, recoiled in terror; but Marche-a-Terre caught sight of the pallid face of the silent traveller rising from the floor of the coach.

"You've got another fowl in your coop," he said in a low voice to Coupiau.

"Yes," said the driver; "but I make it a condition of my joining you that I be allowed to take that worthy man safe and sound to Fougeres. I'm pledged to it in the name of Saint Anne of Auray."

"Who is he?" asked Pille-Miche.

"That I can't tell you," replied Coupiau.

"Let him alone!" said Marche-a-Terre, shoving Pille-Miche with his elbow; "he has vowed by Saint Anne of Auray, and he must keep his word."

"Very good," said Pille-Miche, addressing Coupiau; "but mind you don't go down the mountain too fast; we shall overtake you,—a good reason why; I want to see the cut of your traveller, and give him his passport."

Just then the gallop of a horse coming rapidly up the slopes of La Pelerine was heard, and the young chief presently reappeared. The lady hastened to conceal the bag of plunder which she held in her hand.

"You can keep that money without any scruple," said the young man, touching the arm which the lady had put behind her. "Here is a letter for you which I have just found among mine which were waiting for me at La Vivetiere; it is from your mother." Then, looking at the Chouans who were disappearing into the woods, and at the *turgotine* which was now on its way to the valley of Couesnon, he added: "After all my haste I see I am too late. God grant I am deceived in my suspicions!"

"It was my poor mother's money!" cried the lady, after opening her letter, the first lines of which drew forth her exclamation.

A smothered laugh came from the woods, and the young man himself could not help smiling as he saw the lady holding in her hand the bag containing her share in the pillage of her own money. She herself began to laugh.

"Well, well, marquis, God be praised! this time, at least, you can't blame me," she said, smiling.

"Levity in everything! even your remorse!" said the young man.

She coloured and looked at the marquis with so genuine a contrition that he was softened. The *abbe* politely returned to her, with an equivocal manner, the sum he had received; then he followed the young leader who took the by-way through which he had come. Before following them the lady made a sign to Marche-a-Terre, who came to her.

"Advance towards Mortagne," she said to him in a low voice. "I know that the Blues are constantly sending large sums of money in coin to Alencon to pay for their supplies of war. If I allow you and your comrades to keep what you captured today it is only on condition that you repay it later. But be careful that the *Gars* knows nothing of the object of the expedition; he would certainly oppose it; in case of ill-luck, I will pacify him."

"Madame," said the marquis, after she had rejoined him and had mounted his horse *en croupe*, giving her own to the *abbe*, "my friends in Paris write me to be very careful of what we do; the Republic, they say, is preparing to fight us with spies and treachery."

"It wouldn't be a bad plan," she replied; "they have clever ideas, those fellows. I could take part in that sort of war and find foes."

"I don't doubt it!" cried the marquis. "Pichegru advises me to be cautious and watchful in my friendships and relations of every kind. The Republic does me the honour to think me more dangerous than all the Vendeans put together, and counts on certain of my weaknesses to lay hands upon me."

"Surely you will not distrust me?" she said, striking his heart with the hand by which she held to him.

"Are you a traitor, *madame?*" he said, bending towards her his forehead, which she kissed.

"In that case," said the *abbe*, referring to the news, "Fouche's police will be more dangerous for us than their battalions of recruits and counter-Chouans."

"Yes, true enough, father," replied the marquis.

"Ah! ah!" cried the lady. "Fouche means to send women against you, does he? I shall be ready for them," she added in a deeper tone of voice and after a slight pause.

****

At a distance of three or four gunshots from the plateau, now abandoned, a little scene was taking place which was not uncommon in those days on the high-roads. After leaving the little village of La Pelerine, Pille-Miche and Marche-a-Terre again stopped the *turgotine* at a dip in the road. Coupiau got off his seat after making a faint resistance. The silent traveller, extracted from his hiding place by the two Chouans, found himself on his knees in a furze bush.

"Who are you?" asked Marche-a-Terre in a threatening voice.

The traveller kept silence until Pille-Miche put the question again and enforced it with the butt end of his gun.

47

"I am Jacques Pinaud," he replied, with a glance at Coupiau; "a poor linen-draper."

Coupiau made a sign in the negative, not considering it an infraction of his promise to Saint Anne. The sign enlightened Pille-Miche, who took aim at the luckless traveller, while Marche-a-Terre laid before him categorically a terrible ultimatum.

"You are too fat to be poor. If you make me ask you your name again, here's my friend Pille-Miche, who will obtain the gratitude and good-will of your heirs in a second. Who are you?" he added, after a pause.

"I am d'Orgemont, of Fougeres."

"Ah! ah!" cried the two Chouans.

"I didn't tell your name, Monsieur d'Orgemont," said Coupiau. "The Holy Virgin is my witness that I did my best to protect you."

"Inasmuch as you are Monsieur d'Orgemont, of Fougeres," said Marche-a-Terre, with an air of ironical respect, "we shall let you go in peace. Only, as you are neither a good Chouan nor a true Blue (thought it was you who bought the property of the Abbey de Juvigny), you will pay us three hundred crowns of six *francs* each for your ransom. Neutrality is worth that, at least."

"Three hundred crowns of six *francs* each!" chorussed the luckless banker, Pille-Miche, and Coupiau, in three different tones.

"Alas, my good friend," continued d'Orgemont, "I'm a ruined man. The last forced loan of that devilish Republic for a hundred millions sucked me dry, taxed as I was already."

"How much did your Republic get out of you?"

"A thousand crowns, my dear man," replied the banker, with a piteous air, hoping for a reduction.

"If your Republic gets forced loans out of you for such big sums as that you must see that you would do better with us; our government would cost you less. Three hundred crowns, do you call that dear for your skin?"

"Where am I to get them?"

"Out of your strong-box," said Pille-Miche; "and mind that the money is forthcoming, or we'll singe you still."

"How am I to pay it to you?" asked d'Orgemont.

"Your country-house at Fougeres is not far from Gibarry's farm where my cousin Galope-Chopine, otherwise called Cibot, lives. You can pay the money to him," said Pille-Miche.

"That's not business-like," said d'Orgemont.

"What do we care for that?" said Marche-a-Terre. "But mind you

48

remember that if that money is not paid to Galope-Chopine within two weeks we shall pay you a little visit which will cure your gout. As for you, Coupiau," added Marche-a-Terre, "your name in future is to be Mene-a-Bien."

So saying, the two Chouans departed. The traveller returned to the vehicle, which, thanks to Coupiau's whip, now made rapid progress to Fougeres.

"If you'd only been armed," said Coupiau, "we might have made some defence."

"Idiot!" cried d'Orgemont, pointing to his heavy shoes. "I have ten thousand *francs* in those soles; do you think I would be such a fool as to fight with that sum about me?"

Mene-a-Bien scratched his ear and looked behind him, but his new comrades were out of sight.

Hulot and his command stopped at Ernee long enough to place the wounded in the hospital of the little town, and then, without further hindrance, they reached Mayenne. There the commandant cleared up his doubts as to the action of the Chouans, for on the following day the news of the pillage of the *turgotine* was received.

A few days later the government despatched to Mayenne so strong a force of "patriotic conscripts," that Hulot was able to fill the ranks of his brigade. Disquieting rumours began to circulate about the insurrection. A rising had taken place at all the points where, during the late war, the Chouans and Bretons had made their chief centres of insurrection. The little town of Saint-James, between Pontorson and Fougeres was occupied by them, apparently for the purpose of making it for the time being a headquarters of operations and supplies. From there they were able to communicate with Normandy and the Morbihan without risk. Their subaltern leaders roamed the three provinces, roused all the partisans of monarchy, and gave consistence and unity to their plans. These proceedings coincided with what was going on in La Vendee, where the same intrigues, under the influence of four famous leaders (the Abbe Vernal, the Comte de Fontaine, De Chatillon, and Suzannet), were agitating the country. The Chevalier de Valois, the Marquis d'Esgrignon, and the Troisvilles were, it was said, corresponding with these leaders in the department of the Orne. The chief of the great plan of operations which was thus developing slowly but in formidable proportions was really "the Gars,"—a name given by the Chouans to the Marquis de Montauran on his arrival from England. The information sent to Hulot by the War department proved correct in all particulars. The marquis

49

gained after a time sufficient ascendancy over the Chouans to make them understand the true object of the war, and to persuade them that the excesses of which they were guilty brought disgrace upon the cause they had adopted. The daring nature, the nerve, coolness, and capacity of this young nobleman awakened the hopes of all the enemies of the Republic, and suited so thoroughly the grave and even solemn enthusiasm of those regions that even the least zealous partisans of the king did their part in preparing a decisive blow in behalf of the defeated monarchy.

Hulot received no answer to the questions and the frequent reports which he addressed to the government in Paris.

But the news of the almost magical return of General Bonaparte and the events of the 18th Brumaire were soon current in the air. The military commanders of the West understood then the silence of the ministers. Nevertheless, they were only the more impatient to be released from the responsibility that weighed upon them; and they were in every way desirous of knowing what measures the new government was likely to take. When it was known to these soldiers that General Bonaparte was appointed First Consul of the Republic their joy was great; they saw, for the first time, one of their own profession called to the management of the nation. France, which had made an idol of this young hero, quivered with hope. The vigour and energy of the nation revived. Paris, weary of its long gloom, gave itself up to fetes and pleasures of which it had been so long deprived. The first acts of the Consulate did not diminish any hopes, and Liberty felt no alarm. The First Consul issued a proclamation to the inhabitants of the West. The eloquent allocutions addressed to the masses which Bonaparte had, as it were, invented, produced effects in those days of patriotism and miracle that were absolutely startling. His voice echoed through the world like the voice of a prophet, for none of his proclamations had, as yet, been belied by defeat.

Inhabitants:

An impious war again inflames the West.

The makers of these troubles are traitors sold to the English, or brigands who seek in civil war opportunity and license for misdeeds.

To such men the government owes no forbearance, nor any declaration of its principles.

But there are citizens, dear to France, who have been misled by their wiles. It is so such that truth and light are due.

Unjust laws have been promulgated and executed; arbitrary acts have threatened the safety of citizens and the liberty of consciences; mistaken entries on the list of *émigrés* imperil citizens; the great principles of social order have been violated.

The Consuls declare that liberty of worship having been guaranteed by the Constitution, the law of 11 Prairial, year III., which gives the use of edifices built for religious worship to all citizens, shall be executed.

The government will pardon; it will be merciful to repentance; its mercy will be complete and absolute; but it will punish whosoever, after this declaration, shall dare to resist the national sovereignty.

"Well," said Hulot, after the public reading of this Consular manifesto, "Isn't that paternal enough? But you'll see that not a single royalist brigand will be changed by it."

The commandant was right. The proclamation merely served to strengthen each side in their own convictions. A few days later Hulot and his colleagues received reinforcements. The new minister of war notified them that General Brune was appointed to command the troops in the west of France. Hulot, whose experience was known to the government, had provisional control in the departments of the Orne and Mayenne. An unusual activity began to show itself in the government offices.

Circulars from the minister of war and the minister of police gave notice that vigorous measures entrusted to the military commanders would be taken to stifle the insurrection at its birth. But the Chouans and the Vendeans had profited by the inaction of the Directory to rouse the whole region and virtually take possession of it. A new Consular proclamation was therefore issued. This time, it was the general speaking to his troops:—

Soldiers:

There are none but brigands, *émigrés*, and hirelings of England now remaining in the West.

The army is composed of more than fifty thousand brave men. Let me speedily hear from them that the rebel chiefs have ceased to live. Glory is won by toil alone; if it could be had by living in barracks in a town, all would have it.

Soldiers, whatever be the rank you hold in the army, the gratitude of the nation awaits you. To be worthy of it, you must brave the inclemencies of weather, ice, snow, and the excessive coldness of the nights; you must surprise your enemies at day-break, and exterminate those wretches, the disgrace of France.

Make a short and sure campaign; be inexorable to those brigands, and maintain strict discipline.

National Guards, join the strength of your arms to that of the line.

If you know among you any men who fraternize with the brigands, arrest them. Let them find no refuge; pursue them; if traitors dare to harbour and defend them, let them perish together.

"What a man!" cried Hulot. "It is just as it was in the army of Italy—he rings in the mass, and he says it himself. Don't you call that talking, hey?"

"Yes, but he speaks by himself and in his own name," said Gerard, who began to feel alarmed at the possible results of the 18th Brumaire.

"And where's the harm, since he's a soldier?" said Merle.

A group of soldiers were clustered at a little distance before the same proclamation posted on a wall. As none of them could read, they gazed at it, some with a careless eye, others with curiosity, while two or three hunted about for a citizen who looked learned enough to read it to them.

"Now you tell us, Clef-des-Coeurs, what that rag of a paper says," cried Beau-Pied, in a saucy tone to his comrade.

"Easy to guess," replied Clef-des-Coeurs.

At these words the other men clustered round the pair, who were always ready to play their parts.

"Look there," continued Clef-des-Coeurs, pointing to a coarse woodcut which headed the proclamation and represented a pair of compasses,—which had lately superseded the level of 1793. "It means that the troops—that's us—are to march firm; don't you see the com-passes are open, both legs apart?—that's an emblem."

"Such much for your learning, my lad; it isn't an emblem—it's called a problem. I've served in the artillery," continued Beau-Pied, "and problems were meat and drink to my officers."

"I say it's an emblem."

"It's a problem."

"What will you bet?"

"Anything."

"Your German pipe?"

"Done!"

"By your leave, adjutant, isn't that thing an emblem, and not a problem?" said Clef-des-Coeurs, following Gerard, who was thoughtfully walking away.

"It is both," he replied, gravely.

"The adjutant was making fun of you," said Beau-Pied. "That paper means that our general in Italy is promoted Consul, which is a fine grade, and we are to get shoes and overcoats."

2

One of Fouche's Ideas

One morning towards the end of Brumaire just as Hulot was exer-
cising his brigade, now by order of his superiors wholly concentrated
at Mayenne, a courier arrived from Alencon with despatches, at the
reading of which his face betrayed extreme annoyance.

"Forward, then!" he cried in an angry tone, sticking the papers into
the crown of his hat. "Two companies will march with me towards
Mortagne. The Chouans are there. You will accompany me," he said to
Merle and Gerard. "May be I created a nobleman if I can understand
one word of that despatch. Perhaps I'm a fool! well, anyhow, forward,
march! there's no time to lose."

"Commandant, by your leave," said Merle, kicking the cover of
the ministerial despatch with the toe of his boot, "what is there so
exasperating in that?"

"God's thunder! nothing at all—except that we are fooled."

When the commandant gave vent to this military oath (an object
it must be said of Republican atheistical remonstrance) it gave warning of a storm; the diverse intonations of the words were degrees of
a thermometer by which the brigade could judge of the patience of
its commander; the old soldier's frankness of nature had made this
knowledge so easy that the veriest little drummer-boy knew his
Hulot by heart, simply by observing the variations of the grimace
with which the commander screwed up his cheek and snapped his
eyes and vented his oath. On this occasion the tone of smothered
rage with which he uttered the words made his two friends silent
and circumspect. Even the pits of the small-pox which dented that
veteran face seemed deeper, and the skin itself browner than usual.
His broad queue, braided at the edges, had fallen upon one of his
epaulettes as he replaced his three-cornered hat, and he flung it
back with such fury that the ends became untied. However, as he

stood stock-still, his hands clenched, his arms crossed tightly over his breast, his moustache bristling, Gerard ventured to ask him presently: "Are we to start at once?"

"Yes, if the men have ammunition."

"They have."

"Shoulder arms! Left wheel, forward, march!" cried Gerard, at a sign from the commandant.

The drum-corps marched at the head of the two companies designated by Gerard. At the first roll of the drums the commandant, who still stood plunged in thought, seemed to rouse himself, and he left the town accompanied by his two officers, to whom he said not a word. Merle and Gerard looked at each other silently as if to ask, "How long is he going to keep us in suspense?" and, as they marched, they cautiously kept an observing eye on their leader, who continued to vent rambling words between his teeth. Several times these vague phrases sounded like oaths in the ears of his soldiers, but not one of them dared to utter a word; for they all, when occasion demanded, maintained the stern discipline to which the veterans who had served under Bonaparte in Italy were accustomed. The greater part of them had belonged, like Hulot, to the famous battalions which capitulated at Mayenne under a promise not to serve again on the frontier, and the army called them *Les Mayencais*. It would be difficult to find leaders and men who more thoroughly understood each other.

At dawn of the day after their departure Hulot and his troop were on the high-road to Alencon, about three miles from that town towards Mortagne, at a part of the road which leads through pastures watered by the Sarthe. A picturesque vista of these meadows lay to the left, while the woodlands on the right which flank the road and join the great forest of Menil-Broust, serve as a foil to the delightful aspect of the river-scenery. The narrow causeway is bordered on each side by ditches the soil of which, being constantly thrown out upon the fields, has formed high banks covered with furze,—the name given throughout the West to this prickly gorse. This shrub, which spreads itself in thorny masses, makes excellent fodder in winter for horses and cattle; but as long as it was not cut the Chouans hid themselves behind its breastwork of dull green. These banks bristling with gorse, signifying to travellers their approach to Brittany, made this part of the road at the period of which we write as dangerous as it was beautiful; it was these dangers which compelled the hasty departure of Hulot and his soldiers, and it was here that he at last let out the secret of his wrath.

He was now on his return, escorting an old mail-coach drawn by post-horses, which the weariness of his soldiers, after their forced march, was compelling to advance at a snail's pace. The company of Blues from the garrison at Mortagne, who had escorted the rickety vehicle to the limits of their district, where Hulot and his men had met them, could be seen in the distance, on their way back to their quarters, like so many black specks. One of Hulot's companies was in the rear, the other in advance of the carriage. The commandant, who was marching with Merle and Gerard between the advance guard and the carriage, suddenly growled out: "Ten thousand thunders! would you believe that the general detached us from Mayenne to escort two petticoats?"

"But, commandant," remarked Gerard, "when we came up just now and took charge I observed that you bowed to them not ungraciously."

"Ha! that's the infamy of it. Those dandies in Paris ordered the greatest attention paid to their damned females. How dare they dishonour good and brave patriots by trailing us after petticoats? As for me, I march straight, and I don't choose to have to do with other people's zigzags. When I saw Danton taking mistresses, and Barras too, I said to them: 'Citizens, when the Republic called you to govern, it was not that you might authorize the vices of the old regime!' You may tell me that women—oh yes! we must have women, that's all right. Good soldiers of course must have women, and good women; but in times of danger, no! Besides, where would be the good of sweeping away the old abuses if patriots bring them back again? Look at the First Consul, there's a man! no women for him; always about his business. I'd bet my left moustache that he doesn't know the fool's errand we've been sent on!"

"But, commandant," said Merle, laughing, "I have seen the tip-end of the nose of the young lady, and I'll declare the whole world needn't be ashamed to feel an itch, as I do, to revolve round that carriage and get up a bit of a conversation."

"Look out, Merle," said Gerard; "the veiled beauties have a man accompanying them who seems wily enough to catch you in a trap."

"Who? that *incroyable* whose little eyes are ferreting from one side of the road to the other, as if he saw Chouans? The fellow seems to have no legs; the moment his horse is hidden by the carriage, he looks like a duck with its head sticking out of a pate. If that booby can hinder me from kissing the pretty linnet—"

"'Duck'! 'linnet'! oh, my poor Merle, you have taken wings indeed!

56

But don't trust the duck. His green eyes are as treacherous as the eyes of a snake, and as sly as those of a woman who forgives her husband. I distrust the Chouans much less than I do those lawyers whose faces are like bottles of lemonade."

"Pooh!" cried Merle, gaily. "I'll risk it—with the commandant's permission. That woman has eyes like stars, and it's worth playing any stakes to see them."

"Caught, poor fellow!" said Gerard to the commandant; "he is beginning to talk nonsense!"

Hulot made a face, shrugged his shoulders, and said: "Before he swallows the soup, I advise him to smell it."

"Bravo, Merle," said Gerard, judging by his friend's lagging step that he meant to let the carriage overtake him. Isn't he a happy fellow? He is the only man I know who can laugh over the death of a comrade without being thought unfeeling."

"He's the true French soldier," said Hulot, in a grave tone.

"Just look at him pulling his epaulets back to his shoulders, to show he is a captain," cried Gerard, laughing,—"as if his rank mattered!"

The coach toward which the officer was pivoting did, in fact, contain two women, one of whom seemed to be the servant of the other.

"Such women always run in couples," said Hulot.

A lean and sharp-looking little man ambled his horse sometimes before, sometimes behind the carriage; but, though he was evidently accompanying these privileged women, no one had yet seen him speak to them. This silence, a proof either of respect or contempt, as the case might be; the quantity of baggage belonging to the lady, whom the commandant sneeringly called "the princess"; everything, even to the clothes of her attendant squire, stirred Hulot's bile. The dress of the unknown man was a good specimen of the fashions of the day then being caricatured as *incroyable*,—unbelievable, unless seen. Imagine a person trussed up in a coat, the front of which was so short that five or six inches of the waistcoat came below it, while the skirts were so long that they hung down behind like the tail of a cod,—the term then used to describe them. An enormous cravat was wound about his neck in so many folds that the little head which protruded from that muslin labyrinth certainly did justify Captain Merle's comparison. The stranger also wore tight-fitting trousers and Suwaroff boots. A huge blue-and-white cameo pinned his shirt; two watch-chains hung from his belt; his hair, worn in ringlets on each side of his face, concealed nearly the whole forehead; and, for a last adornment, the collar of his shirt and that of his coat came so high that his head seemed enveloped

like a bunch of flowers in a horn of paper. Add to these queer accessories, which were combined in utter want of harmony, the burlesque
contradictions in colour of yellow trousers, scarlet waistcoat, cinna-
mon coat, and a correct idea will be gained of the supreme good taste
which all dandies blindly obeyed in the first years of the Consulate.
This costume, utterly uncouth, seemed to have been invented as a
final test of grace, and to show that there was nothing too ridiculous
for fashion to consecrate. The rider seemed to be about thirty years
old, but he was really twenty-two; perhaps he owed this appearance of
age to debauchery, possibly to the perils of the period. In spite of his
preposterous dress, he had a certain elegance of manner which proved
him to be a man of some breeding.

When the captain had dropped back close to the carriage, the
dandy seemed to fathom his design, and favoured it by checking his
horse. Merle, who had flung him a sardonic glance, encountered one
of those impenetrable faces, trained by the vicissitudes of the Revolution to hide all, even the most insignificant, emotion. The moment the
curved end of the old triangular hat and the captain's epaulets were
seen by the occupants of the carriage, a voice of angelic sweetness said:
"*Monsieur l'officier*, will you have the kindness to tell us at what part of
the road we now are?"

There is some inexpressible charm in the question of an unknown
traveller, if a woman,—a world of adventure is in every word; but if
the woman asks for assistance or information, proving her weakness or
ignorance of certain things, every man is inclined to construct some
impossible tale which shall lead to his happiness. The words, "*Monsieur
l'officier*," and the polite tone of the question stirred the captain's heart
in a manner hitherto unknown to him. He tried to examine the lady,
but was cruelly disappointed, for a jealous veil concealed her features;
he could barely see her eyes, which shone through the gauze like onyx
gleaming in the sunshine.

"You are now three miles from Alencon, *madame*," he replied.

"Alencon! already!" and the lady threw herself, or, rather, she gently leaned back in the carriage, and said no more.

"Alencon?" said the other woman, apparently waking up; "then
you'll see it again."

She caught sight of the captain and was silent. Merle, disappointed
in his hope of seeing the face of the beautiful incognita, began to examine that of her companion. She was a girl about twenty-six years
of age, fair, with a pretty figure and the sort of complexion, fresh
and white and well-fed, which characterizes the women of Valognes,

Bayeux, and the environs of Alencon. Her blue eyes showed no great intelligence, but a certain firmness mingled with tender feeling. She wore a gown of some common woollen stuff. The fashion of her hair, done up closely under a Norman cap, without any pretension, gave a charming simplicity to her face. Her attitude, without, of course, having any of the conventional nobility of society, was not without the natural dignity of a modest young girl, who can look back upon her past life without a single cause for repentance. Merle knew her at a glance for one of those wild flowers which are sometimes taken from their native fields to Parisian hot-houses, where so many blasting rays are concentrated, without ever losing the purity of their colour or their rustic simplicity. The naive attitude of the girl and her modest glance showed Merle very plainly that she did not wish a listener. In fact, no sooner had he withdrawn than the two women began a conversation in so low a tone that only a murmur of it reached his ear.

"You came away in such a hurry," said the country-girl, "that you hardly took time to dress. A pretty-looking sight you are now! If we are going beyond Alencon, you must really make your toilet."

"Oh! oh! Francine!" cried the lady.

"What is it?"

"This is the third time you have tried to make me tell you the reasons for this journey and where we are going."

"Have I said one single word which deserves that reproach?"

"Oh, I've noticed your manoeuvring. Simple and truthful as you are, you have learned a little cunning from me. You are beginning to hold questioning in horror; and right enough, too, for of all the known ways of getting at a secret, questions are, to my mind, the silliest."

"Well," said Francine, "since nothing escapes you, you must admit, Marie, that your conduct would excite the curiosity of a saint. Yesterday without a penny, today your hands are full of gold; at Mortagne they give you the mail-coach which was pillaged and the driver killed, with government troops to protect you, and you are followed by a man whom I regard as your evil genius."

"Who? Corentin?" said the young lady, accenting the words by two inflections of her voice expressive of contempt, a sentiment which appeared in the gesture with which she waved her hand towards the rider. "Listen, Francine," she said. "Do you remember Patriot, the monkey I taught to imitate Danton?"

"Yes, *mademoiselle*."

"Well, were you afraid of him?"

"He was chained."

"And Corentin is muzzled, my dear."

"We used to play with Patriot by the hour," said Francine,—"I know that; but he always ended by serving us some bad trick." So saying, Francine threw herself hastily back close to her mistress, whose hands she caught and kissed in a coaxing way; saying in a tone of deep affection: "You know what I mean, Marie, but you will not answer me. How can you, after all that sadness which did so grieve me—oh, indeed it grieved me!—how can you, in twenty-four hours, change about and become so gay? you, who talked of suicide! Why have you changed? I have a right to ask these questions of your soul—it is mine, my claim to it is before that of others, for you will never be better loved than you are by me. Speak, *mademoiselle*."

"Why, Francine, don't you see all around you the secret of my good spirits? Look at the yellowing tufts of those distant tree-tops; not one is like another. As we look at them from this distance don't they seem like an old bit of tapestry? See the hedges from behind which the Chouans may spring upon us at any moment. When I look at that gorse I fancy I can see the muzzles of their guns. Every time the road is shady under the trees I fancy I shall hear firing, and then my heart beats and a new sensation comes over me. It is neither the shuddering of fear nor an emotion of pleasure; no, it is better than either, it is the stirring of everything within me—it is life! Why shouldn't I be gay when a little excitement is dropped into my monotonous existence?"

"Ah! you are telling me nothing, cruel girl! Holy Virgin!" added Francine, raising her eyes in distress to heaven; "to whom will she confess herself if she denies the truth to me?"

"Francine," said the lady, in a grave tone, "I can't explain to you my present enterprise; it is horrible."

"Why do wrong when you know it to be wrong?"

"How can I help it? I catch myself thinking as if I were fifty, and acting as if I were still fifteen. You have always been my better self, my poor Francine, but in this affair I must stifle conscience. And," she added after a pause, "I cannot. Therefore, how can you expect me to take a confessor as stern as you?" and she patted the girl's hand.

"When did I ever blame your actions?" cried Francine. "Evil is so mixed with good in your nature. Yes, Saint Anne of Auray, to whom I pray to save you, will absolve you for all you do. And, Marie, am I not here beside you, without so much as knowing where you go?" and she kissed her hands with effusion.

"But," replied Marie, "you may yet desert me, if your conscience—"

"Hush, hush, *mademoiselle,*" cried Francine, with a hurt expression. "But surely you will tell me—"

"Nothing!" said the young lady, in a resolute voice. "Only—and I wish you to know it—I hate this enterprise even more than I hate him whose gilded tongue induced me to undertake it. I will be rank and own to you that I would never have yielded to their wishes if I had not foreseen, in this ignoble farce, a mingling of love and danger which tempted me. I cannot bear to leave this empty world without at least attempting to gather the flowers that it owes me,—whether I perish in the attempt or not. But remember, for the honour of my memory, that had I ever been a happy woman, the sight of their great knife, ready to fall upon my neck, would not have driven me to accept a part in this tragedy—for it is a tragedy. But now," she said, with a gesture of disgust, "if it were countermanded, I should instantly fling myself into the Sarthe. It would not be destroying life, for I have never lived."

"Oh, Saint Anne of Auray, forgive her!"

"What are you so afraid of? You know very well that the dull round of domestic life gives no opportunity for my passions. That would be bad in most women, I admit; but my soul is made of a higher sensibility and can bear great tests. I might have been, perhaps, a gentle being like you. Why, why have I risen above or sunk beneath the level of my sex? Ah! the wife of Bonaparte is a happy woman! Yes, I shall die young, for I am gay, as you say,—gay at this pleasure-party, where there is blood to drink, as that poor Danton used to say. There, there, forget what I am saying; it is the woman of fifty who speaks. Thank God! the girl of fifteen is still within me."

The young country-girl shuddered. She alone knew the fiery, impetuous nature of her mistress. She alone was initiated into the mysteries of a soul rich with enthusiasm, into the secret emotions of a being who, up to this time, had seen life pass her like a shadow she could not grasp, eager as she was to do so. After sowing broadcast with full hands and harvesting nothing, this woman was still virgin in soul, but irritated by a multitude of baffled desires. Weary of a struggle without an adversary, she had reached in her despair to the point of preferring good to evil, if it came in the form of enjoyment; evil to good, if it offered her some poetic emotion; misery to mediocrity, as something nobler and higher; the gloomy and mysterious future of present death to a life without hopes or even without sufferings. Never in any heart was so much powder heaped ready for the spark, never were so many riches for love to feed on; no daughter of Eve was ever moulded, with a greater mixture of gold in her clay. Francine, like an angel of earth, watched

61

over this being whose perfections she adored, believing that she obeyed a celestial mandate in striving to bring that spirit back among the choir of seraphim whence it was banished for the sin of pride.

"There is the clock-tower of Alencon," said the horseman, riding up to the carriage.

"I see it," replied the young lady, in a cold tone.

"Ah, well," he said, turning away with all the signs of servile submission, in spite of his disappointment.

"Go faster," said the lady to the postilion. "There is no longer any danger; go at a fast trot, or even a gallop, if you can; we are almost into Alencon."

As the carriage passed the commandant, she called out to him, in a sweet voice:—

"We will meet at the inn, commandant. Come and see me."

"Yes, yes," growled the commandant. "'The inn'! 'Come and see me'! Is that how you speak to an officer in command of the army?" and he shook his fist at the carriage, which was now rolling rapidly along the road.

"Don't be vexed, commandant, she has got your rank as general up her sleeve," said Corentin, laughing, as he endeavoured to put his horse into a gallop to overtake the carriage.

"I sha'n't let myself be fooled by any such folks as they," said Hulot to his two friends, in a growling tone. "I'd rather throw my general's coat into that ditch than earn it out of a bed. What are these birds after? Have you any idea, either of you?"

"Yes," said Merle, "I've an idea that that's the handsomest women I ever saw! I think you're reading the riddle all wrong. Perhaps she's the wife of the First Consul."

"Pooh! the First Consul's wife is old, and this woman is young," said Hulot. "Besides, the order I received from the minister gives her name as Mademoiselle de Verneuil. She is a *ci-devant.* Don't I know 'em? They all plied one trade before the Revolution, and any man could make himself a major, or a general in double-quick time; all he had to do was to say 'Dear heart' to them now and then."

While each soldier opened his compasses, as the commandant was wont to say, the miserable vehicle which was then used as the mail-coach drew up before the inn of the Trois Maures, in the middle of the main street of Alencon. The sound of the wheels brought the landlord to the door. No one in Alencon could have expected the arrival of the mail-coach at the Trois Maures, for the murderous attack upon the coach at Mortagne was already known, and so many

62

people followed it along the street that the two women, anxious to escape the curiosity of the crowd, ran quickly into the kitchen, which forms the inevitable antechamber to all Western inns. The landlord was about to follow them, after examining the coach, when the postilion caught him by the arm.

"Attention, citizen Brutus," he said; "there's an escort of the Blues behind us; but it is I who bring you these female citizens; they'll pay like *ci-devant* princesses, therefore—"

"Therefore, we'll drink a glass of wine together presently, my lad," said the landlord.

After glancing about the kitchen, blackened with smoke, and noticing a table bloody from raw meat, Mademoiselle de Verneuil flew into the next room with the celerity of a bird; for she shuddered at the sight and smell of the place, and feared the inquisitive eyes of a dirty *chef*, and a fat little woman who examined her attentively.

"What are we to do, wife?" said the landlord. "Who the devil could have supposed we would have so many on our hands in these days? Before I serve her a decent breakfast that woman will get impatient. Stop, an idea! evidently she is a person of quality. I'll propose to put her with the one we have upstairs. What do you think?"

When the landlord went to look for the new arrival he found only Francine, to whom he spoke in a low voice, taking her to the farther end of the kitchen, so as not to be overheard.

"If the ladies wish," he said, "to be served in private, as I have no doubt they wish to do, I have a very nice breakfast all ready for a lady and her son, and I dare say wouldn't mind sharing it with you; they are persons of condition," he added, mysteriously.

He had hardly said the words before he felt a tap on his back from the handle of a whip. He turned hastily and saw behind him a short, thick-set man, who had noiselessly entered from a side room,—an apparition which seemed to terrify the hostess, the cook, and the scullion. The landlord turned pale when he saw the intruder, who shook back the hair which concealed his forehead and eyes, raised himself on the points of his toes to reach the other's ears, and said to him in a whisper: "You know the cost of an imprudence or a betrayal, and the colour of the money we pay it in. We are generous in that coin."

He added a gesture which was like a horrible commentary to his words. Though the rotundity of the landlord prevented Francine from seeing the stranger, who stood behind him, she caught certain words of his threatening speech, and was thunderstruck at hearing the hoarse tones of a Breton voice. She sprang towards the man, but he, seeming to move with the agility of a wild animal, had already darted through a side door which opened on the courtyard. Utterly amazed, she ran to the window. Through its panes, yellowed with smoke, she caught sight of the stranger as he was about to enter the stable. Before doing so, however, he turned a pair of black eyes to the upper story of the inn, and thence to the mail-coach in the yard, as if to call some friend's attention to the vehicle. In spite of his muffling goatskin and thanks to this movement which allowed her to see his face, Francine recognized the Chouan, Marche-a-Terre, with his heavy whip; she saw him, indistinctly, in the obscurity of the stable, fling himself down on a pile of straw, in a position which enabled him to keep an eye on all that happened at the inn. Marche-a-Terre curled himself up in such a way that the cleverest spy, at any distance far or near, might have taken him for one of those huge dogs that drag the hand-carts, lying asleep with his muzzle on his paws.

The behaviour of the Chouan proved to Francine that he had not recognized her. Under the hazardous circumstances which she felt her mistress to be in, she scarcely knew whether to regret or to rejoice in this unconsciousness. But the mysterious connection between the landlord's offer (not uncommon among innkeepers, who can thus kill two birds with one stone), and the Chouan's threats, piqued her curiosity. She left the dirty window from which she could see the formless heap which she knew to be Marche-a-Terre, and returned to the landlord, who was still standing in the attitude of a man who feels he has made a blunder, and does not know how to get out of it. The Chouan's gesture had petrified the poor fellow. No one in the West was ignorant of the cruel refinements of torture with which the "Chasseurs du Roi" punished those who were even suspected of indiscretion; the landlord felt their knives already at his throat. The cook looked with a shudder at the iron stove on which they often "warmed" (*chauffaient*) the feet of those they suspected. The fat landlady held a knife in one hand and a half-peeled potato in the other, and gazed at her husband with a stupefied air. Even the scullion puzzled himself to know the reason of their speechless terror. Francine's curiosity was naturally excited by this silent scene, the principal actor of which was visible to all, though departed. The girl was gratified at the evident power of the Chouan, and though by nature too simple and humble for the tricks of a lady's maid, she was also far too anxious to penetrate the mystery not to profit by her advantages on this occasion.

"Mademoiselle accepts your proposal," she said to the landlord, who jumped as if suddenly awakened by her words.

"What proposal?" he asked with genuine surprise.

"What proposal?" asked Corentin, entering the kitchen.

"What proposal?" asked Mademoiselle de Verneuil, returning to it.

"What proposal?" asked a fourth individual on the lower step of the staircase, who now sprang lightly into the kitchen.

"Why, the breakfast with your persons of distinction," replied Francine, impatiently.

"Distinction!" said the ringing and ironical voice of the person who had just come down the stairway. "My good fellow, that strikes me as a very poor inn joke; but if it's the company of this young female citizen that you want to give us, we should be fools to refuse it. In my mother's absence, I accept," he added, striking the astonished innkeeper on the shoulder.

The charming heedlessness of youth disguised the haughty insolence of the words, which drew the attention of every one present to the new-comer. The landlord at once assumed the countenance of Pilate washing his hands of the blood of that just man; he slid back two steps to reach his wife's ear, and whispered, "You are witness, if any harm comes of it, that it is not my fault. But, anyhow," he added, in a voice that was lower still, "go and tell Monsieur Marche-a-Terre what has happened."

The traveller, who was a young man of medium height, wore a dark blue coat and high black gaiters coming above the knee and over the breeches, which were also of blue cloth. This simple uniform, without epaulets, was that of the pupils of the *Ecole Polytechnique*. Beneath this plain attire Mademoiselle de Verneuil could distinguish at a glance the elegant shape and nameless *something* that tells of natural nobility. The face of the young man, which was rather ordinary at first sight, soon attracted the eye by the conformation of certain features which revealed a soul capable of great things. A bronzed skin, curly fair hair, sparkling blue eyes, a delicate nose, motions full of ease, all disclosed a life guided by noble sentiments and trained to the habit of command. But the most characteristic signs of his nature were in the chin, which was dented like that of Bonaparte, and in the lower lip, which joined the upper one with a graceful curve, like that of an acanthus leaf on the capital of a Corinthian column. Nature had given to these two features of his face an irresistible charm.

"This young man has singular distinction if he is really a republican," thought Mademoiselle de Verneuil.

To see all this at a glance, to brighten at the thought of pleasing, to bend her head softly and smile coquettishly and cast a soft look able

65

to revive a heart that was dead to love, to veil her long black eyes with lids whose curving lashes made shadows on her cheeks, to choose the melodious tones of her voice and give a penetrating charm to the formal words, "Monsieur, we are very much obliged to you,"—all this charming by-play took less time than it has taken to describe it. After this, Mademoiselle de Verneuil, addressing the landlord, asked to be shown to a room, saw the staircase, and disappeared with Francine, leaving the stranger to discover whether her reply was intended as an acceptance or a refusal.

"Who is that woman?" asked the *Polytechnique* student, in an airy manner, of the landlord, who still stood motionless and bewildered.

"That's the female citizen Verneuil," replied Corentin, sharply, looking jealously at the questioner; "a *ci-devant*; what is she to you?"

The stranger, who was humming a revolutionary tune, turned his head haughtily towards Corentin. The two young men looked at each other for a moment like cocks about to fight, and the glance they exchanged gave birth to a hatred which lasted forever. The blue eye of the young soldier was as frank and honest as the green eye of the other man was false and malicious; the manners of the one had native grandeur, those of the other were insinuating; one was eager in his advance, the other deprecating; one commanded respect, the other sought it.

"Is the citizen du Gua Saint-Cyr here?" said a peasant, entering the kitchen at that moment.

"What do you want of him?" said the young man, coming forward.

The peasant made a low bow and gave him a letter, which the young cadet read and threw into the fire; then he nodded his head and the man withdrew.

"No doubt you've come from Paris, citizen?" said Corentin, approaching the stranger with a certain ease of manner, and a pliant, affable air which seemed intolerable to the citizen du Gua.

"Yes," he replied, shortly.

"I suppose you have been graduated into some grade of the artillery?"

"No, citizen, into the navy."

"Ah! then you are going to Brest?" said Corentin, interrogatively.

But the young sailor turned lightly on the heels of his shoes without deigning to reply, and presently disappointed all the expectations which Mademoiselle de Verneuil had based on the charm of his appearance. He applied himself to ordering his breakfast with the eagerness of a boy, questioned the cook and the landlady about their receipts, wondered at provincial customs like a Parisian just out of his shell, made as many objections as any fine lady, and showed the more lack of mind and character because his face and manner had seemed to promise them. Corentin smiled with pity when he saw the face he made on tasting the best cider of Normandy.

"*Heu!*" he cried; "how can you swallow such stuff as that? It is meat and drink both. I don't wonder the Republic distrusts a province where they knock their harvest from trees with poles, and shoot travellers from the ditches. Pray don't put such medicine as that on the table; give us some good Bordeaux, white and red. And above all, do see if there is a good fire upstairs. These country-people are so backward in civilization!" he added. "Alas!" he sighed, "there is but one Paris in the world; what a pity it is I can't transport it to sea! Heavens! spoil-sauce!" he suddenly cried out to the cook; "what makes you put vinegar in that fricassee when you have lemons? And, *madame*," he added, "you gave me such coarse sheets I couldn't close my eyes all night." Then he began to twirl a huge cane, executing with a silly sort of care a variety of evolutions, the greater or less precision and agility of which were considered proofs of a young man's standing in the class of the *incroyables*, so-called.

"And it is with such dandies as that," said Corentin to the landlord confidentially, watching his face, "that the Republic expects to improve her navy!"

"That man," said the young sailor to the landlady, in a low voice, "is a spy of Fouche's. He has 'police' stamped on his face, and I'll swear that spot he has got on his chin is Paris mud. Well, set a thief to catch—"

Just then a lady to whom the young sailor turned with every sign of outward respect, entered the kitchen of the inn.

"My dear mamma," he said. "I am glad you've come. I have recruited some guests in your absence."

"Guests?" she replied; "what folly!"

"It is Mademoiselle de Verneuil," he said in a low voice.

"She perished on the scaffold after the affair of Savenay; she went to Mans to save her brother the Prince de Loudon," returned his mother, rather brusquely.

"You are mistaken, *madame*," said Corentin, gently, emphasizing the word "*madame*"; "there are two demoiselles de Verneuil; all great houses, as you know, have several branches."

The lady, surprised at this freedom, drew back a few steps to examine the speaker; she turned her black eyes upon him, full of the keen sagacity so natural to women, seeking apparently to discover in

67

what interest he stepped forth to explain Mademoiselle de Verneuil's birth. Corentin, on the other hand, who was studying the lady cautiously, denied her in his own mind the joys of motherhood and gave her those of love; he refused the possession of a son of twenty to a woman whose dazzling skin, and arched eyebrows, and lashes still unblemished, were the objects of his admiration, and whose abundant black hair, parted on the forehead into simple bands, bought out the youthfulness of an intelligent head. The slight lines of the brow, far from indicating age, revealed young passions. Though the piercing eyes were somewhat veiled, it was either from the fatigue of travelling or the too frequent expression of excitement. Corentin remarked that she was wrapped in a mantle of English material, and that the shape of her hat, foreign no doubt, did not belong to any of the styles called Greek, which ruled the Parisian fashions of the period. Corentin was one of those beings who are compelled by the bent of their natures to suspect evil rather than good, and he instantly doubted the citizenship of the two travellers. The lady, who, on her side, had made her observations on the person of Corentin with equal rapidity, turned to her son with a significant look which may be faithfully translated into the words: "Who is this queer man? Is he of our stripe?"

To this mute inquiry the youth replied by an attitude and a gesture which said: "Faith! I can't tell; but I distrust him." Then, leaving his mother to fathom the mystery, he turned to the landlady and whispered: "Try to find out who that fellow is; and whether he is really accompanying the young lady; and why."

"So," said Madame du Gua, looking at Corentin, "you are quite sure, citizen, that Mademoiselle de Verneuil is living?"

"She is living in flesh and blood as surely, *madame*, as the citizen du Gua Saint-Cyr."

This answer contained a sarcasm, the hidden meaning of which was known to none but the lady herself, and any one but herself would have been disconcerted by it. Her son looked fixedly at Corentin, who coolly pulled out his watch without appearing to notice the effect of his answer. The lady, uneasy and anxious to discover at once if the speech meant danger or was merely accidental, said to Corentin in a natural tone and manner; "How little security there is on these roads. We were attacked by Chouans just beyond Mortagne. My son came very near being killed; he received two balls in his hat while protecting me."

"Is it possible, *madame*? were you in the mail-coach which those brigands robbed in spite of the escort,—the one we have just come by? You must know the vehicle well. They told me at Mortagne that the Chouans numbered a couple of thousands and that every one in the coach was killed, even the travellers. That's how history is written! Alas! *madame*," he continued, "if they murder travellers so near to Paris you can fancy how unsafe the roads are in Brittany. I shall return to Paris and not risk myself any farther."

"Is Mademoiselle de Verneuil young and handsome?" said the lady to the hostess, struck suddenly with an idea.

Just then the landlord interrupted the conversation, in which there was something of an angry element, by announcing that breakfast was ready. The young sailor offered his hand to his mother with an air of false familiarity that confirmed the suspicions of Corentin, to whom the youth remarked as he went up the stairway: "Citizen, if you are travelling with the female citizen de Verneuil, and she accepts the landlord's proposal, you can come too."

Though the words were said in a careless tone and were not inviting, Corentin followed. The young man squeezed the lady's hand when they were five or six steps above him, and said, in a low voice: "Now you see the dangers to which your imprudent enterprises, which have no glory in them, expose us. If we are discovered, how are we to escape? And what a contemptible role you force me to play!"

All three reached a large room on the upper floor. Any one who has travelled in the West will know that the landlord had, on such an occasion, brought forth his best things to do honour to his guests, and prepared the meal with no ordinary luxury. The table was carefully laid. The warmth of a large fire took the dampness from the room. The linen, glass, and china were not too dingy. Corentin saw at once that the landlord had, as they say familiarly, cut himself into quarters to please the strangers. "Consequently," thought he, "these people are not what they pretend to be. That young man is clever. I took him for a fool, but I begin to believe him as shrewd as myself."

The sailor, his mother, and Corentin awaited Mademoiselle de Verneuil, whom the landlord went to summon. But the handsome traveller did not come. The youth expected that she would make difficulties, and he left the room, humming the popular song, "Guard the nation's safety," and went to that of Mademoiselle de Verneuil, prompted by a keen desire to get the better of her scruples and take her back with him. Perhaps he wanted to solve the doubts which filled his mind; or else to exercise the power which all men like to think they wield over a pretty woman.

"May I be hanged if he's a Republican," thought Corentin, as he saw him go. "He moves his shoulders like a courtier. And if that's his mother," he added, mentally, looking at Madame du Gua, "I'm the Pope! They are Chouans; and I'll make sure of their quality."

The door soon opened and the young man entered, holding the hand of Mademoiselle de Verneuil, whom he led to the table with an air of self-conceit that was nevertheless courteous. The devil had not allowed that hour which had elapsed since the lady's arrival to be wasted. With Francine's assistance, Mademoiselle de Verneuil had armed herself with a travelling-dress more dangerous, perhaps, than any ball-room attire. Its simplicity had precisely that attraction which comes of the skill with which a woman, handsome enough to wear no ornaments, reduces her dress to the position of a secondary charm. She wore a green gown, elegantly cut, the jacket of which, braided and frogged, defined her figure in a manner that was hardly suitable for a young girl, allowing her supple waist and rounded bust and graceful motions to be fully seen. She entered the room smiling, with the natural amenity of women who can show a fine set of teeth, transparent as porcelain between rosy lips, and dimpling cheeks as fresh as those of childhood. Having removed the close hood which had almost concealed her head at her first meeting with the young sailor, she could now employ at her ease the various little artifices, apparently so artless, with which a woman shows off the beauties of her face and the grace of her head, and attracts admiration for them. A certain harmony between her manners and her dress made her seem so much younger than she was that Madame du Gua thought herself beyond the mark in supposing her over twenty. The coquetry of her apparel, evidently worn to please, was enough to inspire hope in the young man's breast; but Mademoiselle de Verneuil bowed to him, as she took her place, with a slight inclination of her head and without looking at him, putting him aside with an apparently light-hearted carelessness which disconcerted him. This coolness might have seemed to an observer neither caution nor coquetry, but indifference, natural or feigned. The candid expression on the young lady's face only made it the more impenetrable. She showed no consciousness of her charms, and was apparently gifted with the pretty manners that win all hearts, and had already duped the natural self-conceit of the young sailor. Thus baffled, the youth returned to his own seat with a sort of vexation.

Mademoiselle de Verneuil took Francine, who accompanied her, by the hand and said, in a caressing voice, turning to Madame de Gua: "Madame, will you have the kindness to allow this young girl, who is more a friend than a servant to me, to sit with us? In these perilous times such devotion as hers can only be repaid by the heart; indeed, that is very nearly all that is left to us."

Madame du Gua replied to the last words, which were said half aside, with a rather unceremonious bow that betrayed her annoyance at the beauty of the new-comer. Then she said, in a low voice, to her son: "'Perilous times,' 'devotion,' '*madame*,' 'servant'! that is not Mademoiselle de Verneuil; it is some girl sent here by Fouché."

The guests were about to sit down when Mademoiselle de Verneuil noticed Corentin, who was still employed in a close scrutiny of the mother and son, who were showing some annoyance at his glances.

"Citizen," she said to him, "you are no doubt too well bred to dog my steps. The Republic, when it sent my parents to the scaffold, did not magnanimously provide me with a guardian. Though you have, from extreme and chivalric gallantry accompanied me against my will to this place" (she sighed), "I am quite resolved not to allow your protecting care to become a burden to you. I am safe now, and you can leave me."

She gave him a fixed and contemptuous look. Corentin understood her; he repressed the smile which almost curled the corners of his wily lips as he bowed to her respectfully.

"*Citoyenne*," he said, "it is always an honour to obey you. Beauty is the only queen a Republican can serve."

Mademoiselle de Verneuil's eyes, as she watched him depart, shone with such natural pleasure, she looked at Francine with a smile of intelligence which betrayed so much real satisfaction, that Madame du Gua, who grew prudent as she grew jealous, felt disposed to relinquish the suspicions which Mademoiselle de Verneuil's great beauty had forced into her mind.

"It may be Mademoiselle de Verneuil, after all," she whispered to her son.

"But that escort?" answered the young man, whose vexation at the young lady's indifference allowed him to be cautious. "Is she a prisoner or an emissary, a friend or an enemy of the government?"

Madame du Gua made a sign as if to say that she would soon clear up the mystery.

However, the departure of Corentin seemed to lessen the young man's distrust, and he began to cast on Mademoiselle de Verneuil certain looks which betrayed an immoderate admiration for women, rather than the respectful warmth of a dawning passion. The young girl grew more and more reserved, and gave all her attentions to Madame du Gua. The youth, angry with himself, tried, in his vexation, to turn the tables and seem indifferent. Mademoiselle de Verneuil appeared not to notice this manoeuvre; she continued to be simple without shyness and reserved without prudery.

This chance meeting of personages who, apparently, were not destined to become intimate, awakened no agreeable sympathy on either side. There was even a sort of vulgar embarrassment, an awkwardness which destroyed all the pleasure which Mademoiselle de Verneuil and the young sailor had begun by expecting. But women have such wonderful conventional tact, they are so intimately allied with each other, or they have such keen desires for emotion, that they always know how to break the ice on such occasions. Suddenly, as if the two beauties had the same thought, they began to tease their solitary knight in a playful way, and were soon vying with each other in the jesting attention which they paid to him; this unanimity of action left them free. At the end of half an hour, the two women, already secret enemies, were apparently the best of friends. The young man then discovered that he felt as angry with Mademoiselle de Verneuil for her friendliness and freedom as he had been with her reserve. In fact, he was so annoyed by it that he regretted, with a sort of dumb anger, having allowed her to breakfast with them.

"Madame," said Mademoiselle de Verneuil, "is your son always as gloomy as he is at this moment?"

"Mademoiselle," he replied, "I ask myself what is the good of a fleeting happiness. The secret of my gloom is the evanescence of my pleasure."

"That is a madrigal," she said, laughing, "which rings of the Court rather than the *Polytechnique.*"

"My son only expressed a very natural thought, *mademoiselle,*" said Madame du Gua, who had her own reasons for placating the stranger.

"Then laugh while you may," said Mademoiselle de Verneuil, smiling at the young man. "How do you look when you have really something to weep for, if what you are pleased to call a happiness makes you so dismal?"

This smile, accompanied by a provoking glance which destroyed the consistency of her reserve, revived the youth's feelings. But inspired by her nature, which often impels a woman to do either too much or too little under such circumstances, Mademoiselle de Verneuil, having covered the young man with that brilliant look full of love's promises, immediately withdrew from his answering expression into a cold and severe modesty,—a conventional performance by which a woman sometimes hides a true emotion. In a moment, a single moment, when each expected to see the eyelids of the other lowered, they had communicated to one another their real thoughts; but they veiled their glances as quickly as they had mingled them in that one flash which convulsed their hearts and enlightened them. Confused at having said so many things in a single glance, they dared no longer look at each other. Mademoiselle de Verneuil withdrew into cold politeness, and seemed to be impatient for the conclusion of the meal.

"Mademoiselle, you must have suffered very much in prison?" said Madame du Gua.

"Alas, *madame*, I sometimes think that I am still there."

"Is your escort sent to protect you, *mademoiselle*, or to watch you? Are you still suspected by the Republic?"

Mademoiselle felt instinctively that Madame du Gua had no real interest in her, and the question alarmed her.

"Madame," she replied, "I really do not know myself the exact nature of my relations to the Republic."

"Perhaps it fears you?" said the young man, rather satirically.

"We must respect her secrets," interposed Madame du Gua.

"Oh, *madame*, the secrets of a young girl who knows nothing of life but its misfortunes are not interesting."

"But," answered Madame du Gua, wishing to continue a conversation which might reveal to her all that she wanted to know, "the First Consul seems to have excellent intentions. They say that he is going to remove the disabilities of the *émigrés*."

"That is true, *madame*," she replied, with rather too much eagerness, "and if so, why do we rouse Brittany and La Vendee? Why bring civil war into France?"

This eager cry, in which she seemed to share her own reproach, made the young sailor quiver. He looked earnestly at her, but was unable to detect either hatred or love upon her face. Her beautiful skin, the delicacy of which was shown by the colour beneath it, was impenetrable. A sudden and invincible curiosity attracted him to this strange creature, to whom he was already drawn by violent desires.

"Madame," said Mademoiselle de Verneuil, after a pause, "may I ask if you are going to Mayenne?"

"Yes, *mademoiselle*," replied the young man with a questioning look.

"Then, *madame*," she continued, "as your son serves the Republic" (she said the words with an apparently indifferent air, but she gave her companions one of those furtive glances the art of which belongs to women and diplomatists), "you must fear the Chouans, and an escort

73

is not to be despised. We are now almost travelling companions, and I hope you will come with me to Mayenne."

Mother and son hesitated, and seemed to consult each other's faces.

"I am not sure, *mademoiselle*," said the young man, "that it is prudent in me to tell you that interests of the highest importance require our presence tonight in the neighbourhood of Fougeres, and we have not yet been able to find a means of conveyance; but women are so naturally generous that I am ashamed not to confide in you. Nevertheless," he added, "before putting ourselves in your hands, I ought to know whether we shall get out of them safe and sound. In short, *mademoiselle*, are you the sovereign or the slave of your Republican escort? Pardon my frankness, but your position does not seem to me exactly natural—"

"We live in times, *monsieur*, when nothing takes place naturally. You can accept my proposal without anxiety. Above all," she added, emphasizing her words, "you need fear no treachery in an offer made by a woman who has no part in political hatreds."

"A journey thus made is not without danger," he said, with a look which gave significance to that commonplace remark.

"What is it you fear?" she answered, smiling sarcastically. "I see no peril for any one."

"Is this the woman who a moment ago shared my desires in her eyes?" thought the young man. "What a tone in her voice! she is laying a trap for me."

At that instant a shrill cry of an owl which appeared to have perched on the chimney top vibrated in the air like a warning.

"What does that mean?" said Mademoiselle de Verneuil. "Our journey together will not begin under favourable auspices. Do owls in these woods screech by daylight?" she added, with a surprised gesture.

"Sometimes," said the young man, coolly. "Mademoiselle," he continued, "we may bring you ill-luck; you are thinking of that, I am sure. We had better not travel together."

These words were said with a calmness and reserve which puzzled Mademoiselle de Verneuil.

"Monsieur," she replied, with truly aristocratic insolence, "I am far from wishing to compel you. Pray let us keep the little liberty the Republic leaves us. If Madame were alone, I should insist—"

The heavy step of a soldier was heard in the passage, and the Commandant Hulot presently appeared in the doorway with a frowning brow.

"Come here, colonel," said Mademoiselle de Verneuil, smiling and pointing to a chair beside her. "Let us talk over the affairs of State. But what is the matter with you? Are there Chouans here?"

The commandant stood speechless on catching sight of the young man, at whom he looked with peculiar attention.

"Mamma, will you take some more hare? Mademoiselle, you are not eating," said the sailor to Francine, seeming busy with the guests.

But Hulot's astonishment and Mademoiselle de Verneuil's close observation had something too dangerously serious about them to be ignored.

"What is it, citizen?" said the young man, abruptly; "do you know me?"

"Perhaps I do," replied the Republican.

"You are right; I remember you at the School."

"I never went to any school," said the soldier, roughly. "What school do you mean?"

"The *Polytechnique*."

"Ha, ha, those barracks where they expect to make soldiers in dormitories," said the veteran, whose aversion for officers trained in that nursery was insurmountable. "To what arm do you belong?"

"I am in the navy."

"Ha!" cried Hulot, smiling vindictively, "how many of your fellow-students are in the navy? Don't you know," he added in a serious tone, "that none but the artillery and the engineers graduate from there?"

The young man was not disconcerted.

"An exception was made in my favour, on account of the name I bear," he answered. "We are all naval men in our family."

"What is the name of your family, citizen?" asked Hulot.

"Du Gua Saint-Cyr."

"Then you were not killed at Mortagne?"

"He came very near being killed," said Madame du Gua, quickly; "my son received two balls in—"

"Where are your papers?" asked Hulot, not listening to the mother.

"Do you propose to read them?" said the young man, cavalierly; his blue eye, keen with suspicion, studied alternately the gloomy face of the commandant and that of Mademoiselle de Verneuil.

"A stripling like you to pretend to fool me! Come, produce your papers, or—"

"La! la! citizen, I'm not such a babe as I look to be. Why should I answer you? Who are you?"

"The commander of this department," answered Hulot.

"Oh, then, of course, the matter is serious; I am taken with arms in my hand," and he held a glass full of Bordeaux to the soldier.

"I am not thirsty," said Hulot. "Come, your papers."

At that instant the rattle of arms and the tread of men was heard in the street. Hulot walked to the window and gave a satisfied look which made Mademoiselle de Verneuil tremble. That sign of interest on her part seemed to fire the young man, whose face had grown cold and haughty. After feeling in the pockets of his coat he drew forth an elegant portfolio and presented certain papers to the commandant, which the latter read slowly, comparing the description given in the passport with the face and figure of the young man before him. During this prolonged examination the owl's cry rose again; but this time there was no difficulty whatever in recognizing a human voice. The commandant at once returned the papers to the young man, with a scoffing look.

"That's all very fine," he said; "but I don't like the music. You will come with me to headquarters."

"Why do you take him there?" asked Mademoiselle de Verneuil, in a tone of some excitement.

"My good lady," replied the commandant, with his usual grimace, "that's none of your business."

Irritated by the tone and words of the old soldier, but still more at the sort of humiliation offered to her in presence of a man who was under the influence of her charms, Mademoiselle de Verneuil rose, abandoning the simple and modest manner she had hitherto adopted; her cheeks glowed and her eyes shone as she said in a quiet tone but with a trembling voice: "Tell me, has this young man met all the requirements of the law?"

"Yes—apparently," said Hulot ironically.

"Then, I desire that you will leave him, *apparently*, alone," she said. "Are you afraid he will escape you? You are to escort him with me to Mayenne; he will be in the coach with his mother. Make no objection; it is my will—Well, what?" she added, noticing Hulot's grimace; "do you suspect him still?"

"Rather."

"What do you want to do with him?"

"Oh, nothing; balance his head with a little lead perhaps. He's a giddy-pate!" said the commandant, ironically.

"Are you joking, colonel?" cried Mademoiselle de Verneuil.

"Come!" said the commandant, nodding to the young man, "make haste, let us be off."

At this impertinence Mademoiselle de Verneuil became calm and smiling.

"Do not go," she said to the young man, protecting him with a gesture that was full of dignity.

"Oh, what a beautiful head!" said the youth to his mother, who frowned heavily.

Annoyance, and many other sentiments, aroused and struggled with, did certainly bring fresh beauties to the young woman's face. Francine, Madame du Gua, and her son had all risen from their seats. Mademoiselle de Verneuil hastily advanced and stood between them and the commandant, who smiled amusedly; then she rapidly unfastened the frogged fastenings of her jacket. Acting with that blindness which often seizes women when their self-love is threatened and they are anxious to show their power, as a child is impatient to play with a toy that has just been given to it, she took from her bosom a paper and presented it to Hulot.

"Read that," she said, with a sarcastic laugh.

Then she turned to the young man and gave him, in the excitement of her triumph, a look in which mischief was mingled with an expression of love. Their brows cleared, joy flushed each agitated face, and a thousand contradictory thoughts rose in their hearts. Madame du Gua noted in that one look far more of love than of pity in Mademoiselle de Verneuil's intervention; and she was right. The handsome creature blushed beneath the other woman's gaze, understanding its meaning, and dropped her eyelids; then, as if aware of some threatening accusation, she raised her head proudly and defied all eyes. The commandant, petrified, returned the paper, countersigned by ministers, which enjoined all authorities to obey the orders of this mysterious lady. Having done so, he drew his sword, laid it across his knees, broke the blade, and flung away the pieces.

"Mademoiselle, you probably know what you are about; but a Republican has his own ideas, and his own dignity. I cannot serve where women command. The First Consul will receive my resignation to-morrow; others, who are not of my stripe, may obey you. I do not understand my orders and therefore I stop short,—all the more because I am supposed to understand them."

There was silence for a moment, but it was soon broken by the young lady, who went up to the commandant and held out her hand, saying, "Colonel, though your beard is somewhat long, you may kiss my hand; you are, indeed, a man!"

"I flatter myself I am, *mademoiselle*," he replied, depositing a kiss upon the hand of this singular young woman rather awkwardly. "As for you, friend," he said, threatening the young man with his finger, "you have had a narrow escape this time."

"Commandant," said the youth, "it is time all this nonsense should cease; I am ready to go with you, if you like, to headquarters."

"And bring your invisible owl, Marche-a-Terre?"

"Who is Marche-a-Terre?" asked the young man, showing all the signs of genuine surprise.

"Didn't he hoot just now?"

"What did that hooting have to do with me, I should like to know? I supposed it was your soldiers letting you know of their arrival."

"Nonsense, you did not think that."

"Yes, I did. But do drink that glass of Bordeaux; the wine is good."

Surprised at the natural behaviour of the youth and also by the frivolity of his manners and the youthfulness of his face, made even more juvenile by the careful curling of his fair hair, the commandant hesitated in the midst of his suspicions. He noticed that Madame du Gua was intently watching the glances that her son gave to Mademoiselle de Verneuil, and he asked her abruptly: "How old are you, *citoyenne*?"

"*Ah, Monsieur l'officier,*" she said, "the rules of the Republic are very severe; must I tell you that I am thirty-eight?"

"May I be shot if I believe it! Marche-a-Terre is here; it was he who gave that cry; you are Chouans in disguise. God's thunder! I'll search the inn and make sure of it!"

Just then a hoot, somewhat like those that preceded it, came from the courtyard; the commandant rushed out, and missed seeing the pallor that covered Madame du Gua's face as he spoke. Hulot saw at once that the sound came from a postilion harnessing his horses to the coach, and he cast aside his suspicions, all the more because it seemed absurd to suppose that the Chouans would risk themselves in Alencon. He returned to the house confounded.

"I forgive him now, but later he shall pay dear for the anxiety he has given us," said the mother to the son, in a low voice, as Hulot reentered the room.

The brave old officer showed on his worried face the struggle that went on in his mind betwixt a stern sense of duty and the natural kindness of his heart. He kept his gruff air, partly, perhaps, because he fancied he had deceived himself, but he took the glass of Bordeaux, and said: "Excuse me, comrade, but your *Polytechnique* does send such young officers—"

"The Chouans have younger ones," said the youth, laughing.

"For whom did you take my son?" asked Madame du Gua.

"For the *Gars*, the leader sent to the Chouans and the Vendeans by the British cabinet; his real name is Marquis de Montauran."

The commandant watched the faces of the suspected pair, who looked at each other with a puzzled expression that seemed to say: "Do you know that name?"

"No, do you?"

"What is he talking about?"

"He's dreaming."

The sudden change in the manner of Marie de Verneuil, and her torpor as she heard the name of the royalist general was observed by no one but Francine, the only person to whom the least shade on that young face was visible. Completely routed, the commandant picked up the bits of his broken sword, looked at Mademoiselle de Verneuil, whose ardent beauty was beginning to find its way to his heart, and said: "As for you, *mademoiselle*, I take nothing back, and tomorrow these fragments of my sword will reach Bonaparte, unless—"

"Pooh! what do I care for Bonaparte, or your republic, or the king, or the *Gars*?" she cried, scarcely repressing an explosion of ill-bred temper.

A mysterious emotion, the passion of which gave to her face a dazzling colour, showed that the whole world was nothing to the girl the moment that one individual was all in all to her. But she suddenly subdued herself into forced calmness, observing, like a trained actor, that the spectators were watching her. The commandant rose hastily and went out. Anxious and agitated, Mademoiselle de Verneuil followed him, stopped him in the corridor, and said, in an almost solemn tone: "Have you any good reason to suspect that young man of being the *Gars*?"

"God's thunder! *mademoiselle*, that fellow who rode here with you came back to warn me that the travellers in the mail-coach had all been murdered by the Chouans; I knew that, but what I didn't know was the name of the murdered persons,—it was Gua de Saint-Cyr!"

"Oh! if Corentin is at the bottom of all this, nothing surprises me," she cried, with a gesture of disgust.

The commandant went his way without daring to look at Mademoiselle de Verneuil, whose dangerous beauty began to affect him.

"If I had stayed two minutes longer I should have committed the folly of taking back my sword and escorting her," he was saying to himself as he went down the stairs.

As Madame du Gua watched the young man, whose eyes were fixed on the door through which Mademoiselle de Verneuil had passed, she said to him in a low voice: "You are incorrigible. You will perish through a woman. A doll can make you forget everything. Why did you allow her to breakfast with us? Who is a Demoiselle de Verneuil escorted by the Blues, who accepts a breakfast from strangers and disarms an officer with a piece of paper hidden in the bosom of her gown like a love-letter? She is one of those contemptible creatures by whose aid Fouche expects to lay hold of you, and the paper she showed the commandant ordered the Blues to assist her against you."

"Eh! *madame*," he replied in a sharp tone which went to the lady's heart and turned her pale; "her generous action disproves your supposition. Pray remember that the welfare of the king is the sole bond between us. You, who have had Charette at your feet must find the world without him empty; are you not living to avenge him?"

The lady stood still and pensive, like one who sees from the shore the wreck of all her treasures, and only the more eagerly longs for the vanished property.

Mademoiselle de Verneuil re-entered the room; the young man exchanged a smile with her and gave her a glance full of gentle meaning. However uncertain the future might seem, however ephemeral their union, the promises of their sudden love were only the more endearing to them. Rapid as the glance was, it did not escape the sagacious eye of Madame du Gua, who instantly understood it; her brow clouded, and she was unable to wholly conceal her jealous anger. Francine was observing her; she saw the eyes glitter, the cheeks flush; she thought she perceived a diabolical spirit in the face, stirred by some sudden and terrible revulsion. But lightning is not more rapid, nor death more prompt than this brief exhibition of inward emotion. Madame du Gua recovered her lively manner with such immediate self-possession that Francine fancied herself mistaken. Nevertheless, having once perceived in this woman a violence of feeling that was fully equal to that of Mademoiselle de Verneuil, she trembled as she foresaw the clash with which such natures might come together, and the girl shuddered when she saw Mademoiselle de Verneuil go up to the young man with a passionate look and, taking him by the hand, draw him close beside her and into the light, with a coquettish glance that was full of witchery.

"Now," she said, trying to read his eyes, "own to me that you are not the citizen du Gua Saint-Cyr."

"Yes, I am, *mademoiselle*."

"But he and his mother were killed yesterday."

"I am very sorry for that," he replied, laughing. "However that may be, I am none the less under a great obligation to you, for which I shall always feel the deepest gratitude and only wish I could prove it to you."

"I thought I was saving an *émigré*, but I love you better as a Republican."

The words escaped her lips as it were impulsively; she became confused; even her eyes blushed, and her face bore no other expression than one of exquisite simplicity of feeling; she softly released the young man's hand, not from shame at having pressed it, but because of a thought too weighty, it seemed, for her heart to bear, leaving him drunk with hope. Suddenly she appeared to regret this freedom, permissible as it might be under the passing circumstances of a journey. She recovered her conventional manner, bowed to the lady and her son, and taking Francine with her, left the room. When they reached their own chamber Francine wrung her hands and tossed her arms, as she looked at her mistress, saying: "Ah, Marie, what a crowd of things in a moment of time! who but you would have such adventures?"

Mademoiselle de Verneuil sprang forward and clasped Francine round the neck.

"Ah! this is life indeed—I am in heaven!"

"Or hell," retorted Francine.

"Yes, hell if you like!" cried Mademoiselle de Verneuil. "Here, give me your hand; feel my heart, how it beats. There's fever in my veins; the whole world is now a mere nothing to me! How many times have I not seen that man in my dreams! Oh! how beautiful his head is— how his eyes sparkle!"

"Will he love you?" said the simple peasant-woman, in a quivering voice, her face full of sad foreboding.

"How can you ask me that!" cried Mademoiselle de Verneuil. "But, Francine, tell me," she added throwing herself into a pose that was half serious, half comic, "will it be very hard to love me?"

"No, but will he love you always?" replied Francine, smiling.

They looked at each other for a moment speechless,—Francine at revealing so much knowledge of life, and Marie at the perception, which now came to her for the first time, of a future of happiness in her passion. She seemed to herself hanging over a gulf of which she had wanted to know the depth, and listening to the fall of the stone she had flung, at first heedlessly, into it.

"Well, it is my own affair," she said, with the gesture of a gambler. "I should never pity a betrayed woman; she has no one but herself to blame if she is abandoned. I shall know how to keep, either living or dead, the man whose heart has once been mine. But," she added, with some surprise and after a moment's silence, "where did you get your knowledge of love, Francine?"

"Mademoiselle," said the peasant-woman, hastily, "hush, I hear steps in the passage."

"Ah! not *his* steps!" said Marie, listening. "But you are evading an answer; well, well, I'll wait for it, or guess it."

Francine was right, however. Three taps on the door interrupted the conversation. Captain Merle appeared, after receiving Mademoiselle de Verneuil's permission to enter.

With a military salute to the lady, whose beauty dazzled him, the soldier ventured on giving her a glance, but he found nothing better to say than: "Mademoiselle, I am at your orders."

"Then you are to be my protector, in place of the commander, who retires; is that so?"

"No, my superior is the adjutant-major Gerard, who has sent me here."

"Your commandant must be very much afraid of me," she said.

"Beg pardon, *mademoiselle*, Hulot is afraid of nothing. But women, you see, are not in his line; it ruffled him to have a general in a mob-cap."

"And yet," continued Mademoiselle de Verneuil, "it was his duty to obey his superiors. I like subordination, and I warn you that I shall allow no one to disobey me."

"That would be difficult," replied Merle, gallantly.

"Let us consult," said Mademoiselle de Verneuil. "You can get fresh troops here and accompany me to Mayenne, which I must reach this evening. Shall we find other soldiers there, so that I might go on at once, without stopping at Mayenne? The Chouans are quite ignorant of our little expedition. If we travel at night, we can avoid meeting any number of them, and so escape an attack. Do you think this feasible?"

"Yes, *mademoiselle.*"

"What sort of road is it between Mayenne and Fougeres?"

"Rough; all up and down, a regular squirrel-wheel."

"Well, let us start at once. As we have nothing to fear near Alencon, you can go before me; we'll join you soon."

"One would think she had seen ten years' service," thought Merle, as he departed. "Hulot is mistaken; that young girl is not earning her living out of a feather-bed. Ten thousand carriages! if I want to be adjutant-major I mustn't be such a fool as to mistake Saint-Michael for the devil."

82

During Mademoiselle de Verneuil's conference with the captain, Francine had slipped out for the purpose of examining, through a window of the corridor, the spot in the courtyard which had excited her curiosity on arriving at the inn. She watched the stable and the heaps of straw with the absorption of one who was saying her prayers to the Virgin, and she presently saw Madame du Gua approaching Marche-a-Terre with the precaution of a cat that dislikes to wet its feet. When the Chouan caught sight of the lady, he rose and stood before her in an attitude of deep respect. This singular circumstance aroused Francine's curiosity; she slipped into the courtyard and along the walls, avoiding Madame du Gua's notice, and trying to hide herself behind the stable door. She walked on tiptoe, scarcely daring to breathe, and succeeded in posting herself close to Marche-a-Terre, without exciting his attention.

"If, after all this information," the lady was saying to the Chouan, "it proves not to be her real name, you are to fire upon her without pity, as you would on a mad dog."

"Agreed!" said Marche-a-Terre.

The lady left him. The Chouan replaced his red woollen cap upon his head, remained standing, and was scratching his ear as if puzzled when Francine suddenly appeared before him, apparently by magic.

"Saint Anne of Auray!" he exclaimed. Then he dropped his whip, clasped his hands, and stood as if in ecstasy. A faint colour illuminated his coarse face, and his eyes shone like diamonds dropped on a muck-heap. "Is it really the brave girl from Cottin?" he muttered, in a voice so smothered that he alone heard it. "You *are* fine," he said, after a pause, using the curious word, *godaine,* a superlative in the dialect of those regions used by lovers to express the combination of fine clothes and beauty.

"I daren't touch you," added Marche-a-Terre, putting out his big hand nevertheless, as if to weigh the gold chain which hung round her neck and below her waist.

"You had better not, Pierre," replied Francine, inspired by the instinct which makes a woman despotic when not oppressed. She drew back haughtily, after enjoying the Chouan's surprise; but she compensated for the harshness of her words by the softness of her glance, saying, as she once more approached him: "Pierre, that lady was talking to you about my young mistress, wasn't she?"

Marche-a-Terre was silent; his face struggled, like the dawn, between clouds and light. He looked in turn at Francine, at the whip he had dropped, and at the chain, which seemed to have as powerful an attraction for him as the Breton girl herself. Then, as if to put a stop to his own uneasiness, he picked up his whip and still kept silence.

"Well, it is easy to see that that lady told you to kill my mistress," resumed Francine, who knew the faithful discretion of the peasant, and wished to relieve his scruples.

Marche-a-Terre lowered his head significantly. To the Cottin girl that was answer enough.

"Very good, Pierre," she said; "if any evil happens to her, if a hair of her head is injured, you and I will have seen each other for the last time; for I shall be in heaven, and you will go to hell."

The possessed of devils whom the Church in former days used to exorcise with great pomp were not more shaken and agitated than Marche-a-Terre at this prophecy, uttered with a conviction that gave it certainty. His glance, which at first had a character of savage tenderness, counteracted by a fanaticism as powerful in his soul as love, suddenly became surly, as he felt the imperious manner of the girl he had long since chosen. Francine interpreted his silence in her own way.

"Won't you do anything for my sake?" she said in a tone of reproach.

At these words the Chouan cast a glance at his mistress from eyes that were black as a crow's wing.

"Are you free?" he asked in a growl that Francine alone could have understood.

"Should I be here if I were not?" she replied indignantly. "But you, what are you doing here? Still playing bandit, still roaming the country like a mad dog wanting to bite. Oh! Pierre, if you were wise, you would come with me. This beautiful young lady, who, I ought to tell you, was nursed when a baby in our home, has taken care of me. I have two hundred *francs* a year from a good investment. And Mademoiselle has bought me my uncle Thomas's big house for fifteen hundred *francs*, and I have saved two thousand beside."

But her smiles and the announcement of her wealth fell dead before the dogged immovability of the Chouan.

"The priests have told us to go to war," he replied. "Every Blue we shoot earns one indulgence."

"But suppose the Blues shoot you?"

He answered by letting his arms drop at his sides, as if regretting the poverty of the offering he should thus make to God and the king.

"What will become of me?" exclaimed the young girl, sorrowfully.

Marche-a-Terre looked at her stupidly; his eyes seemed to enlarge; tears rolled down his hairy cheeks upon the goatskin which covered him, and a low moan came from his breast.

"Saint Anne of Auray!—Pierre, is this all you have to say to me after a parting of seven years? You have changed indeed."

"I love you the same as ever," said the Chouan, in a gruff voice.

"No," she whispered, "the king is first."

"If you look at me like that I shall go," he said.

"Well, then, *adieu*," she replied, sadly.

"*Adieu*," he repeated.

He seized her hand, wrung it, kissed it, made the sign of the cross, and rushed into the stable, like a dog who fears that his bone will be taken from him.

"Pille-Miche," he said to his comrade. "Where's your tobacco-box?"

"Ho! *sacre bleu!* what a fine chain!" cried Pille-Miche, fumbling in a pocket constructed in his goatskin.

Then he held out to Marche-a-Terre the little horn in which Bretons put the finely powdered tobacco which they prepare themselves during the long winter nights. The Chouan raised his thumb and made a hollow in the palm of his hand, after the manner in which an *invalide* takes his tobacco; then he shook the horn, the small end of which Pille-Miche had unscrewed. A fine powder fell slowly from the little hole pierced in the point of this Breton utensil. Marche-a-Terre went through the same process seven or eight times silently, as if the powder had power to change the current of his thoughts. Suddenly he flung the horn to Pille-Miche with a gesture of despair, and caught up a gun which was hidden in the straw.

"Seven or eight shakes at once! I suppose you think that costs nothing!" said the stingy Pille-Miche.

"Forward!" cried Marche-a-Terre in a hoarse voice. "There's work before us."

Thirty or more Chouans who were sleeping in the straw under the mangers, raised their heads, saw Marche-a-Terre on his feet, and disappeared instantly through a door which led to the garden, from which it was easy to reach the fields.

When Francine left the stable she found the mail-coach ready to start. Mademoiselle de Verneuil and her new fellow-travellers were already in it. The girl shuddered as she saw her young mistress sitting side by side with the woman who had just ordered her death. The young man had taken his seat facing Marie, and as soon as Francine was in hers the heavy vehicle started at a good pace.

The sun had swept away the grey autumnal mists, and its rays were brightening the gloomy landscape with a look of youth and holiday. Many lovers fancy that such chance accidents of the sky are premonitions. Francine was surprised at the strange silence which fell upon the travellers. Mademoiselle de Verneuil had recovered her cold manner, and sat with her eyes lowered, her head slightly inclined, and her hands hidden under a sort of mantle in which she had wrapped herself. If she raised her eyes it was only to look at the passing scenery. Certain of being admired, she rejected admiration; but her apparent indifference was evidently more coquettish than natural. Purity, which gives such harmony to the diverse expressions by which a simple soul reveals itself, could lend no charm to a being whose every instinct predestined her to the storms of passion. Yielding himself up to the pleasures of this dawning intrigue, the young man did not try to explain the contradictions which were obvious between the coquetry and the enthusiasm of this singular young girl. Her assumed indifference allowed him to examine at his ease a face which was now as beautiful in its calmness as it had been when agitated. Like the rest of us, he was not disposed to question the sources of his enjoyment.

It is difficult for a pretty woman to avoid the glances of her companions in a carriage when their eyes fasten upon her as a visible distraction to the monotony of a journey. Happy, therefore, in being able to satisfy the hunger of his dawning passion, without offence or avoidance on the part of its object, the young man studied the pure and brilliant lines of the girl's head and face. To him they were a picture. Sometimes the light brought out the transparent rose of the nostrils and the double curve which united the nose with the upper lip; at other times a pale glint of sunshine illuminated the tints of the skin, pearly beneath the eyes and round the mouth, rosy on the cheeks, and ivory-white about the temples and throat. He admired the contrasts of light and shade caused by the masses of black hair surrounding her face and giving it an ephemeral grace,—for all is fleeting in a woman; her beauty of today is often not that of yesterday, fortunately for herself, perhaps! The young man, who was still at an age when youth delights in the nothings which are the all of love, watched eagerly for each movement of the eyelids, and the seductive rise and fall of her bosom as she breathed. Sometimes he fancied, suiting the tenor of his thoughts, that he could see a meaning in the expression of the eyes and the imperceptible inflection of the lips. Every gesture betrayed to him the soul, every motion a new aspect of the young girl. If a thought stirred those mobile features, if a sudden blush suffused the cheeks, or a smile brought life into the face, he found a fresh delight in trying to discover the secrets of this mysterious creature. Everything about her was a snare to the soul and a snare to the senses. Even the silence that fell between them, far from raising an obstacle to the understanding of their hearts, became the common ground for mutual thoughts. But after a while the many looks in which their eyes encountered each other warned Marie de Verneuil that the silence was compromising her, and she turned to Madame du Gua with one of those commonplace remarks which open the way to conversation; but even in so doing she included the young man.

"Madame," she said, "how could you put your son into the navy? have you not doomed yourself to perpetual anxiety?"

"Mademoiselle, the fate of women, of mothers, I should say, is to tremble for the safety of their dear ones."

"Your son is very like you."

"Do you think so, *mademoiselle?*"

The smile with which the young man listened to these remarks increased the vexation of his pretended mother. Her hatred grew with every passionate glance he turned on Marie. Silence or conversation, all increased the dreadful wrath which she carefully concealed beneath a cordial manner.

"Mademoiselle," said the young man, "you are quite mistaken. Naval men are not more exposed to danger than soldiers. Women ought not to dislike the navy; we sailors have a merit beyond that of the military,—we are faithful to our mistresses."

"Oh, from necessity," replied Mademoiselle de Verneuil, laughing.

"But even so, it is fidelity," said Madame du Gua, in a deep voice.

The conversation grew lively, touching upon subjects that were interesting to none but the three travellers, for under such circumstances intelligent persons given new meanings to commonplace talk; but every word, insignificant as it might seem, was a mutual interrogation, hiding the desires, hopes, and passions which agitated them. Marie's cleverness and quick perception (for she was fully on her guard) showed Madame du Gua that calumny and treachery could alone avail to triumph over a rival as formidable through her intellect as by her beauty. The mail-coach presently overtook the escort, and then advanced more slowly. The young man, seeing a long hill before them, proposed to the young lady that they should walk. The friendly politeness of his offer decided her, and her consent flattered him.

"Is Madame of our opinion?" she said, turning to Madame du Gua. "Will she walk, too?"

"Coquette!" said the lady to herself, as she left the coach.

Marie and the young man walked together, but a little apart. The sailor, full of ardent desires, was determined to break the reserve that checked him, of which, however, he was not the dupe. He fancied that he could succeed by dallying with the young lady in that tone

of courteous amiability and wit, sometimes frivolous, sometimes serious, which characterized the men of the exiled aristocracy. But the
smiling Parisian beauty parried him so mischievously, and rejected
his frivolities with such disdain, evidently preferring the stronger
ideas and enthusiasms which he betrayed from time to time in spite
of himself, that he presently began to understand the true way of
pleasing her. The conversation then changed. He realized the hopes
her expressive face had given him; yet, as he did so, new difficulties
arose, and he was still forced to suspend his judgment on a girl who
seemed to take delight in thwarting him, a siren with whom he grew
more and more in love. After yielding to the seduction of her beauty,
he was still more attracted to her mysterious soul, with a curiosity
which Marie perceived and took pleasure in exciting. Their intercourse assumed, insensibly, a character of intimacy far removed from
the tone of indifference which Mademoiselle de Verneuil endeavoured in vain to give to it.

Though Madame du Gua had followed the lovers, the latter had
unconsciously walked so much more rapidly than she that a distance
of several hundred feet soon separated them. The charming pair trod
the fine sand beneath their feet, listening with childlike delight to
the union of their footsteps, happy in being wrapped by the same
ray of a sunshine that seemed spring-like, in breathing with the same
breath autumnal perfumes laden with vegetable odours which seemed
a nourishment brought by the breezes to their dawning love. Though
to them it may have been a mere circumstance of their fortuitous
meeting, yet the sky, the landscape, the season of the year, did communicate to their emotions a tinge of melancholy gravity which gave
them an element of passion. They praised the weather and talked of its
beauty; then of their strange encounter, of the coming rupture of an
intercourse so delightful; of the ease with which, in travelling, friendships, lost as soon as made, are formed. After this last remark, the young
man profited by what seemed to be a tacit permission to make a few
tender confidences, and to risk an avowal of love like a man who was
not unaccustomed to such situations.

"Have you noticed, *mademoiselle*," he said, "how little the feelings
of the heart follow the old conventional rules in the days of terror in
which we live? Everything about us bears the stamp of suddenness.
We love in a day, or we hate on the strength of a single glance. We are
bound to each other for life in a moment, or we part with the celerity of death itself. All things are hurried, like the convulsions of the
nation. In the midst of such dangers as ours the ties that bind should

be stronger than under the ordinary course of life. In Paris during the Terror, every one came to know the full meaning of a clasp of the hand as men do on a battle-field."

"People felt the necessity of living fast and ardently," she answered, "for they had little time to live." Then, with a glance at her companion which seemed to tell him that the end of their short intercourse was approaching, she added, maliciously: "You are very well informed as to the affairs of life, for a young man who has just left the *Ecole Polytechnique!*"

"What are you thinking of me?" he said after a moment's silence. "Tell me frankly, without disguise."

"You wish to acquire the right to speak to me of myself," she said laughing.

"You do not answer me," he went on after a slight pause. "Take care, silence is sometimes significant."

"Do you think I cannot guess all that you would like to say to me? Good heavens! you have already said enough."

"Oh, if we understand each other," he replied, smiling, "I have obtained more than I dared hope for."

She smiled in return so graciously that she seemed to accept the courteous struggle into which all men like to draw a woman. They persuaded themselves, half in jest, half in earnest, that they never could be more to each other than they were at that moment. The young man fancied, therefore, he might give reins to a passion that could have no future; the young woman felt she might smile upon it. Marie suddenly struck her foot against a stone and stumbled.

"Take my arm," said her companion.

"It seems I must," she replied; "you would be too proud if I refused; you would fancy I feared you."

"Ah, *mademoiselle*," he said, pressing her arm against his heart that she might feel the beating of it, "you flatter my pride by granting such a favour."

"Well, the readiness with which I do so will cure your illusions."

"Do you wish to save me from the danger of the emotions you cause?"

"Stop, stop!" she cried; "do not try to entangle me in such boudoir riddles. I don't like to find the wit of fools in a man of your character. See! here we are beneath the glorious sky, in the open country; before us, above us, all is grand. You wish to tell me that I am beautiful, do you not? Well, your eyes have already told me so; besides, I know it; I am not a woman whom mere compliments can please. But perhaps you would like," this with satirical emphasis, "to talk about your *sentiments*?

Do you think me so simple as to believe that sudden sympathies are powerful enough to influence a whole life through the recollections of one morning?"

"Not the recollections of a morning," he said, "but those of a beautiful woman who has shown herself generous."

"You forget," she retorted, laughing, "half my attractions,—a mysterious woman, with everything odd about her, name, rank, situation, freedom of thought and manners."

"You are not mysterious to me!" he exclaimed. "I have fathomed you; there is nothing that could be added to your perfections except a little more faith in the love you inspire."

"Ah, my poor child of eighteen, what can you know of love?" she said smiling. "Well, well, so be it!" she added, "it is a fair subject of conversation, like the weather when one pays a visit. You shall find that I have neither false modesty nor petty fears. I can hear the word love without blushing; it has been so often said to me without one echo of the heart that I think it quite unmeaning. I have met with it everywhere, in books, at the theatre, in society,—yes, everywhere, and never have I found in it even a semblance of its magnificent ideal."

"Did you seek that ideal?"

"Yes."

The word was said with such perfect ease and freedom that the young man made a gesture of surprise and looked at Marie fixedly, as if he had suddenly changed his opinion on her character and real position.

"Mademoiselle," he said with ill-concealed devotion, "are you maid or wife, angel or devil?"

"All," she replied, laughing. "Isn't there something diabolic and also angelic in a young girl who has never loved, does not love, and perhaps will never love?"

"Do you think yourself happy thus?" he asked with a free and easy tone and manner, as though already he felt less respect for her.

"Oh, happy, no," she replied. "When I think that I am alone, hampered by social conventions that make me deceitful, I envy the privileges of a man. But when I also reflect on the means which nature has bestowed on us women to catch and entangle you men in the invisible meshes of a power which you cannot resist, then the part assigned to me in the world is not displeasing to me. And then again, suddenly, it does seem very petty, and I feel that I should despise a man who allowed himself to be duped by such vulgar seductions. No sooner do I perceive our power and like it, than I know it to be horrible and I

90

abhor it. Sometimes I feel within me that longing towards devotion which makes my sex so nobly beautiful; and then I feel a desire, which consumes me, for dominion and power. Perhaps it is the natural struggle of the good and the evil principle in which all creatures live here below. Angel or devil! you have expressed it. Ah! today is not the first time that I have recognized my double nature. But we women understand better than you men can do our own shortcomings. We have an instinct which shows us a perfection in all things to which, nevertheless, we fail to attain. But," she added, sighing as she glanced at the sky; "that which enhances us in your eyes is—"

"Is what?" he said.

"—that we are all struggling, more or less," she answered, "against a thwarted destiny."

"Mademoiselle, why should we part tonight?"

"Ah!" she replied, smiling at the passionate look which he gave her, "let us get into the carriage; the open air does not agree with us."

Marie turned abruptly; the young man followed her, and pressed her arm with little respect, but in a manner that expressed his imperious admiration. She hastened her steps. Seeing that she wished to escape an importune declaration, he became the more ardent; being determined to win a first favour from this woman, he risked all and said, looking at her meaningly:—

"Shall I tell you a secret?"

"Yes, quickly, if it concerns you."

"I am not in the service of the Republic. Where are you going? I shall follow you."

At the words Marie trembled violently. She withdrew her arm and covered her face with both hands to hide either the flush or the pallor of her cheeks; then she suddenly uncovered her face and said in a voice of deep emotion:—

"Then you began as you would have ended, by deceiving me?"

"Yes," he said.

At this answer she turned again from the carriage, which was now overtaking them, and began to almost run along the road.

"I thought," he said, following her, "that the open air did not agree with you?"

"Oh! it has changed," she replied in a grave tone, continuing to walk on, a prey to agitating thoughts.

"You do not answer me," said the young man, his heart full of the soft expectation of coming pleasure.

"Oh!" she said, in a strained voice, "the tragedy begins."

"What tragedy?" he asked.

She stopped short, looked at the young student from head to foot with a mingled expression of fear and curiosity; then she concealed her feelings that were agitating her under the mask of an impenetrable calmness, showing that for a girl of her age she had great experience of life.

"Who are you?" she said,—"but I know already; when I first saw you I suspected it. You are the royalist leader whom they call the *Gars*. The ex-bishop of Autun was right in saying we should always believe in presentiments which give warning of evil."

"What interest have you in knowing the *Gars*?"

"What interest has he in concealing himself from me who have already saved his life?" She began to laugh, but the merriment was forced. "I have wisely prevented you from saying that you love me. Let me tell you, *monsieur*, that I abhor you. I am republican, you are royalist; I would deliver you up if you were not under my protection, and if I had not already saved your life, and if—" she stopped. These violent extremes of feeling and the inward struggle which she no longer attempted to conceal alarmed the young man, who tried, but in vain, to observe her calmly. "Let us part here at once,—I insist upon it; farewell!" she said. She turned hastily back, made a few steps, and then returned to him. "No, no," she continued, "I have too great an interest in knowing who you are. Hide nothing from me; tell me the truth. Who are you? for you are no more a pupil of the *Ecole Polytechnique* than you are eighteen years old."

"I am a sailor, ready to leave the ocean and follow you wherever your imagination may lead you. If I have been so lucky as to rouse your curiosity in any particular I shall be very careful not to lessen it. Why mingle the serious affairs of real life with the life of the heart in which we are beginning to understand each other?"

"Our souls might have understood each other," she said in a grave voice. "But I have no right to exact your confidence. You will never know the extent of your obligations to me; I shall not explain them."

They walked a few steps in silence.

"My life does interest you," said the young man.

"Monsieur, I implore you, tell me your name or else be silent. You are a child," she added, with an impatient movement of her shoulders, "and I feel a pity for you."

The obstinacy with which she insisted on knowing his name made the pretended sailor hesitate between prudence and love. The vexation of a desired woman is powerfully attractive; her anger, like her submission, is imperious; many are the fibres she touches in a man's heart, penetrating and subjugating it. Was this scene only another aspect of Mademoiselle de Verneuil's coquetry? In spite of his sudden passion the unnamed lover had the strength to distrust a woman thus bent on forcing from him a secret of life and death.

"Why has my rash indiscretion, which sought to give a future to our present meeting, destroyed the happiness of it?" he said, taking her hand, which she left in his unconsciously.

Mademoiselle de Verneuil, who seemed to be in real distress, was silent.

"How have I displeased you?" he said. "What can I do to soothe you?"

"Tell me your name."

He made no reply, and they walked some distance in silence. Suddenly Mademoiselle de Verneuil stopped short, like one who has come to some serious determination.

"Monsieur le Marquis de Montauran," she said, with dignity, but without being able to conceal entirely the nervous trembling of her features, "I desire to do you a great service, whatever it may cost me. We part here. The coach and its escort are necessary for your protection, and you must continue your journey in it. Fear nothing from the Republicans; they are men of honour, and I shall give the adjutant certain orders which he will faithfully execute. As for me, I shall return on foot to Alencon with my maid, and take a few of the soldiers with me. Listen to what I say, for your life depends on it. If, before you reach a place of safety, you meet that odious man you saw in my company at the inn, escape at once, for he will instantly betray you. As for me,—" she paused, "as for me, I fling myself back into the miseries of life. Farewell, *monsieur*, may you be happy; farewell."

She made a sign to Captain Merle, who was just then reaching the brow of the hill behind her. The marquis was taken unawares by her sudden action.

"Stop!" he cried, in a tone of despair that was well acted.

This singular caprice of a girl for whom he would at that instant have thrown away his life so surprised him that he invented, on the spur of the moment, a fatal fiction by which to hide his name and satisfy the curiosity of his companion.

"You have almost guessed the truth," he said. "I am an *émigré*, condemned to death, and my name is Vicomte de Bauvan. Love of my country has brought me back to France to join my brother. I hope to be taken off the list of *émigrés* through the influence of Madame de Beauharnais, now the wife of the First Consul; but if I fail in this, I mean to

93

die on the soil of my native land, fighting beside my friend Montauran. I am now on my way secretly, by means of a passport he has sent me, to learn if any of my property in Brittany is still unconfiscated."

While the young man spoke Mademoiselle de Verneuil examined him with a penetrating eye. She tried at first to doubt his words, but being by nature confiding and trustful, she slowly regained an expression of serenity, and said eagerly, "Monsieur, are you telling me the exact truth?"

"Yes, the exact truth," replied the young man, who seemed to have no conscience in his dealings with women.

Mademoiselle de Verneuil gave a deep sigh, like a person who returns to life.

"Ah!" she exclaimed, "I am very happy."

"Then you hate that poor Montauran?"

"No," she said; "but I could not make you understand my meaning. I was not willing that *you* should meet the dangers from which I will try to protect him,—since he is your friend."

"Who told you that Montauran was in danger?"

"Ah, *monsieur*, even if I had not come from Paris, where his enterprise is the one thing talked of, the commandant at Alencon said enough to show his danger."

"Then let me ask you how you expect to save him from it."

"Suppose I do not choose to answer," she replied, with the haughty air that women often assume to hide an emotion. "What right have you to know my secrets?"

"The right of a man who loves you."

"Already?" she said. "No, you do not love me. I am only an object of passing gallantry to you,—that is all. I am clear-sighted; did I not penetrate your disguise at once? A woman who knows anything of good society could not be misled, in these days, by a pupil of the *Polytechnique* who uses choice language, and conceals as little as you do the manners of a *grand seigneur* under the mask of a Republican. There is a trifle of powder left in your hair, and a fragrance of nobility clings to you which a woman of the world cannot fail to detect. Therefore, fearing that the man whom you saw accompanying me, who has all the shrewdness of a woman, might make the same discovery, I sent him away. Monsieur, let me tell you that a true Republican officer just from the *Polytechnique* would not have made love to me as you have done, and would not have taken me for a pretty adventuress. Allow me, Monsieur de Bauvan, to preach you a little sermon from a woman's point of view. Are you too juvenile to know that of all the creatures of my sex the most difficult to subdue is that same adventuress,—she whose price is ticketed and who is weary of pleasure. That sort of woman requires, they tell me, constant seduction; she yields only to her own caprices; any attempt to please her argues, I should suppose, great conceit on the part of a man. But let us put aside that class of women, among whom you have been good enough to rank me; you ought to understand that a young woman, handsome, brilliant, and of noble birth (for, I suppose, you will grant me those advantages), does not sell herself, and can only be won by the man who loves her in one way. You understand me? If she loves him and is willing to commit a folly, she must be justified by great and heroic reasons. Forgive me this logic, rare in my sex; but for the sake of your happiness,—and my own," she added, dropping her head,—"I will not allow either of us to deceive the other, nor will I permit you to think that Mademoiselle de Verneuil, angel or devil, maid or wife, is capable of being seduced by commonplace gallantry."

"Mademoiselle," said the marquis, whose surprise, though he concealed it, was extreme, and who at once became a man of the great world, "I entreat you to believe that I take you to be a very noble person, full of the highest sentiments, or—a charming girl, as you please."

"I don't ask all that," she said, laughing. "Allow me to keep my incognito. My mask is better than yours, and it pleases me to wear it,—if only to discover whether those who talk to me of love are sincere. Therefore, beware of me! Monsieur," she cried, catching his arm vehemently, "listen to me; if you were able to prove that your love is true, nothing, no human power, could part us. Yes, I would fain unite myself to the noble destiny of some great man, and marry a vast ambition, glorious hopes! Noble hearts are never faithless, for constancy is in their fibre; I should be forever loved, forever happy,—I would make my body a stepping-stone by which to raise the man who loved me; I would sacrifice all things to him, bear all things from him, and love him forever,—even if he ceased to love me. I have never before dared to confess to another heart the secrets of mine, nor the passionate enthusiasms which exhaust me; but I tell you something of them now because, as soon as I have seen you in safety, we shall part forever."

"Part? never!" he cried, electrified by the tones of that vigorous soul which seemed to be fighting against some overwhelming thought.

"Are you free?" she said, with a haughty glance which subdued him.

"Free! yes, except for the sentence of death which hangs over me."

She added presently, in a voice full of bitter feeling: "If all this were not a dream, a glorious life might indeed be ours. But I have been talking folly; let us beware of committing any. When I think of all you would have to be before you could rate me at my proper value I doubt everything—"

"I doubt nothing if you will only grant me—"

"Hush!" she cried, hearing a note of true passion in his voice, "the open air is decidedly disagreeing with us; let us return to the coach."

That vehicle soon came up; they took their places and drove on several miles in total silence. Both had matter for reflection, but henceforth their eyes no longer feared to meet. Each now seemed to have an equal interest in observing the other, and in mutually hiding important secrets; but for all that they were drawn together by one and the same impulse, which now, as a result of this interview, assumed the dimensions of a passion. They recognized in each other qualities which promised to heighten all the pleasures to be derived from either their contest or their union. Perhaps both of them, living a life of adventure, had reached the singular moral condition in which, either from weariness or in defiance of fate, the mind rejects serious reflection and flings itself on chance in pursuing an enterprise precisely because the issues of chance are unknown, and the interest of expecting them vivid. The moral nature, like the physical nature, has its abysses into which strong souls love to plunge, risking their future as gamblers risk their fortune. Mademoiselle de Verneuil and the young marquis had obtained a revelation of each other's minds as a consequence of this interview, and their intercourse thus took rapid strides, for the sympathy of their souls succeeded to that of their senses. Besides, the more they felt fatally drawn to each other, the more eager they were to study the secret action of their minds. The so-called Vicomte de Bauvan, surprised at the seriousness of the strange girl's ideas, asked himself how she could possibly combine such acquired knowledge of life with so much youth and freshness. He thought he discovered an extreme desire to appear chaste in the modesty and reserve of her attitudes. He suspected her of playing a part; he questioned the nature of his own pleasure; and ended by choosing to consider her a clever actress. He was right; Mademoiselle de Verneuil, like other women of the world, grew the more reserved the more she felt the warmth of her own feelings, assuming with perfect naturalness the appearance of prudery, beneath which such women veil their desires. They all wish to offer themselves as virgins on love's altar; and if they are not so, the deception they seek to practise is at least a homage which they pay to their lovers. These thoughts passed rapidly through the mind of the young man and gratified him. In fact, for both, this mutual examination was an advance in their intercourse, and the lover soon came to that phase of passion in which a man finds in the defects of his mistress a reason for loving her the more.

Mademoiselle de Verneuil was thoughtful. Perhaps her imagination led her over a greater extent of the future than that of the young *émigré*, who was merely following one of the many impulses of his life as a man; whereas Marie was considering a lifetime, thinking to make it beautiful, and to fill it with happiness and with grand and noble sentiments. Happy in such thoughts, more in love with her ideal than with the actual reality, with the future rather than with the present, she desired now to return upon her steps so as to better establish her power. In this she acted instinctively, as all women act. Having agreed with her soul that she would give herself wholly up, she wished— if we may so express it—to dispute every fragment of the gift; she longed to take back from the past all her words and looks and acts and make them more in harmony with the dignity of a woman beloved. Her eyes at times expressed a sort of terror as she thought of the interview just over, in which she had shown herself aggressive. But as she watched the face before her, instinct with power, and felt that a being so strong must also be generous, she glowed at the thought that her part in life would be nobler than that of most women, inasmuch as her lover was a man of character, a man condemned to death, who had come to risk his life in making war against the Republic. The thought of occupying such a soul to the exclusion of all rivals gave a new aspect to many matters. Between the moment, only five hours earlier, when she composed her face and toned her voice to allure the young man, and the present moment, when she was able to convulse him with a look, there was all the difference to her between a dead world and a living one.

In the condition of soul in which Mademoiselle de Verneuil now existed external life seemed to her a species of phantasmagoria. The carriage passed through villages and valleys and mounted hills which left no impressions on her mind. They reached Mayenne; the soldiers of the escort were changed; Merle spoke to her; she replied; they crossed the whole town and were again in the open country; but the faces, houses, streets, landscape, men, swept past her like the figments of a dream. Night came, and Marie was travelling beneath a diamond sky, wrapped in soft light, and yet she was not aware that darkness had succeeded day; that Mayenne was passed; that Fougeres was near; she knew not even where she was going. That she should part in a few hours from the man she had chosen, and who, she believed, had chosen her, was not for her a possibility. Love is the only passion which looks to neither past nor future. Occasionally her thoughts escaped in broken words, in phrases devoid of meaning, though to her lover's ears they sounded like promises of love. To the two witnesses of this birth of passion she seemed to be rushing onward with fearful rapidity. Francine knew Marie as well as Madame du Gua knew the marquis, and their experience of the past made them await in silence some terrible finale. It was, indeed, not long before the end came to the drama which Mademoiselle de Verneuil had called, without perhaps imagining the truth of her words, a tragedy.

When the travellers were about three miles beyond Mayenne they heard a horseman riding after them with great rapidity. When he reached the carriage he leaned towards it to look at Mademoiselle de Verneuil, who recognized Corentin. That offensive personage made her a sign of intelligence, the familiarity of which was deeply mortifying; then he turned away, after chilling her to the bone with a look full of some base meaning. The young *émigré* seemed painfully affected by this circumstance, which did not escape the notice of his pretended mother; but Marie softly touched him, seeming by her eyes to take refuge in his heart as thought it were her only haven. His brow cleared at this proof of the full extent of his mistress's attachment, coming to him as it were by accident. An inexplicable fear seemed to have overcome her coyness, and her love was visible for a moment without a veil. Unfortunately for both of them, Madame du Gua saw it all; like a miser who gives a feast, she seemed to count the morsels and begrudge the wine.

Absorbed in their happiness the lovers arrived, without any consciousness of the distance they had traversed, at that part of the road which passed through the valley of Ernee. There Francine noticed and showed to her companions a number of strange forms which seemed to move like shadows among the trees and gorse that surrounded the fields. When the carriage came within range of these shadows a volley of musketry, the balls of which whistled above their heads, warned the travellers that the shadows were realities. The escort had fallen into a trap.

Captain Merle now keenly regretted having adopted Mademoiselle de Verneuil's idea that a rapid journey by night would be a safe one,—an error which had led him to reduce his escort from Mayenne to sixty men. He at once, under Gerard's orders, divided his little troop into two columns, one on each side of the road, which the two officers marched at a quick step among the gorse hedges, eager to meet the assailants, though ignorant of their number. The Blues beat the thick bushes right and left with rash intrepidity, and replied to the Chouans with a steady fire.

Mademoiselle de Verneuil's first impulse was to jump from the carriage and run back along the road until she was out of sight of the battle; but ashamed of her fears, and moved by the feeling which impels us all to act nobly under the eyes of those we love, she presently stood still, endeavouring to watch the combat coolly.

The marquis followed her, took her hand, and placed it on his breast.

"I was afraid," she said, smiling, "but now—"

Just then her terrified maid cried out: "Marie, take care!"

But as she said the words, Francine, who was springing from the carriage, felt herself grasped by a strong hand. The sudden weight of that enormous hand made her shriek violently; she turned, and was instantly silenced on recognizing Marche-a-Terre.

"Twice I owe to chance," said the marquis to Mademoiselle de Verneuil, "the revelation of the sweetest secrets of the heart. Thanks to Francine I now know you bear the gracious name of Marie,—Marie, the name I have invoked in my distresses,—Marie, a name I shall henceforth speak in joy, and never without sacrifice, mingling religion and love. There can be no wrong where prayer and love go together."

They clasped hands, looked silently into each other's eyes, and the excess of their emotion took away from them the power to express it.

"There's no danger for *the rest of you*," Marche-a-Terre was saying roughly to Francine, giving to his hoarse and guttural voice a reproachful tone, and emphasizing his last words in a way to stupefy the innocent peasant-girl. For the first time in her life she saw ferocity in that face. The moonlight seemed to heighten the effect of it. The savage Breton, holding his cap in one hand and his heavy carbine in the other, dumpy and thickset as a gnome, and bathed in that white light the shadows of which give such fantastic aspects to forms, seemed to belong more to a world of goblins than to reality. This apparition and its tone of reproach came upon Francine with the suddenness of a phantom. He turned rapidly to Madame du Gua, with whom he exchanged a few eager words, which Francine, who had somewhat forgotten the dialect of Lower Brittany, did not understand. The lady seemed to be giving him a series of orders. The short conference ended by an imperious gesture of the lady's hand pointing out to the Chouan the lovers standing a little distance apart. Before obeying, Marche-a-Terre glanced at Francine whom he seemed to pity; he wished to speak to her, and the girl was aware that his silence was compulsory. The rough and sunburnt skin of his forehead wrinkled, and his eyebrows were drawn violently together. Did he think of disobeying a renewed order to kill Mademoiselle de Verneuil? The contortion of his face made him all the more hideous to Madame du Gua, but to Francine the flash of his eye seemed almost gentle, for it taught her to feel intuitively that the violence of his savage nature would yield to her will as a woman, and that she reigned, next to God, in that rough heart.

The lovers were interrupted in their tender interview by Madame du Gua, who ran up to Marie with a cry, and pulled her away as though some danger threatened her. Her real object however, was to enable a member of the royalist committee of Alencon, whom she saw approaching them, to speak privately to the *Gars*.

"Beware of the girl you met at the hotel in Alencon; she will betray you," said the Chevalier de Valois, in the young man's ear; and immediately he and his little Breton horse disappeared among the bushes from which he had issued.

The firing was heavy at that moment, but the combatants did not come to close quarters.

"Adjutant," said Clef-des-Coeurs, "isn't it a sham attack, to capture our travellers and get a ransom."

"The devil is in it, but I believe you are right," replied Gerard, darting back towards the highroad.

Just then the Chouan fire slackened, for, in truth, the whole object of the skirmish was to give the chevalier an opportunity to utter his warning to the *Gars*. Merle, who saw the enemy disappearing across the hedges, thought best not to follow them nor to enter upon a fight that was uselessly dangerous. Gerard ordered the escort to take its former position on the road, and the convoy was again in motion without the loss of a single man. The captain offered his hand to Mademoiselle de Verneuil to replace her in the coach, for the young nobleman stood motionless, as if thunderstruck. Marie, amazed at his attitude, got into the carriage alone without accepting the politeness of the Republican; she turned her head towards her lover, saw him still motionless, and was stupefied at the sudden change which had evidently come over him. The young man slowly returned, his whole manner betraying deep disgust.

"Was I not right?" said Madame du Gua in his ear, as she led him to the coach. "We have fallen into the hands of a creature who is trafficking for your head; but since she is such a fool as to have fallen

100

in love with you, for heaven's sake don't behave like a boy; pretend to love her at least till we reach La Vivetiere; once there—But," she thought to herself, seeing the young man take his place with a dazed air, as if bewildered, "can it be that he already loves her?"

The coach rolled on over the sandy road. To Mademoiselle de Verneuil's eyes all seemed changed. Death was gliding beside her love. Perhaps it was only fancy, but, to a woman who loves, fancy is as vivid as reality. Francine, who had clearly understood from Marche-a-Terre's glance that Mademoiselle de Verneuil's fate, over which she had commanded him to watch, was in other hands than his, looked pale and haggard, and could scarcely restrain her tears when her mistress spoke to her. To her eyes Madame du Gua's female malignancy was scarcely concealed by her treacherous smiles, and the sudden changes which her obsequious attentions to Mademoiselle de Verneuil made in her manners, voice, and expression was of a nature to frighten a watchful observer. Mademoiselle de Verneuil herself shuddered instinctively, asking herself, "Why should I fear? She is his mother." Then she trembled in every limb as the thought crossed her mind, "Is she really his mother?" An abyss suddenly opened before her, and she cast a look upon the mother and son, which finally enlightened her. "That woman loves him!" she thought. "But why has she begun these attentions after showing me such coolness? Am I lost? or—is she afraid of me?"

As for the young man, he was flushed and pale by turns; but he kept a quiet attitude and lowered his eyes to conceal the emotions which agitated him. The graceful curve of his lips was lost in their close compression, and his skin turned yellow under the struggle of his stormy thoughts. Mademoiselle de Verneuil was unable to decide whether any love for her remained in his evident anger. The road, flanked by woods at this particular point, became darker and more gloomy, and the obscurity prevented the eyes of the silent travellers from questioning each other. The sighing of the wind, the rustling of the trees, the measured step of the escort, gave that almost solemn character to the scene which quickens the pulses. Mademoiselle de Verneuil could not long try in vain to discover the reason of this change. The recollection of Corentin came to her like a flash, and reminded her suddenly of her real destiny. For the first time since the morning she reflected seriously on her position. Until then she had yielded herself up to the delight of loving, without a thought of the past or of the future. Unable to bear the agony of her mind, she sought, with the patience of love, to obtain a look from the young man's eyes, and when she did so her paleness and the quiver in her face had so penetrating an influence over him that he wavered; but the softening was momentary.

"Are you ill, *mademoiselle?*" he said, but his voice had no gentleness; the very question, the look, the gesture, all served to convince her that the events of this day belonged to a mirage of the soul which was fast disappearing like mists before the wind.

"Am I ill?" she replied, with a forced laugh. "I was going to ask you the same question."

"I supposed you understood each other," remarked Madame du Gua with specious kindliness.

Neither the young man nor Mademoiselle de Verneuil replied. The girl, doubly insulted, was angered at feeling her powerful beauty powerless. She knew she could discover the cause of the present situation the moment she chose to do so; but, for the first time, perhaps, a woman recoiled before a secret. Human life is sadly fertile in situations where, as a result of either too much meditation or of some catastrophe, our thoughts seem to hold to nothing; they have no substance, no point of departure, and the present has no hooks by which to hold to the past or fasten on the future. This was Mademoiselle de Verneuil's condition at the present moment. Leaning back in the carriage, she sat there like an uprooted shrub. Silent and suffering, she looked at no one, wrapped herself in her grief, and buried herself so completely in the unseen world, the refuge of the miserable, that she saw nothing around her. Crows crossed the road in the air above them cawing, but although, like all strong hearts, hers had a superstitious corner, she paid no attention to the omen. The party travelled on in silence. "Already parted?" Mademoiselle de Verneuil was saying to herself. "Yet no one about us has uttered one word. Could it be Corentin? It is not his interest to speak. Who can have come to this spot and accused me? Just loved, and already abandoned! I sow attraction, and I reap contempt. Is it my perpetual fate to see happiness and ever lose it?" Pangs hitherto unknown to her wrung her heart, for she now loved truly and for the first time. Yet she had not so wholly delivered herself to her lover that she could not take refuge from her pain in the natural pride and dignity of a young and beautiful woman. The secret of her love—a secret often kept by women under torture itself—had not escaped her lips. Presently she rose from her reclining attitude, ashamed that she had shown her passion by her silent sufferings; she shook her head with a light-hearted action, and showed a face, or rather a mask, that was gay and smiling, then she raised her voice to disguise the quiver of it.

"Where are we?" she said to Captain Merle, who kept himself at a certain distance from the carriage.

"About six miles from Fougeres, *mademoiselle*."

"We shall soon be there, shall we not?" she went on, to encourage a conversation in which she might show some preference for the young captain.

"A Breton mile," said Merle much delighted, "has the disadvantage of never ending; when you are at the top of one hill you see a valley and another hill. When you reach the summit of the slope we are now ascending you will see the plateau of Mont Pelerine in the distance. Let us hope the Chouans won't take their revenge there. Now, in going up hill and going down hill one doesn't make much headway. From La Pelerine you will still see—"

The young *émigré* made a movement at the name which Marie alone noticed.

"What is La Pelerine?" she asked hastily, interrupting the captain's description of Breton topography.

"It is the summit of a mountain," said Merle, "which gives its name to the Maine valley through which we shall presently pass. It separates this valley from that of Couesnon, at the end of which is the town of Fougeres, the chief town in Brittany. We had a fight there last Vendemiaire with the *Gars* and his brigands. We were escorting Breton conscripts, who meant to kill us sooner than leave their own land; but Hulot is a rough Christian, and he gave them—"

"Did you see the *Gars*?" she asked. "What sort of man is he?"

Her keen, malicious eyes never left the so-called *vicomte*'s face.

"Well, *mademoiselle*," replied Merle, nettled at being always interrupted, "he is so like citizen du Gua, that if your friend did not wear the uniform of the *Ecole Polytechnique* I could swear it was he."

Mademoiselle de Verneuil looked fixedly at the cold, impassable young man who had scorned her, but she saw nothing in him that betrayed the slightest feeling of alarm. She warned him by a bitter smile that she had now discovered the secret so treacherously kept; then in a jesting voice, her nostrils dilating with pleasure, and her head so turned that she could watch the young man and yet see Merle, she said to the Republican: "That new leader gives a great deal of anxiety to the First Consul. He is very daring, they say; but he has the weakness of rushing headlong into adventures, especially with women."

"We are counting on that to get even with him," said the captain. "If we catch him for only an hour we shall put a bullet in his head. He'll do the same to us if he meets us, so *par pari*—"

"Oh!" said the *émigré*, "we have nothing to fear. Your soldiers cannot go as far as La Pelerine, they are tired, and, if you consent, we can all rest a short distance from here. My mother stops at La Vivetiere, the road to which turns off a few rods farther on. These ladies might like to stop there too; they must be tired with their long drive from Alencon without resting; and as *mademoiselle*," he added, with forced politeness, "has had the generosity to give safety as well as pleasure to our journey, perhaps she will deign to accept a supper from my mother; and I think, captain," he added, addressing Merle, "the times are not so bad but what we can find a barrel of cider for your men. The *Gars* can't have taken all, at least my mother thinks not—"

"Your mother?" said Mademoiselle de Verneuil, interrupting him in a tone of irony, and making no reply to his invitation.

"Does my age seem more improbable to you this evening, *mademoiselle*?" said Madame du Gua. "Unfortunately I was married very young, and my son was born when I was fifteen."

"Are you not mistaken, *madame*?—when you were thirty, perhaps."

Madame du Gua turned livid as she swallowed the sarcasm. She would have liked to revenge herself on the spot, but was forced to smile, for she was determined at any cost, even that of insult, to discover the nature of the feelings that actuated the young girl; she therefore pretended not to have understood her.

"The Chouans have never had a more cruel leader than the *Gars*, if we are to believe the stories about him," she said, addressing herself vaguely to both Francine and her mistress.

"Oh, as for cruel, I don't believe that," said Mademoiselle de Verneuil; "he knows how to lie, but he seems rather credulous himself. The leader of a party ought not to be the plaything of others."

"Do you know him?" asked the *émigré*, quietly.

"No," she replied, with a disdainful glance, "but I thought I did."

"Oh, *mademoiselle*, he's a *malin*, yes a *malin*," said Captain Merle, shaking his head and giving with an expressive gesture the peculiar meaning to the word which it had in those days but has since lost. "Those old families do sometimes send out vigorous shoots. He has just returned from a country where, they say, the *ci-devants* didn't find life too easy, and men ripen like medlars in the straw. If that fellow is really clever he can lead us a pretty dance. He has already formed companies of light infantry who oppose our troops and neutralize the efforts of the government. If we burn a royalist village he burns two of ours. He can hold an immense tract of country and force us to spread out our men at the very moment when we want them on one spot. Oh, he knows what he is about."

"He is cutting his country's throat," said Gerard in a loud voice, interrupting the captain.

"Then," said the émigré, "if his death would deliver the nation, why don't you catch him and shoot him?"

As he spoke he tried to look into the depths of Mademoiselle de Verneuil's soul, and one of those voiceless scenes the dramatic vividness and fleeting sagacity of which cannot be reproduced in language passed between them in a flash. Danger is always interesting. The worst criminal threatened with death excites pity. Though Mademoiselle de Verneuil was now certain that the lover who had cast her off was this very leader of the Chouans, she was not ready to verify her suspicions by giving him up; she had quite another curiosity to satisfy. She preferred to doubt or to believe as her passion led her, and she now began deliberately to play with peril. Her eyes, full of scornful meaning, bade the young chief notice the soldiers of the escort; by thus presenting to his mind triumphantly an image of his danger she made him feel that his life depended on a word from her, and her lips seemed to quiver on the verge of pronouncing it. Like an American Indian, she watched every muscle of the face of her enemy, tied, as it were, to the stake, while she brandished her tomahawk gracefully, enjoying a revenge that was still innocent, and torturing like a mistress who still loves.

"If I had a son like yours, madame," she said to Madame du Gua, who was visibly frightened, "I should wear mourning from the day when I had yielded him to danger; I should know no peace of mind."

No answer was made to this speech. She turned her head repeatedly to the escort and then suddenly to Madame du Gua, without detecting the slightest secret signal between the lady and the Gars which might have confirmed her suspicions on the nature of their intimacy, which she longed to doubt. The young chief calmly smiled, and bore without flinching the scrutiny she forced him to undergo; his attitude and the expression of his face were those of a man indifferent to danger; he even seemed to say at times: "This is your chance to avenge your wounded vanity—take it! I have no desire to lessen my contempt for you."

Mademoiselle de Verneuil began to study the young man from the vantage-ground of her position with coolness and dignity; at the bottom of her heart she admired his courage and tranquillity. Happy in discovering that the man she loved bore an ancient title (the distinctions of which please every woman), she also found pleasure in meeting him in their present situation, where, as champion of a cause ennobled by misfortune, he was fighting with all the faculties of a strong soul against a Republic that was constantly victorious. She rejoiced to see him brought face to face with danger, and still displaying the courage and bravery so powerful on a woman's heart; again and again she put him to the test, obeying perhaps the instinct which induces a woman to play with her victim as a cat plays with a mouse.

"By virtue of what law do you put the Chouans to death?" she said to Merle.

"That of the 14th of last Fructidor, which outlaws the insurgent departments and proclaims martial law," replied the Republican.

"May I ask why I have the honour to attract your eyes?" she said presently to the young chief, who was attentively watching her.

"Because of a feeling which a man of honour cannot express to any woman, no matter who she is," replied the Marquis de Montauran, in a low voice, bending down to her. "We live in times," he said aloud, "when women do the work of the executioner and wield the axe with even better effect."

She looked at de Montauran fixedly; then, delighted to be attacked by the man whose life she held in her hands, she said in a low voice, smiling softly: "Your head is a very poor one; the executioner does not want it; I shall keep it myself."

The marquis looked at the inexplicable girl, whose love had overcome all, even insult, and who now avenged herself by forgiving that which women are said never to forgive. His eyes grew less stern, less cold; a look of sadness came upon his face. His love was stronger than he suspected. Mademoiselle de Verneuil, satisfied with these faint signs of a desired reconciliation, glanced at him tenderly, with a smile that was like a kiss; then she leaned back once more in the carriage, determined not to risk the future of this happy drama, believing she had assured it with her smile. She was so beautiful! She knew so well how to conquer all obstacles to love! She was so accustomed to take all risks and push on at all hazards! She loved the unexpected, and the tumults of life—why should she fear?

Before long the carriage, under the young chief's directions, left the highway and took a road cut between banks planted with apple-trees, more like a ditch than a roadway, which led to La Vivetiere. The carriage now advanced rapidly, leaving the escort to follow slowly towards the manor-house, the grey roofs of which appeared and disappeared among the trees. Some of the men lingered on the way to knock the stiff clay of the road-bed from their shoes.

"This is devilishly like the road to Paradise," remarked Beau-Pied.

Thanks to the impatience of the postilion, Mademoiselle de Verneuil soon saw the chateau of La Vivetiere. This house, standing at the end of a sort of promontory, was protected and surrounded by two deep lakelets, and could be reached only by a narrow causeway. That part of the little peninsula on which the house and gardens were placed was still further protected by a moat filled with water from the two lakes which it connected. The house really stood on an island that was well-nigh impregnable,—an invaluable retreat for a chieftain, who could be surprised there only by treachery.

Mademoiselle de Verneuil put her head out of the carriage as she heard the rusty hinges of the great gates open to give entrance to an arched portal which had been much injured during the late war. The gloomy colours of the scene which met her eyes almost extinguished the thoughts of love and coquetry in which she had been indulging. The carriage entered a large courtyard that was nearly square, bordered on each side by the steep banks of the lakelets. Those sterile shores, washed by water, which was covered with large green patches, had no other ornament than aquatic trees devoid of foliage, the twisted trunks and hoary heads of which, rising from the reeds and rushes, gave them a certain grotesque likeness to gigantic marmosets. These ugly growths seemed to waken and talk to each other when the frogs deserted them with much croaking, and the water-fowl, startled by the sound of the wheels, flew low upon the surface of the pools. The courtyard, full of rank and seeded grasses, reeds, and shrubs, either dwarf or parasite, excluded all impression of order or of splendour. The house appeared to have been long abandoned. The roof seemed to bend beneath the weight of the various vegetations which grew upon it. The walls, though built of the smooth, slatey stone which abounds in that region, showed many rifts and chinks where ivy had fastened its rootlets. Two main buildings, joined at the angle by a tall tower which faced the lake, formed the whole of the chateau, the doors and swinging, rotten shutters, rusty balustrades, and broken windows of which seemed ready to fall at the first tempest. The north wind whistled through these ruins, to which the moon, with her indefinite light, gave the character and outline of a great spectre. But the colours of those grey-blue granites, mingling with the black and tawny *schists*, must have been seen in order to understand how vividly a spectral image was suggested by the empty and gloomy carcass of the building. Its disjointed stones and paneless windows, the battered tower and broken roofs gave it the aspect of a skeleton; the birds of prey which flew from it, shrieking, added another feature to this vague resemblance. A few tall pine-trees standing behind the house waved their dark foliage above the roof, and several yews cut into formal shapes at the angles of the building, festooned it gloomily like the ornaments on a hearse. The style of the doors, the coarseness of the decorations, the want of harmony in the architecture, were all characteristic of the feudal manors of which Brittany was proud; perhaps justly proud, for they maintained upon that Gaelic ground a species of monumental history of the nebulous period which preceded the establishment of the French monarchy.

Mademoiselle de Verneuil, to whose imagination the word "chateau" brought none but its conventional ideas, was affected by the funereal aspect of the scene. She sprang from the carriage and stood apart gazing at in terror, and debating within herself what action she ought to take. Francine heard Madame du Gua give a sigh of relief as she felt herself in safety beyond reach of the Blues; an exclamation escaped her when the gates were closed, and she saw the carriage and its occupants within the walls of this natural fortress.

The Marquis de Montauran turned hastily to Mademoiselle de Verneuil, divining the thoughts that crowded in her mind.

"This chateau," he said, rather sadly, "was ruined by the war, just as my plans for our happiness have been ruined by you."

"How ruined?" she asked in surprise.

"Are you indeed 'beautiful, brilliant, and of noble birth'?" he asked ironically, repeating the words she had herself used in their former conversation.

"Who has told you to the contrary?"

"Friends, in whom I put faith; who care for my safety and are on the watch against treachery."

"Treachery!" she exclaimed, in a sarcastic tone. "Have you forgotten Hulot and Alencon already? You have no memory,—a dangerous defect in the leader of a party. But if friends," she added, with increased sarcasm, "are so all-powerful in your heart, keep your friends. Nothing is comparable to the joys of friendship. *Adieu*; neither I nor the soldiers of the Republic will stop here."

She turned towards the gateway with a look of wounded pride and scorn, and her motions as she did so displayed a dignity and also a despair which changed in an instant the thoughts of the young man; he felt that the cost of relinquishing his desires was too great, and he gave himself up deliberately to imprudence and credulity. He loved; and the lovers had no desire now to quarrel with each other.

"Say but one word and I will believe you," he said, in a supplicating voice.

"One word?" she answered, closing her lips tightly, "not a single word; not even a gesture."

"At least, be angry with me," he entreated, trying to take the hand she withheld from him,—"that is, if you dare to be angry with the leader of the rebels, who is now as sad and distrustful as he was lately happy and confiding."

Marie gave him a look that was far from angry, and he added: "You have my secret, but I have not yours."

The alabaster brow appeared to darken at these words; she cast a look of annoyance on the young chieftain, and answered, hastily: "Tell you my secret? Never!"

In love every word, every glance has the eloquence of the moment; but on this occasion Mademoiselle de Verneuil's exclamation revealed nothing, and, clever as Montauran might be, its secret was impenetrable to him, though the tones of her voice betrayed some extraordinary and unusual emotion which piqued his curiosity.

"You have a singular way of dispelling suspicion," he said.

"Do you still suspect me?" she replied, looking him in the eye, as if to say, "What rights have you over me?"

"Mademoiselle," said the young man, in a voice that was submissive and yet firm, "the authority you exercise over Republican troops, this escort—"

"Ah, that reminds me! My escort and I," she asked, in a slightly satirical tone, "your protectors, in short,—will they be safe here?"

"Yes, on the word of a gentleman. Whoever you be, you and your party have nothing to fear in my house."

The promise was made with so loyal and generous an air and manner that Mademoiselle de Verneuil felt absolutely secure as to the safety of the Republican soldiers. She was about to speak when Madame du Gua's approach silenced her. That lady had either overheard or guessed part of their conversation, and was filled with anxiety at no longer perceiving any signs of animosity between them. As soon as the marquis caught sight of her, he offered his hand to Mademoiselle de Verneuil and led her hastily towards the house, as if to escape an undesired companion.

"I am in their way," thought Madame du Gua, remaining where she was. She watched the lovers walking slowly towards the portico, where they stopped, as if satisfied to have placed some distance between themselves and her. "Yes, yes, I am in their way," she repeated, speaking to herself; "but before long that creature will not be in mine; the lake, God willing, shall have her. I'll help him keep his word as a gentleman; once under the water, she has nothing to fear,—what can be safer than that?"

She was looking fixedly at the still mirror of the little lake to the right when suddenly she heard a rustling among the rushes and saw in the moonlight the face of Marche-a-Terre rising behind the gnarled trunk of an old willow. None but those who knew the Chouan well could have distinguished him from the tangle of branches of which he seemed a part. Madame du Gua looked about her with some distrust; she saw the postilion leading his horses to a stable in the wing of the chateau which was opposite to the bank where Marche-a-Terre was hiding; Francine, with her back to her, was going towards the two lovers, who at that moment had forgotten the whole earth. Madame du Gua, with a finger on her lip to demand silence, walked towards the Chouan, who guessed rather than heard her question, "How many of you are here?"

"Eighty-seven."

"They are sixty-five; I counted them."

"Good," said the savage, with sullen satisfaction.

Attentive to all Francine's movements, the Chouan disappeared behind the willow, as he saw her turn to look for the enemy over whom she was keeping an instinctive watch.

Six or eight persons, attracted by the noise of the carriage-wheels, came out on the portico, shouting: "It is the *Gars*! it is he; here he is!" On this several other men ran out, and their coming interrupted the lovers. The Marquis de Montauran went hastily up to them, making an imperative gesture for silence, and pointing to the farther end of the causeway, where the Republican escort was just appearing. At the sight of the well-known blue uniforms with red facings, and the glittering bayonets, the amazed conspirators called out hastily, "You have surely not betrayed us?"

"If I had, I should not warn you," said the marquis, smiling bitterly. "Those Blues," he added, after a pause, "are the escort of this young lady, whose generosity has delivered us, almost miraculously, from a danger we were in at Alencon. I will tell you about it later. Mademoiselle and her escort are here in safety, on my word as a gentleman, and we must all receive them as friends."

Madame du Gua and Francine were now on the portico; the marquis offered his hand to Mademoiselle de Verneuil, the group of gentlemen parted in two lines to allow them to pass, endeavouring, as they did so, to catch sight of the young lady's features; for Madame du Gua, who was following behind, excited their curiosity by secret signs.

110

Mademoiselle de Verneuil saw, with surprise, that a large table was set in the first hall, for about twenty guests. The dining-room opened into a vast salon, where the whole party were presently assembled. These rooms were in keeping with the dilapidated appearance of the outside of the house. The walnut panels, polished by age, but rough and coarse in design and badly executed, were loose in their places and ready to fall. Their dingy colour added to the gloom of these apartments, which were barren of curtains and mirrors; a few venerable bits of furniture in the last stages of decay alone remained, and harmonized with the general destruction. Marie noticed maps and plans stretched out upon long tables, and in the corners of the room a quantity of weapons and stacked carbines. These things bore witness, though she did not know it, to an important conference between the leaders of the Vendeans and those of the Chouans.

The marquis led Mademoiselle de Verneuil to a large and worm-eaten armchair placed beside the fireplace; Francine followed and stood behind her mistress, leaning on the back of that ancient bit of furniture.

"You will allow me for a moment to play the part of master of the house," he said, leaving the two women and mingling with the groups of his other guests.

Francine saw the gentlemen hasten, after a few words from Montauran, to hide their weapons, maps, and whatever else might arouse the suspicions of the Republican officers. Some took off their broad leather belts containing pistols and hunting-knives. The marquis requested them to show the utmost prudence, and went himself to see to the reception of the troublesome guests whom fate had bestowed upon him.

Mademoiselle de Verneuil, who had raised her feet to the fire and was now warming them, did not turn her head as Montauran left the room, thus disappointing those present, who were anxious to see her. Francine alone saw the change produced upon the company by the departure of the young chief. The gentlemen gathered hastily round Madame du Gua, and during a conversation carried on in an undertone between them, they all turned several times to look curiously at the stranger.

"You know Montauran," Madame du Gua said to them; "he has fallen in love with that worthless girl, and, as you can easily understand, he thinks all my warnings selfish. Our friends in Paris, Messieurs de Valois and d'Esgrignon, have warned him of a trap set for him by throwing some such creature at his head; but in spite of this

111

he allows himself to be fooled by the first woman he meets,—a girl who, if my information is correct, has stolen a great name only to disgrace it."

The speaker, in whom our readers have already recognized the lady who instigated the attack on the "*turgotine*," may be allowed to keep the name which she used to escape the dangers that threatened her in Alencon. The publication of her real name would only mortify a noble family already deeply afflicted at the misconduct of this woman; whose history, by the bye, has already been given on another scene.

The curiosity manifested by the company of men soon became impertinent and almost hostile. A few harsh words reached Francine's ear, and after a word said to her mistress the girl retreated into the embrasure of a window. Marie rose, turned towards the insolent group, and gave them a look full of dignity and even disdain. Her beauty, the elegance of her manners, and her pride changed the behaviour of her enemies, and won her the flattering murmur which escaped their lips. Two or three men, whose outward appearance seemed to denote the habits of polite society and the gallantry acquired in courts, came towards her; but her propriety of demeanour forced them to respect her, and none dared speak to her; so that, instead of being herself arraigned by the company, it was she who appeared to judge of them. These chiefs of a war undertaken for God and the king bore very little resemblance to the portraits her fancy had drawn of them. The struggle, really great in itself, shrank to mean proportions as she observed these provincial noblemen, all, with one or two vigorous exceptions, devoid of significance and virility. Having made to herself a poem of such heroes, Marie suddenly awakened to the truth. Their faces expressed to her eyes more a love of scheming than a love of glory; self-interest had evidently put arms into their hands. Still, it must be said that these men did become heroic when brought into action. The loss of her illusions made Mademoiselle de Verneuil unjust, and prevented her from recognizing the real devotion which rendered several of these men remarkable. It is true that most of those now present were commonplace. A few original and marked faces appeared among them, but even these were belittled by the artificiality and the etiquette of aristocracy. If Marie generously granted intellect and perception to the latter, she also discerned in them a total absence of the simplicity, the grandeur, to which she had been accustomed among the triumphant men of the Republic. This nocturnal assemblage in the old ruined castle made her smile; the scene seemed symbolic of the monarchy.

But the thought came to her with delight that the marquis at least played a noble part among these men, whose only remaining merit in her eyes was devotion to a lost cause. She pictured her lover's face upon the background of this company, rejoicing to see it stand forth among those paltry and puny figures who were but the instruments of his great designs.

The footsteps of the marquis were heard in the adjoining room. Instantly the company separated into little groups and the whisperings ceased. Like schoolboys who have plotted mischief in the master's absence, they hurriedly became silent and orderly. Montauran entered. Marie had the happiness of admiring him among his fellows, of whom he was the youngest, the handsomest, and the chief. Like a king in his court, he went from group to group, distributing looks and nods and words of encouragement or warning, with pressure of the hands and smiles; doing his duty as leader of a party with a grace and self-possession hardly to be expected in the young man whom Marie had so lately accused of heedlessness.

The presence of the marquis put an end to the open curiosity bestowed on Mademoiselle de Verneuil, but Madame du Gua's scandalous suggestions bore fruit. The Baron du Guenic, familiarly called "l'Intime," who by rank and name had the best right among those present to treat Montauran familiarly, took the young leader by the arm and led him apart.

"My dear marquis," he said; "we are much disturbed at seeing you on the point of committing an amazing folly."

"What do you mean by that?"

"Do you know where that girl comes from, who she is, and what her schemes about you are?"

"Don't trouble yourself, my dear l'Intime; between you and me my fancy for her will be over tomorrow."

"Yes; but suppose that creature betrays you tonight?"

"I'll answer that when you tell me why she has not done it already," said Montauran, assuming with a laugh an air of conceit. "My dear fellow, look at that charming girl, watch her manners, and dare to tell me she is not a woman of distinction. If she gave you a few favourable looks wouldn't you feel at the bottom of your soul a respect for her? A certain lady has prejudiced you. I will tell you this: if she were the lost creature our friends are trying to make her out, I would, after what she and I have said to each other, kill her myself."

"Do you suppose," said Madame du Gua, joining them, "that Fouche is fool enough to send you a common prostitute out of the

113

streets? He has provided seductions according to your deserts. You may choose to be blind, but your friends are keeping their eyes open to protect you."

"Madame," replied the *Gars*, his eyes flashing with anger, "be warned; take no steps against that lady, nor against her escort; if you do, nothing shall save you from my vengeance. I choose that Mademoiselle de Verneuil is to be treated with the utmost respect, and as a lady belonging to my family. We are, I believe, related to the de Verneuils."

The opposition the marquis was made to feel produced the usual effect of such obstacles on all young men. Though he had, apparently, treated Mademoiselle de Verneuil rather lightly, and left it to be supposed that his passion for her was a mere caprice, he now, from a feeling of pride, made immense strides in his relation to her. By openly protecting her, his honour became concerned in compelling respect to her person; and he went from group to group assuring his friends, in the tone of a man whom it was dangerous to contradict, that the lady was really Mademoiselle de Verneuil. The doubts and gossip ceased at once. As soon as Montauran felt that harmony was restored and anxiety allayed, he returned to his mistress eagerly, saying in a low voice:—

"Those mischievous people have robbed me of an hour's happiness."

"I am glad you have come back to me," she said, smiling. "I warn you that I am inquisitive; therefore you must not get tired of my questions. Tell me, in the first place, who is that worthy in a green cloth jacket?"

"That is the famous Major Brigaut, a man from the Marais, a comrade of the late Mercier, called La Vendee."

"And that fat priest with the red face to whom he is talking at this moment about me?" she went on.

"Do you want to know what they are saying?"

"Do I want to know it? What a useless question!"

"But I could not tell it without offending you."

"If you allow me to be insulted in your house without avenging me, marquis, *adieu!*" she said. "I will not stay another moment. I have some qualms already about deceiving these poor Republicans, loyal and confiding as they are!"

She made a few hasty steps; the marquis followed her.

"Dear Marie, listen to me. On my honour, I have silenced their evil speaking, without knowing whether it was false or true. But, placed as

114

I am, if friends whom we have in all the ministries in Paris warn me to beware of every woman I meet, and assure me that Fouche has employed against me a Judith of the streets, it is not unnatural that my best friends here should think you too beautiful to be an honest woman."

As he spoke the marquis plunged a glance into Mademoiselle de Verneuil's eyes. She coloured, and was unable to restrain her tears.

"I deserve these insults," she said. "I wish you really thought me that despicable creature and still loved me; then, indeed, I could no longer doubt you. I believed in you when you were deceiving me, and you will not believe me now when I am true. Let us make an end of this, *monsieur*," she said, frowning, but turning pale as death,—"*adieu!*"

She rushed towards the dining-room with a movement of despair.

"Marie, my life is yours," said the young marquis in her ear.

She stopped short and looked at him.

"No, no," she said, "I will be generous. Farewell. In coming with you here I did not think of my past nor of your future—I was beside myself."

"You cannot mean that you will leave me now when I offer you my life?"

"You offer it in a moment of passion—of desire."

"I offer it without regret, and forever," he replied.

She returned to the room they had left. Hiding his emotions the marquis continued the conversation.

"That fat priest whose name you asked is the Abbe Gudin, a Jesuit, obstinate enough—perhaps I ought to say devoted enough,—to remain in France in spite of the decree of 1793, which banished his order. He is the firebrand of the war in these regions and a propagandist of the religious association called the *Sacre-Coeur*. Trained to use religion as an instrument, he persuades his followers that if they are killed they will be brought to life again, and he knows how to rouse their fanaticism by shrewd sermons. You see, it is necessary to work upon every man's selfish interests to attain a great end. That is the secret of all political success."

"And that vigorous, muscular old man, with the repulsive face, who is he? I mean the one in the ragged gown of a barrister."

"Barrister! he aspires to be considered a brigadier-general. Did you never hear of de Longuy?"

"Is that he!" exclaimed Mademoiselle de Verneuil, horrified. "You employ such men as that?"

"Hush! he'll hear you. Do you see that other man in malignant conversation with Madame du Gua?"

"The one in black who looks like a judge?"

115

"That is one of our go-betweens, La Billardiere, son of a councillor to the Breton Parliament, whose real name is something like Flamet; he is in close correspondence with the princes."

"And his neighbour? the one who is just putting up his white clay pipe, and uses all the fingers of his right hand to snap the box, like a countryman."

"By Jove, you are right; he was game-keeper to the deceased husband of that lady, and now commands one of the companies I send against the Republican militia. He and Marche-a-Terre are the two most conscientious vassals the king has here."

"But she—who is she?"

"Charette's last mistress," replied the marquis. "She wields great influence over all these people."

"Is she faithful to his memory?"

For all answer the marquis gave a dubious smile.

"Do you think well of her?"

"You are very inquisitive."

"She is my enemy because she can no longer be my rival," said Mademoiselle de Verneuil, laughing. "I forgive her her past errors if she forgives mine. Who is that officer with the long moustache?"

"Permit me not to name him; he wants to get rid of the First Consul by assassination. Whether he succeeds or not you will hear of him. He is certain to become famous."

"And you have come here to command such men as these!" she exclaimed in horror. "Are *they* the king's defenders? Where are the gentlemen and the great lords?"

"Where?" said the marquis, coolly, "they are in all the courts of Europe. Who else should win over kings and cabinets and armies to serve the Bourbon cause and hurl them at that Republic which threatens monarchies and social order with death and destruction?"

"Ah!" she said, with generous emotion, "be to me henceforth the source from which I draw the ideas I must still acquire about your cause—I consent. But let me still remember that you are the only noble who does his duty in fighting France with Frenchmen, without the help of foreigners. I am a woman; I feel that if my child struck me in anger I could forgive him; but if he saw me beaten by a stranger, and consented to it, I should regard him as a monster."

"You shall remain a Republican," said the marquis, in the ardour produced by the generous words which confirmed his hopes.

"Republican! no, I am that no longer. I could not now respect you if you submitted to the First Consul," she replied. "But neither do I like to see you at the head of men who are pillaging a corner of France, instead of making war against the whole Republic. For whom are you fighting? What do you expect of a king restored to his throne by your efforts? A woman did that great thing once, and the liberated king allowed her to be burned. Such men are the anointed of the Lord, and there is danger in meddling with sacred things. Let God take care of his own, and place, displace, and replace them on their purple seats. But if you have counted the cost, and seen the poor return that will come to you, you are tenfold greater in my eyes than I thought you—"

"Ah! you are bewitching. Don't attempt to indoctrinate my followers, or I shall be left without a man."

"If you would let me convert you, only you," she said, "we might live happily a thousand leagues away from all this."

"These men whom you seem to despise," said the marquis, in a graver tone, "will know how to die when the struggle comes, and all their misdeeds will be forgotten. Besides, if my efforts are crowned with some success, the laurel leaves of victory will hide all."

"I see no one but you who is risking anything."

"You are mistaken; I am not the only one," he replied, with true modesty. "See, over there, the new leaders from La Vendee. The first, whom you must have heard of as 'Le Grand Jacques,' is the Comte de Fontain; the other is La Billardiere, whom I mentioned to you just now."

"Have you forgotten Quiberon, where La Billardiere played so equivocal a part?" she said, struck by a sudden recollection.

"La Billardiere took a great deal upon himself. Serving princes is far from lying on a bed of roses."

"Ah! you make me shudder!" cried Marie. "Marquis," she continued, in a tone which seemed to indicate some mysterious personal reticence, "a single instant suffices to destroy illusions and to betray secrets on which the life and happiness of many may depend—" she stopped, as though she feared she had said too much; then she added, in another tone, "I wish I could be sure that those Republican soldiers were in safety."

"I will be prudent," he said, smiling to disguise his emotion; "but say no more about your soldiers; have I not answered for their safety on my word as a gentleman?"

"And after all," she said, "what right have I to dictate to you? Be my master henceforth. Did I not tell you it would drive me to despair to rule a slave?"

117

"Monsieur le marquis," said Major Brigaut, respectfully, interrupting the conversation, "how long are the Blues to remain here?"

"They will leave as soon as they are rested," said Marie.

The marquis looked about the room and noticed the agitation of those present. He left Mademoiselle de Verneuil, and his place beside her was taken at once by Madame du Gua, whose smiling and treacherous face was in no way disconcerted by the young chief's bitter smile. Just then Francine, standing by the window, gave a stifled cry. Marie, noticing with amazement that the girl left the room, looked at Madame du Gua, and her surprise increased as she saw the pallor on the face of her enemy. Anxious to discover the meaning of Francine's abrupt departure, she went to the window, where Madame du Gua followed her, no doubt to guard against any suspicions which might arise in her mind. They returned together to the chimney, after each had cast a look upon the shore and the lake,—Marie without seeing anything that could have caused Francine's flight, Madame du Gua seeing that which satisfied her she was being obeyed.

The lake, at the edge of which Marche-a-Terre had shown his head, where Madame du Gua had seen him, joined the moat in misty curves, sometimes broad as ponds, in other places narrow as the artificial streamlets of a park. The steep bank, washed by its waters, lay a few rods from the window. Francine, watching on the surface of the water the black lines thrown by the willows, noticed, carelessly at first, the uniform trend of their branches, caused by a light breeze then prevailing. Suddenly she thought she saw against the glassy surface a figure moving with the spontaneous and irregular motion of life. The form, vague as it was, seemed to her that of a man. At first she attributed what she saw to the play of the moonlight upon the foliage, but presently a second head appeared, then several others in the distance. The shrubs upon the bank were bent and then violently straightened, and Francine saw the long hedge undulating like one of those great Indian serpents of fabulous size and shape. Here and there, among the gorse and taller brambles, points of light could be seen to come and go. The girl's attention redoubled, and she thought she recognized the foremost of the dusky figures; indistinct as its outlines were, the beating of her heart convinced her it was no other than her lover, Marche-a-Terre. Eager to know if this mysterious approach meant treachery, she ran to the courtyard. When she reached the middle of its grass plot she looked alternately at the two wings of the building and along the steep shores, without discovering, on the inhabited side of the house, any sign of this silent approach. She listened attentively and heard a

118

slight rustling, like that which might be made by the footfalls of some wild animal in the silence of the forest. She quivered, but did not tremble. Though young and innocent, her anxious curiosity suggested a ruse. She saw the coach and slipped into it, putting out her head to listen, with the caution of a hare giving ear to the sound of the distant hunters. She saw Pille-Miche come out of the stable, accompanied by two peasants, all three carrying bales of straw; these they spread on the ground in a way to form a long bed of litter before the inhabited wing of the house, parallel with the bank, bordered by dwarf trees.

"You're spreading straw as if you thought they'd sleep here! Enough, Pille-Miche, enough!" said a low, gruff voice, which Francine recognized.

"And won't they sleep here?" returned Pille-Miche with a laugh. "I'm afraid the *Gars* will be angry!" he added, too low for Francine to hear.

"Well, let him," said Marche-a-Terre, in the same tone, "we shall have killed the Blues anyway. Here's that coach, which you and I had better put up."

Pille-Miche pulled the carriage by the pole and Marche-a-Terre pushed it by one of the wheels with such force that Francine was in the barn and about to be locked up before she had time to reflect on her situation. Pille-Miche went out to fetch the barrel of cider, which the marquis had ordered for the escort; and Marche-a-Terre was passing along the side of the coach, to leave the barn and close the door, when he was stopped by a hand which caught and held the long hair of his goatskin. He recognized a pair of eyes the gentleness of which exercised a power of magnetism over him, and he stood stock-still for a moment under their spell. Francine sprang from the carriage, and said, in the nervous tone of an excited woman: "Pierre, what news did you give to that lady and her son on the road? What is going on here? Why are you hiding? I must know all."

These words brought a look on the Chouan's face which Francine had never seen there before. The Breton led his innocent mistress to the door; there he turned her towards the blanching light of the moon, and answered, as he looked in her face with terrifying eyes: "Yes, by my damnation, Francine, I will tell you, but not until you have sworn on these beads (and he pulled an old chaplet from beneath his goatskin)—on this relic, which *you know well*," he continued, "to answer me truly one question."

Francine coloured as she saw the chaplet, which was no doubt a token of their love. "It was on that," he added, much agitated, "that you swore—"

119

He did not finish the sentence. The young girl placed her hand on the lips of her savage lover and silenced him.

"Need I swear?" she said.

He took his mistress gently by the hand, looked at her for a moment and said: "Is the lady you are with really Mademoiselle de Verneuil?"

Francine stood with hanging arms, her eyelids lowered, her head bowed, pale and speechless.

"She is a strumpet!" cried Marche-a-Terre, in a terrifying voice.

At the word the pretty hand once more covered his lips, but this time he sprang back violently. The girl no longer saw a lover; he had turned to a wild beast in all the fury of its nature. His eyebrows were drawn together, his lips drew apart, and he showed his teeth like a dog which defends its master.

"I left you pure, and I find you muck. Ha! why did I ever leave you! You are here to betray us; to deliver up the *Gars!*"

These sentences sounded more like roars than words. Though Francine was frightened, she raised her angelic eyes at this last accusation and answered calmly, as she looked into his savage face: "I will pledge my eternal safety that that is false. That's an idea of the lady you are serving."

He lowered his head; then she took his hand and nestling to him with a pretty movement said: "Pierre, what is all this to you and me? I don't know what you understand about it, but I can't make it out. Recollect one thing: that noble and beautiful young lady has been my benefactress; she is also yours—we live together like two sisters. No harm must ever come to her where we are, you and I—in our lifetime at least. Swear it! I trust no one here but you."

"I don't command here," said the Chouan, in a surly tone.

His face darkened. She caught his long ears and twisted them gently as if playing with a cat.

"At least," she said, seeing that he looked less stern, "promise me to use all the power you have to protect our benefactress."

He shook his head as if he doubted of success, and the motion made her tremble. At this critical moment the escort was entering the courtyard. The tread of the soldiers and the rattle of their weapons awoke the echoes and seemed to put an end to Marche-a-Terre's indecision.

"Perhaps I can save her," he said, "if you make her stay in the house. And mind," he added, "whatever happens, you must stay with her and keep silence; if not, no safety."

"I promise it," she replied in terror.

"Very good; then go in—go in at once, and hide your fears from every one, even your mistress."

"Yes."

She pressed his hand; he stood for a moment watching her with an almost paternal air as she ran with the lightness of a bird up the portico; then he slipped behind the bushes, like an actor darting behind the scenes as the curtain rises on a tragedy.

"Do you know, Merle," said Gerard as they reached the chateau, "that this place looks to me like a mousetrap?"

"So I think," said the captain, anxiously.

The two officers hastened to post sentinels to guard the gate and the causeway; then they examined with great distrust the precipitous banks of the lakes and the surroundings of the chateau.

"Pooh!" said Merle, "we must do one of two things: either trust ourselves in this barrack with perfect confidence, or else not enter it at all."

"Come, let's go in," replied Gerard.

The soldiers, released at the word of command, hastened to stack their muskets in conical sheaves, and to form a sort of line before the litter of straw, in the middle of which was the promised barrel of cider. They then divided into groups, to whom two peasants began to distribute butter and rye-bread. The marquis appeared in the portico to welcome the officers and take them to the salon. As Gerard went up the steps he looked at both ends of the portico, where some venerable larches spread their black branches; and he called up Clef-des-Coeurs and Beau-Pied.

"You will each reconnoitre the gardens and search the bushes, and post a sentry before your line."

"May we light our fire before starting, adjutant?" asked Clef-des-Coeurs.

Gerard nodded.

"There! you see, Clef-des-Coeurs," said Beau-Pied, "the adjutant's wrong to run himself into this wasp's-nest. If Hulot was in command we shouldn't be cornered here—in a saucepan!"

"What a stupid you are!" replied Clef-des-Coeurs, "haven't you guessed, you knave of tricks, that this is the home of the beauty our jovial Merle has been whistling round? He'll marry her to a certainty—that's as clear as a well-rubbed bayonet. A woman like that will do honour to the brigade."

"True for you," replied Beau-Pied, "and you may add that she gives pretty good cider—but I can't drink it in peace till I know what's behind those devilish hedges. I always remember poor Larose and Vieux-Chapeau rolling down the ditch at La Pelerine. I shall recollect Larose's queue to the end of my days; it went hammering down like the knocker of a front door."

"Beau-Pied, my friend; you have too much imagination for a soldier; you ought to be making songs at the national Institute."

"If I've too much imagination," retorted Beau-Pied, "you haven't any; it will take you some time to get your degree as consul."

A general laugh put an end to the discussion, for Clef-des-Coeurs found no suitable reply in his pouch with which to floor his adversary.

"Come and make our rounds; I'll go to the right," said Beau-Pied.

"Very good, I'll take the left," replied his comrade. "But stop one minute, I must have a glass of cider; my throat is glued together like the oiled-silk of Hulot's best hat."

The left bank of the gardens, which Clef-des-Coeurs thus delayed searching at once, was, unhappily, the dangerous slope where Francine had seen the moving line of men. All things go by chance in war.

As Gerard entered the salon and bowed to the company he cast a penetrating eye on the men who were present. Suspicions came forcibly to his mind, and he went at once to Mademoiselle de Verneuil and said in a low voice: "I think you had better leave this place immediately. We are not safe here."

"What can you fear while I am with you?" she answered, laughing. "You are safer here than you would be at Mayenne."

A woman answers for her lover in good faith. The two officers were reassured. The party now moved into the dining-room after some discussion about a guest, apparently of some importance, who had not appeared. Mademoiselle de Verneuil was able, thanks to the silence which always reigns at the beginning of a meal, to give some attention to the character of the assemblage, which was curious enough under existing circumstances. One thing struck her with surprise. The Republican officers seemed superior to the rest of the assembly by reason of their dignified appearance. Their long hair tied behind in a queue drew lines beside their foreheads which gave, in those days, an expression of great candour and nobleness to young heads. Their threadbare blue uniforms with the shabby red facings, even their epaulets flung back behind their shoulders (a sign throughout the army, even among the leaders, of a lack of overcoats),—all these things brought the two Republican officers into strong relief against the men who surrounded them.

"Oh, they are the Nation, and that means liberty!" thought Marie;

then, with a glance at the royalists, she added, "on the other side is a man, a king, and privileges." She could not refrain from admiring Merle, so thoroughly did that gay soldier respond to the ideas she had formed of the French trooper who hums a tune when the balls are whistling, and jests when a comrade falls. Gerard was more imposing. Grave and self-possessed, he seemed to have one of those truly Republican spirits which, in the days of which we write, crowded the French armies, and gave them, by means of these noble individual devotions, an energy which they had never before possessed. "That is one of my men with great ideals," thought Mademoiselle de Verneuil. "Relying on the present, which they rule, they destroy the past for the benefit of the future."

The thought saddened her because she could not apply it to her lover; towards whom she now turned, to discard by a different admiration, these beliefs in the Republic she was already beginning to dislike. Looking at the marquis, surrounded by men who were bold enough, fanatical enough, and sufficiently long-headed as to the future to give battle to a victorious Republic in the hope of restoring a dead monarchy, a proscribed religion, fugitive princes, and lost privileges, "He," thought she, "has no less an aim than the others; clinging to those fragments, he wants to make a future from the past." Her mind, thus grasped by conflicting images, hesitated between the new and the old wrecks. Her conscience told her that the one was fighting for a man, the other for a country; but she had now reached, through her feelings, the point to which reason will also bring us, namely: to a recognition that the king *is* the Nation.

The steps of a man echoed in the adjoining room, and the marquis rose from the table to greet him. He proved to be the expected guest, and seeing the assembled company he was about to speak, when the *Gars* made him a hasty sign, which he concealed from the Republicans, to take his place and say nothing. The more the two officers analyzed the faces about them, the more their suspicions increased. The clerical dress of the Abbe Gudin and the singularity of the Chouan garments were so many warnings to them; they redoubled their watchfulness, and soon discovered many discrepancies between the manners of the guests and the topics of their conversation. The republicanism of some was quite as exaggerated as the aristocratic bearing of others was unmistakable. Certain glances which they detected between the marquis and his guests, certain words of double meaning imprudently uttered, but above all the fringe of beard which was round the necks of several of the men and was very

123

ill-concealed by their cravats, brought the officers at last to a full conviction of the truth, which flashed upon their minds at the same instant. They gave each other one look, for Madame du Gua had cleverly separated them and they could only impart their thoughts by their eyes. Such a situation demanded the utmost caution. They did not know whether they and their men were masters of the situation, or whether they had been drawn into a trap, or whether Mademoiselle de Verneuil was the dupe or the accomplice of this inexplicable state of things. But an unforeseen event precipitated a crisis before they had fully recognized the gravity of their situation.

The new guest was one of those solid men who are square at the base and square at the shoulders, with ruddy skins; men who lean backward when they walk, seeming to displace much atmosphere about them, and who appear to think that more than one glance of the eye is needful to take them in. Notwithstanding his rank, he had taken life as a joke from which he was to get as much amusement as possible; and yet, although he knelt at his own shrine only, he was kind, polite, and witty, after the fashion of those noblemen who, having finished their training at court, return to live on their estates, and never suspect that they have, at the end of twenty years, grown rusty. Men of this type fail in tact with imperturbable coolness, talk folly wittily, distrust good with extreme shrewdness, and take incredible pains to fall into traps.

When, by a play of his knife and fork which proclaimed him a good feeder, he had made up for lost time, he began to look round on the company. His astonishment was great when he observed the two Republican officers, and he questioned Madame du Gua with a look, while she, for all answer, showed him Mademoiselle de Verneuil in the same way. When he saw the siren whose demeanour had silenced the suspicions Madame du Gua had excited among the guests, the face of the stout stranger broke into one of those insolent, ironical smiles which contain a whole history of scandal. He leaned to his next neighbour and whispered a few words, which went from ear to ear and lip to lip, passing Marie and the two officers, until they reached the heart of one whom they struck to death. The leaders of the Vendeans and the Chouans assembled round that table looked at the Marquis de Montauran with cruel curiosity. The eyes of Madame du Gua, flashing with joy, turned from the marquis to Mademoiselle de Verneuil, who was speechless with surprise. The Republican officers, uneasy in mind, questioned each other's thoughts as they awaited the result of this extraordinary scene. In a moment the forks remained inactive in every hand, silence reigned, and every eye was turned to the *Gars*. A frightful anger showed upon his face, which turned waxen in tone. He leaned towards the guest from whom the rocket had started and said, in a voice that seemed muffled in crape, "Death of my soul! count, is that true?"

"On my honour," said the count, bowing gravely.

The marquis lowered his eyes for a moment, then he raised them and looked fixedly at Marie, who, watchful of his struggle, knew that look to be her death-warrant.

"I would give my life," he said in a low voice, "for revenge on the spot."

Madame du Gua understood the words from the mere movement of the young man's lips, and she smiled upon him as we smile at a friend whose regrets are about to cease. The scorn felt for Mademoiselle de Verneuil and shown on every face, brought to its height the growing indignation of the two Republicans, who now rose hastily:—

"Do you want anything, citizens?" asked Madame du Gua.

"Our swords, *citoyenne*," said Gerard, sarcastically.

"You do not need them at table," said the marquis, coldly.

"No, but we are going to play at a game you know very well," replied Gerard. "This is La Pelerine over again."

The whole party seemed dumfounded. Just then a volley, fired with terrible regularity, echoed through the courtyard. The two officers sprang to the portico; there they beheld a hundred or so of Chouans aiming at the few soldiers who were not shot down at the first discharge; these they fired upon as upon so many hares. The Bretons swarmed from the bank, where Marche-a-Terre had posted them at the peril of their lives; for after the last volley, and mingling with the cries of the dying, several Chouans were heard to fall into the lake, where they were lost like stones in a gulf. Pille-Miche took aim at Gerard; Marche-a-Terre held Merle at his mercy.

"Captain," said the marquis to Merle, repeating to the Republican his own words, "you see that men are like medlars, they ripen on the straw." He pointed with a wave of his hand to the entire escort of the Blues lying on the bloody litter where the Chouans were despatching those who still breathed, and rifling the dead bodies with incredible rapidity. "I was right when I told you that your soldiers will not get as far as La Pelerine. I think, moreover, that your head will fill with lead before mine. What say you?"

Montauran felt a horrible necessity to vent his rage. His bitter sarcasm, the ferocity, even the treachery of this military execution, done without his orders, but which he now accepted, satisfied in some

125

degree the craving of his heart. In his fury he would fain have anni-hilated France. The dead Blues, the living officers, all innocent of the crime for which he demanded vengeance, were to him the cards by which a gambler cheats his despair.

"I would rather perish than conquer as you are conquering," said Gerard. Then, seeing the naked and bloody corpses of his men, he cried out, "Murdered basely, in cold blood!"

"That was how you murdered Louis XVI., *monsieur*," said the marquis.

"Monsieur," replied Gerard, haughtily, "there are mysteries in a king's trial which you could never comprehend."

"Do you dare to accuse the king?" exclaimed the marquis.

"Do you dare to fight your country?" retorted Gerard.

"Folly!" said the marquis.

"Parricide!" exclaimed the Republican.

"Well, well," cried Merle, gaily, "a pretty time to quarrel at the mo-ment of your death."

"True," said Gerard, coldly, turning to the marquis. "Monsieur, if it is your intention to put us to death, at least have the goodness to shoot us at once."

"Ah! that's like you, Gerard," said Merle, "always in a hurry to fin-ish things. But if one has to travel far and can't breakfast on the mor-row, at least we might sup."

Gerard sprang forward without a word towards the wall. Pille-Miche covered him, glancing as he did so at the motionless marquis, whose silence he took for an order, and the adjutant-major fell like a tree. Marche-a-Terre ran to share the fresh booty with Pille-Miche; like two hungry crows they disputed and clamoured over the still warm body.

"If you really wish to finish your supper, captain, you can come with me," said the marquis to Merle.

The captain followed him mechanically, saying in a low voice: "It is that devil of a strumpet that caused all this. What will Hulot say?"

"Strumpet!" cried the marquis in a strangled voice, "then she is one?"

The captain seemed to have given Montauran a death-blow, for he re-entered the house with a staggering step, pale, haggard, and undone.

Another scene had meanwhile taken place in the dining-room, which assumed, in the marquis's absence, such a threatening character that Marie, alone without her protector, might well fancy she read her death-warrant in the eyes of her rival. At the noise of the volley the guests all sprang to their feet, but Madame du Gua remained seated.

"It is nothing," she said; "our men are despatching the Blues." Then,

126

seeing the marquis outside on the portico, she rose. "Mademoiselle whom you here see," she continued, with the calmness of concentrated fury, "came here to betray the *Gars*! She meant to deliver him up to the Republic."

"I could have done so twenty times today and yet I saved his life," said Mademoiselle de Verneuil.

Madame du Gua sprang upon her rival like lightning; in her blind excitement she tore apart the fastenings of the young girl's spencer, the stuff, the embroidery, the corset, the chemise, and plunged her savage hand into the bosom where, as she well knew, a letter lay hidden. In doing this her jealousy so bruised and tore the palpitating throat of her rival, taken by surprise at the sudden attack, that she left the bloody marks of her nails, feeling a sort of pleasure in making her submit to so degrading a prostitution. In the feeble struggle which Marie made against the furious woman, her hair became unfastened and fell in undulating curls about her shoulders; her face glowed with outraged modesty, and tears made their burning way along her cheeks, heightening the brilliancy of her eyes, as she quivered with shame before the looks of the assembled men. The hardest judge would have believed in her innocence when he saw her sorrow.

Hatred is so uncalculating that Madame du Gua did not perceive she had overshot her mark, and that no one listened to her as she cried triumphantly: "You shall now see, gentlemen, whether I have slandered that horrible creature."

"Not so horrible," said the bass voice of the guest who had thrown the first stone. "But for my part, I like such horrors."

"Here," continued the cruel woman, "is an order signed by Laplace, and counter-signed by Dubois, minister of war." At these names several heads were turned to her. "Listen to the wording of it," she went on.

"'The military citizen commanders of all grades, the district administrators, the *procureur-syndics, et cetera*, of the insurgent departments, and particularly those of the localities in which the *ci-devant* Marquis de Montauran, leader of the brigands and otherwise known as the *Gars*, may be found, are hereby commanded to give aid and assistance to the *citoyenne* Marie Verneuil and to obey the orders which she may give them at her discretion.'

"A worthless hussy takes a noble name to soil it with such treachery," added Madame du Gua.

A movement of astonishment ran through the assembly.

"The fight is not even if the Republic employs such pretty women against us," said the Baron du Guenic gaily.

"Especially women who have nothing to lose," said Madame du Gua.

"Nothing?" cried the Chevalier du Vissard. "Mademoiselle has a property which probably brings her in a pretty good sum."

"The Republic must like a joke, to send strumpets for ambassadors," said the Abbe Gudin.

"Unfortunately, Mademoiselle seeks the joys that kill," said Madame du Gua, with a horrible expression of pleasure at the end she foresaw.

"Then why are you still living?" said her victim, rising to her feet, after repairing the disorder of her clothes.

This bitter sarcasm excited a sort of respect for so brave a victim, and silenced the assembly. Madame du Gua saw a satirical smile on the lips of the men, which infuriated her, and paying no attention to the marquis and Merle who were entering the room, she called to the Chouan who followed them. "Pille-Miche!" she said, pointing to Mademoiselle de Verneuil, "take her; she is my share of the booty, and I turn her over to you—do what you like with her."

At these words the whole assembly shuddered, for the hideous heads of Pille-Miche and Marche-a-Terre appeared behind the marquis, and the punishment was seen in all its horror.

Francine was standing with clasped hands as though paralyzed. Mademoiselle de Verneuil, who recovered her presence of mind before the danger that threatened her, cast a look of contempt at the assembled men, snatched the letter from Madame du Gua's hand, threw up her head with a flashing eye, and darted towards the door where Merle's sword was still leaning. There she came upon the marquis, cold and motionless as a statue. Nothing pleaded for her on his fixed, firm features. Wounded to the heart, life seemed odious to her. The man who had pledged her so much love must have heard the odious jests that were cast upon her, and stood there silently a witness of the infamy she had been made to endure. She might, perhaps, have forgiven him his contempt, but she could not forgive his having seen her in so humiliating a position, and she flung him a look that was full of hatred, feeling in her heart the birth of an unutterable desire for vengeance. With death beside her, the sense of impotence almost strangled her. A whirlwind of passion and madness rose in her head; the blood which boiled in her veins made everything about her seem like a conflagration. Instead of killing herself, she seized the sword and thrust it though the marquis. But the weapon slipped between his arm and side; he caught her by the wrist and dragged her from the room, aided by Pille-Miche, who had flung himself upon the furious creature when she attacked his master. Francine shrieked aloud. "Pierre! Pierre! Pierre!" she cried in heart-rending tones, as she followed her mistress.

The marquis closed the door on the astonished company. When he reached the portico he was still holding the woman's wrist, which he clasped convulsively, while Pille-Miche had almost crushed the bones of her arm with his iron fingers, but Marie felt only the burning hand of the young leader.

"You hurt me," she said.

For all answer he looked at her a moment.

"Have you some base revenge to take—like that woman?" she said. Then, seeing the dead bodies on the heap of straw, she cried out, shuddering: "The faith of a gentleman! ha! ha! ha!" With a frightful laugh she added: "Ha! the glorious day!"

"Yes," he said, "a day without a morrow."

He let go her hand and took a long, last look at the beautiful creature he could scarcely even then renounce. Neither of these proud natures yielded. The marquis may have looked for a tear, but the eyes of the girl were dry and scornful. Then he turned quickly, and left the victim to Pille-Miche.

"God will hear me, marquis," she called. "I will ask Him to give you a glorious day without a morrow."

Pille-Miche, not a little embarrassed with so rich a prize, dragged her away with some gentleness and a mixture of respect and scorn. The marquis, with a sigh, re-entered the dining-room, his face like that of a dead man whose eyes have not been closed.

Merle's presence was inexplicable to the silent spectators of this tragedy; they looked at him in astonishment and their eyes questioned each other. Merle saw their amazement, and, true to his native character, he said, with a smile: "Gentlemen, you will scarcely refuse a glass of wine to a man who is about to make his last journey."

It was just as the company had calmed down under the influence of these words, said with a true French carelessness which pleased the Vendeans, that Montauran returned, his face pale, his eyes fixed.

"Now you shall see," said Merle, "how death can make men lively."

"Ah!" said the marquis, with a gesture as if suddenly awaking, "here you are, my dear councillor of war," and he passed him a bottle of *vin de Grave*.

"Oh, thanks, citizen marquis," replied Merle. "Now I can divert myself."

At this sally Madame du Gua turned to the other guests with a smile, saying, "Let us spare him the dessert."

"That is a very cruel vengeance, *madame*," he said. "You forget my murdered friend who is waiting for me; I never miss an appointment."

"Captain," said the marquis, throwing him his glove, "you are free; that's your passport. The Chasseurs du Roi know that they must not kill all the game."

"So much the better for me!" replied Merle, "but you are making a mistake; we shall come to close quarters before long, and I'll not let you off. Though your head can never pay for Gerard's, I want it and I shall have it. *Adieu.* I could drink with my own assassins, but I cannot stay with those of my friend"; and he disappeared, leaving the guests astonished at his coolness.

"Well, gentlemen, what do you think of the lawyers and surgeons and bailiffs who manage the Republic," said the *Gars*, coldly.

"God's-death! marquis," replied the Comte de Bauvan; "they have shocking manners; that fellow presumed to be impertinent, it seems to me."

The captain's hasty retreat had a motive. The despised, humiliated woman, who was even then, perhaps, being put to death, had so won upon him during the scene of her degradation that he said to himself, as he left the room, "If she is a prostitute, she is not an ordinary one, and I'll marry her." He felt so sure of being able to rescue her from the savages that his first thought, when his own life was given to him, was to save hers. Unhappily, when he reached the portico, he found the courtyard deserted. He looked about him, listened to the silence, and could hear nothing but the distant shouts and laughter of the Chouans, who were drinking in the gardens and dividing their booty. He turned the corner to the fatal wing before which his men had been shot, and from there he could distinguish, by the feeble light of a few stray lanterns, the different groups of the Chasseurs du Roi. Neither Pille-Miche, nor Marche-a-Terre, nor the girl were visible; but he felt himself gently pulled by the flap of his uniform, and, turning round, saw Francine on her knees.

"Where is she?" he asked.

"I don't know; Pierre drove me back and told me not to stir from here."

"Which way did they go?"

"That way," she replied, pointing to the causeway.

The captain and Francine then noticed in that direction a line of strong shadows thrown by the moonlight on the lake, and among them that of a female figure.

"It is she!" cried Francine.

Mademoiselle de Verneuil seemed to be standing, as if resigned, in the midst of other figures, whose gestures denoted a debate.

"There are several," said the captain. "Well, no matter, let us go to them."

"You will get yourself killed uselessly," said Francine.

"I have been killed once before today," he said gaily.

They both walked towards the gloomy gateway which led to the causeway; there Francine suddenly stopped short.

"No," she said, gently, "I'll go no farther; Pierre told me not to meddle; I believe in him; if we go on we shall spoil all. Do as you please, officer, but leave me. If Pierre saw us together he would kill you."

Just then Pille-Miche appeared in the gateway and called to the postilion who was left in the stable. At the same moment he saw the captain and covered him with his musket, shouting out, "By Saint Anne of Auray! the rector was right enough in telling us the Blues had signed a compact with the devil. I'll bring you to life, I will!"

"Stop! my life is sacred," cried Merle, seeing his danger. "There's the glove of your *Gars*," and he held it out.

"Ghosts' lives are not sacred," replied the Chouan, "and I sha'n't give you yours. *Ave Maria!*"

He fired, and the ball passed through his victim's head. The captain fell. When Francine reached him she heard him mutter the words, "I'd rather die with them than return without them."

The Chouan sprang upon the body to strip it, saying, "There's one good thing about ghosts, they come to life in their clothes." Then, recognizing the *Gars'* glove, that sacred safeguard, in the captain's hand, he stopped short, terrified. "I wish I wasn't in the skin of my mother's son!" he exclaimed, as he turned and disappeared with the rapidity of a bird.

To understand this scene, so fatal to poor Merle, we must follow Mademoiselle de Verneuil after the marquis, in his fury and despair, had abandoned her to Pille-Miche. Francine had caught Marche-a-Terre by the arm and reminded him, with sobs, of the promise he had made her. Pille-Miche was already dragging away his victim like a heavy bundle. Marie, her head and hair hanging back, turned her eyes to the lake; but held as she was in a grasp of iron she was forced to follow the Chouan, who turned now and then to hasten her steps, and each time that he did so a jovial thought brought a hideous smile upon his face.

"Isn't she a morsel!" he cried, with a coarse laugh.

Hearing the words, Francine recovered speech.

"Pierre?"

"Well, what?"

"He'll kill her."

"Not at once."

"Then she'll kill herself, she will never submit; and if she dies I shall die too."

"Then you love her too much, and she shall die," said Marche-a-Terre.

"Pierre! if we are rich and happy we owe it all to her; but, whether or no, you promised me to save her."

"Well, I'll try; but you must stay here, and don't move."

Francine at once let go his arm, and waited in horrible suspense in the courtyard where Merle found her. Meantime Marche-a-Terre joined his comrade at the moment when the latter, after dragging his victim to the barn, was compelling her to get into the coach. Pille-Miche called to him to help in pulling out the vehicle.

"What are you going to do with all that?" asked Marche-a-Terre.

"The Grande Garce gave me the woman, and all that belongs to her is mine."

"The coach will put a *sou* or two in your pocket; but as for the woman, she'll scratch your eyes out like a cat."

Pille-Miche burst into a roar of laughter.

"Then I'll tie her up and take her home," he answered.

"Very good; suppose we harness the horses," said Marche-a-Terre.

A few moments later Marche-a-Terre, who had left his comrade mounting guard over his prey, led the coach from the stable to the causeway, where Pille-Miche got into it beside Mademoiselle de Verneuil, not perceiving that she was on the point of making a spring into the lake.

"I say, Pille-Miche!" cried Marche-a-Terre.

"What!"

"I'll buy all your booty."

"Are you joking?" asked the other, catching his prisoner by the petticoat, as a butcher catches a calf that is trying to escape him.

"Let me see her, and I'll set a price."

The unfortunate creature was made to leave the coach and stand between the two Chouans, who each held a hand and looked at her as the Elders must have looked at Susannah.

"Will you take thirty *francs* in good coin?" said Marche-a-Terre, with a groan.

"Really?"

"Done?" said Marche-a-Terre, holding out his hand.

"Yes, done; I can get plenty of Breton girls for that, and choice morsels, too. But the coach; whose is that?" asked Pille-Miche, beginning to reflect upon his bargain.

"Mine!" cried Marche-a-Terre, in a terrible tone of voice, which showed the sort of superiority his ferocious character gave him over his companions.

"But suppose there's money in the coach?"

"Didn't you say, 'Done'?"

"Yes, I said, 'Done.'"

"Very good; then go and fetch the postilion who is gagged in the stable over there."

"But if there's money in the—"

"Is there any?" asked Marche-a-Terre, roughly, shaking Marie by the arm.

"Yes, about a hundred crowns."

The two Chouans looked at each other.

"Well, well, friend," said Pille-Miche, "we won't quarrel for a female Blue; let's pitch her into the lake with a stone around her neck, and divide the money."

"I'll give you that money as my share in d'Orgemont's ransom," said Marche-a-Terre, smothering a groan, caused by such sacrifice.

Pille-Miche uttered a sort of hoarse cry as he started to find the postilion, and his glee brought death to Merle, whom he met on his way.

Hearing the shot, Marche-a-Terre rushed in the direction where he had left Francine, and found her praying on her knees, with clasped hands, beside the poor captain, whose murder had deeply horrified her.

"Run to your mistress," said the Chouan; "she is saved."

He ran himself to fetch the postilion, returning with all speed, and, as he re-passed Merle's body, he noticed the *Gars'* glove, which was still convulsively clasped in the dead hand.

"Oho!" he cried. "Pille-Miche has blundered horribly—he won't live to spend his crowns."

He snatched up the glove and said to Mademoiselle de Verneuil, who was already in the coach with Francine: "Here, take this glove. If any of our men attack you on the road, call out 'Ho, the *Gars!*' show the glove, and no harm can happen to you. Francine," he said, turning towards her and seizing her violently, "you and I are quits with that woman; come with me and let the devil have her."

"You can't ask me to abandon her just at this moment!" cried Francine, in distress.

Marche-a-Terre scratched his ear and forehead, then he raised his

133

head, and his mistress saw the ferocious expression of his eyes. "You are right," he said; "I leave you with her one week; if at the end of that time you don't come with me—" he did not finish the sentence, but he slapped the muzzle of his gun with the flat of his hand. After making the gesture of taking aim at her, he disappeared, without waiting for her reply.

No sooner was he gone than a voice, which seemed to issue from the lake, called, in a muffled tone: "Madame, *madame!*"

The postilion and the two women shuddered, for several corpses were floating near them. A Blue, hidden behind a tree, cautiously appeared.

"Let me get up behind the coach, or I'm a dead man. That damned cider which Clef-des-Coeurs would stop to drink cost more than a pint of blood. If he had done as I did, and made his round, our poor comrades there wouldn't be floating dead in the pond."

****

While these events were taking place outside the chateau, the leaders sent by the Vendeans and those of the Chouans were holding a council of war, with their glasses in their hands, under the presidency of the Marquis de Montauran. Frequent libations of Bordeaux animated the discussion, which, however, became more serious and important at the end of the meal. After the general plan of military operations had been decided on, the Royalists drank to the health of the Bourbons. It was at that moment that the shot which killed Merle was heard, like an echo of the disastrous war which these gay and noble conspirators were about to make against the Republic. Madame du Gua quivered with pleasure at the thought that she was freed from her rival; the guests looked at each other in silence; the marquis rose from the table and went out.

"He loved her!" said Madame du Gua, sarcastically. "Follow him, Monsieur de Fontaine, and keep him company; he will be as irritating as a fly if we let him sulk."

She went to a window which looked on the courtyard to endeavour to see Marie's body. There, by the last gleams of the sinking moon, she caught sight of the coach being rapidly driven down the avenue of apple-trees. Mademoiselle de Verneuil's veil was fluttering in the wind. Madame du Gua, furious at the sight, left the room hurriedly. The marquis, standing on the portico absorbed in gloomy thought, was watching about a hundred and fifty Chouans, who, having divided their booty in the gardens, were now returning to finish the cider and the rye-bread provided for the Blues. These soldiers of a new species, on whom the monarchy was resting its hopes, dispersed into groups. Some drank the cider; others, on the bank before the portico, amused themselves by flinging into the lake the dead bodies of the Blues, to which they fastened stones. This sight, joined to the other aspects of the strange scene,—the fantastic dress, the savage expressions of the barbarous and uncouth *gars*,—was so new and so amazing to Monsieur de Fontaine, accustomed to the nobler and better-regulated appearance of the Vendean troops, that he seized the occasion to say to the Marquis de Montauran, "What do you expect to do with such brutes?"

"Not very much, my dear count," replied the *Gars*.

"Will they ever be fit to manoeuvre before the enemy?"

"Never."

"Can they understand or execute an order?"

"No."

"Then what good will they be to you?"

"They will help me to plunge my sword into the entrails of the Republic," replied the marquis in a thundering voice. "They will give me Fougeres in three days, and all Brittany in ten! Monsieur," he added in a gentler voice, "start at once for La Vendee; if d'Auticamp, Suzannet, and the Abbe Bernier will act as rapidly as I do, if they'll not negotiate with the First Consul, as I am afraid they will" (here he wrung the hand of the Vendean chief) "we shall be within reach of Paris in a fortnight."

"But the Republic is sending sixty thousand men and General Brune against us."

"Sixty thousand men! indeed!" cried the marquis, with a scoffing laugh. "And how will Bonaparte carry on the Italian campaign? As for General Brune, he is not coming. The First Consul has sent him against the English in Holland, and General Hedouville, *the friend of our friend Barras*, takes his place here. Do you understand?"

As Monsieur de Fontaine heard these words he gave Montauran a look of keen intelligence which seemed to say that the marquis had not himself understood the real meaning of the words addressed to him. The two leaders then comprehended each other perfectly, and the *Gars* replied with an indefinable smile to the thoughts expressed in both their eyes: "Monsieur de Fontaine, do you know my arms? our motto is 'Persevere unto death.'"

The Comte de Fontaine took Montauran's hand and pressed it, saying: "I was left for dead at Quatre-Chemins, therefore you need never doubt me. But believe in my experience—times have changed."

"Yes," said La Billardiere, who now joined them. "You are young, marquis. Listen to me; your property has not yet been sold—"

"Ah!" cried Montauran, "can you conceive of devotion without sacrifice?"

"Do you really know the king?"

"I do."

"Then I admire your loyalty."

"The king," replied the young chieftain, "is the priest; I am fighting not for the man, but for the faith."

They parted,—the Vendean leader convinced of the necessity of yielding to circumstances and keeping his beliefs in the depths of his heart; La Billardiere to return to his negotiations in England; and Montauran to fight savagely and compel the Vendeans, by the victories he expected to win, to co-operate in his enterprise.

****

The events of the day had excited such violent emotions in Mademoiselle de Verneuil's whole being that she lay back almost fainting in the carriage, after giving the order to drive to Fougeres. Francine was as silent as her mistress. The postilion, dreading some new disaster, made all the haste he could to reach the high-road, and was soon on the summit of La Pelerine. Through the thick white mists of morning Marie de Verneuil crossed the broad and beautiful valley of Couesnon (where this history began) scarcely able to distinguish the slatey rock on which the town of Fougeres stands from the slopes of La Pelerine. They were still eight miles from it. Shivering with cold herself, Mademoiselle de Verneuil recollected the poor soldier behind the carriage, and insisted, against his remonstrances, in taking him into the carriage beside Francine.

The sight of Fougeres drew her for a time out of her reflections. The sentinels stationed at the Porte Saint-Leonard refused to allow ingress to the strangers, and she was therefore obliged to exhibit the ministerial order. This at once gave her safety in entering the town, but the postilion could find no other place for her to stop at than the Poste inn.

"Madame," said the Blue whose life she had saved. "If you ever want a sabre to deal some special blow, my life is yours. I am good for that. My name is Jean Falcon, otherwise called Beau-Pied, sergeant of the first company of Hulot's veterans, seventy-second half-brigade, nicknamed 'Les Mayencais.' Excuse my vanity; I can only offer you the soul of a sergeant, but that's at your service."

He turned on his heel and walked off whistling.

"The lower one goes in social life," said Marie, bitterly, "the more we find generous feelings without display. A marquis returns death for life, and a poor sergeant—but enough of that."

When the weary woman was at last in a warm bed, her faithful Francine waited in vain for the affectionate good-night to which she was accustomed; but her mistress, seeing her still standing and evidently uneasy, made her a sign of distress.

"This is called a day, Francine," she said; "but I have aged ten years in it."

The next morning, as soon as she had risen, Corentin came to see her and she admitted him.

"Francine," she exclaimed, "my degradation is great indeed, for the thought of that man is not disagreeable to me."

Still, when she saw him, she felt once more, for the hundredth time, the instinctive repulsion which two years' intercourse had increased rather than lessened.

"Well," he said, smiling, "I felt certain you were succeeding. Was I mistaken? did you get hold of the wrong man?"

"Corentin," she replied, with a dull look of pain, "never mention that affair to me unless I speak of it myself."

He walked up and down the room casting oblique glances at her, endeavouring to guess the secret thoughts of the singular woman whose mere glance had the power of discomfiting at times the cleverest men.

"I foresaw this check," he replied, after a moment's silence. "If you would be willing to establish your headquarters in this town, I have already found a suitable place for you. We are in the very centre of *Chouannerie*. Will you stay here?"

She answered with an affirmative sign, which enabled Corentin to make conjectures, partly correct, as to the events of the preceding evening.

"I can hire a house for you, a bit of national property still unsold. They are behind the age in these parts. No one has dared buy the old barrack because it belonged to an *émigré* who was thought to be harsh. It is close to the church of Saint Leonard; and on my word of honour the view from it is delightful. Something can really be made of the old place; will you try it?"

"Yes, at once," she cried.

"I want a few hours to have it cleaned and put in order for you, so that you may like it."

"What matter?" she said. "I could live in a cloister or a prison without caring. However, see that everything is in order before night, so that I may sleep there in perfect solitude. Go, leave me; your presence is intolerable. I wish to be alone with Francine; she is better for me than my own company, perhaps. *Adieu*; go—go, I say."

These words, said volubly with a mingling of coquetry, despotism, and passion, showed she had entirely recovered her self-possession. Sleep had no doubt classified the impressions of the preceding day, and reflection had determined her on vengeance. If a few reluctant signs appeared on her face they only proved the ease with which certain women can bury the better feelings of their souls, and the cruel dissimulation which enables them to smile sweetly while planning the destruction of a victim. She sat alone after Corentin had left her, thinking how she could get the marquis still living into her toils. For the first time in her life this woman had lived according to her inmost desires; but of that life nothing remained but one craving,— that of vengeance,—vengeance complete and infinite. It was her one thought, her sole desire. Francine's words and attentions were unnoticed. Marie seemed to be sleeping with her eyes open; and the long day passed without an action or even a gesture that bore testimony to her thoughts. She lay on a couch which she had made of chairs and pillows. It was late in the evening when a few words escaped her, as if involuntarily.

"My child," she said to Francine, "I understood yesterday what it was to live for love; today I know what it means to die for vengeance. Yes, I will give my life to seek him wherever he may be, to meet him, seduce him, make him mine! If I do not have that man, who dared to despise me, at my feet humble and submissive, if I do not make him my lackey and my slave, I shall indeed be base; I shall not be a woman; I shall not be myself."

The house which Corentin now hired for Mademoiselle de Verneuil offered many gratifications to the innate love of luxury and elegance that was part of this girl. The capricious creature took possession of it with regal composure, as of a thing which already belonged to her; she appropriated the furniture and arranged it with intuitive sympathy, as though she had known it all her life. This is a vulgar detail, but one that is not unimportant in sketching the character of so exceptional a person. She seemed to have been already familiarized in a dream with the house in which she now lived on her hatred as she might have lived on her love.

"At least," she said to herself, "I did not rouse insulting pity in him; I do not owe him my life. Oh, my first, my last, my only love! what an end to it!" She sprang upon Francine, who was terrified. "Do you love a man? Oh, yes, yes, I remember; you do. I am glad I have a woman here who can understand me. Ah, my poor Francette, man is a miserable being. Ha! he said he loved me, and his love could not bear the slightest test! But I,—if all men had accused him I would have defended him; if the universe rejected him my soul should have been his refuge. In the old days life was filled with human beings coming and going for whom I did not care; it was sad and dull, but not horrible; but now, now, what is life without him? He will live on, and I not near him! I shall not see him, speak to him, feel him, hold him, press him,—ha! I would rather strangle him myself in his sleep!"

Francine, horrified, looked at her in silence.

"Kill the man you love?" she said, in a soft voice.

"Yes, yes, if he ceases to love me."

But after those ruthless words she hid her face in her hands, and sat down silently.

The next day a man presented himself without being announced. His face was stern. It was Hulot, followed by Corentin. Mademoiselle de Verneuil looked at the commandant and trembled.

"You have come," she said, "to ask me to account for your friends. They are dead."

"I know it," he replied, "and not in the service of the Republic."

"For me, and by me," she said. "You preach the nation to me. Can the nation bring to life those who die for her? Can she even avenge them? But I—I will avenge them!" she cried. The awful images of the catastrophe filled her imagination suddenly, and the graceful creature who held modesty to be the first of women's wiles forgot herself in a moment of madness, and marched towards the amazed commandant brusquely.

"In exchange for a few murdered soldiers," she said, "I will bring to the block a head that is worth a million heads of other men. It is not a woman's business to wage war; but you, old as you are, shall learn good stratagems from me. I'll deliver a whole family to your bayonets—him, his ancestors, his past, his future. I will be as false and treacherous to him as I was good and true. Yes, commandant, I will bring that little noble to my arms, and he shall leave them to go to death. I have no other rival. The wretch himself pronounced his doom,—*a day without a morrow.* Your Republic and I shall be avenged. The Republic!" she cried in a voice the strange intonations of which horrified Hulot. "Is

139

he to die for bearing arms against the nation? Shall I suffer France to rob me of my vengeance? Ah! what a little thing is life! death can expiate but one crime. He has but one head to fall, but I will make him know in one night that he loses more than life. Commandant, you who will kill him," and she sighed, "see that nothing betrays my betrayal; he must die convinced of my fidelity. I ask that of you. Let him know only me—me, and my caresses!"

She stopped; but through the crimson of her cheeks Hulot and Corentin saw that rage and delirium had not entirely smothered all sense of shame. Marie shuddered violently as she said the words; she seemed to listen to them as though she doubted whether she herself had said them, and she made the involuntary movement of a woman whose veil is falling from her.

"But you had him in your power," said Corentin.

"Very likely."

"Why did you stop me when I had him?" asked Hulot.

"I did not know what he would prove to be," she cried. Then, suddenly, the excited woman, who was walking up and down with hurried steps and casting savage glances at the spectators of the storm, calmed down. "I do not know myself," she said, in a man's tone. "Why talk? I must go and find him."

"Go and find him?" said Hulot. "My dear woman, take care; we are not yet masters of this part of the country; if you venture outside of the town you will be taken or killed before you've gone a hundred yards."

"There's never any danger for those who seek vengeance," she said, driving from her presence with a disdainful gesture the two men whom she was ashamed to face.

"What a woman!" cried Hulot as he walked away with Corentin. "A queer idea of those police fellows in Paris to send her here; but she'll never deliver him up to us," he added, shaking his head.

"Oh yes, she will," replied Corentin.

"Don't you see she loves him?" said Hulot.

"That's just why she will. Besides," looking at the amazed commandant, "I am here to see that she doesn't commit any folly. In my opinion, comrade, there is no love in the world worth the three hundred thousand *francs* she'll make out of this."

When the police diplomatist left the soldier the latter stood looking after him, and as the sound of the man's steps died away he gave a sigh, muttering to himself, "It may be a good thing after all to be such a dullard as I am. God's thunder! if I meet the *Gars* I'll fight him hand to hand, or my name's not Hulot; for if that fox brings him

140

before me in any of their new-fangled councils of war, my honour will be as soiled as the shirt of a young trooper who is under fire for the first time."

The massacre at La Vivetiere, and the desire to avenge his friends had led Hulot to accept a reinstatement in his late command; in fact, the new minister, Berthier, had refused to accept his resignation under existing circumstances. To the official despatch was added a private letter, in which, without explaining the mission of Mademoiselle de Verneuil, the minister informed him that the affair was entirely outside of the war, and not to interfere with any military operations. The duty of the commanders, he said, was limited to giving assistance to that honourable *citoyenne*, if occasion arose. Learning from his scouts that the movements of the Chouans all tended towards a concentration of their forces in the neighbourhood of Fougeres, Hulot secretly and with forced marches brought two battalions of his brigade into the town. The nation's danger, his hatred of aristocracy, whose partisans threatened to convulse so large a section of country, his desire to avenge his murdered friends, revived in the old veteran the fire of his youth.

****

"So this is the life I craved," exclaimed Mademoiselle de Verneuil, when she was left alone with Francine. "No matter how fast the hours go, they are to me like centuries of thought."

Suddenly she took Francine's hand, and her voice, soft as that of the first red-throat singing after a storm, slowly gave sound to the following words:

"Try as I will to forget them, I see those two delicious lips, that chin just raised, those eyes of fire; I hear the *'Hue!'* of the postilion; I dream, I dream,—why then such hatred on awakening!"

She drew a long sigh, rose, and then for the first time looked out upon the country delivered over to civil war by the cruel leader whom she was plotting to destroy. Attracted by the scene she wandered out to breathe at her ease beneath the sky; and though her steps conducted her at a venture, she was surely led to the Promenade of the town by one of those occult impulses of the soul which lead us to follow hope irrationally. Thoughts conceived under the dominion of that spell are often realized; but we then attribute their pre-vision to a power we call presentiment,—an inexplicable power, but a real one,—which our passions find accommodating, like a flatterer who, among his many lies, does sometimes tell the truth.

3

A Day Without a Morrow

The preceding events of this history having been greatly influenced by the formation of the regions in which they happened, it is desirable to give a minute description of them, without which the closing scenes might be difficult of comprehension.

The town of Fougeres is partly built upon a slate rock, which seems to have slipped from the mountains that hem in the broad valley of Couesnon to the west and take various names according to their localities. The town is separated from the mountains by a gorge, through which flows a small river called the Nancon. To the east, the view is the same as from the summit of La Pelerine; to the west, the town looks down into the tortuous valley of the Nancon; but there is a spot from which a section of the great valley and the picturesque windings of the gorge can be seen at the same time. This place, chosen by the inhabitants of the town for their Promenade, and to which the steps of Mademoiselle de Verneuil were now turned, was destined to be the theatre on which the drama begun at La Vivetiere was to end. Therefore, however picturesque the other parts of Fougeres may be, attention must be particularly given to the scenery which meets the eye from this terrace.

To give an idea of the rock on which Fougeres stands, as seen on this side, we may compare it to one of those immense towers circled by Saracen architects with balconies on each story, which were reached by spiral stairways. To add to this effect, the rock is capped by a Gothic church, the small spires, clock-tower, and buttresses of which make its shape almost precisely that of a sugar-loaf. Before the portal of this church, which is dedicated to Saint-Leonard, is a small, irregular square, where the soil is held up by a buttressed wall, which forms a balustrade and communicates by a flight of steps with the Promenade. This public walk, like a second cornice, extends round the rock a few rods below the square of Saint-Leonard; it is a broad piece of ground planted with trees, and it joins the fortifications of the town. About ten rods below the walls and rocks which support this Promenade (due to a happy combination of indestructible slate and patient industry) another circular road exists, called the "Queen's Staircase"; this is cut in the rock itself and leads to a bridge built across the Nancon by Anne of Brittany. Below this road, which forms a third cornice, gardens descend, terrace after terrace, to the river, like shelves covered with flowers.

Parallel with the Promenade, on the other side of the Nancon and across its narrow valley, high rock-formations, called the heights of Saint-Sulpice, follow the stream and descend in gentle slopes to the great valley, where they turn abruptly to the north. Towards the south, where the town itself really ends and the *faubourg* Saint- Leonard begins, the Fougeres rock makes a bend, becomes less steep, and turns into the great valley, following the course of the river, which it hems in between itself and the heights of Saint-Sulpice, forming a sort of pass through which the water escapes in two streamlets to the Couesnon, into which they fall. This pretty group of rocky hills is called the "Nid-aux-Crocs"; the little vale they surround is the "Val de Gibarry," the rich pastures of which supply the butter known to epicures as that of the "Pree-Valaye."

At the point where the Promenade joins the fortifications is a tower called the "Tour de Papegaut." Close to this square erection, against the side of which the house now occupied by Mademoiselle de Verneuil rested, is a wall, partly built by hands and partly formed of the native rock where it offered a smooth surface. Here stands a gateway leading to the *faubourg* of Saint-Sulpice and bearing the same name. Above, on a breastwork of granite which commands the three valleys, rise the battlements and feudal towers of the ancient castle of Fougeres,—one of those enormous erections built by the Dukes of Brittany, with lofty walls fifteen feet thick, protected on the east by a pond from which flows the Nancon, the waters of which fill its moats, and on the west by the inaccessible granite rock on which it stands.

Seen from the Promenade, this magnificent relic of the Middle Ages, wrapped in its ivy mantle, adorned with its square or rounded towers, in either of which a whole regiment could be quartered,—the castle, the town, and the rock, protected by walls with sheer surfaces, or by the glacis of the fortifications, form a huge horseshoe, lined with precipices, on which the Bretons have, in course of ages, cut various narrow footways. Here and there the rocks push out like architec-

143

tural adornments. Streamlets issue from the fissures, where the roots of stunted trees are nourished. Farther on, a few rocky slopes, less perpendicular than the rest, afford a scanty pasture for the goats. On all sides heather, growing from every crevice, flings its rosy garlands over the dark, uneven surface of the ground. At the bottom of this vast funnel the little river winds through meadows that are always cool and green, lying softly like a carpet.

Beneath the castle and among the granite boulders is a church dedicated to Saint-Sulpice, whose name is given to the suburb which lies across the Nancon. This suburb, flung as it were to the bottom of a precipice, and its church, the spire of which does not rise to the height of the rocks which threaten to crush it, are picturesquely watered by several affluents of the Nancon, shaded by trees and brightened by gardens. The whole region of Fougeres, its suburbs, its churches, and the hills of Saint-Sulpice are surrounded by the heights of Rille, which form part of a general range of mountains enclosing the broad valley of Couesnon.

Such are the chief features of this landscape, the principal characteristic of which is a rugged wildness softened by smiling accidents, by a happy blending of the finest works of men's hands with the capricious lay of a land full of unexpected contrasts, by a something, hardly to be explained, which surprises, astonishes, and puzzles. In no other part of France can the traveller meet with such grandiose contrasts as those offered by the great basin of the Couesnon, and the valleys hidden among the rocks of Fougeres and the heights of Rille. Their beauty is of that unspeakable kind in which chance triumphs and all the harmonies of Nature do their part. The clear, limpid, flowing waters, the mountains clothed with the vigorous vegetation of those regions, the sombre rocks, the graceful buildings, the fortifications raised by nature, and the granite towers built by man; combined with all the artifices of light and shade, with the contrasts of the varieties of foliage, with the groups of houses where an active population swarms, with the lonely barren places where the granite will not suffer even the lichen to fasten on its surface, in short, with all the ideas we ask a landscape to possess: grace and awfulness, poesy with its renascent magic, sublime pictures, delightful ruralities,—all these are here; it is Brittany in bloom.

The tower called the Papegaut, against which the house now occupied by Mademoiselle de Verneuil rested, has its base at the very bottom of the precipice, and rises to the esplanade which forms the cornice or terrace before the church of Saint-Leonard. From Marie's

144

house, which was open on three sides, could be seen the horseshoe (which begins at the tower itself), the winding valley of the Nancon, and the square of Saint-Leonard. It is one of a group of wooden buildings standing parallel with the western side of the church, with which they form an alley-way, the farther end of which opens on a steep street skirting the church and leading to the gate of Saint-Leonard, along which Mademoiselle de Verneuil now made her way.

Marie naturally avoided entering the square of the church which was then above her, and turned towards the Promenade. The magnificence of the scene which met her eyes silenced for a moment the tumult of her passions. She admired the vast trend of the valley, which her eyes took in, from the summit of La Pelerine to the plateau where the main road to Vitry passes; then her eyes rested on the Nid-aux-Crocs and the winding gorges of the Val de Gibarry, the crests of which were bathed in the misty glow of the setting sun. She was almost frightened by the depth of the valley of the Nancon, the tallest poplars of which scarcely reached to the level of the gardens below the Queen's Staircase. At this time of day the smoke from the houses in the suburbs and in the valleys made a vapour in the air, through which the various objects had a bluish tinge; the brilliant colours of the day were beginning to fade; the firmament took a pearly tone; the moon was casting its veil of light into the ravine; all things tended to plunge the soul into reverie and bring back the memory of those beloved.

In a moment the scene before her was powerless to hold Marie's thoughts. In vain did the setting sun cast its gold-dust and its crimson sheets to the depths of the river and along the meadows and over the graceful buildings strewn among the rocks; she stood immovable, gazing at the heights of the Mont Saint-Sulpice. The frantic hope which had led her to the Promenade was miraculously realized. Among the gorse and bracken which grew upon those heights she was certain that she recognized, in spite of the goatskins which they wore, a number of the guests at La Vivetiere, and among them the *Gars*, whose every moment became vivid to her eyes in the softened light of the sinking sun. A few steps back of the ground of men she distinguished her enemy, Madame du Gua. For a moment Marie fancied that she dreamed, but her rival's hatred soon proved to her that the dream was a living one. The attention she was giving to the least little gesture of the marquis prevented her from observing the care with which Madame du Gua aimed a musket at her. But a shot which woke the echoes of the mountains, and a ball that whistled past her warned Mademoiselle de Verneuil of her rival's determination. "She sends me

145

her card," thought Marie, smiling. Instantly a *Qui vive?* echoing from sentry to sentry, from the castle to the Porte Saint-Leonard, proved to the Chouans the alertness of the Blues, inasmuch as the least accessible of their ramparts was so well guarded.

"It is she—and he," muttered Marie to herself.

To seek the marquis, follow his steps and overtake him, was a thought that flashed like lightning through her mind. "I have no weapon!" she cried. She remembered that on leaving Paris she had flung into a trunk an elegant dagger formerly belonging to a sultana, which she had jestingly brought with her to the theatre of war, as some persons take note-books in which to jot down their travelling ideas; she was less attracted by the prospect of shedding blood than by the pleasure of wearing a pretty weapon studded with precious stones, and playing with a blade that was stainless. Three days earlier she had deeply regretted having put this dagger in a trunk, when to escape her enemies at La Vivetiere she had thought for a moment of killing herself. She now returned to the house, found the weapon, put it in her belt, wrapped a large shawl round her shoulders and a black lace scarf about her hair, and covered her head with one of those broad-brimmed hats distinctive of Chouans which belonged to a servant of the house. Then, with the presence of mind which excited passions often give, she took the glove which Marche-a-Terre had given her as a safeguard, and saying, in reply to Francine's terrible looks, "I would seek him in hell," she returned to the Promenade.

The *Gars* was still at the same place, but alone. By the direction of his telescope he seemed to be examining with the careful attention of a commander the various paths across the Nancon, the Queen's Stair-case, and the road leading through the Porte Saint-Sulpice and round the church of that name, where it meets the high-road under range of the guns at the castle. Mademoiselle de Verneuil took one of the little paths made by goats and their keepers leading down from the Prom-enade, reached the Staircase, then the bottom of the ravine, crossed the Nancon and the suburb, and divining like a bird in the desert her right course among the dangerous precipices of the Mont Saint-Sulpice, she followed a slippery track defined upon the granite, and in spite of the prickly gorse and reeds and loose stones which hindered her, she climbed the steep ascent with an energy greater perhaps than that of a man,—the energy momentarily possessed by a woman under the influence of passion.

Night overtook her as she endeavoured by the failing moonlight to make out the path the marquis must have taken; an obstinate quest without reward, for the dead silence about her was sufficient proof of the withdrawal of the Chouans and their leader. This effort of passion collapsed with the hope that inspired it. Finding herself alone, after nightfall, in a hostile country, she began to reflect; and Hulot's advice, together with the recollection of Madame du Gua's attempt, made her tremble with fear. The stillness of the night, so deep in mountain regions, enabled her to hear the fall of every leaf even at a distance, and these slight sounds vibrated on the air as though to give a measure of the silence or the solitude. The wind was blowing across the heights and sweeping away the clouds with violence, producing an alternation of shadows and light, the effect of which increased her fears, and gave fantastic and terrifying semblances to the most harmless objects. She turned her eyes to the houses of Fougeres, where the domestic lights were burning like so many earthly stars, and she presently saw distinctly the tower of Papegaut. She was but a very short distance from her own house, but within that space was the ravine. She remembered the declivities by which she had come, and wondered if there were not more risk in attempting to return to Fougeres than in following out the purpose which had brought her. She reflected that the marquis's glove would surely protect her from the Chouans, and that Madame du Gua was the only enemy to be really feared. With this idea in her mind, Marie clasped her dagger, and tried to find the way to a country house the roofs of which she had noticed as she climbed Saint-Sulpice; but she walked slowly, for she suddenly became aware of the majestic solemnity which oppresses a solitary being in the night time in the midst of wild scenery, where lofty mountains nod their heads like assembled giants. The rustle of her gown, caught by the brambles, made her tremble more than once, and more than once she hastened her steps only to slacken them again as she thought her last hour had come. Before long matters assumed an aspect which the boldest men could not have faced without alarm, and which threw Mademoiselle de Verneuil into the sort of terror that so affects the very springs of life that all things become excessive, weakness as well as strength. The feeblest beings will then do deeds of amazing power; the strongest go mad with fear.

Marie heard at a short distance a number of strange sounds, distinct yet vague, indicative of confusion and tumult, fatiguing to the ear which tried to distinguish them. They came from the ground, which seemed to tremble beneath the feet of a multitude of marching men. A momentary clearness in the sky enabled her to perceive at a little distance long files of hideous figures waving like ears of corn

147

and gliding like phantoms; but she scarcely saw them, for darkness fell again, like a black curtain, and hid the fearful scene which seemed to her full of yellow, dazzling eyes. She turned hastily and ran to the top of a bank to escape meeting three of these horrible figures who were coming towards her.

"Did you see it?" said one.

"I felt a cold wind as it rushed past me," replied a hoarse voice.

"I smelt a damp and graveyard smell," said the third.

"Was it white?" asked the first.

"Why should only *he* come back out of all those we left dead at La Pelerine?" said the second.

"Why indeed?" replied the third. "Why do the *Sacre-Coeur* men have the preference? Well, at any rate, I'd rather die without confession than wander about as he does, without eating or drinking, and no blood in his body or flesh on his bones."

"Ah!"

This exclamation, or rather this fearful cry, issued from the group as the three Chouans pointed to the slender form and pallid face of Mademoiselle de Verneuil, who fled away with terrified rapidity without a sound.

"Here he is!"

"There he is!"

"Where?"

"There!"

"He's gone!"

"No!"

"Yes!"

"Can you see him?"

These cries reverberated like the monotonous murmur of waves upon a shore.

Mademoiselle de Verneuil walked bravely in the direction of the house she had seen, and soon came in sight of a number of persons, who all fled away at her approach with every sign of panic fear. She felt impelled to advance by a mysterious power which coerced her; the lightness of her body, which seemed to herself inexplicable, was another source of terror. These forms which rose in masses at her approach, as if from the ground on which she trod, uttered moans which were scarcely human. At last she reached, not without difficulty, a trampled garden, the hedges and fences of which were broken down. Stopped by a sentry, she showed the glove. The moon lighted her face, and the muzzle of the gun already pointed at her was dropped by the

Chouan, who uttered a hoarse cry, which echoed through the place. She now saw large buildings, where a few lighted windows showed the rooms that were occupied, and presently reached the walls without further hindrance. Through the window into which she looked, she saw Madame du Gua and the leaders who were convoked at La Vivetiere. Bewildered at the sight, also by the conviction of her danger, she turned hastily to a little opening protected by iron bars, and saw in a long vaulted hall the marquis, alone and gloomy, within six feet of her. The reflection of the fire, before which he was sitting in a clumsy chair, lighted his face with a vacillating ruddy glow that gave the character of a vision to the scene. Motionless and trembling, the girl stood clinging to the bars, to catch his words if he spoke. Seeing him so depressed, disheartened, and pale, she believed herself to be the cause of his sadness. Her anger changed to pity, her pity to tenderness, and she suddenly knew that it was not revenge alone which had brought her there.

The marquis rose, turned his head, and stood amazed when he saw, as if in a cloud, Mademoiselle de Verneuil's face; then he shook his head with a gesture of impatience and contempt, exclaiming: "Must I forever see the face of that devil, even when awake?"

This utter contempt for her forced a half-maddened laugh from the unhappy girl which made the young leader quiver. He sprang to the window, but Mademoiselle de Verneuil was gone. She heard the steps of a man behind her, which she supposed to be those of the marquis, and, to escape him, she knew no obstacles; she would have scaled walls and flown through air; she would have found and followed a path to hell sooner than have seen again, in flaming letters on the forehead of that man, "I despise you,"—words which an inward voice sounded in her soul with the noise of a trumpet.

After walking a short distance without knowing where she went, she stopped, conscious of a damp exhalation. Alarmed by the sound of voices, she went down some steps which led into a cellar. As she reached the last of them, she stopped to listen and discover the direction her pursuers might take. Above the sounds from the outside, which were somewhat loud, she could hear within the lugubrious moans of a human being, which added to her terror. Rays of light coming down the steps made her fear that this retreat was only too well known to her enemies, and, to escape them, she summoned fresh energy. Some moments later, after recovering her composure of mind, it was difficult for her to conceive by what means she had been able to climb a little wall, in a recess of which she was now hidden. She took no notice at first of the cramped position in which she was, but before long the pain of it became intolerable, for she was bending double under the arched opening of a vault, like the crouching Venus which ignorant persons attempt to squeeze into too narrow a niche. The wall, which was rather thick and built of granite, formed a low partition between the stairway and the cellar whence the groans were issuing. Presently she saw an individual, clothed in a goatskin, enter the cave beneath her, and move about, without making any sign of eager search. Impatient to discover if she had any chance of safety, Mademoiselle de Verneuil waited with anxiety till the light brought by the new-comer lighted the whole cave, where she could partly distinguish a formless but living mass which was trying to reach a part of the wall, with violent and repeated jerks, something like those of a carp lying out of water on a shore.

A small pine torch threw its blue and hazy light into the cave. In spite of the gloomy poetic effects which Mademoiselle de Verneuil's imagination cast about this vaulted chamber, which was echoing to the sounds of a pitiful prayer, she was obliged to admit that the place was nothing more than an underground kitchen, evidently long abandoned. When the formless mass was distinguishable it proved to be a short and very fat man, whose limbs were carefully bound before he had been left lying on the damp stone floor of the kitchen by those who had seized him. When he saw the new-comer approach him with a torch in one hand and a fagot of sticks in the other, the captive gave a dreadful groan, which so wrought upon the sensibilities of Mademoiselle de Verneuil that she forgot her own terror and despair and the cramped position of her limbs, which were growing numb. But she made a great effort and remained still. The Chouan flung the sticks into the fireplace, after trying the strength of an old crane which was fastened to a long iron bar; then he set fire to the wood with his torch. Marie saw with terror that the man was the same Pille-Miche to whom her rival had delivered her, and whose figure, illuminated by the flame, was like that of the little boxwood men so grotesquely carved in Germany. The moans of his prisoner produced a broad grin upon features that were ribbed with wrinkles and tanned by the sun.

"You see," he said to his victim, "that we Christians keep our promises, which you don't. That fire is going to thaw out your legs and tongue and hands. Hey! hey! I don't see a dripping-pan to put under your feet; they are so fat the grease may put out the fire. Your house must be badly furnished if it can't give its master all he wants to warm him."

The victim uttered a sharp cry, as if he hoped someone would hear him through the ceiling and come to his assistance.

"Ho! sing away, Monsieur d'Orgemont; they are all asleep upstairs, and Marche-a-Terre is just behind me; he'll shut the cellar door."

While speaking Pille-Miche was sounding with the butt-end of his musket the mantel-piece of the chimney, the tiles of the floor, the walls and the ovens, to discover, if possible, where the miser hid his gold. This search was made with such adroitness that d'Orgemont kept silence, as if he feared to have been betrayed by some frightened servant; for, though he trusted his secrets to no one, his habits gave plenty of ground for logical deductions. Pille-Miche turned several times sharply to look at his victim, as children do when they try to guess, by the conscious expression of the comrade who has hidden an article, whether they are nearer to or farther away from it. D'Orgemont pretended to be alarmed when the Chouan tapped the ovens, which sounded hollow, and seemed to wish to play upon his eager credulity. Just then three other Chouans rushed down the steps and entered the kitchen. Seeing Marche-a-Terre among them Pille-Miche discontinued his search, after casting upon d'Orgemont a look that conveyed the wrath of his balked covetousness.

"Marie Lambrequin has come to life!" cried Marche-a-Terre, proclaiming by his manner that all other interests were of no account beside this great piece of news.

"I'm not surprised," said Pille-Miche, "he took the sacrament so often; the good God belonged to him."

"Ha! ha!" observed Mene-a-Bien, "that didn't stand him in anything at his death. He hadn't received absolution before the affair at La Pelerine. He had cheapened Goguelu's daughter, and was living in mortal sin. The Abbe Gudin said he'd have to roam round two months as a ghost before he could come to life. We saw him pass us,—he was pale, he was cold, he was thin, he smelt of the cemetery."

"And his Reverence says that if a ghost gets hold of a living man he can force him to be his companion," said the fourth Chouan.

The grotesque appearance of this last speaker drew Marche-a-Terre from the pious reflections he had been making on the accomplishment of this miracle of coming to life which, according to the Abbe Gudin would happen to every true defender of religion and the king.

"You see, Galope-Chopine," he said to the fourth man gravely, "what comes of omitting even the smallest duty commanded by our holy religion. It is a warning to us, given by Saint Anne of Auray, to be rigorous with ourselves for the slightest sin. Your cousin Pille-Miche

151

has asked the *Gars* to give you the surveillance of Fougeres, and the *Gars* consents, and you'll be well paid—but you know with what flour we bake a traitor's bread."

"Yes, Monsieur Marche-a-Terre."

"And you know why I tell you that. Some say you like cider and gambling, but you can't play heads or tails now, remember; you must belong to us only, or—"

"By your leave, Monsieur Marche-a-Terre, cider and stakes are two good things which don't hinder a man's salvation."

"If my cousin commits any folly," said Pille-Miche, "it will be out of ignorance."

"In any way he commits it, if harm comes," said Marche-a-Terre, in a voice which made the arched roof tremble, "my gun won't miss him. You will answer for him to me," he added, turning to Pille-Miche; "for if he does wrong I shall take it out on the thing that fills your goatskin."

"But, Monsieur Marche-a-Terre, with all due respect," said Galope-Chopine, "haven't you sometimes taken a counterfeit Chouan for a real one."

"My friend," said Marche-a-Terre in a curt tone, "don't let that happen in your case, or I'll cut you in two like a turnip. As to the emissaries of the *Gars*, they all carry his glove, but since that affair at La Vivetiere the Grande Garce has added a green ribbon to it."

Pille Miche nudged his comrade by the elbow and showed him d'Orgemont, who was pretending to be asleep; but Pille-Miche and Marche-a-Terre both knew by experience that no one ever slept by the corner of their fire, and though the last words said to Galope-Chopine were almost whispered, they must have been heard by the victim, and the four Chouans looked at him fixedly, thinking perhaps that fear had deprived him of his senses.

Suddenly, at a slight sign from Marche-a-Terre, Pille-Miche pulled off d'Orgemont's shoes and stockings, Mene-a-Bien and Galope-Chopine seized him round the body and carried him to the fire. Then Marche-a-Terre took one of the thongs that tied the fagots and fastened the miser's feet to the crane. These actions and the horrible celerity with which they were done brought cries from the victim, which became heart-rending when Pille-Miche gathered the burning sticks under his legs.

"My friends, my good friends," screamed d'Orgemont, "you hurt me, you kill me! I'm a Christian like you."

"You lie in your throat!" replied Marche-a-Terre. "Your brother denied God; and as for you, you bought the abbey of Juvigny. The Abbe Gudin says we can roast apostates when we find them."

"But, my brothers in God, I don't refuse to pay."

"We gave you two weeks, and it is now two months, and Galope-Chopine here hasn't received the money."

"Haven't you received any of it, Galope-Chopine?" asked the miser, in despair.

"None of it, Monsieur d'Orgemont," replied Galope-Chopine, frightened.

The cries, which had sunk into groans, continuous as the rattle in a dying throat, now began again with dreadful violence. Accustomed to such scenes, the four Chouans looked at d'Orgemont, who was twisting and howling, so coolly that they seemed like travellers watching before an inn fire till the roast meat was done enough to eat.

"I'm dying, I'm dying!" cried the victim, "and you won't get my money."

In spite of these agonizing cries, Pille-Miche saw that the fire did not yet scorch the skin; he drew the sticks cleverly together so as to make a slight flame. On this d'Orgemont called out in a quavering voice: "My friends, unbind me! How much do you want? A hundred crowns—a thousand crowns—ten thousand crowns—a hundred thousand crowns—I offer you two hundred thousand crowns!"

The voice became so lamentable that Mademoiselle de Verneuil forgot her own danger and uttered an exclamation.

"Who spoke?" asked Marche-a-Terre.

The Chouans looked about them with terrified eyes. These men, so brave in fight, were unable to face a ghost. Pille-Miche alone continued to listen to the promises which the flames were now extracting from his victim.

"Five hundred thousand crowns—yes, I'll give them," cried the victim.

"Well, where are they?" answered Pille-Miche, tranquilly.

"Under the first apple-tree—Holy Virgin! at the bottom of the garden to the left—you are brigands—thieves! Ah! I'm dying—there's ten thousand *francs*—"

"*Francs*! we don't want *francs*," said Marche-a-Terre; "those Republican coins have pagan figures which oughtn't to pass."

"They are not *francs*, they are good *louis d'or*. But oh! undo me, unbind me! I've told you where my life is—my money."

The four Chouans looked at each other as if thinking which of their number they could trust sufficiently to disinter the money.

The cannibal cruelty of the scene so horrified Mademoiselle de Verneuil that she could bear it no longer. Though doubtful whether the role of ghost, which her pale face and the Chouan superstitions evidently assigned to her, would carry her safely through the danger, she called out, courageously, "Do you not fear God's anger? Unbind him, brutes!"

The Chouans raised their heads and saw in the air above them two eyes which shone like stars, and they fled, terrified. Mademoiselle de Verneuil sprang into the kitchen, ran to d'Orgemont, and pulled him so violently from the crane that the thong broke. Then with the blade of her dagger she cut the cords which bound him. When the miser was free and on his feet, the first expression of his face was a painful but sardonic grin.

"Apple-tree! yes, go to the apple-tree, you brigands," he said. "Ho, ho! this is the second time I've fooled them. They won't get a third chance at me."

So saying, he caught Mademoiselle de Verneuil's hand, drew her under the mantel-shelf to the back of the hearth in a way to avoid disturbing the fire, which covered only a small part of it; then he touched a spring; the iron back was lifted, and when their enemies returned to the kitchen the heavy door of the hiding-place had already fallen noiselessly. Mademoiselle de Verneuil then understood the carp-like movements she had seen the miser making.

"The ghost has taken the Blue with him," cried the voice of Marche-a-Terre.

The fright of the Chouans must have been great, for the words were followed by a stillness so profound that d'Orgemont and his companion could hear them muttering to themselves: *"Ave, sancta Anna Auriaca gratia plena, Dominus tecum,"* etc.

"They are praying, the fools!" cried d'Orgemont.

"Hush! are you not afraid they will discover us?" said Mademoiselle de Verneuil, checking her companion.

The old man's laugh dissipated her fears.

"That iron back is set in a wall of granite two feet thick," he said. "We can hear them, but they can't hear us."

Then he took the hand of his preserver and placed it near a crevice through which a current of fresh air was blowing. She then perceived that the opening was made in the shaft of the chimney.

"Ai! ai!" cried d'Orgemont. "The devil! how my legs smart!"

The Chouans, having finished their prayer, departed, and the old miser again caught the hand of his companion and helped her to climb some narrow winding steps cut in the granite wall. When they had mounted some twenty of these steps the gleam of a lamp dimly lighted their heads. The miser stopped, turned to his companion, examined her face as if it were a bank note he was doubtful about cashing, and heaved a heavy sigh.

"By bringing you here," he said, after a moment's silence, "I have paid you in full for the service you did me; I don't see why I should give you—"

"Monsieur, I ask nothing of you," she said.

These words, and also, perhaps, the disdainful expression on the beautiful face, reassured the old man, for he answered, not without a sigh, "Ah! if you take it that way, I have gone too far not to continue on."

He politely assisted Marie to climb a few more steps rather strangely constructed, and half willingly, half reluctantly, ushered her into a small closet about four feet square, lighted by a lamp hanging from the ceiling. It was easy to see that the miser had made preparations to spend more than one day in this retreat if the events of the civil war compelled him to hide himself.

"Don't brush against that wall, you might whiten yourself," said d'Orgemont suddenly, as he hurriedly put his hand between the girl's shawl and the stones which seemed to have been lately whitewashed. The old man's action produced quite another effect from that he intended. Marie looked about her and saw in one corner a sort of projection, the shape of which forced from her a cry of terror, for she fancied it was that of a human being standing erect and mortared into the wall. D'Orgemont made a violent sign to her to hold her tongue, and his little eyes of a porcelain blue showed as much fear as those of his companion.

"Fool! do you think I murdered him? It is the body of my brother," and the old man gave a lugubrious sigh. "He was the first sworn-in priest; and this was the only asylum where he was safe against the fury of the Chouans and the other priests. He was my elder brother, and he alone had the patience to teach me the decimal calculus. Oh! he was a good priest! He was economical and laid by money. It is four years since he died; I don't know what was the matter with him; perhaps it was that priests are so in the habit of kneeling down to pray that he couldn't get accustomed to standing upright here as I do. I walled him up there; *they'd* have dug him up elsewhere. Some day perhaps I can put him in holy ground, as he used to call it,—poor man, he only took the oath out of fear."

A tear rolled from the hard eyes of the little old man, whose rusty wig suddenly seemed less hideous to the girl, and she turned her eyes respectfully away from his distress. But, in spite of these tender reminiscences, d'Orgemont kept on saying, "Don't go near the wall, you might—"

His eyes never ceased to watch hers, hoping thus to prevent her from examining too closely the walls of the closet, where the close air was scarcely enough to inflate the lungs. Marie succeeded, however, in getting a sufficiently good look in spite of her Argus, and she came to the conclusion that the strange protuberances in the walls were neither more nor less than sacks of coin which the miser had placed there and plastered up.

Old d'Orgemont was now in a state of almost grotesque bewilderment. The pain in his legs, the terror he felt at seeing a human being in the midst of his hoards, could be read in every wrinkle of his face, and yet at the same time his eyes expressed, with unaccustomed fire, a lively emotion excited in him by the presence of his liberator, whose white and rosy cheek invited kisses, and whose velvety black eye sent waves of blood to his heart, so hot that he was much in doubt whether they were signs of life or of death.

"Are you married?" he asked, in a trembling voice.

"No," she said, smiling.

"I have a little something," he continued, heaving a sigh, "though I am not so rich as people think for. A young girl like you must love diamonds, trinkets, carriages, money. I've got all that to give—after my death. Hey! if you will—"

The old man's eyes were so shrewd and betrayed such calculation in this ephemeral love that Mademoiselle de Verneuil, as she shook her head in sign of refusal, felt that his desire to marry her was solely to bury his secret in another himself.

"Money!" she said, with a look of scorn which made him satisfied and angry both; "money is nothing to me. You would be three times as rich as you are, if you had all the gold that I have refused—" she stopped suddenly.

"Don't go near that wall, or—"

"But I hear a voice," she said; "it echoes through that wall,—a voice that is more to me than all your riches."

Before the miser could stop her Marie had laid her hand on a small coloured engraving of Louis XV. on horseback; to her amazement it turned, and she saw, in a room beneath her, the Marquis de Montauran, who was loading a musket. The opening, hidden by a little panel on which the picture was gummed, seemed to form some opening in the ceiling of the adjoining chamber, which, no doubt, was the bedroom of the royalist general. D'Orgemont closed the opening with much precaution, and looked at the girl sternly.

"Don't say a word if you love your life. You haven't thrown your grappling-iron on a worthless building. Do you know that the Marquis de Montauran is worth more than one hundred thousand *francs* a year from lands which have not yet been confiscated? And I read in the *Primidi de l'Ille-et-Vilaine* a decree of the Consuls putting an end to confiscation. Ha! ha! you'll think the *Gars* a prettier fellow than ever, won't you? Your eyes are shining like two new *louis d'or.*"

Mademoiselle de Verneuil's face was, indeed, keenly excited when she heard that well-known voice so near her. Since she had been standing there, erect, in the midst as it were of a silver mine, the spring of her mind, held down by these strange events, recovered itself. She seemed to have formed some sinister resolution and to perceive a means of carrying it out.

"There is no return from such contempt," she was saying to herself; "and if he cannot love me, I will kill him—no other woman shall have him."

"No, *abbe*, no!" cried the young chief, in a loud voice which was heard through the panel, "it must be so."

"Monsieur le marquis," replied the Abbe Gudin, haughtily; "you will scandalize all Brittany if you give that ball at Saint James. It is preaching, not dancing, which will rouse our villagers. Take guns, not fiddles."

"Abbe, you have sense enough to know that it is not in a general assembly of our partisans that I can learn to know these people, or judge of what I may be able to undertake with them. A supper is better for examining faces than all the spying in the world, of which, by the bye, I have a horror; they can be made to talk with glasses in their hand."

Marie quivered, as she listened, and conceived the idea of going to the ball and there avenging herself.

"Do you take me for an idiot with your sermon against dancing?" continued Montauran. "Wouldn't you yourself dance a reed if it would restore your order under its new name of Fathers of the Faith? Don't you know that Bretons come away from the mass and go to dancing? Are you aware that Messieurs Hyde de Neuville and d'Andigne had a conference, five days ago, with the First Consul, on the question of restoring his Majesty Louis XVIII.? Ah, *monsieur*, the princes are deceived as to the true state of France. The devotions which uphold them are solely those of rank. Abbe, if I have set my feet in blood, at least I will not go into it to my middle without full knowledge of what I do. I am devoted to the king, but not to four hot-heads, not to a man crippled with debt like Rifoel, not to 'chauffeurs,' not to—"

"Say frankly, *monsieur*, not to abbes who force contributions on the highway to carry on the war," retorted the Abbe Gudin.

"Why should I not say it?" replied the marquis, sharply; "and I'll say, further, that the great and heroic days of La Vendee are over."

"Monsieur le marquis, we can perform miracles without you."

"Yes, like that of Marie Lambrequin, whom I hear you have brought to life," said the marquis, smiling. "Come, come, let us have no rancour, *abbe*. I know that you run all risks and would shoot a Blue as readily as you say an *oremus*. God willing, I hope to make you assist with a mitre on your head at the king's coronation."

This last remark must have had some magic power, for the click of a musket was heard as the *abbe* exclaimed, "I have fifty cartridges in my pocket, *monsieur* le marquis, and my life is the king's."

"He's a debtor of mine," whispered the usurer to Marie. "I don't mean the five or six hundred crowns he has borrowed, but a debt of blood which I hope to make him pay. He can never suffer as much evil as I wish him, the damned Jesuit! He swore the death of my brother, and raised the country against him. Why? Because the poor man was afraid of the new laws." Then, after applying his ear to another part of his hiding-place, he added, "They are all decamping, those brigands. I suppose they are going to do some other miracle elsewhere. I only hope they won't bid me good-bye as they did the last time, by setting fire to my house."

After the lapse of about half an hour, during which time the usurer and Mademoiselle de Verneuil looked at each other as if they were studying a picture, the coarse, gruff voice of Galope-Chopine was heard saying, in a muffled tone: "There's no longer any danger, Monsieur d'Orgemont. But this time, you must allow that I have earned my thirty crowns."

"My dear," said the miser to Marie, "swear to shut your eyes."

Mademoiselle de Verneuil placed one hand over her eyelids; but for greater security d'Orgemont blew out the lamp, took his liberator by the hand, and helped her to make seven or eight steps along a difficult passage. At the end of some minutes he gently removed her hand, and she found herself in the very room the Marquis de Montauran had just quitted, and which was, in fact, the miser's own bedroom.

"My dear girl," said the old man, "you can safely go now. Don't look about you that way. I dare say you have no money with you. Here are ten crowns; they are a little shaved, but they'll pass. When you leave the garden you will see a path that leads straight to the town, or, as they say now, the district. But the Chouans will be at Fougeres, and it is to be presumed that you can't get back there at once. You may want some safe place to hide in. Remember what I say to you, but don't make use of it unless in some great emergency. You will see on the road which leads to Nid-aux-Crocs through the Val de Gibarry, a farmhouse belonging to Cibot—otherwise called Galope-Chopine. Go in, and say to his wife: 'Good-day, Becaniere,' and Barbette will hide you. If Galope-Chopine discovers you he will either take you for the ghost, if it is dark, or ten crowns will master him if it is light. *Adieu*, our account is squared. But if you choose," he added, waving his hand about him, "all this is yours."

Mademoiselle de Verneuil gave the strange old man a look of thanks, and succeeded in extracting a sigh from him, expressing a variety of emotions.

"You will of course return me my ten crowns; and please remark that I ask no interest. You can pay them to my credit with Maitre Patrat, the notary at Fougeres, who would draw our marriage contract if you consented to be mine. *Adieu*."

"*Adieu*," she said, smiling and waving her hand.

"If you ever want money," he called after her, "I'll lend it to you at five per cent; yes, only five—did I say five?—why, she's gone! That girl looks to me like a good one; nevertheless, I'll change the secret opening of my chimney."

Then he took a twelve-pound loaf and a ham, and returned to his hiding-place.

****

As Mademoiselle de Verneuil walked through the country she seemed to breathe a new life. The freshness of the night revived her after the fiery experience of the last few hours. She tried to follow the path explained to her by d'Orgemont, but the darkness became so dense after the moon had gone down that she was forced to walk haphazard, blindly. Presently the fear of falling down some precipice seized her and saved her life, for she stopped suddenly, fancying the ground would disappear before her if she made another step. A cool breeze lifting her hair, the murmur of the river, and her instinct all combined to warn her that she was probably on the verge of the Saint-Sulpice rocks. She slipped her arm around a tree and waited for dawn with keen anxiety, for she heard a noise of arms and horses and human voices; she was grateful to the darkness which saved her from the Chouans, who were evidently, as the miser had said, surrounding Fougeres.

Like fires lit at night as signals of liberty, a few gleams, faintly crimsoned, began to show upon the summits, while the bases of the mountains still retained the bluish tints which contrasted with the rosy clouds that were floating in the valley. Soon a ruby disk rose slowly on the horizon and the skies greeted it; the varied landscape, the bell-tower of Saint-Leonard, the rocks, the meadows buried in shadow, all insensibly reappeared, and the trees on the summits were defined against the skies in the rising glow. The sun freed itself with a graceful spring from the ribbons of flame and ochre and sapphire. Its vivid light took level lines from hill to hill and flowed into the vales. The dusk dispersed, day mastered Nature. A sharp breeze crisped the air, the birds sang, life wakened everywhere. But the girl had hardly time to cast her eyes over the whole of this wondrous landscape before, by a phenomenon not infrequent in these cool regions, the mists spread themselves in sheets, filled the valleys, and rose to the tops of the mountains, burying the great valley beneath a mantle of snow. Mademoiselle de Verneuil fancied for a moment she saw a *mer de glace*, like those of the Alps. Then the vaporous atmosphere rolled like the waves of ocean, lifted impenetrable billows which softly swayed, undulated, and were violently whirled, catching from the sun's rays a vivid rosy tint, and showing here and there in their depths the transparencies of a lake of molten silver. Suddenly the north wind swept this phantasmagoric scene and scattered the mists which laid a dew full of oxygen on the meadows.

Mademoiselle de Verneuil was now able to distinguish a dark mass of men on the rocks of Fougeres. Seven or eight hundred Chouans were running like ants through the suburb of Saint-Sulpice. The sleeping town would certainly have been overpowered in spite of its fortifications and its old grey towers, if Hulot had not been alert. A battery, concealed on a height at the farther end of the basin formed by the ramparts, replied to the first fire of the Chouans by taking them diagonally on the road to the castle. The balls swept the road. Then a company of Blues made a sortie from the Saint-Sulpice gate, profited by the surprise of the royalists to form in line upon the high-road, and poured a murderous fire upon them. The Chouans made no attempt to resist, seeing that the ramparts of the castle were covered with soldiers, and that the guns of the fortress sufficiently protected the Republican advance.

Meantime, however, other Chouans, masters of the little valley of the Nancon, had swarmed up the rocks and reached the Promenade, which was soon covered with goatskins, giving it to Marie's eyes the appearance of a thatched roof, brown with age. At the same moment loud reports were heard from the part of the town which overlooks the valley of Couesnon. Evidently, Fougeres was attacked on all sides and completely surrounded. Flames rising on the western side of the rock showed that the Chouans were setting fire to the suburbs; but these soon ceased, and a column of black smoke which succeeded them showed that the fire was extinguished. Brown and white clouds again hid the scene from Mademoiselle de Verneuil, but they were clouds of smoke from the fire and powder, which the wind dispersed. The Republican commander, as soon as he saw his first orders admirably executed, changed the direction of his battery so as to sweep, successively, the valley of the Nancon, the Queen's Staircase, and the base of the rock of Fougeres. Two guns posted at the gate of Saint-Leonard scattered the ant-hill of Chouans who had seized that position, and the national guard of the town, rushing in haste to the square before the Church, succeeded in dislodging the enemy. The fight lasted only half an hour, and cost the Blues a hundred men. The Chouans, beaten on all sides, retreated under orders from the *Gars*, whose bold attempt failed (although he did not know this) in consequence of the massacre at La Vivetiere, which had brought Hulot secretly and in all haste to Fougeres. The artillery had arrived only that evening, and the news had not reached Montauran; otherwise, he would certainly have abandoned an enterprise which, if it failed, could only have bad results. As soon as he heard the guns the marquis knew it would be madness to continue, out of mere pride, a surprise which had missed fire. Therefore, not to lose men uselessly, he sent at once to all points of the attack, ordering an immediate retreat. The commandant, seeing his adversary on the rocks of Saint-Sulpice surrounded by a council of men, endeavoured to pour a volley upon him; but the spot was cleverly selected, and the young leader was out of danger in a moment. Hulot now changed parts with his opponent and became the aggressor. At the first sign of the *Gars'* intention, the company stationed under the walls of the castle were ordered to cut off the Chouans' retreat by seizing the upper outlet of the valley of the Nancon.

Notwithstanding her desire for revenge, Mademoiselle de Verneuil's sympathies were with the men commanded by her lover, and she turned hastily to see if the other end of the valley were clear for them; but the Blues, conquerors no doubt on the opposite side of Fougeres, were returning from the valley of Couesnon and taking possession of the Nid-aux-Crocs and that portion of the Saint-Sulpice rocks which overhang the lower end of the valley of the Nancon. The

Chouans, thus hemmed in to the narrow fields of the gorge, seemed in danger of perishing to the last man, so cleverly and sagaciously were the commandant's measures taken. But Hulot's cannon were powerless at these two points; and here, the town of Fougeres being quite safe, began one of those desperate struggles which denoted the character of Chouan warfare.

Mademoiselle de Verneuil now comprehended the presence of the masses of men she had seen as she left the town, the meeting of the leaders at d'Orgemont's house, and all the other events of the night, wondering how she herself had escaped so many dangers. The attack, prompted by desperation, interested her so keenly that she stood motionless, watching the living pictures as they presented themselves to her sight. Presently the struggle at the foot of the mountain had a deeper interest for her. Seeing the Blues almost masters of the Chouans, the marquis and his friends rushed into the valley of the Nancon to support their men. The rocks were now covered with straggling groups of furious combatants deciding the question of life or death on a ground and with weapons that were more favourable to the Goatskins. Slowly this moving arena widened. The Chouans, recovering themselves, gained the rocks, thanks to the shrubs and bushes which grew here and there among them. For a moment Mademoiselle de Verneuil felt alarmed as she saw, rather late, her enemies swarming over the summit and defending the dangerous paths by which alone she could descend. Every issue on the mountain was occupied by one or other of the two parties; afraid of encountering them she left the tree behind which she had been sheltering, and began to run in the direction of the farm which d'Orgemont had mentioned to her. After running some time on the slope of Saint-Sulpice which overlooks the valley of Couesnon she saw a cow-shed in the distance, and thought it must belong to the house of Galope-Chopine, who had doubtless left his wife at home and alone during the fight. Mademoiselle de Verneuil hoped to be able to pass a few hours in this retreat until it was possible for her to return to Fougeres without danger. According to all appearance Hulot was to triumph. The Chouans were retreating so rapidly that she heard firing all about her, and the fear of being shot made her hasten to the cottage, the chimney of which was her landmark. The path she was following ended at a sort of shed covered with a furze-roof, supported by four stout trees with the bark still on them. A mud wall formed the back of this shed, under which were a cider-mill, a flail to thresh buckwheat, and several agricultural implements.

She stopped before one of the posts, unwilling to cross the dirty bog which formed a sort of courtyard to the house which, in her Parisian ignorance, she had taken for a stable.

The cabin, protected from the north wind by an eminence towering above the roof, which rested against it, was not without a poetry of its own; for the tender shoots of elms, heather, and various rock-flowers wreathed it with garlands. A rustic staircase, constructed between the shed and the house, enabled the inhabitants to go to the top of the rock and breathe a purer air. On the left, the eminence sloped abruptly down, giving to view a series of fields, the first of which belonged no doubt to this farm. These fields were like bowers, separated by banks which were planted with trees. The road which led to them was barred by the trunk of an old, half-rotten tree,—a Breton method of enclosure the name of which may furnish, further on, a digression which will complete the characterization of this region. Between the stairway cut in the schist rock and the path closed by this old tree, in front of the marsh and beneath the overhanging rock, several granite blocks roughly hewn, and piled one upon the other, formed the four corners of the cottage and held up the planks, cobblestones, and pitch amalgam of which the walls were made. The fact that one half of the roof was covered with furze instead of thatch, and the other with shingles or bits of board cut into the form of slates, showed that the building was in two parts; one half, with a broken hurdle for a door, served as a stable, the other half was the dwelling of the owner. Though this hut owed to the neighbourhood of the town a few improvements which were wholly absent from such buildings that were five or six miles further off, it showed plainly enough the instability of domestic life and habits to which the wars and customs of feudality had reduced the serf; even to this day many of the peasants of those parts call a *seignorial chateau*, "The Dwelling."

While examining the place, with an astonishment we can readily conceive, Mademoiselle de Verneuil noticed here and there in the filth of the courtyard a few bits of granite so placed as to form stepping-stones to the house. Hearing the sound of musketry that was evidently coming nearer, she jumped from stone to stone, as if crossing a rivulet, to ask shelter. The house was closed by a door opening in two parts; the lower one of wood, heavy and massive, the upper one a shutter which served as a window. In many of the smaller towns of France the shops have the same type of door though far more decorated, the lower half possessing a call-bell. The door in question opened with a wooden latch worthy of the golden age, and the upper part was never closed except at night, for it was the only opening through which daylight could enter the room. There was, to be sure, a clumsy window, but the glass was thick like the bottom of a bottle, and the lead which held the panes in place took so much room that the opening seemed intended to intercept the light rather than admit it. As soon as Mademoiselle de Verneuil had turned the creaking hinges of the lower door she smelt an intolerable ammoniacal odour, and saw that the beasts in the stable had kicked through the inner partition which separated the stable from the dwelling. The interior of the farmhouse, for such it was, did not belie its exterior.

Mademoiselle de Verneuil was asking herself how it was possible for human beings to live in such habitual filth, when a ragged boy about eight or nine years old suddenly presented his fresh and rosy face, with a pair of fat cheeks, lively eyes, ivory teeth, and a mass of fair hair, which fell in curls upon his half-naked shoulders. His limbs were vigorous, and his attitude had the charm of that amazement and naive curiosity which widens a child's eyes. The little fellow was a picture of beauty.

"Where is your mother?" said Marie, in a gentle voice, stooping to kiss him between the eyes.

After receiving her kiss the child slipped away like an eel, and disappeared behind a muck-heap which was piled at the top of a mound between the path and the house; for, like many Breton farmers who have a system of agriculture that is all their own, Galope-Chopine put his manure in an elevated spot, so that by the time it was wanted for use the rains had deprived it of all its virtue. Alone for a few minutes, Marie had time to make an inventory. The room in which she waited for Barbette was the whole house. The most obvious and sumptuous object was a vast fireplace with a mantle-shelf of blue granite. The etymology of that word was shown by a strip of green serge, edged with a pale-green ribbon, cut in scallops, which covered and overhung the whole shelf, on which stood a coloured plaster cast of the Holy Virgin. On the pedestal of the statuette were two lines of a religious poem very popular in Brittany:—

"I am the mother of God, Protectress of the sod."

Behind the Virgin a hideous image, daubed with red and blue under pretence of painting, represented Saint-Labre. A green serge bed of the shape called "tomb," a clumsy cradle, a spinning-wheel, common chairs, and a carved chest on which lay utensils, were about the whole of Galope-Chopine's domestic possessions. In front of the window stood a chestnut table flanked by two benches of the same wood, to which the sombre light coming through the thick panes gave the tone of mahogany. An immense cask of cider, under the bung of which Mademoiselle de Verneuil noticed a pool of yellow mud, which had decomposed the flooring, although it was made of scraps of granite conglomerated in clay, proved that the master of the house had a right to his Chouan name, and that the pints galloped down either his own throat or that of his friends. Two enormous jugs full of cider stood on the table. Marie's attention, caught at first by the innumerable spider's-webs which hung from the roof, was fixing itself on these pitchers when the noise of fighting, growing more and more distinct, impelled her to find a hiding-place, without waiting for the woman of the house, who, however, appeared at that moment.

"Good-morning, Becaniere," said Marie, restraining a smile at the appearance of a person who bore some resemblance to the heads which architects attach to window-casings.

"Ha! you come from d'Orgemont?" answered Barbette, in a tone that was far from cordial.

"Yes, where can you hide me? for the Chouans are close by—"

"There," replied Barbette, as much amazed at the beauty as by the strange apparel of a being she could hardly believe to be of her own sex,—"there, in the priest's hiding-place."

She took her to the head of the bed, and was putting her behind it, when they were both startled by the noise of a man springing into the courtyard. Barbette had scarcely time to drop the curtain of the bed and fold it about the girl before she was face to face with a fugitive Chouan.

"Where can I hide, old woman? I am the Comte de Bauvan," said the new-comer.

Mademoiselle de Verneuil quivered as she recognized the voice of the belated guest, whose words, still a secret to her, brought about the catastrophe of La Vivetiere.

"Alas! *monseigneur*, don't you see, I have no place? What I'd better do is to keep outside and watch that no one gets in. If the Blues come, I'll let you know. If I stay here, and they find me with you, they'll burn my house down."

Barbette left the hut, feeling herself incapable of settling the interests of two enemies who, in virtue of the double role her husband was playing, had an equal right to her hiding-place.

"I've only two shots left," said the count, in despair. "It will be very unlucky if those fellows turn back now and take a fancy to look under this bed."

165

He placed his gun gently against the headboard behind which Marie was standing among the folds of the green serge, and stooped to see if there was room for him under the bed. He would infallibly have seen her feet, but she, rendered desperate by her danger, seized his gun, jumped quickly into the room, and threatened him. The count broke into a peal of laughter when he caught sight of her, for, in order to hide herself, Marie had taken off her broad-brimmed Chouan hat, and her hair was escaping, in heavy curls, from the lace scarf which she had worn on leaving home.

"Don't laugh, *monsieur le comte*; you are my prisoner. If you make the least movement, you shall know what an offended woman is capable of doing."

As the count and Marie stood looking at each other with differing emotions, confused voices were heard without among the rocks, calling out, "Save the *Gars!* spread out, spread out, save the *Gars!*"

Barbette's voice, calling to her boy, was heard above the tumult with very different sensations by the two enemies, to whom Barbette was really speaking instead of to her son.

"Don't you see the Blues?" she cried sharply. "Come here, you little scamp, or I shall be after you. Do you want to be shot? Come, hide, quick!"

While these things took place rapidly a Blue jumped into the marshy courtyard.

"Beau-Pied!" exclaimed Mademoiselle de Verneuil.

Beau-Pied, hearing her voice, rushed into the cottage, and aimed at the count.

"Aristocrat!" he cried, "don't stir, or I'll demolish you in a wink, like the Bastille."

"Monsieur Beau-Pied," said Mademoiselle de Verneuil, in a persuasive voice, "you will be answerable to me for this prisoner. Do as you like with him now, but you must return him to me safe and sound at Fougeres."

"Enough, *madame!*"

"Is the road to Fougeres clear?"

"Yes, it's safe enough—unless the Chouans come to life."

Mademoiselle de Verneuil picked up the count's gun gaily, and smiled satirically as she said to her prisoner, *"Adieu, monsieur le comte, au revoir!"*

Then she darted down the path, having replaced the broad hat upon her head.

"I have learned too late," said the count, "not to joke about the virtue of a woman who has none."

"Aristocrat!" cried Beau-Pied, sternly, "if you don't want me to send you to your *ci-devant* paradise, you will not say a word against that beautiful lady."

Mademoiselle de Verneuil returned to Fougeres by the paths which connect the rocks of Saint-Sulpice with the Nid-aux-Crocs. When she reached the latter height and had threaded the winding way cut in its rough granite, she stopped to admire the pretty valley of the Nancon, lately so turbulent and now so tranquil. Seen from that point, the vale was like a street of verdure. Mademoiselle de Verneuil re-entered the town by the Porte Saint-Leonard. The inhabitants, still uneasy about the fighting, which, judging by the distant firing, was still going on, were waiting the return of the National Guard, to judge of their losses. Seeing the girl in her strange costume, her hair dishevelled, a gun in her hand, her shawl and gown whitened against the walls, soiled with mud and wet with dew, the curiosity of the people was keenly excited,—all the more because the power, beauty, and singularity of this young Parisian had been the subject of much discussion.

Francine, full of dreadful fears, had waited for her mistress through-out the night, and when she saw her she began to speak; but Marie, with a kindly gesture, silenced her.

"I am not dead, my child," she said. "Ah!" she added, after a pause, "I wanted emotions when I left Paris, and I have had them!"

Francine asked if she should get her some food, observing that she must be in great need of it.

"No, no; a bath, a bath!" cried Mademoiselle de Verneuil. "I must dress at once."

Francine was not a little surprised when her mistress required her to unpack the most elegant of the dresses she had brought with her. Having bathed and breakfasted, Marie made her toilet with all the minute care which a woman gives to that important act when she expects to meet the eyes of her lover in a ball-room. Francine could not explain to herself the mocking gaiety of her mistress. It was not the joy of love,—a woman never mistakes that; it was rather an expression of concentrated maliciousness, which to Francine's mind boded evil. Marie herself drew the curtains of the window from which the glorious panorama could be seen, then she moved the sofa to the chimney corner, turning it so that the light would fall becomingly on her face; then she told Francine to fetch flowers, that the room might have a festive air; and when they came she herself directed their arrangement in a picturesque manner. Giving a last glance of satisfaction at these various preparations she sent Francine to the commandant with a request that he would bring her prisoner to her; then she lay down luxuriously on a sofa, partly to rest, and partly to throw herself into an attitude of graceful weakness, the power of which is irresistible in certain women. A soft languor, the seductive pose of her feet just seen below the drapery of her gown, the plastic ease of her body, the curving of the throat,—all, even the droop of her slender fingers as they hung from the pillow like the buds of a bunch of jasmine, combined with her eyes to produce seduction. She burned certain perfumes to fill the air with those subtle emanations which affect men's fibres powerfully, and often prepare the way for conquests which women seek to make without seeming to desire them. Presently the heavy step of the old soldier resounded in the adjoining room.

"Well, commandant, where is my captive?" she said.

"I have just ordered a picket of twelve men to shoot him, being taken with arms in his hand."

"Why have you disposed of my prisoner?" she asked. "Listen to me, commandant; surely, if I can trust your face, the death of a man *after* a fight is no particular satisfaction to you. Well, then, give my Chouan a reprieve, for which I will be responsible, and let me see him. I assure you that aristocrat has become essential to me, and he can be made to further the success of our plans. Besides, to shoot a mere amateur in *Chouannerie* would be as absurd as to fire on a balloon when a pinprick would disinflate it. For heaven's sake leave cruelty to the aristocracy. Republicans ought to be generous. Wouldn't you and yours have forgiven the victims of Quiberon? Come, send your twelve men to patrol the town, and dine with me and bring the prisoner. There is only an hour of daylight left, and don't you see," she added smiling, "that if you are too late, my toilet will have lost its effect?"

"But, *mademoiselle*," said the commandant, amazed.

"Well, what? But I know what you mean. Don't be anxious; the count shall not escape. Sooner or later that big butterfly will burn himself in your fire."

The commandant shrugged his shoulders slightly, with the air of a man who is forced to obey, whether he will or no, the commands of a pretty woman; and he returned in about half an hour, followed by the Comte de Bauvan.

Mademoiselle de Verneuil feigned surprise and seemed confused that the count should see her in such a negligent attitude; then, after reading in his eyes that her first effect was produced, she rose and busied herself about her guests with well-bred courtesy. There was nothing studied or forced in her motions, smiles, behaviour, or voice, nothing that betrayed premeditation or purpose. All was harmonious; no part was over-acted; an observer could not have supposed that she affected the manners of a society in which she had not lived. When the Royalist and the Republic were seated she looked sternly at the count. He, on his part, knew women sufficiently well to feel certain that the offence he had committed against this woman was equivalent to a sentence of death. But in spite of this conviction, and without seeming either gay or gloomy, he had the air of a man who did not take such serious results into consideration; in fact, he really thought it ridiculous to fear death in presence of a pretty woman. Marie's stern manner roused ideas in his mind.

"Who knows," thought he, "whether a count's coronet wouldn't please her as well as that of her lost marquis? Montauran is as lean as a nail, while I—" and he looked himself over with an air of satisfaction. "At any rate I should save my head."

These diplomatic revelations were wasted. The passion the count proposed to feign for Mademoiselle de Verneuil became a violent caprice, which the dangerous creature did her best to heighten.

"*Monsieur le comte,*" she said, "you are my prisoner, and I have the right to dispose of you. Your execution cannot take place without my consent, and I have too much curiosity to let them shoot you at present."

"And suppose I am obstinate enough to keep silence?" he replied gaily.

"With an honest woman, perhaps, but with a woman of the town, no, no, *monsieur le comte*, impossible!" These words, full of bitter sarcasm, were hissed, as Sully says, in speaking of the Duchesse de Beaufort, from so sharp a beak that the count, amazed, merely looked at his antagonist. "But," she continued, with a scornful glance, "not to contradict you, if I am a creature of that kind I will act like one. Here is your gun," and she offered him his weapon with a mocking air.

"On the honour of a gentleman, *mademoiselle*—"

"Ah!" she said, interrupting him, "I have had enough of the honour of gentlemen. It was on the faith of that that I went to La Vivetiere. Your leader had sworn to me that I and my escort should be safe there."

"What an infamy!" cried Hulot, contracting his brows.

"The fault lies with *monsieur le comte*," said Marie, addressing Hulot. "I have no doubt the *Gars* meant to keep his word, but this gentleman told some calumny about me which confirmed those that Charette's mistress had already invented—"

"Mademoiselle," said the count, much troubled, "with my head under the axe I would swear that I said nothing but the truth."

"In saying what?"

"That you were the—"

"Say the word, mistress of—"

"The Marquis de Lenoncourt, the present duke, a friend of mine," replied the count.

"Now I can let you go to execution," she said, without seeming at all agitated by the outspoken reply of the count, who was amazed at the real or pretended indifference with which she heard his statement. "However," she added, laughing, "you have not wronged me more than that friend of whom you suppose me to have been the—*Fie! monsieur le comte*; surely you used to visit my father, the Duc de Verneuil? Yes? well then—"

Evidently considering Hulot one too many for the confidence she was about to make, Mademoiselle de Verneuil motioned the count to her side, and said a few words in her ear. Monsieur de Bauvan gave a low ejaculation of surprise and looked with bewilderment at Marie, who completed the effect of her words by leaning against the chimney in the artless and innocent attitude of a child.

"Mademoiselle," cried the count, "I entreat your forgiveness, unworthy as I am of it."

"I have nothing to forgive," she replied. "You have no more ground for repentance than you had for the insolent supposition you proclaimed at La Vivetiere. But this is a matter beyond your comprehension. Only, remember this, *monsieur le comte*, the daughter of the Duc de Verneuil has too generous a spirit not to take a lively interest in your fate."

"Even after I have insulted you?" said the count, with a sort of regret.

"Some are placed so high that insult cannot touch them. *Monsieur le comte*,—I am one of them."

As she said the words, the girl assumed an air of pride and nobility which impressed the prisoner and made the whole of this strange intrigue much less clear to Hulot than the old soldier had thought it. He twirled his moustache and looked uneasily at Mademoiselle de Verneuil, who made him a sign, as if to say she was still carrying out her plan.

"Now," continued Marie, after a pause, "let us discuss these matters. Francine, my dear, bring lights."

She adroitly led the conversation to the times which had now, within a few short years, become the *ancien regime*. She brought back that period to the count's mind by the liveliness of her remarks and sketches, and gave him so many opportunities to display his wit, by cleverly throwing repartees in his way, that he ended by thinking he had never been so charming; and that idea having rejuvenated him, he endeavoured to inspire this seductive young woman with his own good opinion of himself. The malicious creature practised, in return, every art of her coquetry upon him, all the more adroitly because it was mere play to her. Sometimes she let him think he was making rapid progress, and then, as if surprised at the sentiment she was feeling, she showed a sudden coolness which charmed him, and served to increase imperceptibly his impromptu passion. She was like a fisherman who lifts his line from time to time to see if the fish is biting. The poor count allowed himself to be deceived by the innocent air with which she accepted two or three neatly turned compliments. Emigration, Brittany, the Republic, and the Chouans were far indeed from his thoughts. Hulot sat erect and silent as the god Thermes. His want of education made him quite incapable of taking part in a conversation of this kind; he supposed that the talking pair were very witty, but his efforts at comprehension were limited to discovering whether they were plotting against the Republic in covert language.

"Montauran," the count was saying, "has birth and breeding, he is a charming fellow, but he doesn't understand gallantry. He is too young to have seen Versailles. His education is deficient. Instead of diplomatically defaming, he strikes a blow. He may be able to love violently, but he will never have that fine flower of breeding in his gallantry which distinguished Lauzun, Adhemar, Coigny, and so many others! He hasn't the winning art of saying those pretty nothings to women which, after all, they like better than bursts of passion, which soon weary them. Yes, though he has undoubtedly had many love-affairs, he has neither the grace nor the ease that should belong to them."

"I have noticed that myself," said Marie.

"Ah!" thought the count, "there's an inflection in her voice, and a look in her eye which shows me plainly I shall soon be *on terms* with her; and faith! to get her, I'll believe all she wants me to."

He offered her his hand, for dinner was now announced. Mademoiselle de Verneuil did the honours with a politeness and tact which could only have been acquired by the life and training of a court.

"Leave us," she whispered to Hulot as they left the table. "You will only frighten him; whereas, if I am alone with him I shall soon find out all I want to know; he has reached the point where a man tells me everything he thinks, and sees through my eyes only."

"But afterwards?" said Hulot, evidently intending to claim the prisoner.

171

"Afterwards, he is to be free—free as air," she replied.

"But he was taken with arms in his hand."

"No," she said, making one of those sophistical jokes with which women parry unanswerable arguments, "I had disarmed him. Count," she said, turning back to him as Hulot departed, "I have just obtained your liberty, but—nothing for nothing," she added, laughing, with her head on one side as if to interrogate him.

"Ask all, even my name and my honour," he cried, intoxicated. "I lay them at your feet."

He advanced to seize her hand, trying to make her take his passion for gratitude; but Mademoiselle de Verneuil was not a woman to be thus misled. So, smiling in a way to give some hope to this new lover, she drew back a few steps and said: "You might make me regret my confidence."

"The imagination of a young girl is more rapid than that of a woman," he answered, laughing.

"A young girl has more to lose than a woman."

"True; those who carry a treasure ought to be distrustful."

"Let us quit such conventional language," she said, "and talk seriously. You are to give a ball at Saint-James. I hear that your headquarters, arsenals, and base of supplies are there. When is the ball to be?"

"Tomorrow evening."

"You will not be surprised if a slandered woman desires, with a woman's obstinacy, to obtain a public reparation for the insults offered to her, in presence of those who witnessed them. I shall go to your ball. I ask you to give me your protection from the moment I enter the room until I leave it. I ask nothing more than a promise," she added, as he laid his hand on his heart. "I abhor oaths; they are too like precautions. Tell me only that you engage to protect my person from all dangers, criminal or shameful. Promise to repair the wrong you did me, by openly acknowledging that I am the daughter of the Duc de Verneuil; but say nothing of the trials I have borne in being illegitimate,—this will pay your debt to me. Ha! two hours' attendance on a woman in a ball-room is not so dear a ransom for your life, is it? You are not worth a ducat more." Her smile took the insult from her words.

"What do you ask for the gun?" said the count, laughing.

"Oh! more than I do for you."

"What is it?"

"Secrecy. Believe me, my dear count, a woman is never fathomed except by a woman. I am certain that if you say one word of this, I shall be murdered on my way to that ball. Yesterday I had warning enough. Yes, that woman is quick to act. Ah! I implore you," she said, "contrive that no harm shall come to me at the ball."

"You will be there under my protection," said the count, proudly. "But," he added, with a doubtful air, "are you coming for the sake of Montauran?"

"You wish to know more than I know myself," she answered, laughing. "Now go," she added, after a pause. "I will take you to the gate of the town myself, for this seems to me a cannibal warfare."

"Then you do feel some interest in me?" exclaimed the count. "Ah! *mademoiselle*, permit me to hope that you will not be insensible to my friendship—for that sentiment must content me, must it not?" he added with a conceited air.

"Ah! diviner!" she said, putting on the gay expression a woman assumes when she makes an avowal which compromises neither her dignity nor her secret sentiments.

Then, having slipped on a *pelisse*, she accompanied him as far as the Nid-aux-Crocs. When they reached the end of the path she said, "Monsieur, be absolutely silent on all this; even to the marquis"; and she laid her finger on both lips.

The count, emboldened by so much kindness, took her hand; she let him do so as though it were a great favour, and he kissed it tenderly.

"Oh! *mademoiselle*," he cried, on knowing himself beyond all danger, "rely on me for life, for death. Though I owe you a gratitude equal to that I owe my mother, it will be very difficult to restrain my feelings to mere respect."

He sprang into the narrow pathway. After watching him till he reached the rocks of Saint-Sulpice, Marie nodded her head in sign of satisfaction, saying to herself in a low voice: "That fat fellow has given me more than his life for his life! I can make him my creator at a very little cost! Creature or creator, that's all the difference there is between one man and another—"

She did not finish her thought, but with a look of despair she turned and re-entered the Porte Saint-Leonard, where Hulot and Corentin were awaiting her.

"Two more days," she cried, "and then—" She stopped, observing that they were not alone—"he shall fall under your guns," she whispered to Hulot.

The commandant recoiled a step and looked with a jeering contempt, impossible to render, at the woman whose features and expression gave no sign whatever of relenting. There is one thing remarkable about women: they never reason about their blameworthy actions,—feeling carries them off their feet; even in their dissimulation there is an element of sincerity; and in women alone crime may exist without baseness, for it often happens that they do not know how it came about that they committed it.

"I am going to Saint-James, to a ball the Chouans give tomorrow night, and—"

"But," said Corentin, interrupting her, "that is fifteen miles distant; had I not better accompany you?"

"You think a great deal too much of something I never think of at all," she replied, "and that is yourself."

Marie's contempt for Corentin was extremely pleasing to Hulot, who made his well-known grimace as she turned away in the direction of her own house. Corentin followed her with his eyes, letting his face express a consciousness of the fatal power he knew he could exercise over the charming creature, by working upon the passions which sooner or later, he believed, would give her to him.

As soon as Mademoiselle de Verneuil reached home she began to deliberate on her ball-dress. Francine, accustomed to obey without understanding her mistress's motives, opened the trunks, and suggested a Greek costume. The Republican fashions of those days were all Greek in style. Marie chose one which could be put in a box that was easy to carry.

"Francine, my dear, I am going on an excursion into the country; do you want to go with me, or will you stay behind?"

"Stay behind!" exclaimed Francine; "then who would dress you?"

"Where have you put that glove I gave you this morning?"

"Here it is."

"Sew this green ribbon into it, and, above all, take plenty of money." Then noticing that Francine was taking out a number of the new Republican coins, she cried out, "Not those; they would get us murdered. Send Jeremie to Corentin—no, stay, the wretch would follow me—send to the commandant; ask him from me for some six-*franc* crowns."

With the feminine sagacity which takes in the smallest detail, she thought of everything. While Francine was completing the arrangements for this extraordinary trip, Marie practised the art of imitating an owl, and so far succeeded in rivalling Marche-a-Terre that the illusion was a good one. At midnight she left Fougeres by the gate of Saint-Leonard, took the little path to Nid-aux-Crocs, and started, followed by Francine, to cross the Val de Gibarry with a firm step, under the impulse of that strong will which gives to the body and its bearing such an expression of force. To leave a ball-room with sufficient care to avoid a cold is an important affair to the health of a woman; but let her have a passion in her heart, and her body becomes adamant. Such an enterprise as Marie had now undertaken would have floated in a bold man's mind for a long time; but Mademoiselle de Verneuil had no sooner thought of it than its dangers became to her attractions.

"You are starting without asking God to bless you," said Francine, turning to look at the tower of Saint-Leonard.

The pious Breton stopped, clasped her hands, and said an *Ave* to Saint Anne of Auray, imploring her to bless their expedition; during which time her mistress waited pensively, looking first at the artless attitude of her maid who was praying fervently, and then at the effects of the vaporous moonlight as it glided among the traceries of the church building, giving to the granite all the delicacy of filigree. The pair soon reached the hut of Galope-Chopine. Light as their steps were they roused one of those huge watch-dogs on whose fidelity the Bretons rely, putting no fastening to their doors but a simple latch. The dog ran to the strangers, and his bark became so threatening that they were forced to retreat a few steps and call for help. But no one came. Mademoiselle de Verneuil then gave the owl's cry, and instantly the rusty hinges of the door made a creaking sound, and Galope-Chopine, who had risen hastily, put out his head.

"I wish to go to Saint-James," said Marie, showing the *Gars'* glove. "Monsieur le Comte de Bauvan told me that you would take me there and protect me on the way. Therefore be good enough to get us two riding donkeys, and make yourself ready to go with us. Time is precious, for if we do not get to Saint-James before tomorrow night I can neither see the ball nor the *Gars*."

Galope-Chopine, completely bewildered, took the glove and turned it over and over, after lighting a pitch candle about a finger thick and the colour of gingerbread. This article of consumption, imported into Brittany from the North, was only one more proof to the eyes in this strange country of a utter ignorance of all commercial principles, even the commonest. After seeing the green ribbon, staring at Mademoiselle de Verneuil, scratching his ear, and drinking a beaker of cider (having first offered a glass to the beautiful lady), Galope-Chopine left her seated before the table and went to fetch the required donkeys.

The violet gleam cast by the pitch candle was not powerful enough to counteract the fitful moonlight, which touched the dark floor and furniture of the smoke-blackened cottage with luminous points. The little boy had lifted his pretty head inquisitively, and above it two cows were poking their rosy muzzles and brilliant eyes through the holes in the stable wall. The big dog, whose countenance was by no means the least intelligent of the family, seemed to be examining the strangers with as much curiosity as the little boy. A painter would have stopped to admire the night effects of this scene, but Marie, not wishing to enter into conversation with Barbette, who sat up in bed and began to show signs of amazement at recognizing her, left the hovel to escape its fetid air and the questions of its mistress. She ran quickly up the stone staircase behind the cottage, admiring the vast details of the landscape, the aspect of which underwent as many changes as spectators made steps either upward to the summits or downward to the valleys. The moonlight was now enveloping like a luminous mist the valley of Couesnon. Certainly a woman whose heart was burdened with a despised love would be sensitive to the melancholy which that soft brilliancy inspires in the soul, by the weird appearance it gives to objects and the colours with which it tints the streams.

The silence was presently broken by the braying of a donkey. Marie went quickly back to the hut, and the party started. Galope-Chopine, armed with a double-barrelled gun, wore a long goatskin, which gave him something the look of Robinson Crusoe. His blotched face, seamed with wrinkles, was scarcely visible under the broad-brimmed hat which the Breton peasants still retain as a tradition of the olden time; proud to have won, after their servitude, the right to wear the former ornament of *seignorial* heads. This nocturnal caravan, protected by a guide whose clothing, attitudes, and person had something patriarchal about them, bore no little resemblance to the Flight into Egypt as we see it represented by the sombre brush of Rembrandt. Galope-Chopine carefully avoided the main-road and guided the two women through the labyrinth of by-ways which intersect Brittany.

Mademoiselle de Verneuil then understood the Chouan warfare. In threading these complicated paths, she could better appreciate the condition of a country which when she saw it from an elevation had seemed to her so charming, but into which it was necessary to penetrate before the dangers and inextricable difficulties of it could be understood. Round each field, and from time immemorial, the peasants have piled mud walls, about six feet high, and prismatic in shape; on the top of which grow chestnuts, oaks and beeches. The walls thus planted are called hedges (Norman hedges) and the long branches of the trees sweeping over the pathways arch them. Sunken between these walls (made of a clay soil) the paths are like the covered ways of a fortification, and where the granite rock, which in these regions comes to the surface of the ground, does not make a sort of rugged natural pavement, they become so impracticable that the smallest vehicles can only be drawn over them by two pairs of oxen or Breton horses, which are small but usually vigorous. These by-ways are so swampy that foot-passengers have gradually by long usage made other paths beside them on the hedge-banks which are called *rotes*; and these begin and end with each division into fields. In order to cross from one field to another it is necessary to climb the clay banks by means of steps which are often very slippery after a rain.

Travellers have many other obstacles to encounter in these intricate paths. Thus surrounded, each field is closed by what is called in the West an *echalier*. That is a trunk or stout branch of a tree, one end of which, being pierced, is fitted to an upright post which serves as a pivot on which it turns. One end of the *echalier* projects far enough beyond the pivot to hold a weight, and this singular rustic gate, the post of which rests in a hole made in the bank, is so easy to work that a child can handle it. Sometimes the peasants economize the stone which forms the weight by lengthening the trunk or branch beyond the pivot. This method of enclosure varies with the genius of each proprietor. Sometimes it consists of a single trunk or branch, both ends of which are embedded in the bank. In other places it looks like a gate, and is made of several slim branches placed at regular distances like the steps of a ladder lying horizontally. The form turns, like the *echalier*, on a pivot. These "hedges" and *echaliers* give the region the appearance of a huge chess-board, each field forming a square, perfectly isolated from the rest, closed like a fortress and protected by ramparts. The gate, which is very easy to defend, is a dangerous spot for assailants. The Breton peasant thinks he improves his fallow land by encouraging the growth of gorse, a shrub so well treated in these regions that it soon attains the height of a man. This delusion, worthy of a population which puts its manure on the highest spot in the courtyard, has covered the soil to a proportion of one fourth with masses of gorse, in the midst of which a thousand men might ambush. Also there is scarcely a field without a number of old apple-trees, the fruit being used for cider, which kill the vegetation wherever their branches cover the ground. Now, if the reader will reflect on the small extent of open ground within these hedges and large trees whose hungry roots impoverish the soil, he will have an idea of the cultivation and general character of the region through which Mademoiselle de Verneuil was now passing.

177

It is difficult to say whether the object of these enclosures is to avoid all disputes of possession, or whether the custom is a lazy one of keeping the cattle from straying, without the trouble of watching them; at any rate such formidable barriers are permanent obstacles, which make these regions impenetrable and ordinary warfare impossible. There lies the whole secret of the Chouan war. Mademoiselle de Verneuil saw plainly the necessity the Republic was under to strangle the disaffection by means of police and by negotiation, rather than by a useless employment of military force. What could be done, in fact, with a people wise enough to despise the possession of towns, and hold to that of an open country already furnished with indestructible fortifications? Surely, nothing except negotiate; especially as the whole active strength of these deluded peasants lay in a single able and enterprising leader. She admired the genius of the minister who, sitting in his study, had been able to grasp the true way of procuring peace. She thought she understood the considerations which act on the minds of men powerful enough to take a bird's-eye view of an empire; men whose actions, criminal in the eyes of the masses, are the outcome of a vast and intelligent thought. There is in these terrible souls some mysterious blending of the force of fate and that of destiny, some prescience which suddenly elevates them above their fellows; the masses seek them for a time in their own ranks, then they raise their eyes and see these lordly souls above them.

Such reflections as these seemed to Mademoiselle de Verneuil to justify and even to ennoble her thoughts of vengeance; this travail of her soul and its expectations gave her vigour enough to bear the unusual fatigues of this strange journey. At the end of each property Galope-Chopine made the women dismount from their donkeys and climb the obstructions; then, mounting again, they made their way through the boggy paths which already felt the approach of winter. The combination of tall trees, sunken paths, and enclosed places, kept the soil in a state of humidity which wrapped the travellers in a mantle of ice. However, after much wearisome fatigue, they managed to reach the woods of Marignay by sunrise. The journey then became less difficult, and led by a broad footway through the forest. The arch formed by the branches, and the great size of the trees protected the travellers from the weather, and the many difficulties of the first half of their way did not recur.

They had hardly gone a couple of miles through the woods before they heard a confused noise of distant voices and the tinkling of a bell, the silvery tones of which did not have the monotonous sound given by the movements of cattle. Galope-Chopine listened with great attention, as he walked along, to this melody; presently a puff of wind brought several chanted words to his ear, which seemed to affect him powerfully, for he suddenly turned the wearied donkeys into a by-path, which led away from Saint-James, paying no attention to the remonstrances of Mademoiselle de Verneuil, whose fears were increased by the darkness of the forest path along which their guide now led them. To right and left were enormous blocks of granite, laid one upon the other, of whimsical shape. Across them huge roots had glided, like monstrous serpents, seeking from afar the juicy nourishment enjoyed by a few beeches. The two sides of the road resembled the subterranean grottos that are famous for stalactites. Immense festoons of stone, where the darkling verdure of ivy and holly allied itself to the green-grey patches of the moss and lichen, hid the precipices and the openings into several caves. When the three travellers had gone a few steps through a very narrow path a most surprising spectacle suddenly unfolded itself to Mademoiselle de Verneuil's eyes, and made her understand the obstinacy of her Chouan guide.

A semi-circular basin of granite blocks formed an amphitheatre, on the rough tiers of which rose tall black pines and yellowing chestnuts, one above the other, like a vast circus, where the wintry sun shed its pale colours rather than poured its light, and autumn had spread her tawny carpet of fallen leaves. About the middle of this hall, which seemed to have had the deluge for its architect, stood three enormous Druid stones,—a vast altar, on which was raised an old church-banner. About a hundred men, kneeling with bared heads, were praying fervently in this natural enclosure, where a priest, assisted by two other ecclesiastics, was saying mass. The poverty of the sacerdotal vestments, the feeble voice of the priest, which echoed like a murmur through the open space, the praying men filled with conviction and united by one and the same sentiment, the bare cross, the wild and barren temple, the dawning day, gave the primitive character of the earlier times of Christianity to the scene. Mademoiselle de Verneuil was struck with admiration. This mass said in the depths of the woods, this worship driven back by persecution to its sources, the poesy of ancient times revived in the midst of this weird and romantic nature, these armed and unarmed Chouans, cruel and praying, men yet children, all these things resembled nothing that she had ever seen or yet imagined. She remembered admiring in her childhood the pomps of the Roman church so pleasing to the senses; but she knew nothing of God *alone*, his cross on the altar, his altar the earth. In place of the carved foliage of a Gothic cathedral, the autumnal trees upheld the sky; instead of a thousand colours thrown through stained glass windows, the sun could barely slide its ruddy rays and dull reflections on altar, priest, and people. The men present were a fact, a reality, and not a system,—it was a prayer, not a religion. But human passions, the momentary repression of which gave harmony to the picture, soon reappeared on this mysterious scene and gave it powerful vitality.

As Mademoiselle de Verneuil reached the spot the reading of the gospel was just over. She recognized in the officiating priest, not without fear, the Abbe Gudin, and she hastily slipped behind a granite block, drawing Francine after her. She was, however, unable to move Galope-Chopine from the place he had chosen, and from which he intended to share in the benefits of the ceremony; but she noticed the nature of the ground around her, and hoped to be able to evade the danger by getting away, when the service was over, before the priests. Through a large fissure of the rock that hid her, she saw the Abbe Gudin mounting a block of granite which served him as a pulpit, where he began his sermon with the words,—

"*In nomine Patris et Filii, et Spiritus Sancti.*"

All present made the sign of the cross.

"My dear friends," continued the *abbe*, "let us pray in the first place for the souls of the dead,—Jean Cochegrue, Nicalos Laferte, Joseph Brouet, Francois Parquoi, Sulpice Coupiau, all of this parish, and dead of wounds received in the fight on Mont Pelerine and at the siege of Fougeres. *De profundis*," etc.

The psalm was recited, according to custom, by the congregation and the priests, taking verses alternately with a fervour which augured well for the success of the sermon. When it was over the *abbe* continued, in a voice which became gradually louder and louder, for the former Jesuit was not unaware that vehemence of delivery was in itself a powerful argument with which to persuade his semi-savage hearers.

"These defenders of our God, Christians, have set you an example of duty," he said. "Are you not ashamed of what will be said of you in paradise? If it were not for these blessed ones, who have just been received with open arms by all the saints, our Lord might have thought that your parish is inhabited by Mahometans!—Do you know, men, what is said of you in Brittany and in the king's presence? What! you don't know? Then I shall tell you. They say: 'Behold, the Blues have cast down altars, and killed priests, and murdered the king and queen; they mean to make the parish folk of Brittany Blues like themselves, and send them to fight in foreign lands, away from their churches, where they run the risk of dying without confession and going eternally to hell; and yet the *gars* of Marignay, whose churches they have burned, stand still with folded arms! Oh! oh! this Republic of damned souls has sold the property of God and that of the nobles at auction; it has shared the proceeds with the Blues; it has decreed, in order to gorge itself with money as it does with blood, that a crown shall be only worth three *francs* instead of six; and yet the *gars* of Marignay haven't seized their weapons and driven the Blues from Brittany! Ha! paradise will be closed to them! they can never save their souls!'That's what they say of you in the king's presence! It is your own salvation, Christians, which is at stake.Your souls are to be saved by fighting for religion and the king. Saint Anne of Auray herself appeared to me yesterday at half-past two o'clock; and she said to me these very words which I now repeat to you:'Are you a priest of Marignay?' 'Yes, *madame*, ready to serve you.' 'I am Saint Anne of Auray, aunt of God, after the manner of Brittany. I have come to bid you warn the people of Marignay that they must not hope for salvation if they do not take arms.You are to refuse them absolution for their sins unless they serve God. Bless their guns, and those who gain absolution will never miss the Blues, because their guns are sanctified.' She disappeared, leaving an odour of incense behind her. I marked the spot. It is under the oak of the Patte d'Oie; just where that beautiful wooden Virgin was placed by the rector of Saint-James; to whom the crippled mother of Pierre Leroi (otherwise called Marche-a-Terre) came to pray, and was cured of all her pains, because of her son's good deeds.You see her there in the midst of you, and you know that she walks without assistance. It was a miracle—a miracle intended, like the resurrection of Marie Lambrequin to prove to you that God will never forsake the Breton cause so long as the people fight for his servants and for the king.Therefore, my dear brothers, if you wish to save your souls and show yourselves defenders of God and the king, you will obey all the orders of the man whom God has sent to us, and whom we call the *Gars*.Then indeed, you will no longer be Mahometans; you will rank with all the *gars* of Brittany under the flag of God.You can take from the pockets of the Blues the money they have stolen from you; for, if the fields have to go uncultivated while you are making war, God and the king will deliver to you the spoils of your enemies. Shall it be said, Christians, that the *gars* of Marignay are behind the *gars* of the Morbihan, the *gars* of Saint-Georges, of Vitre, or Antrain, who are all faithful to God and the king? Will you let them get all the spoils? Will you stand like heretics, with your arms folded, when other Bretons are saving their souls and saving their king? 'Forsake all, and follow me,' says the Gospel. Have we not forsaken our tithes, we priests? And you, I say to you, forsake all for this holy war! You shall be like the Maccabees. All will be forgiven you. You will find the priests and curates in your midst, and you will conquer! Pay attention to these words, Christians," he said, as he ended; "for this day only have we the power to bless your guns. Those who do not take advantage of the Saint's favour will not find her merciful; she will not forgive them or listen to them as she did in the last war."

This appeal, enforced by the power of a loud voice and by many gestures, the vehemence of which bathed the orator in perspiration, produced, apparently, very little effect. The peasants stood motionless, their eyes on the speaker, like statues; but Mademoiselle de Verneuil presently noticed that this universal attitude was the result of a spell cast by the *abbe* on the crowd. He had, like great actors, held his audience as one man by addressing their passions and self-interests. He had absolved excesses before committal, and broken the only bonds which held these boorish men to the practice of religious and social precepts. He had prostituted his sacred office to political interests; but it must be said that, in these times of revolution, every man made a weapon of whatever he possessed for the benefit of his party, and the pacific cross of Jesus became as much an instrument of war as the peasant's plough-share.

Seeing no one with whom to advise, Mademoiselle de Verneuil turned to look for Francine, and was not a little astonished to see that she shared in the rapt enthusiasm, and was devoutly saying her chaplet over some beads which Galope-Chopine had probably given her during the sermon.

"Francine," she said, in a low voice, "are you afraid of being a Mahometan?"

"Oh! *mademoiselle*," replied the girl, "just see Pierre's mother; she is walking!"

Francine's whole attitude showed such deep conviction that Marie understood at once the secret of the homily, the influence of the clergy over the rural masses, and the tremendous effect of the scene which was now beginning.

The peasants advanced one by one and knelt down, presenting their guns to the preacher, who laid them upon the altar. Galope-

Chopine offered his old duck-shooter. The three priests sang the hymn *Veni, Creator*, while the celebrant wrapped the instruments of death in bluish clouds of incense, waving the smoke into shapes that appeared to interlace one another. When the breeze had dispersed the vapour the guns were returned in due order. Each man received his own on his knees from the hands of the priests, who recited a Latin prayer as they returned them. After the men had regained their places, the profound enthusiasm of the congregation, mute till then, broke forth and resounded in a formidable manner.

"Domine salvum fac regem!" was the prayer which the preacher intoned in an echoing voice, and was then sung vehemently by the people. The cry had something savage and warlike in it. The two notes of the word *regem*, readily interpreted by the peasants, were taken with such energy that Mademoiselle de Verneuil's thoughts reverted almost tenderly to the exiled Bourbon family. These recollections awakened those of her past life. Her memory revived the fetes of a court now dispersed, in which she had once a share. The face of the marquis entered her reverie. With the natural mobility of a woman's mind she forgot the scene before her and reverted to her plans of vengeance, which might cost her her life or come to nought under the influence of a look. Seeing a branch of holly the trivial thought crossed her mind that in this decisive moment, when she wished to appear in all her beauty at the ball, she had no decoration for her hair; and she gathered a tuft of the prickly leaves and shining berries with the idea of wearing them.

"Ho! ho! my gun may miss fire on a duck, but on a Blue, never!" cried Galope-Chopine, nodding his head in sign of satisfaction.

Marie examined her guide's face attentively, and found it of the type of those she had just seen. The old Chouan had evidently no more ideas than a child. A naive joy wrinkled his cheeks and forehead as he looked at his gun; but a pious conviction cast upon that expression of his joy a tinge of fanaticism, which brought into his face for an instant the signs of the vices of civilization.

Presently they reached a village, or rather a collection of huts like that of Galope-Chopine, where the rest of the congregation arrived before Mademoiselle de Verneuil had finished the milk and bread and butter which formed the meal. This irregular company was led by the *abbe*, who held in his hand a rough cross draped with a flag, followed by a *gars*, who was proudly carrying the parish banner. Mademoiselle de Verneuil was compelled to mingle with this detachment, which was on its way, like herself, to Saint-James, and would naturally protect her from all danger as soon as Galope-Chopine informed them that the *Gars* glove was in her possession, provided always that the *abbe* did not see her.

Towards sunset the three travellers arrived safely at Saint-James, a little town which owes its name to the English, by whom it was built in the fourteenth century, during their occupation of Brittany. Before entering it Mademoiselle de Verneuil was witness of a strange scene of this strange war, to which, however, she gave little attention; she feared to be recognized by some of her enemies, and this dread hastened her steps. Five or six thousand peasants were camping in a field. Their clothing was not in any degree warlike; in fact, this tumultuous assembly resembled that of a great fair. Some attention was needed to even observe that these Bretons were armed, for their goatskins were so made as to hide their guns, and the weapons that were chiefly visible were the scythes with which some of the men had armed themselves while awaiting the distribution of muskets. Some were eating and drinking, others were fighting and quarrelling in loud tones, but the greater part were sleeping on the ground. An officer in a red uniform attracted Mademoiselle de Verneuil's attention, and she supposed him to belong to the English service. At a little distance two other officers seemed to be trying to teach a few Chouans, more intelligent than the rest, to handle two cannon, which apparently formed the whole artillery of the royalist army. Shouts hailed the coming of the *gars* of Marignay, who were recognized by their banner. Under cover of the tumult which the new-comers and the priests excited in the camp, Mademoiselle de Verneuil was able to make her way past it and into the town without danger. She stopped at a plain-looking inn not far from the building where the ball was to be given. The town was so full of strangers that she could only obtain one miserable room. When she was safely in it Galope-Chopine brought Francine the box which contained the ball dress, and having done so he stood stock-still in an attitude of indescribable irresolution. At any other time Mademoiselle de Verneuil would have been much amused to see what a Breton peasant can be like when he leaves his native parish; but now she broke the charm by opening her purse and producing four crowns of six *francs* each, which she gave him.

"Take it," she said, "and if you wish to oblige me, you will go straight back to Fougeres without entering the camp or drinking any cider."

The Chouan, amazed at her liberality, looked first at the crowns (which he had taken) and then at Mademoiselle de Verneuil; but she made him a sign with her hand and he disappeared.

"How could you send him away, *mademoiselle?*" said Francine. "Don't you see how the place is surrounded? we shall never get away! and who will protect you here?"

"You have a protector of your own," said Marie maliciously, giving in an undertone Marche-a-Terre's owl cry which she was constantly practising.

Francine coloured, and smiled rather sadly at her mistress's gaiety.

"But who is yours?" she said.

Mademoiselle de Verneuil plucked out her dagger, and showed it to the frightened girl, who dropped on a chair and clasped her hands.

"What have you come here for, Marie?" she cried in a supplicating voice which asked no answer.

Mademoiselle de Verneuil was busily twisting the branches of holly which she had gathered.

"I don't know whether this holly will be becoming," she said; "a brilliant skin like mine may possibly bear a dark wreath of this kind. What do you think, Francine?"

Several remarks of the same kind as she dressed for the ball showed the absolute self-possession and coolness of this strange woman. Whoever had listened to her then would have found it hard to believe in the gravity of a situation in which she was risking her life. An Indian muslin gown, rather short and clinging like damp linen, revealed the delicate outlines of her shape; over this she wore a red drapery, numerous folds of which, gradually lengthening as they fell by her side, took the graceful curves of a Greek peplum. This voluptuous garment of the pagan priestesses lessened the indecency of the rest of the attire which the fashions of the time suffered women to wear. To soften its immodesty still further, Marie threw a gauze scarf over her shoulders, left bare and far too low by the red drapery. She wound the long braids of her hair into the flat irregular cone above the nape of the neck which gives such grace to certain antique statues by an artistic elongation of the head, while a few stray locks escaping from her forehead fell in shining curls beside her cheeks. With a form and head thus dressed, she presented a perfect likeness of the noble masterpieces of Greek sculpture. She smiled as she looked with approval at the arrangement of her hair, which brought out the beauties of her face, while the scarlet berries of the holly wreath which she laid upon it repeated charmingly the colour of the peplum. As she twisted and turned a few leaves, to give capricious diversity to their arrangement, she examined her whole costume in a mirror to judge of its general effect.

"I am horrible tonight," she said, as though she were surrounded by flatterers. "I look like a statue of Liberty."

She placed the dagger carefully in her bosom leaving the rubies in the hilt exposed, their ruddy reflections attracting the eye to the hidden beauties of her shape. Francine could not bring herself to leave her mistress. When Marie was ready she made various pretexts to follow her. She must help her to take off her mantle, and the overshoes which the mud and muck in the streets compelled her to wear (though the roads had been sanded for this occasion); also the gauze veil which Mademoiselle de Verneuil had thrown over her head to conceal her features from the Chouans who were collecting in the streets to watch the company. The crowd was in fact so great that they were forced to make their way through two hedges of Chouans. Francine no longer strove to detain her mistress, and after giving a few last touches to a costume the greatest charm of which was its exquisite freshness, she stationed herself in the courtyard that she might not abandon this beloved mistress to her fate without being able to fly to her succour; for the poor girl foresaw only evil in these events.

A strange scene was taking place in Montauran's chamber as Marie was on her way to the ball. The young marquis, who had just finished dressing, was putting on the broad red ribbon which distinguished him as first in rank of the assembly, when the Abbe Gudin entered the room with an anxious air.

"Monsieur le marquis, come quickly," he said. "You alone can quell a tumult which has broken out, I don't know why, among the leaders. They talk of abandoning the king's cause. I think that devil of a Rifoel is at the bottom of it. Such quarrels are always caused by some mere nonsense. Madame du Gua reproached him, so I hear, for coming to the ball ill-dressed."

"That woman must be crazy," cried the marquis, "to try to—"

"Rifoel retorted," continued the *abbe*, interrupting his chief, "that if you had given him the money promised him in the king's name—"

"Enough, enough; I understand it all now. This scene has all been arranged, and you are put forward as ambassador—"

"I, *monsieur* le marquis!" said the *abbe*, again interrupting him. "I am supporting you vigorously, and you will, I hope, do me the justice to believe that the restoration of our altars in France and that of the king upon the throne of his fathers are far more powerful incentives to my humble labours than the bishopric of Rennes which you—"

The *abbe* dared say no more, for the marquis smiled bitterly at his last words. However, the young chief instantly repressed all expression of feeling, his brow grew stern, and he followed the Abbe Gudin into a hall where the worst of the clamour was echoing.

"I recognize no authority here," Rifoel was saying, casting angry looks at all about him and laying his hand on the hilt of his sabre.

"Do you recognize that of common-sense?" asked the marquis, coldly.

The young Chevalier de Vissard, better known under his patronymic of Rifoel, was silent before the general of the Catholic armies.

"What is all this about, gentlemen?" asked the marquis, examining the faces round him.

"This, *monsieur* le marquis," said a famous smuggler, with the awkwardness of a man of the people who long remains under the yoke of respect to a great lord, though he admits no barriers after he has once jumped them, and regards the aristocrat as an equal only, "*this*," he said, "and you have come in the nick of time to hear it. I am no speaker of gilded phrases, and I shall say things plainly. I commanded five hundred men during the late war. Since we have taken up arms again I have raised a thousand heads as hard as mine for the service of the king. It is now seven years that I have risked my life in the good cause; I don't blame you, but I say that the labourer is worthy of his hire. Now, to begin with, I demand that I be called Monsieur de Cottereau. I also demand that the rank of colonel shall be granted me, or I send in my adhesion to the First Consul! Let me tell you, *monsieur* le marquis, my men and I have a devilishly importunate creditor who must be satisfied—he's here!" he added, striking his stomach.

"Have the musicians come?" said the marquis, in a contemptuous tone, turning to Madame du Gua.

But the smuggler had dealt boldly with an important topic, and the calculating, ambitious minds of those present had been too long in suspense as to what they might hope for from the king to allow the scorn of their new leader to put an end to the scene. Rifoel hastily blocked the way before Montauran, and seized his hand to oblige him to remain.

"Take care, *monsieur* le marquis," he said; "you are treating far too lightly men who have a right to the gratitude of him whom you are here to represent. We know that his Majesty has sent you with full powers to judge of our services, and we say that they ought to be recognized and rewarded, for we risk our heads upon the scaffold daily. I know, so far as I am concerned, that the rank of brigadier-general—"

"You mean colonel."

"No, *monsieur* le marquis; Charette made me a colonel. The rank

187

I mention cannot be denied me. I am not arguing for myself, I speak for my brave brothers-in-arms, whose services ought to be recorded. Your signature and your promise will suffice them for the present; though," he added, in a low voice, "I must say they are satisfied with very little. But," he continued, raising his voice, "when the sun rises on the chateau of Versailles to glorify the return of the monarchy after the faithful have conquered France, *in France*, for the king, will they obtain favours for their families, pensions for widows, and the restitution of their confiscated property? I doubt it. But, *monsieur le marquis*, we must have certified proof of our services when that time comes. I will never distrust the king, but I do distrust those cormorants of ministers and courtiers, who tingle his ears with talk about the public welfare, the honour of France, the interests of the crown, and other crochets. They will sneer at a loyal Vendean or a brave Chouan, because he is old and the sword he drew for the good cause dangles on his withered legs, palsied with exposure. Can you say that we are wrong in feeling thus?"

"You talk well, Monsieur du Vissard, but you are over hasty," replied the marquis.

"Listen, marquis," said the Comte de Bauvan, in a whisper. "Rifoel has really, on my word, told the truth. You are sure, yourself, to have the ear of the king, while the rest of us only see him at a distance and from time to time. I will own to you that if you do not give me your word as a gentleman that I shall, in due course of time, obtain the place of Master of Woods and Waters in France, the devil take me if I will risk my neck any longer. To conquer Normandy for the king is not an easy matter, and I demand the Order for it. But," he added, colouring, "there's time enough to think of that. God forbid that I should imitate these poor mercenaries and harass you. Speak to the king for me, and that's enough."

Each of the chiefs found means to let the marquis know, in a more or less ingenious manner, the exaggerated price they set upon their services. One modestly demanded the governorship of Brittany; another a barony; this one a promotion; that one a command; and all wanted pensions.

"Well, baron," said the marquis to Monsieur du Guenic, "don't you want anything?"

"These gentlemen have left me nothing but the crown of France, marquis, but I might manage to put up with that—"

"Gentlemen!" cried the Abbe Gudin, in a loud voice, "remember that if you are too eager you will spoil everything in the day of victory. The king will then be compelled to make concessions to the revolutionists."

"To those Jacobins!" shouted the smuggler. "Ha! if the king would let me have my way, I'd answer for my thousand men; we'd soon wring their necks and be rid of them."

"Monsieur *de* Cottereau," said the marquis, "I see some of our invited guests arriving. We must all do our best by attention and courtesy to make them share our sacred enterprise; you will agree, I am sure, that this is not the moment to bring forward your demands, however just they may be."

So saying, the marquis went to the door, as if to meet certain of the country nobles who were entering the room, but the bold smuggler barred his way in a respectful manner.

"No, no, *monsieur* le marquis, excuse me," he said; "the Jacobins taught me too well in 1793 that it is not he who sows and reaps who eats the bread. Sign this bit of paper for me, and tomorrow I'll bring you fifteen hundred *gars*. If not, I'll treat with the First Consul."

Looking haughtily about him, the marquis saw plainly that the boldness of the old partisan and his resolute air were not displeasing to any of the spectators of this debate. One man alone, sitting by himself in a corner of the room, appeared to take no part in the scene, and to be chiefly occupied in filling his pipe. The contemptuous air with which he glanced at the speakers, his modest demeanour, and a look of sympathy which the marquis encountered in his eyes, made the young leader observe the man, whom he then recognized as Major Brigaut, and he went suddenly up to him.

"And you, what do you want?" he said.

"Oh, *monsieur* le marquis, if the king comes back that's all I want."

"But for yourself?"

"For myself? are you joking?"

The marquis pressed the horny hand of the Breton, and said to Madame du Gua, who was near them: "Madame, I may perish in this enterprise before I have time to make a faithful report to the king on the Catholic armies of Brittany. I charge you, in case you live to see the Restoration, not to forget this honourable man nor the Baron du Guenic. There is more devotion in them than in all those other men put together."

He pointed to the chiefs, who were waiting with some impatience till the marquis should reply to their demands. They were all holding papers in their hands, on which, no doubt, their services were recorded over the signatures of the various generals of the former war;

189

and all were murmuring. The Abbe Gudin, the Comte de Bauvan, and the Baron du Guenic were consulting how best to help the marquis in rejecting these extravagant demands, for they felt the position of the young leader to be extremely delicate.

Suddenly the marquis ran his blue eyes, gleaming with satire, over the whole assembly, and said in a clear voice: "Gentlemen, I do not know whether the powers which the king has graciously assigned to me are such that I am able to satisfy your demands. He doubtless did not foresee such zeal, such devotion, on your part. You shall judge yourselves of the duties put upon me,—duties which I shall know how to accomplish."

So saying, he left the room and returned immediately holding in his hand an open letter bearing the royal seal and signature.

"These are the letters-patent in virtue of which you are to obey me," he said. "They authorize me to govern the provinces of Brittany, Normandy, Maine, and Anjou, in the king's name, and to recognize the services of such officers as may distinguish themselves in his armies."

A movement of satisfaction ran through the assembly. The Chouans approached the marquis and made a respectful circle round him. All eyes fastened on the king's signature. The young chief, who was standing near the chimney, suddenly threw the letters into the fire, and they were burned in a second.

"I do not choose to command any," cried the young man, "but those who see a king in the king, and not a prey to prey upon. You are free, gentlemen, to leave me."

Madame du Gua, the Abbe Gudin, Major Brigaut, the Chevalier du Vissard, the Baron du Guenic, and the Comte de Bauvan raised the cry of *"Vive le roi!"* For a moment the other leaders hesitated; then, carried away by the noble action of the marquis, they begged him to forget what had passed, assuring him that, letters-patent or not, he must always be their leader.

"Come and dance," cried the Comte de Bauvan, "and happen what will! After all," he added, gaily, "it is better, my friends, to pray to God than the saints. Let us fight first, and see what comes of it."

"Ha! that's good advice," said Brigaut. "I have never yet known a day's pay drawn in the morning."

The assembly dispersed about the rooms, where the guests were now arriving. The marquis tried in vain to shake off the gloom which darkened his face. The chiefs perceived the unfavourable impression made upon a young man whose devotion was still surrounded by all the beautiful illusions of youth, and they were ashamed of their action.

However, a joyous gaiety soon enlivened the opening of the ball, at which were present the most important personages of the royalist party, who, unable to judge rightly, in the depths of a rebellious province, of the actual events of the Revolution, mistook their hopes for realities. The bold operations already begun by Montauran, his name, his fortune, his capacity, raised their courage and caused that political intoxication, the most dangerous of all excitements, which does not cool till torrents of blood have been uselessly shed. In the minds of all present the Revolution was nothing more than a passing trouble to the kingdom of France, where, to their belated eyes, nothing was changed. The country belonged as it ever did to the house of Bourbon. The royalists were the lords of the soil as completely as they were four years earlier, when Hoche obtained less a peace than an armistice. The nobles made light of the revolutionists; for them Bonaparte was another, but more fortunate, Marceau. So gaiety reigned. The women had come to dance. A few only of the chiefs, who had fought the Blues, knew the gravity of the situation; but they were well aware that if they talked of the First Consul and his power to their benighted companions, they could not make themselves understood. These men stood apart and looked at the women with indifference. Madame du Gua, who seemed to do the honours of the ball, endeavoured to quiet the impatience of the dancers by dispensing flatteries to each in turn. The musicians were tuning their instruments and the dancing was about to begin, when Madame du Gua noticed the gloom on de Montauran's face and went hurriedly up to him.

"I hope it is not that vulgar scene you have just had with those clodhoppers which depresses you?" she said.

She got no answer; the marquis, absorbed in thought, was listening in fancy to the prophetic reasons which Marie had given him in the midst of the same chiefs at La Vivetiere, urging him to abandon the struggle of kings against peoples. But the young man's soul was too proud, too lofty, too full perhaps of conviction, to abandon an enterprise he had once begun, and he decided at this moment, to continue it boldly in the face of all obstacles. He raised his head haughtily, and for the first time noticed that Madame du Gua was speaking to him.

"Your mind is no doubt at Fougeres," she remarked bitterly, seeing how useless her efforts to attract his attention had been. "Ah, *monsieur*, I would give my life to put *her* within your power, and see you happy with her."

"Then why have you done all you could to kill her?"

191

"Because I wish her dead or in your arms. Yes, I may have loved the Marquis de Montauran when I thought him a hero, but now I feel only a pitying friendship for him; I see him shorn of all his glory by a fickle love for a worthless woman."

"As for love," said the marquis, in a sarcastic tone, "you judge me wrong. If I loved that girl, *madame*, I might desire her less; if it were not for you, perhaps I should not think of her at all."

"Here she is!" exclaimed Madame du Gua, abruptly.

The haste with which the marquis looked round went to the heart of the woman; but the clear light of the wax candles enabled her to see every change on the face of the man she loved so violently, and when he turned back his face, smiling at her woman's trick, she fancied there was still some hope of recovering him.

"What are you laughing at?" asked the Comte de Bauvan.

"At a soap-bubble which has burst," interposed Madame du Gua, gaily. "The marquis, if we are now to believe him, is astonished that his heart ever beat the faster for that girl who presumes to call herself Mademoiselle de Verneuil. You know who I mean."

"That girl!" echoed the count. "Madame, the author of a wrong is bound to repair it. I give you my word of honour that she is really the daughter of the Duc de Verneuil."

"*Monsieur le comte,*" said the marquis, in a changed voice, "which of your statements am I to believe,—that of La Vivetiere, or that now made?"

The loud voice of a servant at the door announced Mademoiselle de Verneuil. The count sprang forward instantly, offered his hand to the beautiful woman with every mark of profound respect, and led her through the inquisitive crowd to the marquis and Madame du Gua. "Believe the one now made," he replied to the astonished young leader.

Madame du Gua turned pale at the unwelcome sight of the girl, who stood for a moment, glancing proudly over the assembled company, among whom she sought to find the guests at La Vivetiere. She awaited the forced salutation of her rival, and, without even looking at the marquis, she allowed the count to lead her to the place of honour beside Madame du Gua, whose bow she returned with an air that was slightly protecting. But the latter, with a woman's instinct, took no offense; on the contrary, she immediately assumed a smiling, friendly manner. The extraordinary dress and beauty of Mademoiselle de Verneuil caused a murmur throughout the ballroom. When the marquis and Madame du Gua looked towards the late guests at La Vivetiere they saw them in an attitude of respectful admiration which was not assumed; each seemed desirous of recovering favour with the misjudged young woman. The enemies were in presence of each other.

"This is really magic, *mademoiselle*," said Madame du Gua; "there is no one like you for surprises. Have you come all alone?"

"All alone," replied Mademoiselle de Verneuil. "So you have only one to kill tonight, *madame*."

"Be merciful," said Madame du Gua. "I cannot express to you the pleasure I have in seeing you again. I have truly been overwhelmed by the remembrance of the wrongs I have done you, and am most anxious for an occasion to repair them."

"As for those wrongs, *madame*, I readily pardon those you did to me, but my heart bleeds for the Blues whom you murdered. However, I excuse all, in return for the service you have done me."

Madame du Gua lost countenance as she felt her hand pressed by her beautiful rival with insulting courtesy. The marquis had hitherto stood motionless, but he now seized the arm of the count.

"You have shamefully misled me," he said; "you have compromised my honour. I am not a Geronte of comedy, and I shall have your life or you will have mine."

"Marquis," said the count, haughtily, "I am ready to give you all the explanations you desire."

They passed into the next room. The witnesses of this scene, even those least initiated into the secret, began to understand its nature, so that when the musicians gave the signal for the dancing to begin no one moved.

"Mademoiselle, what service have I rendered you that deserves a return?" said Madame du Gua, biting her lips in a sort of rage.

"Did you not enlighten me as to the true character of the Marquis de Montauran, *madame*? With what utter indifference that man allowed me to go to my death! I give him up to you willingly!"

"Then why are you here?" asked Madame du Gua, eagerly.

"To recover the respect and consideration you took from me at La Vivetiere, *madame*. As for all the rest, make yourself easy. Even if the marquis returned to me, you know very well that a return is never love."

Madame du Gua took Mademoiselle de Verneuil's hand with that affectionate touch and motion which women practise to each other, especially in the presence of men.

"Well, my poor dear child," she said, "I am glad to find you so reasonable. If the service I did you was rather harsh," she added, pressing the hand she held, and feeling a desire to rend it as her fingers felt its softness and delicacy, "it shall at least be thorough. Listen to me, I know the character of the *Gars*; he meant to deceive you; he neither can nor will marry any woman except—"

"Ah!"

"Yes, *mademoiselle*, he has accepted his dangerous mission to win the hand of Mademoiselle d'Uxelles, a marriage to which his Majesty has promised his countenance."

"Ah! ah!"

Mademoiselle de Verneuil added not a word to that scornful ejaculation. The young and handsome Chevalier du Vissard, eager to be forgiven for the joke which had led to the insults at La Vivetiere, now came up to her and respectfully invited her to dance. She placed her hand in his, and they took their places in a quadrille opposite to Madame du Gua. The gowns of the royalist women, which recalled the fashions of the exiled court, and their creped and powdered hair seemed absurd as soon as they were contrasted with the attire which republican fashions authorized Mademoiselle de Verneuil to wear. This attire, which was elegant, rich, and yet severe, was loudly condemned but inwardly envied by all the women present. The men could not restrain their admiration for the beauty of her natural hair and the adjustment of a dress the charm of which was in the proportions of the form which it revealed.

At that moment the marquis and the count re-entered the ballroom behind Mademoiselle de Verneuil, who did not turn her head. If a mirror had not been there to inform her of Montauran's presence, she would have known it from Madame du Gua's face, which scarcely concealed, under an apparently indifferent air, the impatience with which she awaited the conflict which must, sooner or later, take place between the lovers. Though the marquis talked with the count and other persons, he heard the remarks of all the dancers who from time to time in the mazes of the quadrille took the place of Mademoiselle de Verneuil and her partner.

"Positively, *madame*, she came alone," said one.

"She must be a bold woman," replied the lady.

"If I were dressed like that I should feel myself naked," said another woman.

"Oh, the gown is not decent, certainly," replied her partner; "but it is so becoming, and she is so handsome."

"I am ashamed to look at such perfect dancing, for her sake; isn't it exactly that of an opera girl?" said the envious woman.

"Do you suppose that she has come here to intrigue for the First Consul?" said another.

"A joke if she has," replied the partner.

"Well, she can't offer innocence as a dowry," said the lady, laughing.

The *Gars* turned abruptly to see the lady who uttered this sarcasm, and Madame du Gua looked at him as if to say, "You see what people think of her."

"Madame," said the count, laughing, "so far, it is only women who have taken her innocence away from her."

The marquis privately forgave the count. When he ventured to look at his mistress, whose beauty was, like that of most women, brought into relief by the light of the wax candles, she turned her back upon him as she resumed her place, and went on talking to her partner in a way to let the marquis hear the sweetest and most caressing tones of her voice.

"The First Consul sends dangerous ambassadors," her partner was saying.

"Monsieur," she replied, "you all said that at La Vivetiere."

"You have the memory of a king," replied he, disconcerted at his own awkwardness.

"To forgive injuries one must needs remember them," she said quickly, relieving his embarrassment with a smile.

"Are we all included in that amnesty?" said the marquis, approaching her.

But she darted away in the dance, with the gaiety of a child, leaving him without an answer. He watched her coldly and sadly; she saw it, and bent her head with one of those coquettish motions which the graceful lines of her throat enabled her to make, omitting no movement or attitude which could prove to him the perfection of her figure. She attracted him like hope, and eluded him like a memory. To see her thus was to desire to possess her at any cost. She knew that, and the sense it gave her of her own beauty shed upon her whole person an inexpressible charm. The marquis felt the storm of love, of rage, of madness, rising in his heart; he wrung the count's hand violently, and left the room.

"Is he gone?" said Mademoiselle de Verneuil, returning to her place.

The count gave her a glance and passed into the next room, from which he presently returned accompanied by the *Gars*.

"He is mine!" she thought, observing his face in the mirror.

She received the young leader with a displeased air and said nothing, but she smiled as she turned away from him; he was so superior to all about him that she was proud of being able to rule him; and obeying an instinct which sways all women more or less, she resolved to let him know the value of a few gracious words by making him pay dear for them. As soon as the quadrille was over, all the gentlemen who had been at La Vivetiere surrounded Mademoiselle de Verneuil, wishing by their flattering attentions to obtain her pardon for the mistake they had made; but he whom she longed to see at her feet did not approach the circle over which she now reigned a queen.

"He thinks I still love him," she thought, "and does not wish to be confounded with mere flatterers."

She refused to dance again. Then, as if the ball were given for her, she walked about on the arm of the Comte de Bauvan, to whom she was pleased to show some familiarity. The affair at La Vivetiere was by this time known to all present, thanks to Madame du Gua, and the lovers were the object of general attention. The marquis dared not again address his mistress; a sense of the wrong he had done her and the violence of his returning passion made her seem to him actually terrible. On her side Marie watched his apparently calm face while she seemed to be observing the ball.

"It is fearfully hot here," she said to the count. "Take me to the other side where I can breathe; I am stifling here."

And she motioned towards a small room where a few card-players were assembled. The marquis followed her. He ventured to hope she had left the crowd to receive him, and this supposed favour roused his passion to extreme violence; for his love had only increased through the resistance he had made to it during the last few days. Mademoiselle de Verneuil still tormented him; her eyes, so soft and velvety for the count, were hard and stern when, as if by accident, they met his. Montauran at last made a painful effort and said, in a muffled voice, "Will you never forgive me?"

"Love forgives nothing, or it forgives all," she said, coldly. "But," she added, noticing his joyful look, "it must be love."

She took the count's arm once more and moved forward into a small boudoir which adjoined the card room. The marquis followed her.

"Will you not hear me?" he said.

"One would really think, *monsieur*," she replied, "that I had come here to meet you, and not to vindicate my own self-respect. If you do not cease this odious pursuit I shall leave the ballroom."

"Ah!" he cried, recollecting one of the crazy actions of the last Duc de Lorraine, "let me speak to you so long as I can hold this live coal in my hand."

He stooped to the hearth and picking up a brand held it tightly.

Mademoiselle de Verneuil flushed, took her arm from that of the count, and looked at the marquis in amazement. The count softly withdrew, leaving them alone together. So crazy an action shook Marie's heart, for there is nothing so persuasive in love as courageous folly.

"You only prove to me," she said, trying to make him throw away the brand, "that you are willing to make me suffer cruelly. You are extreme in everything. On the word of a fool and the slander of a woman you suspected that one who had just saved your life was capable of betraying you."

"Yes," he said, smiling, "I have been very cruel to you; but nevertheless, forget it; I shall never forget it. Hear me. I have been shamefully deceived; but so many circumstances on that fatal day told against you—"

"And those circumstances were stronger than your love?"

He hesitated; she made a motion of contempt, and rose.

"Oh, Marie. I shall never cease to believe in you now."

"Then throw that fire away. You are mad. Open your hand; I insist upon it."

He took delight in still resisting the soft efforts of her fingers, but she succeeded in opening the hand she would fain have kissed.

"What good did that do you?" she said, as she tore her handkerchief and laid it on the burn, which the marquis covered with his glove.

Madame du Gua had stolen softly into the card room, watching the lovers with furtive eyes, but escaping theirs adroitly; it was, however, impossible for her to understand their conversation from their actions.

"If all that they said of me was true you must admit that I am avenged at this moment," said Marie, with a look of malignity which startled the marquis.

"What feeling brought you here?" he asked.

"Do you suppose, my dear friend, that you can despise a woman like me with impunity? I came here for your sake and for my own," she continued, after a pause, laying her hand on the hilt of rubies in her bosom and showing him the blade of her dagger.

"What does all that mean?" thought Madame du Gua.

"But," she continued, "you still love me; at any rate, you desire me, and the folly you have just committed," she added, taking his hand, "proves it to me. I will again be that I desired to be; and I return to Fougeres happy. Love absolves everything. You love me; I have regained the respect of the man who represents to me the whole world, and I can die."

"Then you still love me?" said the marquis.

"Have I said so?" she replied with a scornful look, delighting in the torture she was making him endure. "I have run many risks to come here. I have saved Monsieur de Bauvan's life, and he, more grateful than others, offers me in return his fortune and his name. You have never even thought of doing that."

The marquis, bewildered by these words, stifled the worst anger he had ever felt, supposing that the count had played him false. He made no answer.

"Ah! you reflect," she said, bitterly.

"Mademoiselle," replied the young man, "your doubts justify mine."

"Let us leave this room," said Mademoiselle de Verneuil, catching sight of a corner of Madame du Gua's gown, and rising. But the wish to reduce her rival to despair was too strong, and she made no further motion to go.

"Do you mean to drive me to hell?" cried the marquis, seizing her hand and pressing it violently.

"Did you not drive me to hell five days ago? are you not leaving me at this very moment uncertain whether your love is sincere or not?"

"But how do I know whether your revenge may not lead you to obtain my life to tarnish it, instead of killing me?"

"Ah! you do not love me! you think of yourself and not of me!" she said angrily, shedding a few tears.

The coquettish creature well knew the power of her eyes when moistened by tears.

"Well, then," he cried, beside himself, "take my life, but dry those tears."

"Oh, my love! my love!" she exclaimed in a stifled voice: "those are the words, the accents, the looks I have longed for, to allow me to prefer your happiness to mine. But," she added, "I ask one more proof of your love, which you say is so great. I wish to stay here only so long as may be needed to show the company that you are mine. I will not even drink a glass of water in the house of a woman who has twice tried to kill me, who is now, perhaps, plotting mischief against us," and she showed the marquis the floating corner of Madame du Gua's drapery. Then she dried her eyes and put her lips to the ear of the young man, who quivered as he felt the caress of her warm breath. "See that everything is prepared for my departure," she said; "you shall take me yourself to Fougeres and there only will I tell you if I love you. For the second time I trust you. Will you trust me a second time?"

"Ah, Marie, you have brought me to a point where I know not what I do. I am intoxicated by your words, your looks, by you—by you, and I am ready to obey you."

"Well, then, make me for an instant very happy. Let me enjoy the only triumph I desire. I want to breathe freely, to drink of the life I have dreamed, to feed my illusions before they are gone forever. Come—come into the ballroom and dance with me."

They re-entered the room together, and though Mademoiselle de Verneuil was as completely satisfied in heart and vanity as any woman ever could be, the unfathomable gentleness of her eyes, the demure smile on her lips, the rapidity of the motions of a gay dance, kept the secret of her thoughts as the sea swallows those of the criminal who casts a weighted body into its depths. But a murmur of admiration ran through the company as, circling in each other's arms, voluptuously interlaced, with heavy heads, and dimmed sight, they waltzed with a sort of frenzy, dreaming of the pleasures they hoped to find in a future union.

A few moments later Mademoiselle de Verneuil and the marquis were in the latter's travelling-carriage drawn by four horses. Surprised to see these enemies hand in hand, and evidently understanding each other, Francine kept silence, not daring to ask her mistress whether her conduct was that of treachery or love. Thanks to the darkness, the marquis did not observe Mademoiselle de Verneuil's agitation as they neared Fougeres. The first flush of dawn showed the towers of Saint-Leonard in the distance. At that moment Marie was saying to herself: "I am going to my death."

As they ascended the first hill the lovers had the same thought; they left the carriage and mounted the rise on foot, in memory of their first meeting. When Marie took the young man's arm she thanked him by a smile for respecting her silence; then, as they reached the summit of the plateau and looked at Fougeres, she threw off her reverie.

"Don't come any farther," she said; "my authority cannot save you from the Blues today."

Montauran showed some surprise. She smiled sadly and pointed to a block of granite, as if to tell him to sit down, while she herself stood before him in a melancholy attitude. The rending emotions of her soul no longer permitted her to play a part. At that moment she would have knelt on red-hot coals without feeling them any more than the marquis had felt the fire-brand he had taken in his hand to prove the strength of his passion. It was not until she had contemplated her lover with a look of the deepest anguish that she said to him, at last:—

"All that you have suspected of me is true."

The marquis started.

"Ah! I pray you," she said, clasping her hands, "listen to me without interruption. I am indeed the daughter of the Duc de Verneuil,—but his natural daughter. My mother, a Demoiselle de Casteran, who became a nun to escape the reproaches of her family, expiated her fault by fifteen years of sorrow, and died at Seez, where she was abbess. On her death-bed she implored, for the first time and only for me, the help of the man who had betrayed her, for she knew she was leaving me without friends, without fortune, without a future. The duke accepted the charge, and took me from the roof of Francine's mother, who had hitherto taken care of me; perhaps he liked me because I was beautiful; possibly I reminded him of his youth. He was one of those great lords of the old regime, who took pride in showing how they could get their crimes forgiven by committing them with grace. I will say no more, he was my father. But let me explain to you how my life in Paris injured my soul. The society of the Duc de Verneuil, to which he introduced me, was bitten by that scoffing philosophy about which all France was then enthusiastic because it was wittily professed. The brilliant conversations which charmed my ear were marked by subtlety of perception and by witty contempt for all that was true and spiritual. Men laughed at sentiments, and pictured them all the better because they did not feel them; their satirical epigrams were as fascinating as the light-hearted humour with which they could put a whole adventure into a word; and yet they had sometimes too much wit, and wearied women by making love an art, and not a matter of feeling. I could not resist the tide. And yet my soul was too ardent—forgive this pride—not to feel that their minds had withered their hearts; and the life I led resulted in a perpetual struggle between my natural feelings and beliefs and the vicious habits of mind which I there contracted. Several superior men took pleasure in developing in me that liberty of thought and contempt for public opinion which do tear from a woman her modesty of soul, robbed of which she loses her charm. Alas! my subsequent misfortunes have failed to lessen the faults I learned through opulence. My father," she continued, with a sigh, "the Duc de Verneuil, died, after duly recognizing me as his daughter and making provisions for me by his will, which considerably reduced the fortune of my brother, his legitimate son. I found myself one day without a home and without a protector. My brother contested the will which made me rich. Three years of my late life had developed my vanity. By satisfying all my fancies my father had created in my nature a need of luxury, and given me habits of self-indulgence of which my own mind, young and artless as it then was, could not perceive either the danger or the tyranny. A friend of my father, the Marechal Duc de Lenoncourt, then seventy years old, offered to become my guardian, and I found myself, soon after the termination of the odious suit, in a brilliant home, where I enjoyed all the advantages of which my brother's cruelty had deprived me. Every evening the old *marechal* came to sit with me and comfort me with kind and consoling words. His white hair and the many proofs he gave me of paternal tenderness led me to turn all the feelings of my heart upon him, and I felt myself his daughter. I accepted his presents, hiding none of my caprices from him, for I saw how he loved to gratify them. I heard one fatal evening that all Paris believed me the mistress of the poor old man. I was told that it was then beyond my power to recover an innocence thus gratuitously denied me. They said that the man who had abused my inexperience could not be lover, and would not be my husband. The week in which I made this horrible discovery the duke left Paris. I was shamefully ejected from the house where he had placed me, and which did not belong to him. Up to this point I have told you the truth as though I stood before God; but now, do not ask a wretched woman to give account of sufferings which are buried in her heart. The time came when I found myself married to Danton. A few days later the storm uprooted the mighty oak around which I had thrown my arms. Again I was plunged into the worst distress, and I resolved to kill myself. I don't know whether love of life, or the hope of wearying ill-fortune and of finding at the bottom of the abyss the happiness which had always escaped me were, unconsciously to myself, my advisers, or whether I was fascinated by the arguments of a young man from Vendome, who, for the last two years, has wound himself about me like a serpent round a tree,—in short, I know not how it is that I accepted, for a payment of three hundred thousand *francs*, the odious mission of making an unknown man fall in love with me and then betraying him. I met you; I knew you at once by one of those presentiments which never mislead us; yet I tried to doubt my recognition, for the more I came to love you, the more the certainty appalled me. When I saved you from the hands of Hulot, I abjured the part I had taken; I resolved to betray the slaughterers, and not their victim. I did wrong to play with men, with their lives, their principles, with myself, like a thoughtless girl who sees only sentiments in this life. I believed you loved me; I let myself cling to the hope that my life might begin anew; but all things have revealed my past,—even I myself, perhaps, for you must have distrusted a woman

201

so passionate as you have found me. Alas! is there no excuse for my love and my deception? My life was like a troubled sleep; I woke and thought myself a girl; I was in Alencon, where all my memories were pure and chaste. I had the mad simplicity to think that love would baptize me into innocence. For a moment I thought myself pure, for I had never loved. But last night your passion seemed to me true, and a voice cried to me, 'Do not deceive him.' Monsieur le marquis," she said, in a guttural voice which haughtily challenged condemnation, "know this; I am a dishonoured creature, unworthy of you. From this hour I accept my fate as a lost woman. I am weary of playing a part,—the part of a woman to whom you had brought back the sanctities of her soul. Virtue is a burden to me. I should despise you if you were weak enough to marry me. The Comte de Bauvan might commit that folly, but you—you must be worthy of your future and leave me without regret. A courtesan is too exacting; I should not love you like the simple, artless girl who felt for a moment the delightful hope of being your companion, of making you happy, of doing you honour, of becoming a noble wife. But I gather from that futile hope the courage to return to a life of vice and infamy, that I may put an eternal barrier between us. I sacrifice both honour and fortune to you. The pride I take in that sacrifice will support me in my wretchedness,—fate may dispose of me as it will. I will never betray you. I shall return to Paris. There your name will be to me a part of myself, and the glory you win will console my grief. As for you, you are a man, and you will forget me. Farewell."

She darted away in the direction of the gorges of Saint-Sulpice, and disappeared before the marquis could rise to detain her. But she came back unseen, hid herself in a cavity of the rocks, and examined the young man with a curiosity mingled with doubt. Presently she saw him walking like a man overwhelmed, without seeming to know where he went.

"Can he be weak?" she thought, when he had disappeared, and she felt she was parted from him. "Will he understand me?" She quivered. Then she turned and went rapidly towards Fougeres, as though she feared the marquis might follow her into the town, where certain death awaited him.

"Francine, what did he say to you?" she asked, when the faithful girl rejoined her.

"Ah! Marie, how I pitied him. You great ladies stab a man with your tongues."

"How did he seem when he came up to you?"

"As if he saw me not at all! Oh, Marie, he loves you!"

"Yes, he loves me, or he does not love me—there is heaven or hell for me in that," she answered. "Between the two extremes there is no spot where I can set my foot."

After thus carrying out her resolution, Marie gave way to grief, and her face, beautified till then by these conflicting sentiments, changed for the worse so rapidly that in a single day, during which she floated incessantly between hope and despair, she lost the glow of beauty, and the freshness which has its source in the absence of passion or the ardour of joy. Anxious to ascertain the result of her mad enterprise, Hulot and Corentin came to see her soon after her return. She received them smiling.

"Well," she said to the commandant, whose care-worn face had a questioning expression, "the fox is coming within range of your guns; you will soon have a glorious triumph over him."

"What happened?" asked Corentin, carelessly, giving Mademoiselle de Verneuil one of those oblique glances with which diplomatists of his class spy on thought.

"Ah!" she said, "the *Gars* is more in love than ever; I made him come with me to the gates of Fougeres."

"Your power seems to have stopped there," remarked Corentin; "the fears of your *ci-devant* are greater than the love you inspire."

"You judge him by yourself," she replied, with a contemptuous look.

"Well, then," said he, unmoved, "why did you not bring him here to your own house?"

"Commandant," she said to Hulot, with a coaxing smile, "if he really loves me, would you blame me for saving his life and getting him to leave France?"

The old soldier came quickly up to her, took her hand, and kissed it with a sort of enthusiasm. Then he looked at her fixedly and said in a gloomy tone: "You forget my two friends and my sixty-three men."

"Ah, commandant," she cried, with all the naiveté of passion, "he was not accountable for that; he was deceived by a bad woman, Charette's mistress, who would, I do believe, drink the blood of the Blues."

"Come, Marie," said Corentin, "don't tease the commandant; he does not understand such jokes."

"Hold your tongue," she answered, "and remember that the day when you displease me too much will have no morrow for you."

"I see, *mademoiselle*," said Hulot, without bitterness, "that I must prepare for a fight."

"You are not strong enough, my dear colonel. I saw more than six thousand men at Saint-James,—regular troops, artillery, and English officers. But they cannot do much unless *he* leads them? I agree with Fouche, his presence is the head and front of everything."

"Are we to get his head?—that's the point," said Corentin, impatiently.

"I don't know," she answered, carelessly.

"English officers!" cried Hulot, angrily, "that's all that was wanting to make a regular brigand of him. Ha! ha! I'll give him English, I will!"

"It seems to me, citizen-diplomat," said Hulot to Corentin, after the two had taken leave and were at some distance from the house, "that you allow that girl to send you to the right-about when she pleases."

"It is quite natural for you, commandant," replied Corentin, with a thoughtful air, "to see nothing but fighting in what she said to us. You soldiers never seem to know there are various ways of making war. To use the passions of men and women like wires to be pulled for the benefit of the State; to keep the running-gear of the great machine we call government in good order, and fasten to it the desires of human nature, like baited traps which it is fun to watch,—I call *that* creating a world, like God, and putting ourselves at the centre of it!"

"You will please allow me to prefer my calling to yours," said the soldier, curtly. "You can do as you like with your running-gear; I recognize no authority but that of the minister of war. I have my orders; I shall take the field with veterans who don't skulk, and face an enemy you want to catch behind."

"Oh, you can fight if you want to," replied Corentin. "From what that girl has dropped, close-mouthed as you think she is, I can tell you that you'll have to skirmish about, and I myself will give you the pleasure of an interview with the *Gars* before long."

"How so?" asked Hulot, moving back a step to get a better view of this strange individual.

"Mademoiselle de Verneuil is in love with him," replied Corentin, in a thick voice, "and perhaps he loves her. A marquis, a knight of Saint-Louis, young, brilliant, perhaps rich,—what a list of temptations! She would be foolish indeed not to look after her own interests and try to marry him rather than betray him. The girl is attempting to fool us. But I saw hesitation in her eyes. They probably have a rendezvous; perhaps they've met already. Well, tomorrow I shall have him by the forelock. Yesterday he was nothing more than the enemy of the Republic, today he is mine; and I tell you this, every man who has been so rash as to come between that girl and me has died upon the scaffold."

So saying, Corentin dropped into a reverie which hindered him from observing the disgust on the face of the honest soldier as he discovered the depths of this intrigue, and the mechanism of the means employed by Fouché. Hulot resolved on the spot to thwart Corentin in every way that did not conflict essentially with the success of the government, and to give the *Gars* a fair chance of dying honourably, sword in hand, before he could fall a prey to the executioner, for whom this agent of the detective police acknowledged himself the purveyor.

"If the First Consul would listen to me," thought Hulot, as he turned his back on Corentin, "he would leave those foxes to fight aristocrats, and send his solders on other business."

Corentin looked coldly after the old soldier, whose face had brightened at the resolve, and his eyes gleamed with a sardonic expression, which showed the mental superiority of this subaltern Machiavelli.

"Give an ell of blue cloth to those fellows, and hang a bit of iron at their waists," he said to himself, "and they'll think there's but one way to kill people." Then, after walking up and down awhile very slowly, he exclaimed suddenly, "Yes, the time has come, that woman shall be mine! For five years I've been drawing the net round her, and I have her now; with her, I can be a greater man in the government than Fouché himself. Yes, if she loses the only man she has ever loved, grief will give her to me, body and soul; but I must be on the watch night and day."

A few moments later the pale face of this man might have been seen through the window of a house, from which he could observe all who entered the *cul-de-sac* formed by the line of houses running parallel with Saint-Leonard, one of those houses being that now occupied by Mademoiselle de Verneuil. With the patience of a cat watching a mouse Corentin was there in the same place on the following morning, attentive to the slightest noise, and subjecting the passers-by to the closest examination. The day that was now beginning was a market-day. Although in these calamitous times the peasants rarely risked themselves in the towns, Corentin presently noticed a small man with a gloomy face, wrapped in a goatskin, and carrying on his arm a small flat basket; he was making his way in the direction of Mademoiselle de Verneuil's house, casting careless glances about him. Corentin watched him enter the house; then he ran down into the street, meaning to waylay the man as he left; but on second thoughts it occurred to him that if he called unexpectedly on Mademoiselle de Verneuil he might surprise by a single glance the secret that was hidden in the basket of the emissary. Besides, he had already learned that it was impossible to extract anything from the inscrutable answers of Bretons and Normans.

"Galope-Chopine!" cried Mademoiselle de Verneuil, when Francine brought the man to her. "Does he love me?" she murmured to herself, in a low voice.

The instinctive hope sent a brilliant colour to her cheeks and joy into her heart. Galope-Chopine looked alternately from the mistress to the maid with evident distrust of the latter; but a sign from Mademoiselle de Verneuil reassured him.

"Madame," he said, "about two o'clock *he* will be at my house waiting for you."

Emotion prevented Mademoiselle de Verneuil from giving any other reply than a movement of her head, but the man understood her meaning. At that moment Corentin's step was heard in the adjoining room, but Galope-Chopine showed no uneasiness, though Mademoiselle de Verneuil's look and shudder warned him of danger, and as soon as the spy had entered the room the Chouan raised his voice to an ear-splitting tone.

"Ha, ha!" he said to Francine, "I tell you there's Breton butter *and* Breton butter. You want the Gibarry kind, and you won't give more than eleven *sous* a pound; then why did you send me to fetch it? It is good butter that," he added, uncovering the basket to show the pats which Barbette had made. "You ought to be fair, my good lady, and pay one *sou* more."

His hollow voice betrayed no emotion, and his green eyes, shaded by thick grey eyebrows, bore Corentin's piercing glance without flinching.

"Nonsense, my good man, you are not here to sell butter; you are talking to a lady who never bargained for a thing in her life. The trade you run, old fellow, will shorten you by a head in a very few days"; and Corentin, with a friendly tap on the man's shoulder, added, "you can't keep up being a spy of the Blues and a spy of the Chouans very long."

Galope-Chopine needed all his presence of mind to subdue his rage, and not deny the accusation which his avarice had made a just one. He contented himself with saying:

"Monsieur is making game of me."

Corentin turned his back on the Chouan, but, while bowing to Mademoiselle de Verneuil, whose heart stood still, he watched him in the mirror behind her. Galope-Chopine, unaware of this, gave a glance to Francine, to which she replied by pointing to the door, and saying, "Come with me, my man, and we will settle the matter between us."

Nothing escaped Corentin, neither the fear which Mademoiselle de Verneuil could not conceal under a smile, nor her colour and the contraction of her features, nor the Chouan's sign and Francine's reply; he had seen all. Convinced that Galope-Chopine was sent by the marquis, he caught the man by the long hairs of his goatskin as he was leaving the room, turned him round to face him, and said with a keen look: "Where do you live, my man? I want butter, too."

"My good *monsieur*," said the Chouan, "all Fougeres knows where I live. I am—"

"Corentin!" exclaimed Mademoiselle de Verneuil, interrupting Galope-Chopine. "Why do you come here at this time of day? I am scarcely dressed. Let that peasant alone; he does not understand your tricks any more than I understand the motive of them. You can go, my man."

Galope-Chopine hesitated a moment. The indecision, real or feigned, of the poor devil, who knew not which to obey, deceived even Corentin; but the Chouan, finally, after an imperative gesture from the lady, left the room with a dragging step. Mademoiselle de Verneuil and Corentin looked at each other in silence. This time Marie's limpid eyes could not endure the gleam of cruel fire in the man's look. The resolute manner in which the spy had forced his way into her room, an expression on his face which Marie had never seen there before, the deadened tones of his shrill voice, his whole demeanour,— all these things alarmed her; she felt that a secret struggle was about to take place between them, and that he meant to employ against her all the powers of his evil influence. But though she had at this moment a full and distinct view of the gulf into which she was plunging, she gathered strength from her love to shake off the icy chill of these presentiments.

"Corentin," she said, with a sort of gayety, "I hope you are going to let me make my toilet?"

"Marie," he said,—"yes, permit me to call you so,—you don't yet know me. Listen; a much less sagacious man than I would see your love for the Marquis de Montauran. I have several times offered you my heart and hand. You have never thought me worthy of you; and perhaps you are right. But however much you may feel yourself too high, too beautiful, too superior for me, I can compel you to come down to my level. My ambition and my maxims have given you a low opinion of me; frankly, you are mistaken. Men are not worth even what I rate them at, and that is next to nothing. I shall certainly attain a position which will gratify your pride. Who will ever love you better, or make you more absolutely mistress of yourself and of him, than the man who has loved you now for five years? Though I run the risk of exciting your suspicions,—for you cannot conceive that any one should renounce an idolized woman out of excessive love,—I will now prove to you the unselfishness of my passion. If the marquis loves you, marry him; but before you do so, make sure of his sincerity. I could not endure to see you deceived, for I do prefer your happiness to my own. My resolution may surprise you; lay it to the prudence of a man who is not so great a fool as to wish to possess a woman against her will. I blame myself, not you, for the failure of my efforts to win you. I hoped to do so by submission and devotion, for I have long, as you well know, tried to make you happy according to my lights; but you have never in any way rewarded me."

"I have suffered you to be near me," she said, haughtily.

"Add that you regret it."

"After involving me in this infamous enterprise, do you think that I have any thanks to give you?"

"When I proposed to you an enterprise which was not exempt from blame to timid minds," he replied, audaciously, "I had only your own prosperity in view. As for me, whether I succeed or fail, I can make all results further my ends. If you marry Montauran, I shall be delighted to serve the Bourbons in Paris, where I am already a member of the Clichy club. Now, if circumstances were to put me in correspondence with the princes I should abandon the interests of the Republic, which is already on its last legs. General Bonaparte is much too able a man not to know that he can't be in England and in Italy at the same time, and that is how the Republic is about to fall. I have no doubt he made the 18th Brumaire to obtain greater advantages over the Bourbons when it came to treating with them. He is a long-headed fellow, and very keen; but the politicians will get the better of him on their own ground. The betrayal of France is another scruple which men of superiority leave to fools. I won't conceal from you that I have come here with the necessary authority to open negotiations with the Chouans, *or* to further their destruction, as the case may be; for Fouche, my patron, is deep; he has always played a double part; during the Terror he was as much for Robespierre as for Danton—"

"Whom you basely abandoned," she said.

"Nonsense; he is dead,—forget him," replied Corentin. "Come, speak honestly to me; I have set you the example. Old Hulot is deeper than he looks; if you want to escape his vigilance, I can help you. Remember that he holds all the valleys and will instantly detect a rendezvous. If you make one in Fougeres, under his very eyes, you are at the mercy of his patrols. See how quickly he knew that this Chouan had entered your house. His military sagacity will show him that your movements betray those of the Gars—if Montauran loves you."

Mademoiselle de Verneuil had never listened to a more affectionate voice; Corentin certainly seemed sincere, and spoke confidingly. The poor girl's heart was so open to generous impressions that she was on the point of betraying her secret to the serpent who had her in his folds, when it occurred to her that she had no proof beyond his own words of his sincerity, and she felt no scruple in blinding him.

"Yes," she said, "you are right, Corentin. I do love the marquis, but he does not love me—at least, I fear so; I can't help fearing that the appointment he wishes me to make with him is a trap."

"But you said yesterday that he came as far as Fougeres with you," returned Corentin. "If he had meant to do you bodily harm you wouldn't be here now."

"You've a cold heart, Corentin. You can draw shrewd conclusions as to the ordinary events of human life, but not on those of passion. Perhaps that is why you inspire me with such repulsion. As you are so clear-sighted, you may be able to tell me why a man from whom I separated myself violently two days ago now wishes me to meet him in a house at Florigny on the road to Mayenne."

At this avowal, which seemed to escape her with a recklessness that was not unnatural in so passionate a creature, Corentin flushed, for he was still young; but he gave her a sidelong penetrating look, trying to search her soul. The girl's artlessness was so well played, however, that she deceived the spy, and he answered with crafty good-humour, "Shall I accompany you at a distance? I can take a few solders with me, and be ready to help and obey you."

"Very good," she said; "but promise me, on your honour,—no, I don't believe in it; by your salvation,—but you don't believe in God; by your soul,—but I don't suppose you have any! what pledge *can* you give me of your fidelity? and yet you expect me to trust you, and put more than my life—my love, my vengeance—into your hands?"

The slight smile which crossed the pallid lips of the spy showed Mademoiselle de Verneuil the danger she had just escaped. The man, whose nostrils contracted instead of dilating, took the hand of his victim, kissed it with every mark of the deepest respect, and left the room with a bow that was not devoid of grace.

Three hours after this scene Mademoiselle de Verneuil, who feared the man's return, left the town furtively by the Porte Saint-Leonard, and made her way through the labyrinth of paths to the cottage of Galope-Chopine, led by the dream of at last finding happiness, and also by the purpose of saving her lover from the danger that threatened him.

During this time Corentin had gone to find the commandant. He had some difficulty in recognizing Hulot when he found him in a little square, where he was busy with certain military preparations. The brave veteran had made a sacrifice, the full merit of which may be difficult to appreciate. His queue and his moustache were cut off, and his hair had a sprinkling of powder. He had changed his uniform for a goatskin, wore hobnailed shoes, a belt full of pistols, and carried a heavy carbine. In this costume he was reviewing about two hundred of the natives of Fougeres, all in the same kind of dress, which was fitted to deceive the eye of the most practised Chouan. The warlike spirit of the little town and the Breton character were fully displayed in this scene, which was not at all uncommon. Here and there a few mothers and sisters were bringing to their sons and brothers gourds filled with brandy, or forgotten pistols. Several old men were examining into the number and condition of the cartridges of these young national guards dressed in the guise of Chouans, whose gaiety was more in keeping with a hunting expedition than the dangerous duty they were undertaking. To them, such encounters with *Chouannerie*, where the Breton of the town fought the Breton of the country district, had taken the place of the old chivalric tournaments. This patriotic enthusiasm may possibly have been connected with certain purchases of the "national domain." Still, the benefits of the Revolution which were better understood and appreciated in the towns, party spirit, and a certain national delight in war, had a great deal to do with their ardour.

Hulot, much gratified, was going through the ranks and getting information from Gudin, on whom he was now bestowing the confidence and good-will he had formerly shown to Merle and Gerard. A number of the inhabitants stood about watching the preparations, and comparing the conduct of their tumultuous contingent with the regulars of Hulot's brigade. Motionless and silent the Blues were awaiting, under control of their officers, the orders of the commandant, whose figure they followed with their eyes as he passed from rank to rank of the contingent. When Corentin came near the old warrior he could not help smiling at the change which had taken place in him. He looked like a portrait that has little or no resemblance to the original.

"What's all this?" asked Corentin.

"Come with us under fire, and you'll find out," replied Hulot.

"Oh! I'm not a Fougeres man," said Corentin.

"Easy to see that, citizen," retorted Gudin.

A few contemptuous laughs came from the nearest ranks.

"Do you think," said Corentin, sharply, "that the only way to serve France is with bayonets?"

Then he turned his back to the laughers, and asked a woman beside him if she knew the object of the expedition.

"Hey! my good man, the Chouans are at Florigny. They say there are more than three thousand, and they are coming to take Fougeres."

"Florigny?" cried Corentin, turning white; "then the rendezvous is not there! Is Florigny on the road to Mayenne?" he asked.

"There are not two Florignys," replied the woman, pointing in the direction of the summit of La Pelerine.

"Are you going in search of the Marquis de Montauran?" said Corentin to Hulot.

"Perhaps I am," answered the commandant, curtly.

"He is not at Florigny," said Corentin. "Send your troops there by all means; but keep a few of those imitation Chouans of yours with you, and wait for me."

"He is too malignant not to know what he's about," thought Hulot as Corentin made off rapidly, "he's the king of spies."

Hulot ordered the battalion to start. The republican soldiers marched without drums and silently through the narrow suburb which led to the Mayenne high-road, forming a blue and red line among the trees and houses. The disguised guard followed them; but Hulot, detaining Gudin and about a score of the smartest young fellows of the town, remained in the little square, awaiting Corentin, whose mysterious manner had piqued his curiosity. Francine herself told the astute spy, whose suspicions she changed into certainty, of her mistress's departure. Inquiring of the post guard at the Porte Saint-Leonard, he learned that Mademoiselle de Verneuil had passed that way. Rushing to the Promenade, he was, unfortunately, in time to see her movements. Though she was wearing a green dress and hood, to be less easily distinguished, the rapidity of her almost distracted step enabled him to follow her with his eye through the leafless hedges, and to guess the point towards which she was hurrying.

"Ha!" he cried, "you said you were going to Florigny, but you are in the valley of Gibarry! I am a fool, she has tricked me! No matter, I can light my lamp by day as well as by night."

Corentin, satisfied that he knew the place of the lovers' rendezvous, returned in all haste to the little square, which Hulot, resolved not to wait any longer, was just quitting to rejoin his troops.

"Halt, general!" he cried to the commandant, who turned round.

He then told Hulot the events relating to the marquis and Mademoiselle de Verneuil, and showed him the scheme of which he held a thread. Hulot, struck by his perspicacity, seized him by the arm.

"God's thunder! citizen, you are right," he cried. "The brigands are making a false attack over there to keep the coast clear; but the two columns I sent to scour the environs between Antrain and Vitre have not yet returned, so we shall have plenty of reinforcements if we need them; and I dare say we shall, for the *Gars* is not such a fool as to risk his life without a bodyguard of those damned owls. Gudin," he added, "go and tell Captain Lebrun that he must rub those fellows' noses at Florigny without me, and come back yourself in a flash. You know the paths. I'll wait till you return, and *then*—we'll avenge those murders at La Vivetiere. Thunder! how he runs," he added, seeing Gudin disappear as if by magic. "Gerard would have loved him."

On his return Gudin found Hulot's little band increased in numbers by the arrival of several soldiers taken from the various posts in the town. The commandant ordered him to choose a dozen of his compatriots who could best counterfeit the Chouans, and take them out by the Porte Saint-Leonard, so as to creep round the side of the Saint-Sulpice rocks which overlooks the valley of Couesnon and on which was the hovel of Galope-Chopine. Hulot himself went out with the rest of his troop by the Porte Saint-Sulpice, to reach the summit of the same rocks, where, according to his calculations, he ought to meet the men under Beau-Pied, whom he meant to use as a line of sentinels from the suburb of Saint-Sulpice to the Nid-aux-Crocs.

Corentin, satisfied with having delivered over the fate of the *Gars* to his implacable enemies, went with all speed to the Promenade, so as to follow with his eyes the military arrangements of the commandant. He soon saw Gudin's little squad issuing from the valley of the Nancon and following the line of the rocks to the great valley, while Hulot, creeping round the castle of Fougeres, was mounting the dangerous path which leads to the summit of Saint-Sulpice. The two companies were therefore advancing on parallel lines. The trees and shrubs, draped by the rich arabesques of the hoarfrost, threw whitish reflections which enabled the watcher to see the grey lines of the squads in motion. When Hulot reached the summit of the rocks, he detached all the soldiers in uniform from his main body, and made them into a line of sentinels, each communicating with the other, the first with Gudin, the last with Hulot; so that no shrub could escape the bayonets of the three lines which were now in a position to hunt the *Gars* across field and mountain.

"The sly old wolf!" thought Corentin, as the shining muzzle of the last gun disappeared in the bushes. "The *Gars* is done for. If Marie had only betrayed that damned marquis, she and I would have been united in the strongest of all bonds—a vile deed. But she's mine, in any case."

The twelve young men under Gudin soon reached the base of the rocks of Saint-Sulpice. Here Gudin himself left the road with six of them, jumping the stiff hedge into the first field of gorse that he came to, while the other six by his orders did the same on the other side of the road. Gudin advanced to an apple-tree which happened to be in the middle of the field. Hearing the rustle of this movement through the gorse, seven or eight men, at the head of whom was Beau-Pied, hastily hid behind some chestnut-trees which topped the bank of this particular field. Gudin's men did not see them, in spite of the white reflections of the hoar-frost and their own practised sight.

"Hush! here they are," said Beau-Pied, cautiously putting out his head. "The brigands have more men than we, but we have 'em at the muzzles of our guns, and we mustn't miss them, or, by the Lord, we are not fit to be soldiers of the pope."

By this time Gudin's keen eyes had discovered a few muzzles pointing through the branches at his little squad. Just then eight voices cried in derision, *"Qui vive?"* and eight shots followed. The balls whistled round Gudin and his men. One fell, another was shot in the arm. The five others who were safe and sound replied with a volley and the cry, "Friends!" Then they marched rapidly on their assailants so as to reach them before they had time to reload.

"We did not know how true we spoke," cried Gudin, as he recognized the uniforms and the battered hats of his own brigade. "Well, we behaved like Bretons, and fought before explaining."

The other men were stupefied on recognizing the little company.

"Who the devil would have known them in those goatskins?" cried Beau-Pied, dismally.

"It is a misfortune," said Gudin, "but we are all innocent if you were not informed of the sortie. What are you doing here?" he asked.

"A dozen of those Chouans are amusing themselves by picking us off, and we are getting away as best we can, like poisoned rats; but by dint of scrambling over these hedges and rocks—may the lightning blast 'em!—our compasses have got so rusty we are forced to take a rest. I think those brigands are now somewhere near the old hovel where you see that smoke."

"Good!" cried Gudin. "You," he added to Beau-Pied and his men, "fall back towards the rocks through the fields, and join the line of sentinels you'll find there. You can't go with us, because you are in uniform. We mean to make an end of those curs now; the *Gars* is with them. I can't stop to tell you more. To the right, march! and don't administer any more shots to our own goatskins; you'll know ours by their cravats, which they twist round their necks and don't tie."

Gudin left his two wounded men under the apple-tree, and marched towards Galope-Chopine's cottage, which Beau-Pied had pointed out to him, the smoke from the chimney serving as a guide.

While the young officer was thus closing in upon the Chouans, the little detachment under Hulot had reached a point still parallel with that at which Gudin had arrived. The old soldier, at the head of his men, was silently gliding along the hedges with the ardour of a young man; he jumped them from time to time actively enough, casting his wary eyes to the heights and listening with the ear of a hunter to every noise. In the third field to which he came he found a woman about thirty years old, with bent back, hoeing the ground vigorously, while a small boy with a sickle in his hand was knocking the hoarfrost from the rushes, which he cut and laid in a heap. At the noise Hulot made in jumping the hedge, the boy and his mother raised their heads. Hulot mistook the young woman for an old one, naturally enough. Wrinkles, coming long before their time, furrowed her face and neck; she was clothed so grotesquely in a worn-out goatskin that if it had not been for a dirty yellow petticoat, a distinctive mark of sex, Hulot would hardly have known the gender she belonged to; for the meshes of her long black hair were twisted up and hidden by a red worsted cap. The tatters of the little boy did not cover him, but left his skin exposed.

"Ho! old woman!" called Hulot, in a low voice, approaching her, "where is the *Gars*?"

The twenty men who accompanied Hulot now jumped the hedge.

"Hey! if you want the *Gars* you'll have to go back the way you came," said the woman, with a suspicious glance at the troop.

"Did I ask you the road to Fougeres, old carcass?" said Hulot, roughly. "By Saint-Anne of Auray, have you seen the *Gars* go by?"

"I don't know what you mean," replied the woman, bending over her hoe.

"You damned *garce*, do you want to have us eaten up by the Blues who are after us?"

At these words the woman raised her head and gave another look of distrust at the troop as she replied, "How can the Blues be after you? I have just seen eight or ten of them who were going back to Fougeres by the lower road."

"One would think she meant to stab us with that nose of hers!" cried Hulot. "Here, look, you old nanny-goat!"

And he showed her in the distance three or four of his sentinels, whose hats, guns, and uniforms it was easy to recognize.

"Are you going to let those fellows cut the throats of men who are sent by Marche-a-Terre to protect the *Gars*?" he cried, angrily.

"Ah, beg pardon," said the woman; "but it is so easy to be deceived. What parish do you belong to?"

"Saint-Georges," replied two or three of the men, in the Breton patois, "and we are dying of hunger."

"Well, there," said the woman; "do you see that smoke down there? that's my house. Follow the path to the right, and you will come to the rock above it. Perhaps you'll meet my man on the way. Galope-Chopine is sure to be on watch to warn the *Gars*. He is spending the day in our house," she said, proudly, "as you seem to know."

"Thank you, my good woman," replied Hulot. "Forward, march! God's thunder! we've got him," he added, speaking to his men.

The detachment followed its leader at a quick step through the path pointed out to them. The wife of Galope-Chopine turned pale as she heard the un-Catholic oath of the so-called Chouan. She looked at the gaiters and goatskins of his men, then she caught her boy in her arms, and sat down on the ground, saying, "May the holy Virgin of Auray and the ever blessed Saint-Labre have pity upon us! Those men are not ours; their shoes have no nails in them. Run down by the lower road and warn your father; you may save his head," she said to the boy, who disappeared like a deer among the bushes.

****

Mademoiselle de Verneuil met no one on her way, neither Blues nor Chouans. Seeing the column of blue smoke which was rising from the half-ruined chimney of Galope-Chopine's melancholy dwelling, her heart was seized with a violent palpitation, the rapid, sonorous beating of which rose to her throat in waves. She stopped, rested her hand against a tree, and watched the smoke which was serving as a beacon to the foes as well as to the friends of the young chieftain. Never had she felt such overwhelming emotion.

"Ah! I love him too much," she said, with a sort of despair. "Today, perhaps, I shall no longer be mistress of myself—"

She hurried over the distance which separated her from the cottage, and reached the courtyard, the filth of which was now stiffened by the frost. The big dog sprang up barking, but a word from Galope-Chopine silenced him and he wagged his tail. As she entered the house Marie gave a look which included everything. The marquis was not there. She breathed more freely, and saw with pleasure that the Chouan had taken some pains to clean the dirty and only room in his hovel. He now took his duck-gun, bowed silently to his guest and left the house, followed by his dog. Marie went to the threshold of the door and watched him as he took the path to the right of his hut. From there she could overlook a series of fields, the curious openings to which formed a perspective of gates; for the leafless trees and hedges were no longer a barrier to a full view of the country. When the Chouan's broad hat was out of sight Mademoiselle de Verneuil turned round to look for the church at Fougeres, but the shed concealed it. She cast her eyes over the valley of the Couesnon, which lay before her like a vast sheet of muslin, the whiteness of which still further dulled a grey sky laden with snow. It was one of those days when nature seems dumb and noises are absorbed by the atmosphere. Therefore, though the Blues and their contingent were marching through the country in three lines, forming a triangle which drew together as they neared the cottage, the silence was so profound that Mademoiselle de Verneuil was overcome by a presentiment which added a sort of physical pain to her mental torture. Misfortune was in the air.

At last, in a spot where a little curtain of wood closed the perspective of gates, she saw a young man jumping the barriers like a squirrel and running with astonishing rapidity. "It is he!" she thought.

The *Gars* was dressed as a Chouan, with a musket slung from his shoulder over his goatskin, and would have been quite disguised were it not for the grace of his movements. Marie withdrew hastily into the cottage, obeying one of those instinctive promptings which are as little explicable as fear itself. The young man was soon beside her before the chimney, where a bright fire was burning. Both were voiceless, fearing to look at each other, or even to make a movement. One and the same hope united them, the same doubt; it was agony, it was joy.

"Monsieur," said Mademoiselle de Verneuil at last, in a trembling voice, "your safety alone has brought me here."

"My safety!" he said, bitterly.

"Yes," she answered; "so long as I stay at Fougeres your life is threatened, and I love you too well not to leave it. I go tonight."

"Leave me! ah, dear love, I shall follow you."

"Follow me!—the Blues?"

"Dear Marie, what have the Blues got to do with our love?"

"But it seems impossible that you can stay with me in France, and still more impossible that you should leave it with me."

"Is there anything impossible to those who love?"

"Ah, true! true! all is possible—have I not the courage to resign you, for your sake."

"What! you could give yourself to a hateful being whom you did not love, and you refuse to make the happiness of a man who adores you, whose life you fill, who swears to be yours, and yours only. Hear me, Marie, do you love me?"

"Yes," she said.

"Then be mine."

"You forget the infamous career of a lost woman; I return to it, I leave you—yes, that I may not bring upon your head the contempt that falls on mine. Without that fear, perhaps—"

"But if I fear nothing?"

"Can I be sure of that? I am distrustful. Who could be otherwise in a position like mine? If the love we inspire cannot last at least it should be complete, and help us to bear with joy the injustice of the world. But you, what have you done for me? You desire me. Do you think that lifts you above other men? Suppose I bade you renounce your ideas, your hopes, your king (who will, perhaps, laugh when he hears you have died for him, while I would die for you with sacred joy!); or suppose I should ask you to send your submission to the First Consul so that you could follow me to Paris, or go with me to America,—away from the world where all is vanity; suppose I thus tested you, to know if you loved me for myself as at this moment I love you? To say all in a word, if I wished, instead of rising to your level, that you should fall to mine, what would you do?"

"Hush, Marie, be silent, do not slander yourself," he cried. "Poor child, I comprehend you. If my first desire was passion, my passion now is love. Dear soul of my soul, you are as noble as your name, I know it,—as great as you are beautiful. I am noble enough, I feel myself great enough to force the world to receive you. Is it because I foresee in you the source of endless, incessant pleasure, or because I find in your soul those precious qualities which make a man forever love the one woman? I do not know the cause, but this I know—that my love for you is boundless. I know I can no longer live without you. Yes, life would be unbearable unless you are ever with me."

"Ever with you!"

"Ah! Marie, will you not understand me?"

"You think to flatter me by the offer of your hand and name," she said, with apparent haughtiness, but looking fixedly at the marquis as if to detect his inmost thought. "How do you know you would love me six months hence? and then what would be my fate? No, a mistress is the only woman who is sure of a man's heart; duty, law, society, the interests of children, are poor auxiliaries. If her power lasts it gives her joys and flatteries which make the trials of life endurable. But to be your wife and become a drag upon you,—rather than that, I prefer a passing love and a true one, though death and misery be its end. Yes, I could be a virtuous mother, a devoted wife; but to keep those instincts firmly in a woman's soul the man must not marry her in a rush of passion. Besides, how do I know that you will please me tomorrow? No, I will not bring evil upon you; I leave Brittany," she said, observing hesitation in his eyes. "I return to Fougeres now, where you cannot come to me—"

"I can! and if tomorrow you see smoke on the rocks of Saint-Sulpice you will know that I shall be with you at night, your lover, your husband,—what you will that I be to you; I brave all!"

"Ah! Alphonse, you love me well," she said, passionately, "to risk your life before you give it to me."

He did not answer; he looked at her and her eyes fell; but he read in her ardent face a passion equal to his own, and he held out his arms to her. A sort of madness overcame her, and she let herself fall softly on his breast, resolved to yield to him, and turn this yielding to great results,—staking upon it her future happiness, which would become more certain if she came victorious from this crucial test. But her head had scarcely touched her lover's shoulder when a slight noise was heard without. She tore herself from his arms as if suddenly awakened, and sprang from the cottage. Her coolness came back to her, and she thought of the situation.

"He might have accepted me and scorned me," she reflected. "Ah! if I could think that, I would kill him. But not yet!" she added, catching sight of Beau-Pied, to whom she made a sign which the soldier was quick to understand. He turned on his heel, pretending to have seen nothing. Mademoiselle de Verneuil re-entered the cottage, putting her finger to her lips to enjoin silence.

"They are there!" she whispered in a frightened voice.

"Who?"

"The Blues."

"Ah! must I die without one kiss!"

"Take it," she said.

He caught her to him, cold and unresisting, and gathered from her lips a kiss of horror and of joy, for while it was the first, it might also be the last. Then they went together to the door and looked cautiously out. The marquis saw Gudin and his men holding the paths leading to the valley. Then he turned to the line of gates where the first rotten trunk was guarded by five men. Without an instant's pause he jumped on the barrel of cider and struck a hole through the thatch of the roof, from which to spring upon the rocks behind the house; but he drew his head hastily back through the gap he had made, for Hulot was on the height; his retreat was cut off in that direction. The marquis turned and looked at his mistress, who uttered a cry of despair; for she heard the tramp of the three detachments near the house.

"Go out first," he said; "you shall save me."

Hearing the words, to her all-glorious, she went out and stood before the door. The marquis loaded his musket. Measuring with his eye the space between the door of the hut and the old rotten trunk where seven men stood, the *Gars* fired into their midst and sprang forward instantly, forcing a passage through them. The three troops rushed towards the opening through which he had passed, and saw him running across the field with incredible celerity.

"Fire! fire! a thousand devils! You're not Frenchmen! Fire, I say!" called Hulot.

As he shouted these words from the height above, his men and Gudin's fired a volley, which was fortunately ill-aimed. The marquis reached the gate of the next field, but as he did so he was almost caught by Gudin, who was close upon his heels. The *Gars* redoubled his speed. Nevertheless, he and his pursuer reached the next barrier together; but the marquis dashed his musket at Gudin's head with so good an aim that he stopped his rush. It is impossible to depict the anxiety betrayed by Marie, or the interest of Hulot and his troops as they watched the scene. They all, unconsciously or silently, repeated the gestures which they saw the runners making. The *Gars* and Gudin reached the little wood together, but as they did so the latter stopped and darted behind a tree. About twenty Chouans, afraid to fire at a distance lest they should kill their leader, rushed from the copse and riddled the tree with balls. Hulot's men advanced at a run to save Gudin, who, being without arms, retreated from tree to tree, seizing his opportunity as the Chouans reloaded. His danger was soon over. Hulot and the Blues met him at the spot where the marquis had thrown his musket. At this instant Gudin perceived his adversary sitting among the trees and out of breath, and he left his comrades firing at the Chouans, who had retreated behind a lateral hedge; slipping round them, he darted towards the marquis with the agility of a wild animal. Observing this manoeuvre the Chouans set up a cry to warn their leader; then, having fired on the Blues and their contingent with the gusto of poachers, they boldly made a rush for them; but Hulot's men sprang through the hedge which served them as a rampart and took a bloody revenge. The Chouans then gained the road which skirted the fields and took to the heights which Hulot had committed the blunder of abandoning. Before the Blues had time to reform, the Chouans were entrenched behind the rocks, where they could fire with impunity on the Republicans if the latter made any attempt to dislodge them.

While Hulot and his soldiers went slowly towards the little wood to meet Gudin, the men from Fougeres busied themselves in rifling the dead Chouans and dispatching those who still lived. In this fearful war neither party took prisoners. The marquis having made good his escape, the Chouans and the Blues mutually recognized their respective positions and the uselessness of continuing the fight; so that both sides prepared to retreat.

"Ha! ha!" cried one of the Fougeres men, busy about the bodies, "here's a bird with yellow wings."

And he showed his companions a purse full of gold which he had just found in the pocket of a stout man dressed in black.

"What's this?" said another, pulling a breviary from the dead man's coat.

"Communion bread—he's a priest!" cried the first man, flinging the breviary on the ground.

"Here's a wretch!" cried a third, finding only two crowns in the pockets of the body he was stripping, "a cheat!"

"But he's got a fine pair of shoes!" said a soldier, beginning to pull them off.

"You can't have them unless they fall to your share," said the Fougeres man, dragging the dead feet away and flinging the boots on a heap of clothing already collected.

Another Chouan took charge of the money, so that lots might be drawn as soon as the troops were all assembled. When Hulot returned with Gudin, whose last attempt to overtake the *Gars* was useless as well as perilous, he found about a score of his own men and thirty of the contingent standing around eleven of the enemy, whose naked bodies were thrown into a ditch at the foot of the bank.

"Soldiers!" cried Hulot, sternly. "I forbid you to share that clothing. Form in line, quick!"

"Commandant," said a soldier, pointing to his shoes, at the points of which five bare toes could be seen on each foot, "all right about the money, but those boots," motioning to a pair of hobnailed boots with the butt of his gun, "would fit me like a glove."

"Do you want to put English shoes on your feet?" retorted Hulot.

"But," said one of the Fougeres men, respectfully, "we've divided the booty all through the war."

"I don't prevent you civilians from following your own ways," replied Hulot, roughly.

"Here, Gudin, here's a purse with three *louis*," said the officer who was distributing the money. "You have run hard and the commandant won't prevent your taking it."

Hulot looked askance at Gudin, and saw that he turned pale.

"It's my uncle's purse!" exclaimed the young man.

Exhausted as he was with his run, he sprang to the mound of bodies, and the first that met his eyes was that of his uncle. But he had hardly recognized the rubicund face now furrowed with blue lines, and seen the stiffened arms and the gunshot wound before he gave a stifled cry, exclaiming, "Let us be off, commandant."

The Blues started. Hulot gave his arm to his young friend.

"God's thunder!" he cried. "Never mind, it is no great matter."

"But he is dead," said Gudin, "dead! He was my only relation, and though he cursed me, still he loved me. If the king returns, the neighbourhood will want my head, and my poor uncle would have saved it."

"What a fool Gudin is," said one of the men who had stayed behind to share the spoils; "his uncle was rich, and he hasn't had time to make a will and disinherit him."

The division over, the men of Fougeres rejoined the little battalion of the Blues on their way to the town.

****

Towards midnight the cottage of Galope-Chopine, hitherto the scene of life without a care, was full of dread and horrible anxiety. Barbette and her little boy returned at the supper-hour, one with her heavy burden of rushes, the other carrying fodder for the cattle. Entering the hut, they looked about in vain for Galope-Chopine; the miserable chamber never looked to them as large, so empty was it. The fire was out, and the darkness, the silence, seemed to tell of some disaster. Barbette hastened to make a blaze, and to light two *ori-bus*, the name given to candles made of pitch in the region between the villages of Amorique and the Upper Loire, and still used beyond Amboise in the Vendomois districts. Barbette did these things with the slowness of a person absorbed in one overpowering feeling. She listened to every sound. Deceived by the whistling of the wind she went often to the door of the hut, returning sadly. She cleaned two beakers, filled them with cider, and placed them on the long table. Now and again she looked at her boy, who watched the baking of the buckwheat cakes, but did not speak to him. The lad's eyes happened to rest on the nails which usually held his father's duck-gun, and Barbette trembled as she noticed that the gun was gone. The silence was broken only by the lowing of a cow or the splash of the cider as it dropped at regular intervals from the bung of the cask. The poor woman sighed while she poured into three brown earthenware porringers a sort of soup made of milk, biscuit broken into bits, and boiled chestnuts.

"They must have fought in the field next to the Berandiere," said the boy.

"Go and see," replied his mother.

The child ran to the place where the fighting had, as he said, taken place. In the moonlight he found the heap of bodies, but his father was not among them, and he came back whistling joyously, having picked up several five-*franc* pieces trampled in the mud and overlooked by the victors. His mother was sitting on a stool beside the fire, employed in spinning flax. He made a negative sign to her, and then, ten o'clock having struck from the tower of Saint-Leonard, he went to bed, muttering a prayer to the holy Virgin of Auray. At dawn, Barbette, who had not closed her eyes, gave a cry of joy, as she heard in the distance a sound she knew well of hobnailed shoes, and soon after Galope-Chopine's scowling face presented itself.

"Thanks to Saint-Labre," he said, "to whom I owe a candle, the *Gars* is safe. Don't forget that we now owe three candles to the saint."

He seized a beaker of cider and emptied it at a draught without drawing breath. When his wife had served his soup and taken his gun and he himself was seated on the wooden bench, he said, looking at the fire:

"I can't make out how the Blues got here. The fighting was at Fl-origny. Who the devil could have told them that the *Gars* was in our house; no one knew it but he and the handsome *garce* and we—"

Barbette turned white.

"They made me believe they were the *gars* of Saint-Georges," she said, trembling, "it was I who told them the *Gars* was here."

Galope-Chopine turned pale himself and dropped his porringer on the table.

"I sent the boy to warn you," said Barbette, frightened, "didn't you meet him?"

The Chouan rose and struck his wife so violently that she dropped, pale as death, upon the bed.

"You cursed woman," he said, "you have killed me!" Then seized with remorse, he took her in his arms. "Barbette!" he cried, "Barbette!—Holy Virgin, my hand was too heavy!"

"Do you think," she said, opening her eyes, "that Marche-a-Terre will hear of it?"

"The *Gars* will certainly inquire who betrayed him."

"Will he tell it to Marche-a-Terre?"

"Marche-a-Terre and Pille-Miche were both at Florigny."

Barbette breathed a little easier.

"If they touch a hair of your head," she cried, "I'll rinse their glasses with vinegar."

"Ah! I can't eat," said Galope-Chopine, anxiously.

His wife set another pitcher full of cider before him, but he paid no heed to it. Two big tears rolled from the woman's eyes and moistened the deep furrows of her withered face.

"Listen to me, wife; tomorrow morning you must gather fagots on the rocks of Saint-Sulpice, to the right and Saint-Leonard and set fire to them. That is a signal agreed upon between the *Gars* and the old rector of Saint-Georges who is to come and say mass for him."

"Is the *Gars* going to Fougeres?"

"Yes, to see his handsome *garce*. I have been sent here and there all day about it. I think he is going to marry her and carry her off; for he told me to hire horses and have them ready on the road to Saint-Malo."

Thereupon Galope-Chopine, who was tired out, went to bed for an hour or two, at the end of which time he again departed. Later, on the following morning, he returned, having carefully fulfilled all the commissions entrusted to him by the *Gars*. Finding that Marche-a-Terre and Pille-Miche had not appeared at the cottage, he relieved the apprehensions of his wife, who went off, reassured, to the rocks of Saint-Sulpice, where she had collected the night before several piles of fagots, now covered with hoarfrost. The boy went with her, carrying fire in a broken wooden shoe.

Hardly had his wife and son passed out of sight behind the shed when Galope-Chopine heard the noise of men jumping the successive barriers, and he could dimly see, through the fog which was growing thicker, the forms of two men like moving shadows.

"It is Marche-a-Terre and Pille-Miche," he said, mentally; then he shuddered. The two Chouans entered the courtyard and showed their gloomy faces under the broad-brimmed hats which made them look like the figures which engravers introduce into their landscapes.

"Good-morning, Galope-Chopine," said Marche-a-Terre, gravely.

"Good-morning, Monsieur Marche-a-Terre," replied the other, humbly. "Will you come in and drink a drop? I've some cold buckwheat cake and fresh-made butter."

"That's not to be refused, cousin," said Pille-Miche.

The two Chouans entered the cottage. So far there was nothing alarming for the master of the house, who hastened to fill three beakers from his huge cask of cider, while Marche-a-Terre and Pille-Miche, sitting on the polished benches on each side of the long table, cut the cake and spread it with the rich yellow butter from which the milk spurted as the knife smoothed it. Galope-Chopine placed the beakers full of frothing cider before his guests, and the three Chouans began to eat; but from time to time the master of the house cast sidelong glances at Marche-a-Terre as he drank his cider.

"Lend me your snuff-box," said Marche-a-Terre to Pille-Miche.

Having shaken several pinches into the palm of his hand the Breton inhaled the tobacco like a man who is making ready for serious business.

"It is cold," said Pille-Miche, rising to shut the upper half of the door.

The daylight, already dim with fog, now entered only through the little window, and feebly lighted the room and the two seats; the fire, however, gave out a ruddy glow. Galope-Chopine refilled the beakers, but his guests refused to drink again, and throwing aside their large hats looked at him solemnly. Their gestures and the look they gave him terrified Galope-Chopine, who fancied he saw blood in the red woollen caps they wore.

"Fetch your axe," said Marche-a-Terre.

"But, Monsieur Marche-a-Terre, what do you want it for?"

"Come, cousin, you know very well," said Pille-Miche, pocketing his snuff-box which Marche-a-Terre returned to him; "you are condemned."

The two Chouans rose together and took their guns.

"Monsieur Marche-a-Terre, I never said one word about the *Gars*—"

224

"I told you to fetch your axe," said Marche-a-Terre.

The hapless man knocked against the wooden bedstead of his son, and several five-*franc* pieces rolled on the floor. Pille-Miche picked them up.

"Ho! ho! the Blues paid you in new money," cried Marche-a-Terre.

"As true as that's the image of Saint-Labre," said Galope-Chopine, "I have told nothing. Barbette mistook the Fougeres men for the *gars* of Saint-Georges, and that's the whole of it."

"Why do you tell things to your wife?" said Marche-a-Terre, roughly.

"Besides, cousin, we don't want excuses, we want your axe. You are condemned."

At a sign from his companion, Pille-Miche helped Marche-a-Terre to seize the victim. Finding himself in their grasp Galope-Chopine lost all power and fell on his knees holding up his hands to his slayers in desperation.

"My friends, my good friends, my cousin," he said, "what will become of my little boy?"

"I will take charge of him," said Marche-a-Terre.

"My good comrades," cried the victim, turning livid. "I am not fit to die. Don't make me go without confession. You have the right to take my life, but you've no right to make me lose a blessed eternity."

"That is true," said Marche-a-Terre, addressing Pille-Miche.

The two Chouans waited a moment in much uncertainty, unable to decide this case of conscience. Galope-Chopine listened to the rustling of the wind as though he still had hope. Suddenly Pille-Miche took him by the arm into a corner of the hut.

"Confess your sins to me," he said, "and I will tell them to a priest of the true Church, and if there is any penance to do I will do it for you."

Galope-Chopine obtained some respite by the way in which he confessed his sins; but in spite of their number and the circumstances of each crime, he came finally to the end of them.

"Cousin," he said, imploringly, "since I am speaking to you as I would to my confessor, I do assure you, by the holy name of God, that I have nothing to reproach myself with except for having, now and then, buttered my bread on both sides; and I call on Saint-Labre, who is there over the chimney-piece, to witness that I have never said one word about the *Gars*. No, my good friends, I have not betrayed him."

"Very good, that will do, cousin; you can explain all that to God in course of time."

"But let me say good-bye to Barbette."

"Come," said Marche-a-Terre, "if you don't want us to think you worse than you are, behave like a Breton and be done with it."

The two Chouans seized him again and threw him on the bench where he gave no other sign of resistance than the instinctive and convulsive motions of an animal, uttering a few smothered groans, which ceased when the axe fell. The head was off at the first blow. Marche-a-Terre took it by the hair, left the room, sought and found a large nail in the rough casing of the door, and wound the hair about it; leaving the bloody head, the eyes of which he did not even close, to hang there.

The two Chouans then washed their hands, without the least haste, in a pot full of water, picked up their hats and guns, and jumped the gate, whistling the "Ballad of the Captain." Pille-Miche began to sing in a hoarse voice as he reached the field the last verses of that rustic song, their melody floating on the breeze:—

"At the first town
"Her lover dressed her
"All in white satin;

"At the next town
"Her lover dressed her
"In gold and silver.

"So beautiful was she
"They gave her veils
"To wear in the regiment."

The tune became gradually indistinguishable as the Chouans got further away; but the silence of the country was so great that several of the notes reached Barbette's ear as she neared home, holding her boy by the hand. A peasant-woman never listens coldly to that song, so popular is it in the West of France, and Barbette began, unconsciously, to sing the first verses:—

"Come, let us go, my girl,
"Let us go to the war;
"Let us go, it is time.

"Brave captain,
"Let it not trouble you,
"But my daughter is not for you.

"You shall not have her on earth,
"You shall not have her at sea,
"Unless by treachery.

"The father took his daughter,
"He unclothed her
"And flung her out to sea.

"The captain, wiser still,
"Into the waves he jumped
"And to the shore he brought her.

"Come, let us go, my girl,
"Let us go to the war;
"Let us go, it is time.

"At the first town
"Her lover dressed her," Etc., etc.

As Barbette reached this verse of the song, where Pille-Miche had begun it, she was entering the courtyard of her home; her tongue suddenly stiffened, she stood still, and a great cry, quickly repressed, came from her gaping lips.

"What is it, mother?" said the child.

"Walk alone," she cried, pulling her hand away and pushing him roughly; "you have neither father nor mother."

The child, who was rubbing his shoulder and weeping, suddenly caught sight of the thing on the nail; his childlike face kept the nervous convulsion his crying had caused, but he was silent. He opened his eyes wide, and gazed at the head of his father with a stupid look which betrayed no emotion; then his face, brutalized by ignorance, showed savage curiosity. Barbette again took his hand, grasped it violently, and dragged him into the house. When Pille-Miche and Marche-a-Terre threw their victim on the bench one of his shoes, dropping off, fell on the floor beneath his neck and was afterward filled with blood. It was the first thing that met the widow's eye.

"Take off your shoe," said the mother to her son. "Put your foot in that. Good. Remember," she cried, in a solemn voice, "your father's shoe; never put on your own without remembering how the Chouans filled it with his blood, and *kill the Chouans!*"

She swayed her head with so convulsive an action that the meshes of her black hair fell upon her neck and gave a sinister expression to her face.

"I call Saint-Labre to witness," she said, "that I vow you to the Blues. You shall be a soldier to avenge your father. Kill, kill the *Chouans*, and do as I do. Ha! they've taken the head of my man, and I am going to give that of the *Gars* to the Blues."

She sprang at a bound on the bed, seized a little bag of money from a hiding-place, took the hand of the astonished little boy, and dragged him after her without giving him time to put on his shoe, and was on her way to Fougeres rapidly, without once turning her head to look at the home she abandoned. When they reached the summit of the rocks of Saint-Sulpice Barbette set fire to the pile of fagots, and the boy helped her to pile on the green gorse, damp with hoarfrost, to make the smoke more dense.

"That fire will last longer than your father, longer than I, longer than the *Gars*," said Barbette, in a savage voice.

While the widow of Galope-Chopine and her son with his bloody foot stood watching, the one, with a gloomy expression of revenge, the other with curiosity, the curling of the smoke, Mademoiselle de Verneuil's eyes were fastened on the same rock, trying, but in vain, to see her lover's signal. The fog, which had thickened, buried the whole region under a veil, its grey tints obscuring even the outlines of the scenery that was nearest the town. She examined with tender anxiety the rocks, the castle, the buildings, which loomed like shadows through the mist. Near her window several trees stood out against this blue-grey background; the sun gave a dull tone as of tarnished silver to the sky; its rays coloured the bare branches of the trees, where a few last leaves were fluttering, with a dingy red. But too many dear and delightful sentiments filled Marie's soul to let her notice the ill-omens of a scene so out of harmony with the joys she was tasting in advance. For the last two days her ideas had undergone a change. The fierce, undisciplined vehemence of her passions had yielded under the influence of the equable atmosphere which a true love gives to life. The certainty of being loved, sought through so many perils, had given birth to a desire to re-enter those social conditions which sanction love, and which despair alone had made her leave. To love for a moment only now seemed to her a species of weakness. She saw herself lifted from the dregs of society, where misfortune had driven her, to the high rank in which her father had meant to place her. Her vanity, repressed for a time by the cruel alternations of hope and misconception, was awakened and showed her all the benefits of a great position. Born in a certain way to rank, marriage to a marquis meant, to her mind, living and acting in the sphere that belonged to her. Having known the chances and changes of an adventurous life, she could appreciate, better than other women, the grandeur of the feelings which make the Family. Marriage and motherhood with all their cares seemed to her less a task than a rest. She loved the calm and virtuous life she saw through the clouds of this last storm as a woman weary of virtue may sometimes covet an illicit passion. Virtue was to her a new seduction.

"Perhaps," she thought, leaving the window without seeing the signal on the rocks of Saint-Sulpice, "I have been too coquettish with him—but I knew he loved me! Francine, it is not a dream; tonight I shall be Marquise de Montauran. What have I done to deserve such perfect happiness? Oh! I love him, and love alone is love's reward. And yet, I think God means to recompense me for taking heart through all my misery; he means me to forget my sufferings—for you know, Francine, I have suffered."

"Tonight, Marquise de Montauran, you, Marie? Ah! until it is done I cannot believe it! Who has told him your true goodness?"

"Dear child! he has more than his handsome eyes to see me with, he has a soul. If you had seen him, as I have, in danger! Oh! he knows how to love—he is so brave!"

"If you really love him why do you let him come to Fougeres?"

"We had no time to say one word to each other when the Blues surprised us. Besides, his coming is a proof of love. Can I ever have proofs enough? And now, Francine, do my hair."

But she pulled it down a score of times with motions that seemed electric, as though some stormy thoughts were mingling still with the arts of her coquetry. As she rolled a curl or smoothed the shining plaits she asked herself, with a remnant of distrust, whether the marquis were deceiving her; but treachery seemed to her impossible, for did he not expose himself to instant vengeance by entering Fougeres? While studying in her mirror the effects of a sidelong glance, a smile, a gentle frown, an attitude of anger, or of love, or disdain, she was seeking some woman's wile by which to probe to the last instant the heart of the young leader.

"You are right, Francine," she said; "I wish with you that the marriage were over. This is the last of my cloudy days—it is big with death or happiness. Oh! that fog is dreadful," she went on, again looking towards the heights of Saint-Sulpice, which were still veiled in mist.

She began to arrange the silk and muslin curtains which draped the window, making them intercept the light and produce in the room a voluptuous *chiaroscuro*.

"Francine," she said, "take away those knick-knacks on the mantelpiece; leave only the clock and the two Dresden vases. I'll fill those vases myself with the flowers Corentin brought me. Take out the chairs, I want only this sofa and a *fauteuil*. Then sweep the carpet, so as to bring out the colours, and put wax candles in the sconces and on the mantel."

Marie looked long and carefully at the old tapestry on the walls. Guided by her innate taste she found among the brilliant tints of these

229

hangings the shades by which to connect their antique beauty with the furniture and accessories of the boudoir, either by the harmony of colour or the charm of contrast. The same thought guided the arrangement of the flowers with which she filled the twisted vases which decorated her chamber. The sofa was placed beside the fire. On either side of the bed, which filled the space parallel to that of the chimney, she placed on gilded tables tall Dresden vases filled with foliage and flowers that were sweetly fragrant. She quivered more than once as she arranged the folds of the green damask above the bed, and studied the fall of the drapery which concealed it. Such preparations have a secret, ineffable happiness about them; they cause so many de-lightful emotions that a woman as she makes them forgets her doubts; and Mademoiselle de Verneuil forgot hers. There is in truth a religious sentiment in the multiplicity of cares taken for one beloved who is not there to see them and reward them, but who will reward them later with the approving smile these tender preparations (always so fully understood) obtain. Women, as they make them, love in advance; and there are few indeed who would not say to themselves, as Mad-emoiselle de Verneuil now thought: "Tonight I shall be happy!" That soft hope lies in every fold of silk or muslin; insensibly, the harmony the woman makes about her gives an atmosphere of love in which she breathes; to her these things are beings, witnesses; she has made them the sharers of her coming joy. Every movement, every thought brings that joy within her grasp. But presently she expects no longer, she hopes no more, she questions silence; the slightest sound is to her an omen; doubt hooks its claws once more into her heart; she burns, she trembles, she is grasped by a thought which holds her like a physical force; she alternates from triumph to agony, and without the hope of coming happiness she could not endure the torture. A score of times did Mademoiselle de Verneuil raise the window-curtain, hoping to see the smoke rising above the rocks; but the fog only took a greyer tone, which her excited imagination turned into a warning. At last she let fall the curtain, impatiently resolving not to raise it again. She looked gloomily around the charming room to which she had given a soul and a voice, asking herself if it were done in vain, and this thought brought her back to her preparations.

"Francine," she said, drawing her into a little dressing-room which adjoined her chamber and was lighted through a small round window opening on a dark corner of the fortifications where they joined the rock terrace of the Promenade, "put everything in order. As for the salon, you can leave that as it is," she added, with a smile which women reserve for their nearest friends, the delicate senti-ment of which men seldom understand.

"Ah! how sweet you are!" exclaimed the little maid.

"A lover is our beauty—foolish women that we are!" she replied gaily.

Francine left her lying on the ottoman and went away convinced that, whether her mistress were loved or not, she would never betray Montauran.

****

"Are you sure of what you are telling me, old woman?" Hulot was saying to Barbette, who had sought him out as soon as she had reached Fougeres.

"Have you got eyes? Look at the rocks of Saint-Sulpice, there, my good man, to the right of Saint-Leonard."

Corentin, who was with Hulot, looked towards the summit in the direction pointed out by Barbette, and, as the fog was beginning to lift, he could see with some distinctness the column of white smoke the woman told of.

"But when is he coming, old woman?—tonight, or this evening?"

"My good man," said Barbette, "I don't know."

"Why do you betray your own side?" said Hulot, quickly, having drawn her out of hearing of Corentin.

"Ah! general, see my boy's foot—that's washed in the blood of my man, whom the Chouans have killed like a calf, to punish him for the few words you got out of me the other day when I was work-ing in the fields. Take my boy, for you've deprived him of his father and his mother; make a Blue of him, my good man, teach him to kill Chouans. Here, there's two hundred crowns,—keep them for him; if he is careful, they'll last him long, for it took his father twelve years to lay them by."

Hulot looked with amazement at the pale and withered woman, whose eyes were dry.

"But you, mother," he said, "what will become of you? you had better keep the money."

"I?" she replied, shaking her head sadly. "I don't need anything in this world. You might bolt me into that highest tower over there" (pointing to the battlements of the castle) "and the Chouans would contrive to come and kill me."

She kissed her boy with an awful expression of grief, looked at him, wiped away her tears, looked at him again, and disappeared.

"Commandant," said Corentin, "this is an occasion when two heads are better than one. We know all, and yet we know nothing. If you surrounded Mademoiselle de Verneuil's house now, you will only warn her. Neither you, nor I, nor your Blues and your battalions are strong enough to get the better of that girl if she takes it into her head to save the *ci-devant*. The fellow is brave, and consequently wily; he is a young man full of daring. We can never get hold of him as he enters Fougeres. Perhaps he is here already. Domiciliary visit? Absurdity! that's no good, it will only give them warning."

"Well," said Hulot impatiently, "I shall tell the sentry on the Place Saint-Leonard to keep his eye on the house, and pass word along the other sentinels, if a young man enters it; as soon as the signal reaches me I shall take a corporal and four men and—"

"—and," said Corentin, interrupting the old soldier, "if the young man is not the marquis, or if the marquis doesn't go in by the front door, or if he is already there, if—if—if—what then?"

Corentin looked at the commandant with so insulting an air of superiority that the old soldier shouted out: "God's thousand thunders! get out of here, citizen of hell! What have I got to do with your intrigues? If that cockchafer buzzes into my guard-room I shall shoot him; if I hear he is in a house I shall surround that house and take him when he leaves it and shoot him, but may the devil get me if I soil my uniform with any of your tricks."

"Commandant, the order of the ministers states that you are to obey Mademoiselle de Verneuil."

"Let her come and give them to me herself and I'll see about it."

"Well, citizen," said Corentin, haughtily, "she shall come. She shall tell you herself the hour at which she expects the *ci-devant*. Possibly she won't be easy till you do post the sentinels round the house."

"The devil is made man," thought the old leader as he watched Corentin hurrying up the Queen's Staircase at the foot of which this scene had taken place. "He means to deliver Montauran bound hand and foot, with no chance to fight for his life, and I shall be harassed to death with a court-martial. However," he added, shrugging his shoulders, "the *Gars* certainly is an enemy of the Republic, and he killed my poor Gerard, and his death will make a noble the less—the devil take him!"

He turned on the heels of his boots and went off, whistling the Marseillaise, to inspect his guard-rooms.

****

Mademoiselle de Verneuil was absorbed in one of those meditations the mysteries of which are buried in the soul, and prove by their thousand contradictory emotions, to the woman who undergoes them, that it is possible to have a stormy and passionate existence between four walls without even moving from the ottoman on which her very life is burning itself away. She had reached the final scene of the drama she had come to enact, and her mind was going over and over the phases of love and anger which had so powerfully stirred her during the ten days which had now elapsed since her first meeting with the marquis. A man's step suddenly sounded in the adjoining room and she trembled; the door opened, she turned quickly and saw Corentin.

"You little cheat!" said the police-agent, "when will you stop deceiving? Ah, Marie, Marie, you are playing a dangerous game by not taking me into your confidence. Why do you play such tricks without consulting me? If the marquis escapes his fate—"

"It won't be your fault, will it?" she replied, sarcastically. "Monsieur," she continued, in a grave voice, "by what right do you come into my house?"

"Your house?" he exclaimed.

"You remind me," she answered, coldly, "that I have no home. Perhaps you chose this house deliberately for the purpose of committing murder. I shall leave it. I would live in a desert to get away from—"

"Spies, say the word," interrupted Corentin. "But this house is neither yours nor mine, it belongs to the government; and as for leaving it you will do nothing of the kind," he added, giving her a diabolical look.

Mademoiselle de Verneuil rose indignantly, made a few steps to leave the room, but stopped short suddenly as Corentin raised the curtain of the window and beckoned her, with a smile, to come to him.

"Do you see that column of smoke?" he asked, with the calmness he always kept on his livid face, however intense his feelings might be.

"What has my departure to do with that burning brush?" she asked.

"Why does your voice tremble?" he said. "You poor thing!" he added, in a gentle voice, "I know all. The marquis is coming to Fougeres this evening; and it is not with any intention of delivering him to us that you have arranged this boudoir and the flowers and candles."

Mademoiselle de Verneuil turned pale, for she saw her lover's death in the eyes of this tiger with a human face, and her love for him rose to frenzy. Each hair on her head caused her an acute pain she could not endure, and she fell on the ottoman. Corentin stood looking at her for a moment with his arms folded, half pleased at inflicting a torture which avenged him for the contempt and the sarcasms this woman had heaped upon his head, half grieved by the sufferings of a creature whose yoke was pleasant to him, heavy as it was.

"She loves him!" he muttered.

"Loves him!" she cried. "Ah! what are words? Corentin! he is my life, my soul, my breath!" She flung herself at the feet of the man, whose silence terrified her. "Soul of vileness!" she cried, "I would rather degrade myself to save his life than degrade myself by betraying him. I will save him at the cost of my own blood. Speak, what price must I pay you?"

Corentin quivered.

"I came to take your orders, Marie," he said, raising her. "Yes, Marie, your insults will not hinder my devotion to your wishes, provided you will promise not to deceive me again; you must know by this time that no one dupes me with impunity."

"If you want me to love you, Corentin, help me to save him."

"At what hour is he coming?" asked the spy, endeavouring to ask the question calmly.

"Alas, I do not know."

They looked at each other in silence.

"I am lost!" thought Mademoiselle de Verneuil.

"She is deceiving me!" thought Corentin. "Marie," he continued, "I have two maxims. One is never to believe a single word a woman says to me—that's the only means of not being duped; the other is to find what interest she has in doing the opposite of what she says, and behaving in contradiction to the facts she pretends to confide to me. I think that you and I understand each other now."

"Perfectly," replied Mademoiselle de Verneuil. "You want proofs of my good faith; but I reserve them for the time when you give me some of yours."

"*Adieu, mademoiselle,*" said Corentin, coolly.

"Nonsense," said the girl, smiling; "sit down, and pray don't sulk; but if you do I shall know how to save the marquis without you. As for the three hundred thousand *francs* which are always spread before your eyes, I will give them to you in good gold as soon as the marquis is safe."

Corentin rose, stepped back a pace or two, and looked at Marie.

"You have grown rich in a very short time," he said, in a tone of ill-disguised bitterness.

"Montauran," she continued, "will make you a better offer still for his ransom. Now, then, prove to me that you have the means of guaranteeing him from all danger and—"

234

"Can't you send him away the moment he arrives?" cried Corentin, suddenly. "Hulot does not know he is coming, and—" He stopped as if he had said too much. "But how absurd that you should ask me how to play a trick," he said, with an easy laugh. "Now listen, Marie, I do feel certain of your loyalty. Promise me a compensation for all I lose in furthering your wishes, and I will make that old fool of a commandant so unsuspicious that the marquis will be as safe at Fougères as at Saint-James."

"Yes, I promise it," said the girl, with a sort of solemnity.

"No, not in that way," he said, "swear it by your mother."

Mademoiselle de Verneuil shuddered; raising a trembling hand she made the oath required by the man whose tone to her had changed so suddenly.

"You can command me," he said; "don't deceive me again, and you shall have reason to bless me tonight."

"I will trust you, Corentin," cried Mademoiselle de Verneuil, much moved. She bowed her head gently towards him and smiled with a kindness not unmixed with surprise, as she saw an expression of melancholy tenderness on his face.

"What an enchanting creature!" thought Corentin, as he left the house. "Shall I ever get her as a means to fortune and a source of delight? To fling herself at my feet! Oh, yes, the marquis shall die! If I can't get that woman in any other way than by dragging her through the mud, I'll sink her in it. At any rate," he thought, as he reached the square unconscious of his steps, "she no longer distrusts me. Three hundred thousand *francs* down! she thinks me grasping! Either the offer was a trick or she is already married to him."

Corentin, buried in thought, was unable to come to a resolution. The fog which the sun had dispersed at mid-day was now rolling thicker and thicker, so that he could hardly see the trees at a little distance.

"That's another piece of ill-luck," he muttered, as he turned slowly homeward. "It is impossible to see ten feet. The weather protects the lovers. How is one to watch a house in such a fog? Who goes there?" he cried, catching the arm of a boy who seemed to have clambered up the dangerous rocks which made the terrace of the Promenade.

"It is I," said a childish voice.

"Ah! the boy with the bloody foot. Do you want to revenge your father?" said Corentin.

"Yes," said the child.

"Very good. Do you know the *Gars*?"

"Yes."

"Good again. Now, don't leave me except to do what I bid you, and you will obey your mother and earn some big *sous*—do you like *sous*?"

"Yes."

"You like *sous*, and you want to kill the *Gars* who killed your father—well, I'll take care of you. Ah! Marie," he muttered, after a pause, "you yourself shall betray him, as you engaged to do! She is too violent to suspect me—passion never reflects. She does not know the marquis's writing. Yes, I can set a trap into which her nature will drive her headlong. But I must first see Hulot."

Mademoiselle de Verneuil and Francine were deliberating on the means of saving the marquis from the more than doubtful generosity of Corentin and Hulot's bayonets.

"I could go and warn him," said the Breton girl.

"But we don't know where he is," replied Marie; "even I, with the instincts of love, could never find him."

After making and rejecting a number of plans Mademoiselle de Verneuil exclaimed, "When I see him his danger will inspire me."

She thought, like other ardent souls, to act on the spur of the moment, trusting to her star, or to that instinct of adroitness which rarely, if ever, fails a woman. Perhaps her heart was never so wrung. At times she seemed stupefied, her eyes were fixed, and then, at the least noise, she shook like a half-uprooted tree which the woodsman drags with a rope to hasten its fall. Suddenly, a loud report from a dozen guns echoed from a distance. Marie turned pale and grasped Francine's hand. "I am dying," she cried; "they have killed him!"

The heavy footfall of a man was heard in the antechamber. Francine went out and returned with a corporal. The man, making a military salute to Mademoiselle de Verneuil, produced some letters, the covers of which were a good deal soiled. Receiving no acknowledgment, the Blue said as he withdrew, "Madame, they are from the commandant."

Mademoiselle de Verneuil, a prey to horrible presentiments, read a letter written apparently in great haste by Hulot:—

"Mademoiselle—a party of my men have just caught a messenger from the *Gars* and have shot him. Among the intercepted letters is one which may be useful to you and I transmit it—etc."

"Thank God, it was not he they shot," she exclaimed, flinging the letter into the fire.

She breathed more freely and took up the other letter, enclosed by Hulot. It was apparently written to Madame du Gua by the marquis.

"No, my angel," the letter said, "I cannot go tonight to La Vivetiere.

You must lose your wager with the count. I triumph over the Republic in the person of their beautiful emissary. You must allow that she is worth the sacrifice of one night. It will be my only victory in this campaign, for I have received the news that La Vendee surrenders. I can do nothing more in France. Let us go back to England—but we will talk of all this tomorrow."

The letter fell from Marie's hands; she closed her eyes, and was silent, leaning backward, with her head on a cushion. After a long pause she looked at the clock, which then marked four in the afternoon.

"My lord keeps me waiting," she said, with savage irony.

"Oh! God grant he may not come!" cried Francine.

"If he does not come," said Marie, in a stifled tone, "I shall go to him. No, no, he will soon be here. Francine, do I look well?"

"You are very pale."

"Ah!" continued Mademoiselle de Verneuil, glancing about her, "this perfumed room, the flowers, the lights, this intoxicating air, it is full of that celestial life of which I dreamed—"

"Marie, what has happened?"

"I am betrayed, deceived, insulted, fooled! I will kill him, I will tear him bit by bit! Yes, there was always in his manner a contempt he could not hide and which I would not see. Oh! I shall die of this! Fool that I am," she went on laughing, "he is coming; I have one night in which to teach him that, married or not, the man who has possessed me cannot abandon me. I will measure my vengeance by his offence; he shall die with despair in his soul. I did believe he had a soul of honour, but no! it is that of a lackey. Ah, he has cleverly deceived me, for even now it seems impossible that the man who abandoned me to Pille-Miche should sink to such back-stair tricks. It is so base to deceive a loving woman, for it is so easy. He might have killed me if he chose, but lie to me! to me, who held him in my thoughts so high! The scaffold! the scaffold! ah! could I only see him guillotined! Am I cruel? He shall go to his death covered with caresses, with kisses which might have blessed him for a lifetime—"

"Marie," said Francine, gently, "be the victim of your lover like other women; not his mistress and his betrayer. Keep his memory in your heart; do not make it an anguish to you. If there were no joys in hopeless love, what would become of us, poor women that we are? God, of whom you never think, Marie, will reward us for obeying our vocation on this earth,—to love, and suffer."

"Dear," replied Mademoiselle de Verneuil, taking Francine's hand

and patting it, "your voice is very sweet and persuasive. Reason is attractive from your lips. I should like to obey you, but—"

"You will forgive him, you will not betray him?"

"Hush! never speak of that man again. Compared with him Corentin is a noble being. Do you hear me?"

She rose, hiding beneath a face that was horribly calm the madness of her soul and a thirst for vengeance. The slow and measured step with which she left the room conveyed the sense of an irrevocable resolution. Lost in thought, hugging her insults, too proud to show the slightest suffering, she went to the guard-room at the Porte Saint-Leonard and asked where the commandant lived. She had hardly left her house when Corentin entered it.

"Oh, Monsieur Corentin," cried Francine, "if you are interested in this young man, save him; Mademoiselle has gone to give him up because of this wretched letter."

Corentin took the letter carelessly and asked,—

"Which way did she go?"

"I don't know."

"Yes," he said, "I will save her from her own despair."

He disappeared, taking the letter with him. When he reached the street he said to Galope-Chopine's boy, whom he had stationed to watch the door, "Which way did a lady go who left the house just now?"

The boy went with him a little way and showed him the steep street which led to the Porte Saint-Leonard. "That way," he said.

At this moment four men entered Mademoiselle de Verneuil's house, unseen by either the boy or Corentin.

"Return to your watch," said the latter. "Play with the handles of the blinds and see what you can inside; look about you everywhere, even on the roof."

Corentin darted rapidly in the direction given him, and thought he recognized Mademoiselle de Verneuil through the fog; he did, in fact, overtake her just as she reached the guard-house.

"Where are you going?" he said; "you are pale—what has happened? Is it right for you to be out alone? Take my arm."

"Where is the commandant?" she asked.

Hardly had the words left her lips when she heard the movement of troops beyond the Porte Saint-Leonard and distinguished Hulot's gruff voice in the tumult.

"God's thunder!" he cried, "I never saw such fog as this for a reconnaissance! The *Gars* must have ordered the weather."

"What are you complaining of?" said Mademoiselle de Verneuil, grasping his arm. "The fog will cover vengeance as well as perfidy. Commandant," she added, in a low voice, "you must take measures at once so that the *Gars* may not escape us."

"Is he at your house?" he asked, in a tone which showed his amazement.

"Not yet," she replied; "but give me a safe man and I will send him to you when the marquis comes."

"That's a mistake," said Corentin; "a soldier will alarm him, but a boy, and I can find one, will not."

"Commandant," said Mademoiselle de Verneuil, "thanks to this fog which you are cursing, you can surround my house. Put soldiers everywhere. Place a guard in the church to command the esplanade on which the windows of my salon open. Post men on the Promenade; for though the windows of my bedroom are twenty feet above the ground, despair does sometimes give a man the power to jump even greater distances safely. Listen to what I say. I shall probably send this gentleman out of the door of my house; therefore see that only brave men are there to meet him; for," she added, with a sigh, "no one denies him courage; he will assuredly defend himself."

"Gudin!" called the commandant. "Listen, my lad," he continued in a low voice when the young man joined him, "this devil of a girl is betraying the *Gars* to us—I am sure I don't know why, but that's no matter. Take ten men and place yourself so as to hold the *cul-de-sac* in which the house stands; be careful that no one sees either you or your men."

"Yes, commandant, I know the ground."

"Very good," said Hulot. "I'll send Beau-Pied to let you know when to play your sabres. Try to meet the marquis yourself, and if you can manage to kill him, so that I sha'n't have to shoot him judicially, you shall be a lieutenant in a fortnight or my name's not Hulot."

Gudin departed with a dozen soldiers.

"Do you know what you have done?" said Corentin to Mademoiselle de Verneuil, in a low voice.

She made no answer, but looked with a sort of satisfaction at the men who were starting, under command of the sub-lieutenant, for the Promenade, while others, following the next orders given by Hulot, were to post themselves in the shadows of the church of Saint-Leonard.

"There are houses adjoining mine," she said; "you had better surround them all. Don't lay up regrets by neglecting a single precaution."

"She is mad," thought Hulot.

"Was I not a prophet?" asked Corentin in his ear. "As for the boy I shall send with her, he is the little *gars* with a bloody foot; therefore—"

He did not finish his sentence, for Mademoiselle de Verneuil by a sudden movement darted in the direction of her house, whither he followed her, whistling like a man supremely satisfied. When he overtook her she was already at the door of her house, where Galope-Chopine's little boy was on the watch.

"Mademoiselle," said Corentin, "take the lad with you; you cannot have a more innocent or active emissary. Boy," he added, "when you have seen the *Gars* enter the house come to me, no matter who stops you; you'll find me at the guard-house and I'll give you something that will make you eat cake for the rest of your days."

At these words, breathed rather than said in the child's ear, Corentin felt his hand squeezed by that of the little Breton, who followed Mademoiselle de Verneuil into the house.

"Now, my good friends, you can come to an explanation as soon as you like," cried Corentin when the door was closed. "If you make love, my little marquis, it will be on your winding-sheet."

But Corentin could not bring himself to let that fatal house completely out of sight, and he went to the Promenade, where he found the commandant giving his last orders. By this time it was night. Two hours went by; but the sentinels posted at intervals noticed nothing that led them to suppose the marquis had evaded the triple line of men who surrounded the three sides by which the tower of Papegaut was accessible. Twenty times had Corentin gone from the Promenade to the guard-room, always to find that his little emissary had not appeared. Sunk in thought, the spy paced the Promenade slowly, enduring the martyrdom to which three passions, terrible in their clashing, subject a man,—love, avarice, and ambition. Eight o'clock struck from all the towers in the town. The moon rose late. Fog and darkness wrapped in impenetrable gloom the places where the drama planned by this man was coming to its climax. He was able to silence the struggle of his passions as he walked up and down, his arms crossed, and his eyes fixed on the windows which rose like the luminous eyes of a phantom above the rampart. The deep silence was broken only by the rippling of the Nancon, by the regular and lugubrious tolling from the belfries, by the heavy steps of the sentinels or the rattle of arms as the guard was hourly relieved.

"The night's as thick as a wolf's jaw," said the voice of Pille-Miche.

"Go on," growled Marche-a-Terre, "and don't talk more than a dead dog."

"I'm hardly breathing," said the Chouan.

"If the man who made that stone roll down wants his heart to serve as the scabbard for my knife he'll do it again," said Marche-a-Terre, in a low voice scarcely heard above the flowing of the river.

"It was I," said Pille-Miche.

"Well, then, old money-bag, down on your stomach," said the other, "and wriggle like a snake through a hedge, or we shall leave our carcasses behind us sooner than we need."

"Hey, Marche-a-Terre," said the incorrigible Pille-Miche, who was using his hands to drag himself along on his stomach, and had reached the level of his comrade's ear. "If the Grande-Garce is to be believed there'll be a fine booty today. Will you go shares with me?"

"Look here, Pille-Miche," said Marche-a-Terre stopping short on the flat of his stomach. The other Chouans, who were accompanying the two men, did the same, so wearied were they with the difficulties they had met with in climbing the precipice. "I know you," continued Marche-a-Terre, "for a Jack Grab-All who would rather give blows than receive them when there's nothing else to be done. We have not come here to grab dead men's shoes; we are devils against devils, and sorrow to those whose claws are too short. The Grande-Garce has sent us here to save the *Gars*. He is up there; lift your dog's nose and see that window above the tower."

Midnight was striking. The moon rose, giving the appearance of white smoke to the fog. Pille-Miche squeezed Marche-a-Terre's arm and silently showed him on the terrace just above them, the triangular iron of several shining bayonets.

"The Blues are there already," said Pille-Miche; "we sha'n't gain anything by force."

"Patience," replied Marche-a-Terre; "if I examined right this morning, we must be at the foot of the Papegaut tower between the ramparts and the Promenade,—that place where they put the manure; it is like a feather-bed to fall on."

"If Saint-Labre," remarked Pille-Miche, "would only change into cider the blood we shall shed tonight the citizens might lay in a good stock tomorrow."

Marche-a-Terre laid his large hand over his friend's mouth; then an order muttered by him went from rank to rank of the Chouans suspended as they were in mid-air among the brambles of the slate rocks. Corentin, walking up and down the esplanade had too practiced an ear not to hear the rustling of the shrubs and the light sound of pebbles rolling down the sides of the precipice. Marche-a-Terre, who seemed to possess the gift of seeing in darkness, and whose senses, continually in action, were acute as those of a savage, saw Corentin; like a trained dog he had scented him. Fouche's diplomatist listened but heard nothing; he looked at the natural wall of rock and saw no signs. If the confusing gleam of the fog enabled him to see, here and there, a crouching Chouan, he took him, no doubt, for a fragment of rock, for these human bodies had all the appearance of inert nature. This danger to the invaders was of short duration. Corentin's attention was diverted by a very distinct noise coming from the other end of the Promenade, where the rock wall ended and a steep descent leading down to the Queen's Staircase began. When Corentin reached the spot he saw a figure gliding past it as if by magic. Putting out his hand to grasp this real or fantastic being, who was there, he supposed, with no good intentions, he encountered the soft and rounded figure of a woman.

"The devil take you!" he exclaimed, "if any one else had met you, you'd have had a ball through your head. What are you doing, and where are you going, at this time of night? Are you dumb? It certainly is a woman," he said to himself.

The silence was suspicious, but the stranger broke it by saying, in a voice which suggested extreme fright, "Ah, my good man, I'm on my way back from a wake."

"It is the pretended mother of the marquis," thought Corentin. "I'll see what she's about. Well, go that way, old woman," he replied, feigning not to recognize her. "Keep to the left if you don't want to be shot."

He stood quite still; then observing that Madame du Gua was making for the Papegaut tower, he followed her at a distance with diabolical caution. During this fatal encounter the Chouans had posted themselves on the manure towards which Marche-a-Terre had guided them.

"There's the Grande-Garce!" thought Marche-a-Terre, as he rose to his feet against the tower wall like a bear.

"We are here," he said to her in a low voice.

"Good," she replied, "there's a ladder in the garden of that house about six feet above the manure; find it, and the *Gars* is saved. Do you see that small window up there? It is in the dressing-room; you must get to it. This side of the tower is the only one not watched. The horses are ready; if you can hold the passage over the Nancon, a quarter of an hour will put him out of danger—in spite of his folly. But if that woman tries to follow him, stab her."

Corentin now saw several of the forms he had hitherto supposed

242

to be stones moving cautiously but swiftly. He went at once to the guard-room at the Porte Saint-Leonard, where he found the commandant fully dressed and sound asleep on a camp bed.

"Let him alone," said Beau-Pied, roughly, "he has only just lain down."

"The Chouans are here!" cried Corentin, in Hulot's ear.

"Impossible! but so much the better," cried the old soldier, still half asleep; "then he can fight."

When Hulot reached the Promenade Corentin pointed out to him the singular position taken by the Chouans.

"They must have deceived or strangled the sentries I placed between the castle and the Queen's Staircase. Ah! what a devil of a fog! However, patience! I'll send a squad of men under a lieutenant to the foot of the rock. There is no use attacking them where they are, for those animals are so hard they'd let themselves roll down the precipice without breaking a limb."

The cracked clock of the belfry was ringing two when the commandant got back to the Promenade after giving these orders and taking every military precaution to seize the Chouans. The sentries were doubled and Mademoiselle de Verneuil's house became the centre of a little army. Hulot found Corentin absorbed in contemplation of the window which overlooked the tower.

"Citizen," said the commandant, "I think the *ci-devant* has fooled us; there's nothing stirring."

"He is there," cried Corentin, pointing to the window. "I have seen a man's shadow on the curtain. But I can't think what has become of that boy. They must have killed him or locked him up. There! commandant, don't you see that? there's a man's shadow; come, come on!"

"I sha'n't seize him in bed; thunder of God! He will come out if he went in; Gudin won't miss him," cried Hulot, who had his own reasons for waiting till the *Gars* could defend himself.

"Commandant, I enjoin you, in the name of the law to proceed at once into that house."

"You're a fine scoundrel to try to make me do that."

Without showing any resentment at the commandant's language, Corentin said coolly: "You will obey me. Here is an order in good form, signed by the minister of war, which will force you to do so." He drew a paper from his pocket and held it out. "Do you suppose we are such fools as to leave that girl to do as she likes? We are endeavouring to suppress a civil war, and the grandeur of the purpose covers the pettiness of the means."

"I take the liberty, citizen, of sending you to—you understand me? Enough. To the right-about, march! Let me alone, or it will be the worse for you."

"But read that," persisted Corentin.

"Don't bother me with your functions," cried Hulot, furious at receiving orders from a man he regarded as contemptible.

At this instant Galope-Chopine's boy suddenly appeared among them like a rat from a hole.

"The *Gars* has started!" he cried.

"Which way?"

"The rue Saint-Leonard."

"Beau-Pied," said Hulot in a whisper to the corporal who was near him, "go and tell your lieutenant to draw in closer round the house, and make ready to fire. Left wheel, forward on the tower, the rest of you!" he shouted.

To understand the conclusion of this fatal drama we must re-enter the house with Mademoiselle de Verneuil when she returned to it after denouncing the marquis to the commandant.

When passions reach their crisis they bring us under the dominion of far greater intoxication than the petty excitements of wine or opium. The lucidity then given to ideas, the delicacy of the high-wrought senses, produce the most singular and unexpected effects. Some persons when they find themselves under the tyranny of a single thought can see with extraordinary distinctness objects scarcely visible to others, while at the same time the most palpable things become to them almost as if they did not exist. When Mademoiselle de Verneuil hurried, after reading the marquis's letter, to prepare the way for vengeance just as she had lately been preparing all for love, she was in that stage of mental intoxication which makes real life like the life of a somnambulist. But when she saw her house surrounded, by her own orders, with a triple line of bayonets a sudden flash of light illuminated her soul. She judged her conduct and saw with horror that she had committed a crime. Under the first shock of this conviction she sprang to the threshold of the door and stood there irresolute, striving to think, yet unable to follow out her reasoning. She knew so vaguely what had happened that she tried in vain to remember why she was in the antechamber, and why she was leading a strange child by the hand. A million of stars were floating in the air before her like tongues of fire. She began to walk about, striving to shake off the horrible torpor which laid hold of her; but, like one asleep, no object appeared to her under its natural form or in its own colours. She grasped the hand of the little boy with a violence not natural to her, dragging him along with such precipitate steps that she seemed to have the motions of a madwoman. She saw neither persons nor things in the salon as she crossed it, and yet she was saluted by three men who made way to let her pass.

"That must be she," said one of them.

"She is very handsome," exclaimed another, who was a priest.

"Yes," replied the first; "but how pale and agitated—"

"And beside herself," said the third; "she did not even see us."

At the door of her own room Mademoiselle de Verneuil saw the smiling face of Francine, who whispered to her: "He is here, Marie."

Mademoiselle de Verneuil awoke, reflected, looked at the child whose hand she held, remembered all, and replied to the girl: "Shut up that boy; if you wish me to live do not let him escape you."

As she slowly said the words her eyes were fixed on the door of her bedroom, and there they continued fastened with so dreadful a fixedness that it seemed as if she saw her victim through the wooden panels. Then she gently opened it, passed through and closed it behind her without turning round, for she saw the marquis standing before the fireplace. His dress, without being too choice, had the look of careful arrangement which adds so much to the admiration which a woman feels for her lover. All her self-possession came back to her at the sight of him. Her lips, rigid, although half-open, showed the enamel of her white teeth and formed a smile that was fixed and terrible rather than voluptuous. She walked with slow steps toward the young man and pointed with her finger to the clock.

"A man who is worthy of love is worth waiting for," she said with deceptive gaiety.

Then, overcome with the violence of her emotions, she dropped upon the sofa which was near the fireplace.

"Dear Marie, you are so charming when you are angry," said the marquis, sitting down beside her and taking her hand, which she let him take, and entreating a look, which she refused him. "I hope," he continued, in a tender, caressing voice, "that my wife will not long refuse a glance to her loving husband."

Hearing the words she turned abruptly and looked into his eyes.

"What is the meaning of that dreadful look?" he said, laughing. "But your hand is burning! oh, my love, what is it?"

"Your love!" she repeated, in a dull, changed voice.

"Yes," he said, throwing himself on his knees beside her and taking her two hands which he covered with kisses. "Yes, my love—I am thine for life."

She pushed him violently away from her and rose. Her features contracted, she laughed as mad people laugh, and then she said to him: "You do not mean one word of all you are saying, base man—baser than the lowest villain." She sprang to the dagger which was lying beside a flower-vase, and let it sparkle before the eyes of the amazed young marquis. "Bah!" she said, flinging it away from her, "I do not respect you enough to kill you. Your blood is even too vile to be shed by soldiers; I see nothing fit for you but the executioner."

The words were painfully uttered in a low voice, and she moved her feet like a spoilt child, impatiently. The marquis went to her and tried to clasp her.

"Don't touch me!" she cried, recoiling from him with a look of horror.

"She is mad!" said the marquis in despair.

"Mad, yes!" she repeated, "but not mad enough to be your dupe. What would I not forgive to passion? but to seek to possess me without love, and to write to that woman—"

"To whom have I written?" he said, with an astonishment which was certainly not feigned.

"To that chaste woman who sought to kill me."

The marquis turned pale with anger and said, grasping the back of a chair until he broke it, "If Madame du Gua has committed some dastardly wrong—"

Mademoiselle de Verneuil looked for the letter; not finding it she called to Francine.

"Where is that letter?" she asked.

"Monsieur Corentin took it."

"Corentin! ah! I understand it all; he wrote the letter; he has deceived me with diabolical art—as he alone can deceive."

With a piercing cry she flung herself on the sofa, tears rushing from her eyes. Doubt and confidence were equally dreadful now. The marquis knelt beside her and clasped her to his breast, saying, again and again, the only words he was able to utter:—

"Why do you weep, my darling? there is no harm done; your reproaches were all love; do not weep, I love you—I shall always love you."

Suddenly he felt her press him with almost supernatural force. "Do you still love me?" she said, amid her sobs.

"Can you doubt it?" he replied in a tone that was almost melancholy.

She abruptly disengaged herself from his arms, and fled, as if frightened and confused, to a little distance.

"Do I doubt it?" she exclaimed, but a smile of gentle meaning was on her lover's face, and the words died away upon her lips; she let him take her by the hand and lead her to the salon. There an altar had been hastily arranged during her absence. The priest was robed in his officiating vestments. The lighted tapers shed upon the ceiling a glow as soft as hope itself. She now recognized the two men who had bowed to her, the Comte de Bauvan and the Baron du Guenic, the witnesses chosen by Montauran.

"You will not still refuse?" said the marquis.

But at the sight she stopped, stepped backward into her chamber and fell on her knees; raising her hands towards the marquis she cried out: "Pardon! pardon! pardon!"

Her voice died away, her head fell back, her eyes closed, and she lay in the arms of her lover and Francine as if dead. When she opened her eyes they met those of the young man full of loving tenderness.

"Marie! patience! this is your last trial," he said.

"The last!" she exclaimed, bitterly.

Francine and the marquis looked at each other in surprise, but she silenced them by a gesture.

"Call the priest," she said, "and leave me alone with him."

They did so, and withdrew.

"My father," she said to the priest so suddenly called to her, "in my childhood an old man, white-haired like yourself, used to tell me that God would grant all things to those who had faith. Is that true?"

"It is true," replied the priest; "all things are possible to Him who created all."

Mademoiselle de Verneuil threw herself on her knees before him with incredible enthusiasm.

"Oh, my God!" she cried in ecstasy, "my faith in thee is equal to my love for him; inspire me! do here a miracle, or take my life!"

"Your prayer will be granted," said the priest.

Marie returned to the salon leaning on the arm of the venerable old man. A deep and secret emotion brought her to the arms of her lover more brilliant than on any of her past days, for a serenity like that which painters give to the martyrs added to her face an imposing dignity. She held out her hand to the marquis and together they advanced to the altar and knelt down. The marriage was about to be celebrated beside the nuptial bed, the altar hastily raised, the cross, the vessels, the chalice, secretly brought thither by the priest, the fumes of incense rising to the ceiling, the priest himself, who wore a stole above his cassock, the tapers on an altar in a salon,—all these things combined to form a strange and touching scene, which typified those times of saddest memory, when civil discord overthrew all sacred institutions. Religious ceremonies then had the savour of the mysteries. Children were baptized in the chambers where the mothers were still groaning from their labour. As in the olden time, the Saviour went, poor and lowly, to console the dying. Young girls received their first communion in the home where they had played since infancy. The marriage of the marquis and Mademoiselle de Verneuil was now solemnized, like many other unions, by a service contrary to the recent legal enactments. In after years these marriages, mostly celebrated at the foot of oaks, were scrupulously recognized and considered legal. The priest who thus preserved the ancient usages was one of those men who hold to their principles in the height of the storm. His voice, which never made the oath exacted by the Republic, uttered no word throughout the tempest that did not make for peace. He never incited, like the Abbe Gudin, to fire and sword; but like many others, he devoted himself to the still more dangerous mission of performing his priestly functions for the souls of faithful Catholics. To accomplish this perilous ministry he used all the pious deceptions necessitated by persecution, and the marquis, when he sought his services on this occasion, had found him in one of those excavated caverns which are known, even to the present day, by the name of "the priest's hiding-place." The mere sight of that pale and suffering face was enough to give this worldly room a holy aspect.

All was now ready for the act of misery and of joy. Before beginning the ceremony the priest asked, in the dead silence, the names of the bride.

"Marie-Nathalie, daughter of Mademoiselle Blanche de Casteran, abbess, deceased, of Notre-Dame de Seez, and Victor-Amedee, Duc de Verneuil."

"Where born?"

"At La Chasterie, near Alencon."

"I never supposed," said the baron in a low voice to the count, "that Montauran would have the folly to marry her. The natural daughter of a duke!—horrid!"

"If it were of the king, well and good," replied the Comte de Bauvan, smiling. "However, it is not for me to blame him; I like Charette's mistress full as well; and I shall transfer the war to her—though she's not one to bill and coo."

The names of the marquis had been filled in previously, and the two lovers now signed the document with their witnesses. The ceremony then began. At that instant Marie, and she alone, heard the sound of muskets and the heavy tread of soldiers,—no doubt relieving the guard in the church which she had herself demanded. She trembled violently and raised her eyes to the cross on the altar.

"A saint at last," said Francine, in a low voice.

"Give me such saints, and I'll be devilishly devout," added the count, in a whisper.

When the priest made the customary inquiry of Mademoiselle de Verneuil, she answered by a "yes" uttered with a deep sigh. Bending to her husband's ear she said: "You will soon know why I have broken the oath I made never to marry you."

After the ceremony all present passed into the dining-room, where dinner was served, and as they took their places Jeremie, Marie's footman, came into the room terrified. The poor bride rose and went to him; Francine followed her. With one of those pretexts which never fail a woman, she begged the marquis to do the honours for a moment, and went out, taking Jeremie with her before he could utter the fatal words.

"Ah! Francine, to be dying a thousand deaths and not to die!" she cried.

This absence might well be supposed to have its cause in the ceremony that had just taken place. Towards the end of the dinner, as the marquis was beginning to feel uneasy, Marie returned in all the pomp of a bridal robe. Her face was calm and joyful, while that of Francine who followed her had terror imprinted on every feature, so that the guests might well have thought they saw in these two women a fantastic picture by Salvator Rosa, of Life and Death holding each other by the hand.

"Gentlemen," said Marie to the priest, the baron, and the count, "you are my guests for the night. I find you cannot leave Fougeres; it would be dangerous to attempt it. My good maid has instructions to make you comfortable in your apartments. No, you must not rebel," she added to the priest, who was about to speak. "I hope you will not thwart a woman on her wedding-day."

An hour later she was alone with her husband in the room she had so joyously arranged a few hours earlier. They had reached that fatal bed where, like a tomb, so many hopes are wrecked, where the waking to a happy life is all uncertain, where love is born or dies, according to the natures that are tried there. Marie looked at the clock. "Six hours to live," she murmured.

"Can I have slept?" she cried toward morning, wakening with one of those sudden movements which rouse us when we have made ourselves a promise to wake at a certain hour. "Yes, I have slept," she thought, seeing by the light of the candles that the hands of the clock were pointing to two in the morning. She turned and looked at the sleeping marquis, lying like a child with his head on one hand, the other clasping his wife's hand, his lips half smiling as though he had fallen asleep while she kissed him.

"Ah!" she whispered to herself, "he sleeps like an infant; he does not distrust me—me, to whom he has given a happiness without a name."

She touched him softly and he woke, continuing to smile. He kissed the hand he held and looked at the wretched woman with eyes so sparkling that she could not endure their light and slowly lowered her large eyelids. Her husband might justly have accused her of coquetry if she were not concealing the terrors of her soul by thus evading the fire of his looks. Together they raised their charming heads and made each other a sign of gratitude for the pleasures they had tasted; but after a rapid glance at the beautiful picture his wife presented, the marquis was struck with an expression on her face which seemed to him melancholy, and he said in a tender voice, "Why sad, dear love?"

"Poor Alphonse," she answered, "do you know to what I have led you?"

"To happiness."

"To death!"

Shuddering with horror she sprang from the bed; the marquis, astonished, followed her. His wife motioned him to a window and raised the curtain, pointing as she did so to a score of soldiers. The moon had scattered the fog and was now casting her white light on the muskets and the uniforms, on the impassable Corentin pacing up and down like a jackal waiting for his prey, on the commandant, standing still, his arms crossed, his nose in the air, his lips curling, watchful and displeased.

"Come, Marie, leave them and come back to me."

"Why do you smile? I placed them there."

"You are dreaming."

"No."

They looked at each other for a moment. The marquis divined the whole truth, and he took her in his arms. "No matter!" he said, "I love you still."

"All is not lost!" cried Marie, "it cannot be! Alphonse," she said after a pause, "there is hope."

At this moment they distinctly heard the owl's cry, and Francine entered from the dressing-room.

"Pierre has come!" she said with a joy that was like delirium.

The marquise and Francine dressed Montauran in Chouan clothes with that amazing rapidity that belongs only to women. As soon as Marie saw her husband loading the gun Francine had brought in she slipped hastily from the room with a sign to her faithful maid. Francine then took the marquis to the dressing-room adjoining the bed-chamber. The young man seeing a large number of sheets knotted firmly together, perceived the means by which the girl expected him to escape the vigilance of the soldiers.

"I can't get through there," he said, examining the bull's-eye window.

At that instant it was darkened by a thickset figure, and a hoarse voice, known to Francine, said in a whisper, "Make haste, general, those rascally Blues are stirring."

"Oh! one more kiss," said a trembling voice beside him.

The marquis, whose feet were already on the liberating ladder, though he was not wholly through the window, felt his neck clasped with a despairing pressure. Seeing that his wife had put on his clothes, he tried to detain her; but she tore herself roughly from his arms and he was forced to descend. In his hand he held a fragment of some stuff which the moonlight showed him was a piece of the waistcoat he had worn the night before.

"Halt! fire!"

These words uttered by Hulot in the midst of a silence that was almost horrible broke the spell which seemed to hold the men and their surroundings. A volley of balls coming from the valley and reaching to the foot of the tower succeeded the discharges of the Blues posted on the Promenade. Not a cry came from the Chouans. Between each discharge the silence was frightful.

But Corentin had heard a fall from the ladder on the precipice side of the tower, and he suspected some ruse.

"None of those animals are growling," he said to Hulot; "our lovers are capable of fooling us on this side, and escaping themselves on the other."

The spy, to clear up the mystery, sent for torches; Hulot, understanding the force of Corentin's supposition, and hearing the noise of a serious struggle in the direction of the Porte Saint-Leonard, rushed to the guard-house exclaiming: "That's true, they won't separate."

"His head is well-riddled, commandant," said Beau-Pied, who was the first to meet him, "but he killed Gudin, and wounded two men. Ha! the savage; he got through three ranks of our best men and would

251

have reached the fields if it hadn't been for the sentry at the gate who spitted him on his bayonet."

The commandant rushed into the guard-room and saw on a camp bedstead a bloody body which had just been laid there. He went up to the supposed marquis, raised the hat which covered the face, and fell into a chair.

"I suspected it!" he cried, crossing his arms violently; "she kept him, cursed thunder! too long."

The soldiers stood about, motionless. The commandant himself unfastened the long black hair of a woman. Suddenly the silence was broken by the tramp of men and Corentin entered the guardroom, preceding four soldiers who bore on their guns, crossed to make a litter, the body of Montauran, who was shot in the thighs and arms. They laid him on the bedstead beside his wife. He saw her, and found strength to clasp her hand with a convulsive gesture. The dying woman turned her head, recognized her husband, and shuddered with a spasm that was horrible to see, murmuring in a voice almost extinct: "A day without a morrow! God heard me too well!"

"Commandant," said the marquis, collecting all his strength, and still holding Marie's hand, "I count on your honour to send the news of my death to my young brother, who is now in London. Write him that if he wishes to obey my last injunction he will never bear arms against his country—neither must he abandon the king's service."

"It shall be done," said Hulot, pressing the hand of the dying man.

"Take them to the nearest hospital," cried Corentin.

Hulot took the spy by the arm with a grip that left the imprint of his fingers on the flesh.

"Out of this camp!" he cried; "your business is done here. Look well at the face of Commander Hulot, and never find yourself again in his way if you don't want your belly to be the scabbard of his blade—"

And the older soldier flourished his sabre.

"That's another of the honest men who will never make their way," said Corentin to himself when he was some distance from the guard-room.

The marquis was still able to thank his gallant adversary by a look marking the respect which all soldiers feel for loyal enemies.

****

In 1827 an old man accompanied by his wife was buying cattle in the market-place of Fougeres. Few persons remembered that he had killed a hundred or more men, and that his former name was Marche-

252

a-Terre. A person to whom we owe important information about all the personages of this drama saw him there, leading a cow, and was struck by his simple, ingenuous air, which led her to remark, "That must be a worthy man."

As for Cibot, otherwise called Pille-Miche, we already know his end. It is likely that Marche-a-Terre made some attempt to save his comrade from the scaffold; possibly he was in the square at Alencon on the occasion of the frightful tumult which was one of the events of the famous trial of Rifoel, Briond, and la Chanterie.

Juana

Dedication

To Madame la Comtesse Merlin.

CHAPTER 1

Exposition

Notwithstanding the discipline which Marechal Suchet had introduced into his army corps, he was unable to prevent a short period of
trouble and disorder at the taking of Tarragona. According to certain
fair-minded military men, this intoxication of victory bore a striking
resemblance to pillage, though the *marechal* promptly suppressed it.
Order being re-established, each regiment quartered in its respective
lines, and the commandant of the city appointed, military administra-
tion began. The place assumed a mongrel aspect. Though all things
were organized on a French system, the Spaniards were left free to
follow *in petto* their national tastes.

This period of pillage (it is difficult to determine how long it
lasted) had, like all other sublunary effects, a cause, not so difficult
to discover. In the *marechal's* army was a regiment, composed almost
entirely of Italians and commanded by a certain Colonel Eugene, a
man of remarkable bravery, a second Murat, who, having entered the
military service too late, obtained neither a Grand Duchy of Berg nor
a Kingdom of Naples, nor balls at the Pizzo. But if he won no crown
he had ample opportunity to obtain wounds, and it was not surprising
that he met with several. His regiment was composed of the scattered
fragments of the Italian legion. This legion was to Italy what the co-
lonial battalions are to France. Its permanent cantonments, established
on the island of Elba, served as an honourable place of exile for the
troublesome sons of good families and for those great men who have
just missed greatness, whom society brands with a hot iron and desig-
nates by the term *mauvais sujets*; men who are for the most part misunderstood; whose existence may become either noble through the
smile of a woman lifting them out of their rut, or shocking at the close
of an orgy under the influence of some damnable reflection dropped
by a drunken comrade.

Napoleon had incorporated these vigorous beings in the sixth of the line, hoping to metamorphose them finally into generals,—barring those whom the bullets might take off. But the emperor's calculation was scarcely fulfilled, except in the matter of the bullets. This regiment, often decimated but always the same in character, acquired a great reputation for valour in the field and for wickedness in private life. At the siege of Tarragona it lost its celebrated hero, Bianchi, the man who, during the campaign, had wagered that he would eat the heart of a Spanish sentinel, and did eat it. Though Bianchi was the prince of the devils incarnate to whom the regiment owed its dual reputation, he had, nevertheless, that sort of chivalrous honour which excuses, in the army, the worst excesses. In a word, he would have been, at an earlier period, an admirable pirate. A few days before his death he distinguished himself by a daring action which the *marechal* wished to reward. Bianchi refused rank, pension, and additional decoration, asking, for sole recompense, the favour of being the first to mount the breach at the assault on Tarragona. The *marechal* granted the request and then forgot his promise; but Bianchi forced him to remember Bianchi. The enraged hero was the first to plant our flag on the wall, where he was shot by a monk.

This historical digression was necessary, in order to explain how it was that the 6th of the line was the regiment to enter Tarragona, and why the disorder and confusion, natural enough in a city taken by storm, degenerated for a time into a slight pillage.

This regiment possessed two officers, not at all remarkable among these men of iron, who played, nevertheless, in the history we shall now relate, a somewhat important part.

The first, a captain in the quartermaster's department, an officer half civil, half military, was considered, in soldier phrase, to be fighting his own battle. He pretended bravery, boasted loudly of belonging to the 6th of the line, twirled his moustache with the air of a man who was ready to demolish everything; but his brother officers did not esteem him. The fortune he possessed made him cautious. He was nicknamed, for two reasons, "captain of crows." In the first place, he could smell powder a league off, and took wing at the sound of a musket; secondly, the nickname was based on an innocent military pun, which his position in the regiment warranted. Captain Montefiore, of the illustrious Montefiore family of Milan (though the laws of the Kingdom of Italy forbade him to bear his title in the French service) was one of the handsomest men in the army. This beauty may have been among the secret causes of his prudence on fighting days. A wound which might have injured his nose, cleft his forehead, or scarred his cheek, would have destroyed one of the most beautiful Italian faces which a woman ever dreamed of in all its delicate proportions. This face, not unlike the type which Girodet has given to the dying young Turk, in the "Revolt at Cairo," was instinct with that melancholy by which all women are more or less duped.

The Marquis de Montefiore possessed an entailed property, but his income was mortgaged for a number of years to pay off the costs of certain Italian escapades which are inconceivable in Paris. He had ruined himself in supporting a theatre at Milan in order to force upon a public a very inferior prima donna, whom he was said to love madly. A fine future was therefore before him, and he did not care to risk it for the paltry distinction of a bit of red ribbon. He was not a brave man, but he was certainly a philosopher; and he had precedents, if we may use so parliamentary an expression. Did not Philip the Second register a vow after the battle of Saint Quentin that never again would he put himself under fire? And did not the Duke of Alba encourage him in thinking that the worst trade in the world was the involuntary exchange of a crown for a bullet? Hence, Montefiore was Philippiste in his capacity of rich marquis and handsome man; and in other respects also he was quite as profound a politician as Philip the Second himself. He consoled himself for his nickname, and for the disesteem of the regiment by thinking that his comrades were blackguards, whose opinion would never be of any consequence to him if by chance they survived the present war, which seemed to be one of extermination. He relied on his face to win him promotion; he saw himself made colonel by feminine influence and a carefully managed transition from captain of equipment to orderly officer, and from orderly officer to *aide-de-camp* on the staff of some easy-going marshal. By that time, he reflected, he should come into his property of a hundred thousand *scudi* a year, some journal would speak of him as "the brave Montefiore," he would marry a girl of rank, and no one would dare to dispute his courage or verify his wounds.

Captain Montefiore had one friend in the person of the quartermaster,—a Provencal, born in the neighbourhood of Nice, whose name was Diard. A friend, whether at the galleys or in the garret of an artist, consoles for many troubles. Now Montefiore and Diard were two philosophers, who consoled each other for their present lives by the study of vice, as artists soothe the immediate disappointment of their hopes by the expectation of future fame. Both regarded the war in its results, not its action; they simply considered those who died for

259

glory fools. Chance had made soldiers of them; whereas their natural proclivities would have seated them at the green table of a congress. Nature had poured Montefiore into the mould of a Rizzio, and Diard into that of a diplomatist. Both were endowed with that nervous, feverish, half-feminine organization, which is equally strong for good or evil, and from which may emanate, according to the impulse of these singular temperaments, a crime or a generous action, a noble deed or a base one. The fate of such natures depends at any moment on the pressure, more or less powerful, produced on their nervous systems by violent and transitory passions.

Diard was considered a good accountant, but no soldier would have trusted him with his purse or his will, possibly because of the antipathy felt by all real soldiers against the bureaucrats. The quartermaster was not without courage and a certain juvenile generosity, sentiments which many men give up as they grow older, by dint of reasoning or calculating. Variable as the beauty of a fair woman, Diard was a great boaster and a great talker, talking of everything. He said he was artistic, and he made prizes (like two celebrated generals) of works of art, solely, he declared, to preserve them for posterity. His military comrades would have been puzzled indeed to form a correct judgment of him. Many of them, accustomed to draw upon his funds when occasion obliged them, thought him rich; but in truth, he was a gambler, and gamblers may be said to have nothing of their own. Montefiore was also a gambler, and all the officers of the regiment played with the pair; for, to the shame of men be it said, it is not a rare thing to see persons gambling together around a green table who, when the game is finished, will not bow to their companions, feeling no respect for them. Montefiore was the man with whom Bianchi made his bet about the heart of the Spanish sentinel.

Montefiore and Diard were among the last to mount the breach at Tarragona, but the first in the heart of the town as soon as it was taken. Accidents of this sort happen in all attacks, but with this pair of friends they were customary. Supporting each other, they made their way bravely through a labyrinth of narrow and gloomy little streets in quest of their personal objects; one seeking for painted Madonnas, the other for Madonnas of flesh and blood.

In what part of Tarragona it happened I cannot say, but Diard presently recognized by its architecture the portal of a convent, the gate of which was already battered in. Springing into the cloister to put a stop to the fury of the soldiers, he arrived just in time to prevent two Parisians from shooting a Virgin by Albano. In spite of the moustache with which in their military fanaticism they had decorated her face, he bought the picture. Montefiore, left alone during this episode, noticed, nearly opposite the convent, the house and shop of a draper, from which a shot was fired at him at the moment when his eyes caught a flaming glance from those of an inquisitive young girl, whose head was advanced under the shelter of a blind. Tarragona taken by assault, Tarragona furious, firing from every window, Tarragona violated, with dishevelled hair, and half-naked, was indeed an object of curiosity,—the curiosity of a daring Spanish woman. It was a magnified bull-fight.

Montefiore forgot the pillage, and heard, for the moment, neither the cries, nor the musketry, nor the growling of the artillery. The profile of that Spanish girl was the most divinely delicious thing which he, an Italian libertine, weary of Italian beauty, and dreaming of an impossible woman because he was tired of all women, had ever seen. He could still quiver, he, who had wasted his fortune on a thousand follies, the thousand passions of a young and *blasé* man—the most abominable monster that society generates. An idea came into his head, suggested perhaps by the shot of the draper-patriot, namely,—to set fire to the house. But he was now alone, and without any means of action; the fighting was centred in the market-place, where a few obstinate beings were still defending the town. A better idea then occurred to him. Diard came out of the convent, but Montefiore said not a word of his discovery; on the contrary, he accompanied him on a series of rambles about the streets. But the next day, the Italian had obtained his military billet in the house of the draper,—an appropriate lodging for an equipment captain!

The house of the worthy Spaniard consisted, on the ground-floor, of a vast and gloomy shop, externally fortified with stout iron bars, such as we see in the old storehouses of the rue des Lombards. This shop communicated with a parlour lighted from an interior courtyard, a large room breathing the very spirit of the middle-ages, with smoky old pictures, old tapestries, antique *brazero*, a plumed hat hanging to a nail, the musket of the guerrillas, and the cloak of Bartholo. The kitchen adjoined this unique living-room, where the inmates took their meals and warmed themselves over the dull glow of the brazier, smoking cigars and discoursing bitterly to animate all hearts with hatred against the French. Silver pitchers and precious dishes of plate and porcelain adorned a buttery shelf of the old fashion. But the light, sparsely admitted, allowed these dazzling objects to show but slightly; all things, as in pictures of the Dutch school, looked brown, even the faces. Between the shop and this living-room, so fine in colour and in its tone of patriarchal life, was a dark staircase leading to a ware-room where the light, carefully distributed, permitted the examination of goods. Above this were the apartments of the merchant and his wife. Rooms for an apprentice and a servant-woman were in a garret under the roof, which projected over the street and was supported by buttresses, giving a somewhat fantastic appearance to the exterior of the building. These chambers were now taken by the merchant and his wife who gave up their own rooms to the officer who was billeted upon them,—probably because they wished to avoid all quarrelling.

Montefiore gave himself out as a former Spanish subject, persecuted by Napoleon, whom he was serving against his will; and these semi-lies had the success he expected. He was invited to share the meals of the family, and was treated with the respect due to his name, his birth, and his title. He had his reasons for capturing the good-will of the merchant and his wife; he scented his Madonna as the ogre scented the youthful flesh of Tom Thumb and his brothers. But in spite of the confidence he managed to inspire in the worthy pair the latter maintained the most profound silence as to the said Madonna; and not only did the captain see no trace of the young girl during the first day he spent under the roof of the honest Spaniard, but he heard no sound and came upon no indication which revealed her presence in that ancient building. Supposing that she was the only daughter of the old couple, Montefiore concluded they had consigned her to the garret, where, for the time being, they made their home.

But no revelation came to betray the hiding-place of that precious treasure. The marquis glued his face to the lozenge-shaped leaded panes which looked upon the black-walled enclosure of the inner courtyard; but in vain; he saw no gleam of light except from the windows of the old couple, whom he could see and hear as they went and came and talked and coughed. Of the young girl, not a shadow!

Montefiore was far too wary to risk the future of his passion by exploring the house nocturnally, or by tapping softly on the doors. Discovery by that hot patriot, the mercer, suspicious as a Spaniard must be, meant ruin infallibly. The captain therefore resolved to wait patiently, resting his faith on time and the imperfection of men, which always results—even with scoundrels, and how much more with honest men!—in the neglect of precautions.

The next day he discovered a hammock in the kitchen, showing plainly where the servant-woman slept. As for the apprentice, his bed was evidently made on the shop counter. During supper on the second day Montefiore succeeded, by cursing Napoleon, in smoothing the anxious forehead of the merchant, a grave, black-visaged Spaniard, much like the faces formerly carved on the handles of Moorish lutes; even the wife let a gay smile of hatred appear in the folds of her elderly face. The lamp and the reflections of the brazier illumined fantastically the shadows of the noble room. The mistress of the house offered a *cigarrito* to their semi-compatriot. At this moment the rustle of a dress and the fall of a chair behind the tapestry were plainly heard.

"Ah!" cried the wife, turning pale, "may the saints assist us! God grant no harm has happened!"

"You have some one in the next room, have you not?" said Montefiore, giving no sign of emotion.

The draper dropped a word of imprecation against the girls. Evidently alarmed, the wife opened a secret door, and led in, half fainting, the Italian's Madonna, to whom he was careful to pay no attention; only, to avoid a too-studied indifference, he glanced at the girl before he turned to his host and said in his own language:—

"Is that your daughter, *signore?*"

Perez de Lagounia (such was the merchant's name) had large commercial relations with Genoa, Florence, and Livorno; he knew Italian, and replied in the same language:—

"No; if she were my daughter I should take less precautions. The child is confided to our care, and I would rather die than see any evil happen to her. But how is it possible to put sense into a girl of eighteen?"

"She is very handsome," said Montefiore, coldly, not looking at her face again.

"Her mother's beauty is celebrated," replied the merchant, briefly.

They continued to smoke, watching each other. Though Montefiore compelled himself not to give the slightest look which might contradict his apparent coldness, he could not refrain, at a moment when Perez turned his head to expectorate, from casting a rapid glance at the young girl, whose sparkling eyes met his. Then, with that science of vision which gives to a libertine, as it does to a sculptor, the fatal power of disrobing, if we may so express it, a woman, and divining her shape by inductions both rapid and sagacious, he beheld one of those masterpieces of Nature whose creation appears to demand as its right all the happiness of love. Here was a fair young face, on which the sun of Spain had cast faint tones of bistre which added to its expression of seraphic calmness a passionate pride, like a flash of light infused beneath that diaphanous complexion,—due, perhaps, to

263

the Moorish blood which vivified and coloured it. Her hair, raised to the top of her head, fell thence with black reflections round the delicate transparent ears and defined the outlines of a blue-veined throat. These luxuriant locks brought into strong relief the dazzling eyes and the scarlet lips of a well-arched mouth. The bodice of the country set off the lines of a figure that swayed as easily as a branch of willow. She was not the Virgin of Italy, but the Virgin of Spain, of Murillo, the only artist daring enough to have painted the Mother of God intoxicated with the joy of conceiving the Christ,—the glowing imagination of the boldest and also the warmest of painters.

In this young girl three things were united, a single one of which would have sufficed for the glory of a woman: the purity of the pearl in the depths of ocean; the sublime exaltation of the Spanish Saint Teresa; and a passion of love which was ignorant of itself. The presence of such a woman has the virtue of a talisman. Montefiore no longer felt worn and jaded. That young girl brought back his youthful freshness.

But, though the apparition was delightful, it did not last. The girl was taken back to the secret chamber, where the servant-woman carried to her openly both light and food.

"You do right to hide her," said Montefiore in Italian. "I will keep your secret. The devil! we have generals in our army who are capable of abducting her."

Montefiore's infatuation went so far as to suggest to him the idea of marrying her. He accordingly asked her history, and Perez very willingly told him the circumstances under which she had become his ward. The prudent Spaniard was led to make this confidence because he had heard of Montefiore in Italy, and knowing his reputation was desirous to let him see how strong were the barriers which protected the young girl from the possibility of seduction. Though the goodman was gifted with a certain patriarchal eloquence, in keeping with his simple life and customs, his tale will be improved by abridgment.

At the period when the French Revolution changed the manners and morals of every country which served as the scene of its wars, a street prostitute came to Tarragona, driven from Venice at the time of its fall. The life of this woman had been a tissue of romantic adventures and strange vicissitudes. To her, oftener than to any other woman of her class, it had happened, thanks to the caprice of great lords struck with her extraordinary beauty, to be literally gorged with gold and jewels and all the delights of excessive wealth,—flowers, carriages, pages, maids, palaces, pictures, journeys (like those of Catherine II.); in short, the life of a queen, despotic in her caprices and obeyed, often beyond her own imaginings. Then, without herself, or any one, chemist, physician, or man of science, being able to discover how her gold evaporated, she would find herself back in the streets, poor, denuded of everything, preserving nothing but her all-powerful beauty, yet living on without thought or care of the past, the present, or the future. Cast, in her poverty, into the hands of some poor gambling officer, she attached herself to him as a dog to its master, sharing the discomforts of the military life, which indeed she comforted, as content under the roof of a garret as beneath the silken hangings of opulence. Italian and Spanish both, she fulfilled very scrupulously the duties of religion, and more than once she had said to love:—

"Return tomorrow; today I belong to God."

But this slime permeated with gold and perfumes, this careless indifference to all things, these unbridled passions, these religious beliefs cast into that heart like diamonds into mire, this life begun, and ended, in a hospital, these gambling chances transferred to the soul, to the very existence,—in short, this great alchemy, for which vice lit the fire beneath the crucible in which fortunes were melted up and the gold of ancestors and the honour of great names evaporated, proceeded from a *cause*, a particular heredity, faithfully transmitted from mother to daughter since the middle ages. The name of this woman was La Marana. In her family, existing solely in the female line, the idea, person, name and power of a father had been completely unknown since the thirteenth century. The name Marana was to her what the designation of Stuart is to the celebrated royal race of Scotland, a name of distinction substituted for the patronymic name by the constant heredity of the same office devolving on the family.

Formerly, in France, Spain, and Italy, when those three countries had, in the fourteenth and fifteenth centuries, mutual interests which united and disunited them by perpetual warfare, the name Marana served to express in its general sense, a prostitute. In those days women of that sort had a certain rank in the world of which nothing in our day can give an idea. Ninon de l'Enclos and Marian Delorme have alone played, in France, the role of the Imperias, Catalinas, and Maranas who, in preceding centuries, gathered around them the cassock, gown, and sword. An Imperia built I forget which church in Rome in a frenzy of repentance, as Rhodope built, in earlier times, a pyramid in Egypt. The name Marana, inflicted at first as a disgrace upon the singular family with which we are now concerned, had ended by becoming its veritable name and by ennobling its vice by incontestable antiquity.

One day, a day of opulence or of penury I know not which, for this event was a secret between herself and God, but assuredly it was in a moment of repentance and melancholy, this Marana of the nineteenth century stood with her feet in the slime and her head raised to heaven. She cursed the blood in her veins, she cursed herself, she trembled lest she should have a daughter, and she swore, as such women swear, on the honour and with the will of the galleys—the firmest will, the most scrupulous honour that there is on earth—she swore, before an altar, and believing in that altar, to make her daughter a virtuous creature, a saint, and thus to gain, after that long line of lost women, criminals in love, an angel in heaven for them all.

The vow once made, the blood of the Maranas spoke; the courtesan returned to her reckless life, a thought the more within her heart. At last she loved, with the violent love of such women, as Henrietta Wilson loved Lord Ponsonby, as Mademoiselle Dupuis loved Bolingbroke, as the Marchesa Pescara loved her husband—but no, she did not love, she adored one of those fair men, half women, to whom she gave the virtues which she had not, striving to keep for herself all that there was of vice between them. It was from that weak man, that senseless marriage unblessed by God or man which happiness is thought to justify, but which no happiness absolves, and for which men blush at last, that she had a daughter, a daughter to save, a daughter for whom to desire a noble life and the chastity she had not. Henceforth, happy or not happy, opulent or beggared, she had in her heart a pure, untainted sentiment, the highest of all human feelings because the most disinterested. Love has its egotism, but motherhood has none. La Marana was a mother like none other; for, in her total, her eternal shipwreck, motherhood might still redeem her. To accomplish sacredly through life the task of sending a pure soul to heaven, was not that a better thing than a tardy repentance? was it not, in truth, the only spotless prayer which she could lift to God?

So, when this daughter, when her Marie-Juana-Pepita (she would fain have given her all the saints in the calendar as guardians), when this dear little creature was granted to her, she became possessed of so high an idea of the dignity of motherhood that she entreated vice to grant her a respite. She made herself virtuous and lived in solitude. No more fetes, no more orgies, no more love. All joys, all fortunes were centred now in the cradle of her child. The tones of that infant voice made an oasis for her soul in the burning sands of her existence. That sentiment could not be measured or estimated by any other. Did it not, in fact, comprise all human sentiments, all heavenly hopes? La

Marana was so resolved not to soil her daughter with any stain other than that of birth, that she sought to invest her with social virtues; she even obliged the young father to settle a handsome patrimony upon the child and to give her his name. Thus the girl was not know as Juana Marana, but as Juana di Mancini.

Then, after seven years of joy, and kisses, and intoxicating happiness, the time came when the poor Marana deprived herself of her idol. That Juana might never bow her head under their hereditary shame, the mother had the courage to renounce her child for her child's sake, and to seek, not without horrible suffering, for another mother, another home, other principles to follow, other and saintlier examples to imitate. The abdication of a mother is either a revolting act or a sublime one; in this case, was it not sublime?

At Tarragona a lucky accident threw the Lagounias in her way, under circumstances which enabled her to recognize the integrity of the Spaniard and the noble virtue of his wife. She came to them at a time when her proposal seemed that of a liberating angel. The fortune and honour of the merchant, momentarily compromised, required a prompt and secret succour. La Marana made over to the husband the whole sum she had obtained of the father for Juana's "dot," requiring neither acknowledgment nor interest. According to her own code of honour, a contract, a trust, was a thing of the heart, and God its supreme judge. After stating the miseries of her position to Dona Lagounia, she confided her daughter and her daughter's fortune to the fine old Spanish honour, pure and spotless, which filled the precincts of that ancient house. Dona Lagounia had no child, and she was only too happy to obtain one to nurture. The mother then parted from her Juana, convinced that the child's future was safe, and certain of having found her a mother, a mother who would bring her up as a Mancini, and not as a Marana.

Leaving her child in the simple modest house of the merchant where the burgher virtues reigned, where religion and sacred sentiments and honour filled the air, the poor prostitute, the disinherited mother was enabled to bear her trial by visions of Juana, virgin, wife, and mother, a mother throughout her life. On the threshold of that house Marana left a tear such as the angels garner up.

Since that day of mourning and hope the mother, drawn by some invincible presentiment, had thrice returned to see her daughter. Once when Juana fell ill with a dangerous complaint:

"I knew it," she said to Perez when she reached the house.

Asleep, she had seen her Juana dying. She nursed her and watched her, until one morning, sure of the girl's convalescence, she kissed her, still asleep, on the forehead and left her without betraying whom she was. A second time the Marana came to the church where Juana made her first communion. Simply dressed, concealing herself behind a column, the exiled mother recognized herself in her daughter such as she once had been, pure as the snow fresh-fallen on the Alps. A courtesan even in maternity, the Marana felt in the depths of her soul a jealous sentiment, stronger for the moment than that of love, and she left the church, incapable of resisting any longer the desire to kill Dona Lagounia, as she sat there, with radiant face, too much the mother of her child. A third and last meeting had taken place between mother and daughter in the streets of Milan, to which city the merchant and his wife had paid a visit. The Marana drove through the Corso in all the splendour of a sovereign; she passed her daughter like a flash of lightning and was not recognized. Horrible anguish! To this Marana, surfeited with kisses, one was lacking, a single one, for which she would have bartered all the others: the joyous, girlish kiss of a daughter to a mother, an honoured mother, a mother in whom shone all the domestic virtues. Juana living was dead to her. One thought revived the soul of the courtesan—a precious thought! Juana was henceforth safe. She might be the humblest of women, but at least she was not what her mother was—an infamous courtesan.

The merchant and his wife had fulfilled their trust with scrupulous integrity. Juana's fortune, managed by them, had increased tenfold. Perez de Lagounia, now the richest merchant in the provinces, felt for the young girl a sentiment that was semi-superstitious. Her money had preserved his ancient house from dishonourable ruin, and the presence of so precious a treasure had brought him untold prosperity. His wife, a heart of gold, and full of delicacy, had made the child religious, and as pure as she was beautiful. Juana might well become the wife of either a great *seigneur* or a wealthy merchant; she lacked no virtue necessary to the highest destiny. Perez had intended taking her to Madrid and marrying her to some grandee, but the events of the present war delayed the fulfilment of this project.

"I don't know where the Marana now is," said Perez, ending the above history, "but in whatever quarter of the world she may be living, when she hears of the occupation of our province by your armies, and of the siege of Tarragona, she will assuredly set out at once to come here and see to her daughter's safety."

CHAPTER 2

Auction

The foregoing narrative changed the intentions of the Italian captain; no longer did he think of making a Marchesa di Montefiore of Juana di Mancini. He recognized the blood of the Maranas in the glance the girl had given from behind the blinds, in the trick she had just played to satisfy her curiosity, and also in the parting look she had cast upon him. The libertine wanted a virtuous woman for a wife.

The adventure was full of danger, but danger of a kind that never daunts the least courageous man, for love and pleasure followed it. The apprentice sleeping in the shop, the cook bivouacking in the kitchen, Perez and his wife sleeping, no doubt, the wakeful sleep of the aged, the echoing sonority of the old mansion, the close surveillance of the girl in the day-time,—all these things were obstacles, and made success a thing well-nigh impossible. But Montefiore had in his favour against all impossibilities the blood of the Maranas which gushed in the heart of that inquisitive girl, Italian by birth, Spanish in principles, virgin indeed, but impatient to love. Passion, the girl, and Montefiore were ready and able to defy the whole universe.

Montefiore, impelled as much by the instinct of a man of gallantry as by those vague hopes which cannot be explained, and to which we give the name of presentiments (a word of astonishing verbal accuracy), Montefiore spent the first hours of the night at his window, endeavouring to look below him to the secret apartment where, undoubtedly, the merchant and his wife had hidden the love and joyfulness of their old age. The ware-room of the *entresol* separated him from the rooms on the ground-floor. The captain therefore could not have recourse to noises significantly made from one floor to the other, an artificial language which all lovers know well how to create. But chance, or it may have been the young girl herself, came to his assistance. At the moment when he stationed himself at his window, he saw, on the black wall of the courtyard, a circle of light, in the centre of which the silhouette of Juana was clearly defined; the consecutive movement of the arms, and the attitude, gave evidence that she was arranging her hair for the night.

"Is she alone?" Montefiore asked himself; "could I, without danger, lower a letter filled with coin and strike it against that circular window in her hiding-place?"

At once he wrote a note, the note of a man exiled by his family to Elba, the note of a degraded marquis now a mere captain of equipment. Then he made a cord of whatever he could find that was capable of being turned into string, filled the note with a few silver crowns, and lowered it in the deepest silence to the centre of that spherical gleam.

"The shadows will show if her mother or the servant is with her," thought Montefiore. "If she is not alone, I can pull up the string at once."

But, after succeeding with infinite trouble in striking the glass, a single form, the little figure of Juana, appeared upon the wall. The young girl opened her window cautiously, saw the note, took it, and stood before the window while she read it. In it, Montefiore had given his name and asked for an interview, offering, after the style of the old romances, his heart and hand to the Signorina Juana di Mancini—a common trick, the success of which is nearly always certain. At Juana's age, nobility of soul increases the dangers which surround youth. A poet of our day has said: "Woman succumbs only to her own nobility. The lover pretends to doubt the love he inspires at the moment when he is most beloved; the young girl, confident and proud, longs to make sacrifices to prove her love, and knows the world and men too little to continue calm in the midst of her rising emotions and repel with contempt the man who accepts a life offered in expiation of a false reproach."

Ever since the constitution of societies the young girl finds herself torn by a struggle between the caution of prudent virtue and the evils of wrong-doing. Often she loses a love, delightful in prospect, and the first, if she resists; on the other hand, she loses a marriage if she is imprudent. Casting a glance over the vicissitudes of social life in Paris, it is impossible to doubt the necessity of religion; and yet Paris is situated in the forty-eighth degree of latitude, while Tarragona is in the forty-first. The old question of climates is still useful to narrators to explain the sudden denouements, the imprudences, or the resistances of love.

Montefiore kept his eyes fixed on the exquisite black profile projected by the gleam upon the wall. Neither he nor Juana could see each other; a troublesome cornice, vexatiously placed, deprived them of the mute correspondence which may be established between a pair of lovers as they bend to each other from their windows. Thus the mind and the attention of the captain were concentrated on that luminous circle where, without perhaps knowing it herself, the young girl would, he thought, innocently reveal her thoughts by a series of gestures. But no! The singular motions she proceeded to make gave not a particle of hope to the expectant lover. Juana was amusing herself by cutting up his missive. But virtue and innocence sometimes imitate the clever proceedings inspired by jealousy to the Bartholos of comedy. Juana, without pens, ink, or paper, was replying by snip of scissors. Presently she refastened the note to the string; the officer drew it up, opened it, and read by the light of his lamp one word, carefully cut out of the paper: *come.*

"Come!" he said to himself; "but what of poison? or the dagger or carbine of Perez? And that apprentice not yet asleep, perhaps, in the shop? and the servant in her hammock? Besides, this old house echoes the slightest sound; I can hear old Perez snoring even here. Come, indeed! She can have nothing more to lose."

Bitter reflection! rakes alone are logical and will punish a woman for devotion. Man created Satan and Lovelace; but a virgin is an angel on whom he can bestow naught but his own vices. She is so grand, so beautiful, that he cannot magnify or embellish her; he has only the fatal power to blast her and drag her down into his own mire.

Montefiore waited for a later and more somnolent hour of the night; then, in spite of his reflections, he descended the stairs without boots, armed with his pistols, moving step by step, stopping to question the silence, putting forth his hands, measuring the stairs, peering into the darkness, and ready at the slightest incident to fly back into his room. The Italian had put on his handsomest uniform; he had perfumed his black hair, and now shone with the particular brilliancy which dress and toilet bestow upon natural beauty. Under such circumstances most men are as feminine as a woman.

The marquis arrived without hindrance before the secret door of the room in which the girl was hidden, a sort of cell made in the angle of the house and belonging exclusively to Juana, who had remained there hidden during the day from every eye while the siege lasted. Up to the present time she had slept in the room of her adopted mother, but the limited space in the garret where the merchant and his wife had gone to make room for the officer who was billeted upon them, did not allow of her going with them. Dona Lagounia had therefore left the young girl to the guardianship of lock and key, under the protection of religious ideas, all the more efficacious because they were partly superstitious, and also under the shield of a native pride and sensitive modesty which made the young Mancini in sort an exception among her sex. Juana possessed in an equal degree the most attaching virtues and the most passionate impulses; she had needed the modesty and sanctity of this monotonous life to calm and cool the tumultuous blood of the Maranas which bounded in her heart, the desires of which her adopted mother told her were an instigation of the devil.

A faint ray of light traced along the sill of the secret door guided Montefiore to the place; he scratched the panel softly and Juana opened to him. Montefiore entered, palpitating, but he recognized in the expression of the girl's face complete ignorance of her peril, a sort of naive curiosity, and an innocent admiration. He stopped short, arrested for a moment by the sacredness of the picture which met his eyes.

He saw before him a tapestry on the walls with a grey ground sprinkled with violets, a little coffer of ebony, an antique mirror, an immense and very old arm chair also in ebony and covered with tapestry, a table with twisted legs, a pretty carpet on the floor, near the table a single chair; and that was all. On the table, however, were flowers and embroidery; in a recess at the farther end of the room was the narrow little bed where Juana dreamed. Above the bed were three pictures; and near the pillow a crucifix, with a holy water basin and a prayer, printed in letters of gold and framed. Flowers exhaled their perfume faintly; the candles cast a tender light; all was calm and pure and sacred. The dreamy thoughts of Juana, but above all Juana herself, had communicated to all things her own peculiar charm; her soul appeared to shine there, like the pearl in its matrix. Juana, dressed in white, beautiful with naught but her own beauty, laying down her rosary to answer love, might have inspired respect, even in a Montefiore, if the silence, if the night, if Juana herself had not seemed so amorous. Montefiore stood still, intoxicated with an unknown happiness, possibly that of Satan beholding heaven through a rift of the clouds which form its enclosure.

"As soon as I saw you," he said in pure Tuscan, and in the modest tone of voice so peculiarly Italian, "I loved you. My soul and my life are now in you, and in you they will be forever, if you will have it so."

Juana listened, inhaling from the atmosphere the sound of these words which the accents of love made magnificent.

"Poor child! how have you breathed so long the air of this dismal house without dying of it? You, made to reign in the world, to inhabit the palace of a prince, to live in the midst of fetes, to feel the joys which love bestows, to see the world at your feet, to efface all other beauty by your own which can have no rival—you, to live here, solitary, with those two shopkeepers!"

Adroit question! He wished to know if Juana had a lover.

"True," she replied. "But who can have told you my secret thoughts? For the last few months I have nearly died of sadness. Yes, I would *rather* die than stay longer in this house. Look at that embroidery; there is not a stitch there which I did not set with dreadful thoughts. How many times I have thought of escaping to fling myself into the sea! Why? I don't know why,—little childish troubles, but very keen, though they are so silly. Often I have kissed my mother at night as one would kiss a mother for the last time, saying in my heart: 'Tomorrow I will kill myself.' But I do not die. Suicides go to hell, you know, and I am so afraid of hell that I resign myself to live, to get up in the morning and go to bed at night, and work the same hours, and do the same things. I am not so weary of it, but I suffer—And yet, my father and mother adore me. Oh! I am bad, I am bad; I say so to my confessor."

"Do you always live here alone, without amusement, without pleasures?"

"Oh! I have not always been like this. Till I was fifteen the festivals of the church, the chants, the music gave me pleasure. I was happy, feeling myself like the angels without sin and able to communicate every week—I loved God then. But for the last three years, from day to day, all things have changed. First, I wanted flowers here—and I have them, lovely flowers! Then I wanted—but I want nothing now," she added, after a pause, smiling at Montefiore. "Have you not said that you would love me always?"

"Yes, my Juana," cried Montefiore, softly, taking her round the waist and pressing her to his heart, "yes. But let me speak to you as you speak to God. Are you not as beautiful as Mary in heaven? Listen. I swear to you," he continued, kissing her hair, "I swear to take that forehead for my altar, to make you my idol, to lay at your feet all the luxuries of the world. For you, my palace at Milan; for you my horses, my jewels, the diamonds of my ancient family; for you, each day, fresh jewels, a thousand pleasures, and all the joys of earth!"

"Yes," she said reflectively, "I would like that; but I feel within my

273

soul that I would like better than all the world my husband. *Mio caro sposo!*" she said, as if it were impossible to give in any other language the infinite tenderness, the loving elegance with which the Italian tongue and accent clothe those delightful words. Besides, Italian was Juana's maternal language.

"I should find," she continued, with a glance at Montefiore in which shone the purity of the cherubim, "I should find in *him* my dear religion, him and God—God and him. Is he to be you?" she said. "Yes, surely it will be you," she cried, after a pause. "Come, and see the picture my father brought me from Italy."

She took a candle, made a sign to Montefiore, and showed him at the foot of her bed a Saint Michael overthrowing the demon.

"Look!" she said, "has he not your eyes? When I saw you from my window in the street, our meeting seemed to me a sign from heaven. Every day during my morning meditation, while waiting for my mother to call me to prayer, I have so gazed at that picture, that angel, that I have ended by thinking him my husband—oh! heavens, I speak to you as though you were myself. I must seem crazy to you; but if you only knew how a poor captive wants to tell the thoughts that choke her! When alone, I talk to my flowers, to my tapestry; they can understand me better, I think, than my father and mother, who are so grave."

"Juana," said Montefiore, taking her hands and kissing them with the passion that gushed in his eyes, in his gestures, in the tones of his voice, "speak to me as your husband, as yourself. I have suffered all that you have suffered. Between us two few words are needed to make us comprehend our past, but there will never be enough to express our coming happiness. Lay your hand upon my heart. Feel how it beats. Let us promise before God, who sees and hears us, to be faithful to each other throughout our lives. Here, take my ring—and give me yours."

"Give you my ring!" she said in terror.

"Why not?" asked Montefiore, uneasy at such artlessness.

"But our holy father the Pope has blessed it; it was put upon my finger in childhood by a beautiful lady who took care of me, and who told me never to part with it."

"Juana, you cannot love me!"

"Ah!" she said, "here it is; take it. You, are you not another my-self?"

She held out the ring with a trembling hand, holding it tightly as she looked at Montefiore with a clear and penetrating eye that questioned him. That ring! all of herself was in it; but she gave it to him.

"Oh, my Juana!" said Montefiore, again pressing her in his arms. "I should be a monster indeed if I deceived you. I will love you forever."

Juana was thoughtful. Montefiore, reflecting that in this first interview he ought to venture upon nothing that might frighten a young girl so ignorantly pure, so imprudent by virtue rather than from desire, postponed all further action to the future, relying on his beauty, of which he knew the power, and on this innocent ring-marriage, the hymen of the heart, the lightest, yet the strongest of all ceremonies. For the rest of that night, and throughout the next day, Juana's imagination was the accomplice of her passion.

On this first evening Montefiore forced himself to be as respectful as he was tender. With that intention, in the interests of his passion and the desires with which Juana inspired him, he was caressing and unctuous in language; he launched the young creature into plans for a new existence, described to her the world under glowing colours, talked to her of household details always attractive to the mind of girls, giving her a sense of the rights and realities of love. Then, having agreed upon the hour for their future nocturnal interviews, he left her happy, but changed; the pure and pious Juana existed no longer; in the last glance she gave him, in the pretty movement by which she brought her forehead to his lips, there was already more of passion than a girl should feel. Solitude, weariness of employments contrary to her nature had brought this about. To make the daughter of the Maranas truly virtuous, she ought to have been habituated, little by little, to the world, or else to have been wholly withdrawn from it.

"The day, tomorrow, will seem very long to me," she said, receiving his kisses on her forehead. "But stay in the salon, and speak loud, that I may hear your voice; it fills my soul."

Montefiore, clever enough to imagine the girl's life, was all the more satisfied with himself for restraining his desires because he saw that it would lead to his greater contentment. He returned to his room without accident.

Ten days went by without any event occurring to trouble the peace and solitude of the house. Montefiore employed his Italian cajolery on old Perez, on Dona Lagounia, on the apprentice, even on the cook, and they all liked him; but, in spite of the confidence he now inspired in them, he never asked to see Juana, or to have the door of her mysterious hiding-place opened to him. The young girl, hungry to see her lover, implored him to do so; but he always refused her from an instinct of prudence. Besides, he had used his best powers and fascinations to lull the suspicions of the old couple, and had now accustomed them to see him, a soldier, stay in bed till midday on pretence that he was ill. Thus the lovers lived only in the night-time, when the rest of the household were asleep. If Montefiore had not been one of those libertines whom the habit of gallantry enables to retain their self-possession under all circumstances, he might have been lost a dozen times during those ten days. A young lover, in the simplicity of a first love, would have committed the enchanting imprudences which are so difficult to resist. But he did resist even Juana herself, Juana pouting, Juana making her long hair a chain which she wound about his neck when caution told him he must go.

The most suspicious of guardians would however have been puzzled to detect the secret of their nightly meetings. It is to be supposed that, sure of success, the Italian marquis gave himself the ineffable pleasures of a slow seduction, step by step, leading gradually to the fire which should end the affair in a conflagration. On the eleventh day, at the dinner-table, he thought it wise to inform old Perez, under seal of secrecy, that the reason of his separation from his family was an ill-assorted marriage. This false revelation was an infamous thing in view of the nocturnal drama which was being played under that roof. Montefiore, an experienced rake, was preparing for the finale of that drama which he foresaw and enjoyed as an artist who loves his art. He expected to leave before long, and without regret, the house and his love. It would happen, he thought, in this way: Juana, after waiting for him in vain for several nights, would risk her life, perhaps, in asking Perez what had become of his guest; and Perez would reply, not aware of the importance of his answer,—

"The Marquis de Montefiore is reconciled to his family, who consent to receive his wife; he has gone to Italy to present her to them."

And Juana?—The marquis never asked himself what would become of Juana; but he had studied her character, its nobility, candour, and strength, and he knew he might be sure of her silence.

He obtained a mission from one of the generals. Three days later, on the night preceding his intended departure, Montefiore, instead of returning to his own room after dinner, contrived to enter unseen that of Juana, to make that farewell night the longer. Juana, true Spaniard and true Italian, was enchanted with such boldness; it argued ardour! For herself she did not fear discovery. To find in the pure love of marriage the excitements of intrigue, to hide her husband behind the curtains of her bed, and say to her adopted father and mother, in case of detection: "I am the Marquise de Montefiore!"—was to an igno-

276

rant and romantic young girl, who for three years past had dreamed of love without dreaming of its dangers, delightful. The door closed on this last evening upon her folly, her happiness, like a veil, which it is useless here to raise.

It was nine o'clock; the merchant and his wife were reading their evening prayers; suddenly the noise of a carriage drawn by several horses resounded in the street; loud and hasty raps echoed from the shop where the servant hurried to open the door, and into that venerable salon rushed a woman, magnificently dressed in spite of the mud upon the wheels of her travelling-carriage, which had just crossed Italy, France, and Spain. It was, of course, the Marana,—the Marana who, in spite of her thirty-six years, was still in all the glory of her ravishing beauty; the Marana who, being at that time the mistress of a king, had left Naples, the fetes, the skies of Naples, the climax of her life of luxury, on hearing from her royal lover of the events in Spain and the siege of Tarragona.

"Tarragona! I must get to Tarragona before the town is taken!" she cried. "Ten days to reach Tarragona!"

Then without caring for crown or court, she arrived in Tarragona, furnished with an almost imperial safe-conduct; furnished too with gold which enabled her to cross France with the velocity of a rocket.

"My daughter! my daughter!" cried the Marana.

At this voice, and the abrupt invasion of their solitude, the prayerbook fell from the hands of the old couple.

"She is there," replied the merchant, calmly, after a pause during which he recovered from the emotion caused by the abrupt entrance, and the look and voice of the mother. "She is there," he repeated, pointing to the door of the little chamber.

"Yes, but has any harm come to her; is she still—"

"Perfectly well," said Dona Lagounia.

"O God! send me to hell if it so pleases thee!" cried the Marana, dropping, exhausted and half dead, into a chair.

The flush in her cheeks, due to anxiety, paled suddenly; she had strength to endure suffering, but none to bear this joy. Joy was more violent in her soul than suffering, for it contained the echoes of her pain and the agonies of its own emotion.

"But," she said, "how have you kept her safe? Tarragona is taken."

"Yes," said Perez, "but since you see me living why do you ask that question? Should I not have died before harm could have come to Juana?"

At that answer, the Marana seized the calloused hand of the old man, and kissed it, wetting it with the tears that flowed from her eyes—she who never wept! those tears were all she had most precious under heaven.

"My good Perez!" she said at last. "But have you had no soldiers quartered in your house?"

"Only one," replied the Spaniard. "Fortunately for us the most loyal of men; a Spaniard by birth, but now an Italian who hates Bonaparte; a married man. He is ill, and gets up late and goes to bed early."

"An Italian! What is his name?"

"Montefiore."

"Can it be the Marquis de Montefiore—"

"Yes, Senora, he himself."

"Has he seen Juana?"

"No," said Dona Lagounia.

"You are mistaken, wife," said Perez. "The marquis must have seen her for a moment, a short moment, it is true; but I think he looked at her that evening she came in here during supper."

"Ah, let me see my daughter!"

"Nothing easier," said Perez; "she is now asleep. If she has left the key in the lock we must waken her."

As he rose to take the duplicate key of Juana's door his eyes fell by chance on the circular gleam of light upon the black wall of the inner courtyard. Within that circle he saw the shadow of a group such as Canova alone has attempted to render. The Spaniard turned back.

"I do not know," he said to the Marana, "where to find the key."

"You are very pale," she said.

"And I will show you why," he cried, seizing his dagger and rapping its hilt violently on Juana's door as he shouted,—

"Open! open! open! Juana!"

Juana did not open, for she needed time to conceal Montefiore. She knew nothing of what was passing in the salon; the double portieres of thick tapestry deadened all sounds.

"Madame, I lied to you in saying I could not find the key. Here it is," added Perez, taking it from a sideboard. "But it is useless. Juana's key is in the lock; her door is barricaded. We have been deceived, my wife!" he added, turning to Dona Lagounia. "There is a man in Juana's room."

"Impossible! By my eternal salvation I say it is impossible!" said his wife.

"Do not swear, Dona Lagounia. Our honour is dead, and this woman—" He pointed to the Marana, who had risen and was standing motionless, blasted by his words, "this woman has the right to despise us. She saved our life, our fortune, and our honour, and we have saved nothing for her but her money—Juana!" he cried again, "open, or I will burst in your door."

His voice, rising in violence, echoed through the garrets in the roof. He was cold and calm. The life of Montefiore was in his hands; he would wash away his remorse in the blood of that Italian.

"Out, out, out! out, all of you!" cried the Marana, springing like a tigress on the dagger, which she wrenched from the hand of the astonished Perez. "Out, Perez," she continued more calmly, "out, you and your wife and servants! There will be murder here. You might be shot by the French. Have nothing to do with this; it is my affair, mine only. Between my daughter and me there is none but God. As for the man, he belongs to *me*. The whole earth could not tear him from my grasp. Go, go! I forgive you. I see plainly that the girl is a Marana. You, your religion, your virtue, were too weak to fight against my blood."

She gave a dreadful sigh, turning her dry eyes on them. She had lost all, but she knew how to suffer,—a true courtesan.

The door opened. The Marana forgot all else, and Perez, making a sign to his wife, remained at his post. With his old invincible Spanish honour he was determined to share the vengeance of the betrayed mother. Juana, all in white, and softly lighted by the wax candles, was standing calmly in the centre of her chamber.

"What do you want with me?" she said.

The Marana could not repress a passing shudder.

"Perez," she asked, "has this room another issue?"

Perez made a negative gesture; confiding in that gesture, the mother entered the room.

"Juana," she said, "I am your mother, your judge; you have placed yourself in the only situation in which I could reveal myself to you. You have come down to me, you, whom I thought in heaven. Ah! you have fallen low indeed. You have a lover in this room."

"Madame, there is and can be no one but my husband," answered the girl. "I am the Marquise de Montefiore."

"Then there are two," said Perez, in a grave voice. "He told me he was married."

"Montefiore, my love!" cried the girl, tearing aside the curtain and revealing the officer. "Come! they are slandering you."

The Italian appeared, pale and speechless; he saw the dagger in the Marana's hand, and he knew her well. With one bound he sprang from the room, crying out in a thundering voice,—

"Help! help! they are murdering a Frenchman. Soldiers of the 6th of the line, rush for Captain Diard! Help, help!"

Perez had gripped the man and was trying to gag him with his large hand, but the Marana stopped him, saying,—

"Bind him fast, but let him shout. Open the doors, leave them open, and go, go, as I told you; go, all of you.—As for you," she said, addressing Montefiore, "shout, call for help if you choose; by the time your soldiers get here this blade will be in your heart. Are you married? Answer."

Montefiore, who had fallen on the threshold of the door, scarcely a step from Juana, saw nothing but the blade of the dagger, the gleam of which blinded him.

"Has he deceived me?" said Juana, slowly. "He told me he was free."

"He told me that he was married," repeated Perez, in his solemn voice.

"Holy Virgin!" murmured Dona Lagounia.

"Answer, soul of corruption," said the Marana, in a low voice, bending to the ear of the marquis.

"Your daughter—" began Montefiore.

"The daughter that was mine is dead or dying," interrupted the Marana. "I have no daughter; do not utter that word. Answer, are you married?"

"No, *madame*," said Montefiore, at last, striving to gain time, "I desire to marry your daughter."

"My noble Montefiore!" said Juana, drawing a deep breath.

"Then why did you attempt to fly and cry for help?" asked Perez. Terrible, revealing light!

Juana said nothing, but she wrung her hands and went to her armchair and sat down.

At that moment a tumult rose in the street which was plainly heard in the silence of the room. A soldier of the 6th, hearing Montefiore's cry for help, had summoned Diard. The quartermaster, who was fortunately in his bivouac, came, accompanied by friends.

"Why did I fly?" said Montefiore, hearing the voice of his friend. "Because I told you the truth; I am married—Diard! Diard!" he shouted in a piercing voice.

But, at a word from Perez, the apprentice closed and bolted the doors, so that the soldiers were delayed by battering them in. Before they could enter, the Marana had time to strike her dagger into the guilty man; but anger hindered her aim, the blade slipped upon the Italian's epaulet, though she struck her blow with such force that he fell at the very feet of Juana, who took no notice of him. The Marana sprang upon him, and this time, resolved not to miss her prey, she caught him by the throat.

"I am free and I will marry her! I swear it, by God, by my mother, by all there is most sacred in the world; I am a bachelor; I will marry her, on my honour!"

And he bit the arm of the courtesan.

"Mother," said Juana, "kill him. He is so base that I will not have him for my husband, were he ten times as beautiful."

"Ah! I recognize my daughter!" cried the mother.

"What is all this?" demanded the quartermaster, entering the room.

"They are murdering me," cried Montefiore, "on account of this girl; she says I am her lover. She inveigled me into a trap, and they are forcing me to marry her—"

"And you reject her?" cried Diard, struck with the splendid beauty which contempt, hatred, and indignation had given to the girl, already so beautiful. "Then you are hard to please. If she wants a husband I am ready to marry her. Put up your weapons; there is no trouble here."

The Marana pulled the Italian to the side of her daughter's bed and said to him, in a low voice,—

"If I spare you, give thanks for the rest of your life; but, remember this, if your tongue ever injures my daughter you will see me again. Go!—How much 'dot' do you give her?" she continued, going up to Perez.

"She has two hundred thousand gold *piastres*," replied the Spaniard.

"And that is not all, monsieur," said the Marana, turning to Diard. "Who are you?—Go!" she repeated to Montefiore.

The marquis, hearing this statement of gold *piastres*, came forward once more, saying,—

"I am really free—"

A glance from Juana silenced him.

"You are really free to go," she said.

And he went immediately.

"Alas! monsieur," said the girl, turning to Diard, "I thank you with admiration. But my husband is in heaven. Tomorrow I shall enter a convent—"

"Juana, my Juana, hush!" cried the mother, clasping her in her arms. Then she whispered in the girl's ear. "You *must* have another husband."

Juana turned pale. She freed herself from her mother and sat down once more in her arm-chair.

"Who are you, monsieur?" repeated the Marana, addressing Diard.

"Madame, I am at present only the quartermaster of the 6th of the line. But for such a wife I have the heart to make myself a marshal of France. My name is Pierre-Francois Diard. My father was provost of merchants. I am not—"

"But, at least, you are an honest man, are you not?" cried the Marana, interrupting him. "If you please the Signorina Juana di Mancini, you can marry her and be happy together.—Juana," she continued in a grave tone, "in becoming the wife of a brave and worthy man remember that you will also be a mother. I have sworn that you shall kiss your children without a blush upon your face" (her voice faltered slightly). "I have sworn that you shall live a virtuous life; expect, therefore, many troubles. But, whatever happens, continue pure, and be faithful to your husband. Sacrifice all things to him, for he will be the father of your children—the father of your children! If you take a lover, I, your mother, will stand between you and him. Do you see that dagger? It is in your 'dot,'" she continued, throwing the weapon on Juana's bed. "I leave it there as the guarantee of your honour so long as my eyes are open and my arm free. Farewell," she said, restraining her tears. "God grant that we may never meet again."

At that idea, her tears began to flow.

"Poor child!" she added, "you have been happier than you knew in this dull home.—Do not allow her to regret it," she said, turning to Diard.

The foregoing rapid narrative is not the principal subject of this Study, for the understanding of which it was necessary to explain how it happened that the quartermaster Diard married Juana di Mancini, that Montefiore and Diard were intimately known to each other, and to show plainly what blood and what passions were in Madame Diard.

CHAPTER 3

The History of Madame Diard

By the time that the quartermaster had fulfilled all the long and dilatory formalities without which no French soldier can be married, he was passionately in love with Juana di Mancini, and Juana had had time to think of her coming destiny.

An awful destiny! Juana, who felt neither esteem nor love for Diard, was bound to him forever, by a rash but necessary promise. The man was neither handsome nor well-made. His manners, devoid of all distinction, were a mixture of the worst army tone, the habits of his province, and his own insufficient education. How could she love Diard, she, a young girl all grace and elegance, born with an invincible instinct for luxury and good taste, her very nature tending toward the sphere of the higher social classes? As for esteeming him, she rejected the very thought precisely because he had married her. This repulsion was natural. Woman is a saintly and noble creature, but almost always misunderstood, and nearly always misjudged because she is misunderstood. If Juana had loved Diard she would have esteemed him. Love creates in a wife a new woman; the woman of the day before no longer exists on the morrow. Putting on the nuptial robe of a passion in which life itself is concerned, the woman wraps herself in purity and whiteness. Reborn into virtue and chastity, there is no past for her; she is all future, and should forget the things behind her to relearn life. In this sense the famous words which a modern poet has put into the lips of Marion Delorme is infused with truth,—

"And Love remade me virgin."

That line seems like a reminiscence of a tragedy of Corneille, so truly does it recall the energetic diction of the father of our modern theatre. Yet the poet was forced to sacrifice it to the essentially vaudevillist spirit of the pit.

So Juana loveless was doomed to be Juana humiliated, degraded, hopeless. She could not honour the man who took her thus. She felt, in all the conscientious purity of her youth, that distinction, subtle in appearance but sacredly true, legal with the heart's legality, which women apply instinctively to all their feelings, even the least reflective. Juana became profoundly sad as she saw the nature and the extent of the life before her. Often she turned her eyes, brimming with tears proudly repressed, upon Perez and Dona Lagounia, who fully comprehended, both of them, the bitter thoughts those tears contained. But they were silent: of what good were reproaches now; why look for consolations? The deeper they were, the more they enlarged the wound.

One evening, Juana, stupid with grief, heard through the open door of her little room, which the old couple had thought shut, a pitying moan from her adopted mother.

"The child will die of grief."

"Yes," said Perez, in a shaking voice, "but what can we do? I cannot now boast of her beauty and her chastity to Comte d'Arcos, to whom I hoped to marry her."

"But a single fault is not vice," said the old woman, pitying as the angels.

"Her mother gave her to this man," said Perez.

"Yes, in a moment; without consulting the poor child!" cried Dona Lagounia.

"She knew what she was doing."

"But oh! into what hands our pearl is going!"

"Say no more, or I shall seek a quarrel with that Diard."

"And that would only lead to other miseries."

Hearing these dreadful words Juana saw the happy future she had lost by her own wrongdoing. The pure and simple years of her quiet life would have been rewarded by a brilliant existence such as she had fondly dreamed,—dreams which had caused her ruin. To fall from the height of Greatness to Monsieur Diard! She wept. At times she went nearly mad. She floated for a while between vice and religion. Vice was a speedy solution, religion a lifetime of suffering. The meditation was stormy and solemn. The next day was the fatal day, the day for the marriage. But Juana could still remain free. Free, she knew how far her misery would go; married, she was ignorant of where it went or what it might bring her.

Religion triumphed. Dona Lagounia stayed beside her child and prayed and watched as she would have prayed and watched beside the dying.

"God wills it," she said to Juana.

Nature gives to woman alternately a strength which enables her to suffer and a weakness which leads her to resignation. Juana resigned herself; and without restriction. She determined to obey her mother's prayer, and cross the desert of life to reach God's heaven, knowing well that no flowers grew for her along the way of that painful journey.

She married Diard. As for the quartermaster, though he had no grace in Juana's eyes, we may well absolve him. He loved her distractedly. The Marana, so keen to know the signs of love, had recognized in that man the accents of passion and the brusque nature, the generous impulses, that are common to Southerners. In the paroxysm of her anger and her distress she had thought such qualities enough for her daughter's happiness.

The first days of this marriage were apparently happy; or, to express one of those latent facts, the miseries of which are buried by women in the depths of their souls, Juana would not cast down her husband's joy,—a double role, dreadful to play, but to which, sooner or later, all women unhappily married come. This is a history impossible to recount in its full truth. Juana, struggling hourly against her nature, a nature both Spanish and Italian, having dried up the source of her tears by dint of weeping, was a human type, destined to represent woman's misery in its utmost expression, namely, sorrow undyingly active; the description of which would need such minute observations that to persons eager for dramatic emotions they would seem insipid. This analysis, in which every wife would find some one of her own sufferings, would require a volume to express them all; a fruitless, hopeless volume by its very nature, the merit of which would consist in faintest tints and delicate shadings which critics would declare to be effeminate and diffuse. Besides, what man could rightly approach, unless he bore another heart within his heart, those solemn and touching elegies which certain women carry with them to their tomb; melancholies, misunderstood even by those who cause them; sighs unheeded, devotions unrewarded,—on earth at least,—splendid silences misconstrued; vengeances withheld, disdained; generosities perpetually bestowed and wasted; pleasures longed for and denied; angelic charities secretly accomplished,—in short, all the religions of womanhood and its inextinguishable love.

Juana knew that life; fate spared her nought. She was wholly a wife, but a sorrowful and suffering wife; a wife incessantly wounded, yet forgiving always; a wife pure as a flawless diamond,—she who had the beauty and the glow of the diamond, and in that beauty, that glow, a

285

vengeance in her hand; for she was certainly not a woman to fear the dagger added to her "dot."

At first, inspired by a real love, by one of those passions which for the time being change even odious characters and bring to light all that may be noble in a soul, Diard behaved like a man of honour. He forced Montefiore to leave the regiment and even the army corps, so that his wife might never meet him during the time they remained in Spain. Next, he petitioned for his own removal, and succeeded in entering the Imperial Guard. He desired at any price to obtain a title, honours, and consideration in keeping with his present wealth. With this idea in his mind, he behaved courageously in one of the most bloody battles in Germany, but, unfortunately, he was too severely wounded to remain in the service. Threatened with the loss of a leg, he was forced to retire on a pension, without the title of baron, without those rewards he hoped to win, and would have won had he not been Diard.

This event, this wound, and his thwarted hopes contributed to change his character. His Provencal energy, roused for a time, sank down. At first he was sustained by his wife, in whom his efforts, his courage, his ambition had induced some belief in his nature, and who showed herself, what women are, tender and consoling in the troubles of life. Inspired by a few words from Juana, the retired soldier came to Paris, resolved to win in an administrative career a position to command respect, bury in oblivion the quartermaster of the 6th of the line, and secure for Madame Diard a noble title. His passion for that seductive creature enabled him to divine her most secret wishes. Juana expressed nothing, but he understood her. He was not loved as a lover dreams of being loved; he knew this, and he strove to make himself respected, loved, and cherished. He foresaw a coming happiness, poor man, in the patience and gentleness shown on all occasions by his wife; but that patience, that gentleness, were only the outward signs of the resignation which had made her his wife. Resignation, religion, were they love? Often Diard wished for refusal where he met with chaste obedience; often he would have given his eternal life that Juana might have wept upon his bosom and not disguised her secret thoughts behind a smiling face which lied to him nobly. Many young men—for after a certain age men no longer struggle—persist in the effort to triumph over an evil fate, the thunder of which they hear, from time to time, on the horizon of their lives; and when at last they succumb and roll down the precipice of evil, we ought to do them justice and acknowledge these inward struggles.

Like many men Diard tried all things, and all things were hostile to him. His wealth enabled him to surround his wife with the enjoyments of Parisian luxury. She lived in a fine house, with noble rooms, where she maintained a salon, in which abounded artists (by nature no judges of men), men of pleasure ready to amuse themselves anywhere, a few politicians who swelled the numbers, and certain men of fashion, all of whom admired Juana. Those who put themselves before the eyes of the public in Paris must either conquer Paris or be subject to it. Diard's character was not sufficiently strong, compact, or persistent to command society at that epoch, because it was an epoch when all men were endeavouring to rise. Social classifications ready-made are perhaps a great boon even for the people. Napoleon has confided to us the pains he took to inspire respect in his court, where most of the courtiers had been his equals. But Napoleon was Corsican, and Diard Provencal. Given equal genius, an islander will always be more compact and rounded than the man of terra firma in the same latitude; the arm of the sea which separates Corsica from Provence is, in spite of human science, an ocean which has made two nations.

Diard's mongrel position, which he himself made still more questionable, brought him great troubles. Perhaps there is useful instruction to be derived from the almost imperceptible connection of acts which led to the finale of this history.

In the first place, the sneerers of Paris did not see without malicious smiles and words the pictures with which the former quartermaster adorned his handsome mansion. Works of art purchased the night before were said to be spoils from Spain; and this accusation was the revenge of those who were jealous of his present fortune. Juana comprehended this reproach, and by her advice Diard sent back to Tarragona all the pictures he had brought from there. But the public, determined to see things in the worst light, only said, "That Diard is shrewd; he has sold his pictures." Worthy people continued to think that those which remained in the Diard salons were not honourably acquired. Some jealous women asked how it was that a *Diard* had been able to marry so rich and beautiful a young girl. Hence comments and satires without end, such as Paris contributes. And yet, it must be said, that Juana met on all sides the respect inspired by her pure and religious life, which triumphed over everything, even Parisian calumny; but this respect stopped short with her, her husband received none of it. Juana's feminine perception and her keen eye hovering over her salons, brought her nothing but pain.

This lack of esteem was perfectly natural. Diard's comrades, in spite of the virtues which our imaginations attribute to soldiers, never forgave the former quartermaster of the 6th of the line for becoming suddenly so rich and for attempting to cut a figure in Paris. Now in Paris, from the last house in the *faubourg* Saint-Germain to the last in the rue Saint-Lazare, between the heights of the Luxembourg and the heights of Montmartre, all that clothes itself and gabbles, clothes itself to go out and goes out to gabble. All that world of great and small pretensions, that world of insolence and humble desires, of envy and cringing, all that is gilded or tarnished, young or old, noble of yesterday or noble from the fourth century, all that sneers at a parvenu, all that fears to commit itself, all that wants to demolish power and worships power if it resists,—*all* those ears hear, *all* those tongues say, *all* those minds know, in a single evening, where the new-comer who aspires to honour among them was born and brought up, and what that interloper has done, or has not done, in the course of his life. There may be no court of assizes for the upper classes of society; but at any rate they have the most cruel of public prosecutors, an intangible moral being, both judge and executioner, who accuses and brands. Do not hope to hide anything from him; tell him all yourself; he wants to know all and he will know all. Do not ask what mysterious telegraph it was which conveyed to him in the twinkling of an eye, at any hour, in any place, that story, that bit of news, that scandal; do not ask what prompts him. That telegraph is a social mystery; no observer can report its effects. Of many extraordinary instances thereof, one may suffice: The assassination of the Duc de Berry, which occurred at the Opera-house, was related within ten minutes in the Ile-Saint-Louis. Thus the opinion of the 6th of the line as to its quartermaster filtered through society the night on which he gave his first ball.

Diard was therefore debarred from succeeding in society. Henceforth his wife alone had the power to make anything of him. Miracle of our strange civilization! In Paris, if a man is incapable of being anything himself, his wife, when she is young and clever, may give him other chances for elevation. We sometimes meet with invalid women, feeble beings apparently, who, without rising from sofas or leaving their chambers, have ruled society, moved a thousand springs, and placed their husbands where their ambition or their vanity prompted. But Juana, whose childhood was passed in her retreat in Tarragona, knew nothing of the vices, the meannesses, or the resources of Parisian society; she looked at that society with the curiosity of a girl, but she learned from it only that which her sorrow and her wounded pride revealed to her.

Juana had the tact of a virgin heart which receives impressions in advance of the event, after the manner of what are called *sensitives*. The solitary young girl, so suddenly become a woman and a wife, saw plainly that were she to attempt to compel society to respect her husband, it must be after the manner of Spanish beggars, carbine in hand. Besides, the multiplicity of the precautions she would have to take, would they meet the necessity? Suddenly she divined society as, once before, she had divined life, and she saw nothing around her but the immense extent of an irreparable disaster. She had, moreover, the additional grief of tardily recognizing her husband's peculiar form of incapacity; he was a man unfitted for any purpose that required continuity of ideas. He could not understand a consistent part, such as he ought to play in the world; he perceived it neither as a whole nor in its gradations, and its gradations were everything. He was in one of those positions where shrewdness and tact might have taken the place of strength; when shrewdness and tact succeed, they are, perhaps, the highest form of strength.

Now Diard, far from arresting the spot of oil on his garments left by his antecedents, did his best to spread it. Incapable of studying the phase of the empire in the midst of which he came to live in Paris, he wanted to be made prefect. At that time every one believed in the genius of Napoleon; his favour enhanced the value of all offices. Prefectures, those miniature empires, could only be filled by men of great names, or chamberlains of H.M. the emperor and king. Already the prefects were a species of vizier. The myrmidons of the great man scoffed at Diard's pretensions to a prefecture, whereupon he lowered his demand to a sub-prefecture. There was, of course, a ridiculous discrepancy between this latter demand and the magnitude of his fortune. To frequent the imperial salons and live with insolent luxury, and then to abandon that millionaire life and bury himself as sub-prefect at Issoudun or Savenay was certainly holding himself below his position. Juana, too late aware of our laws and habits and administrative customs, did not enlighten her husband soon enough. Diard, desperate, petitioned successively all the ministerial powers; repulsed everywhere, he found nothing open to him; and society then judged him as the government judged him and as he judged himself. Diard, grievously wounded on the battlefield, was nevertheless not decorated; the quartermaster, rich as he was, was allowed no place in public life, and society logically refused him that to which he pretended in its midst.

Finally, to cap all, the luckless man felt in his own home the superiority of his wife. Though she used great tact—we might say velvet

289

softness if the term were admissible—to disguise from her husband this supremacy, which surprised and humiliated herself, Diard ended by being affected by it.

At a game of life like this men are either unmanned, or they grow the stronger, or they give themselves to evil. The courage or the ardour of this man lessened under the reiterated blows which his own faults dealt to his self-appreciation, and fault after fault he committed. In the first place he had to struggle against his own habits and character. A passionate Provencal, frank in his vices as in his virtues, this man whose fibres vibrated like the strings of a harp, was all heart to his former friends. He succoured the shabby and spattered man as readily as the needy of rank; in short, he accepted everybody, and gave his hand in his gilded salons to many a poor devil. Observing this on one occasion, a general of the empire, a variety of the human species of which no type will presently remain, refused his hand to Diard, and called him, insolently, "my good fellow" when he met him. The few persons of really good society whom Diard knew, treated him with that elegant, polished contempt against which a new-made man has seldom any weapons. The manners, the semi-Italian gesticulations, the speech of Diard, his style of dress,—all contributed to repulse the respect which careful observation of matters of good taste and dignity might otherwise obtain for vulgar persons; the yoke of such conventionalities can only be cast off by great and unthinkable powers. So goes the world.

These details but faintly picture the many tortures to which Juana was subjected; they came upon her one by one; each social nature pricked her with its own particular pin; and to a soul which preferred the thrust of a dagger, there could be no worse suffering than this struggle in which Diard received insults he did not feel and Juana felt those she did not receive. A moment came, an awful moment, when she gained a clear and lucid perception of society, and felt in one instant all the sorrows which were gathering themselves together to fall upon her head. She judged her husband incapable of rising to the honoured ranks of the social order, and she felt that he would one day descend to where his instincts led him. Henceforth Juana felt pity for him.

The future was very gloomy for this young woman. She lived in constant apprehension of some disaster. This presentiment was in her soul as a contagion is in the air, but she had strength of mind and will to disguise her anguish beneath a smile. Juana had ceased to think of herself. She used her influence to make Diard resign his various pretensions and to show him, as a haven, the peaceful and consoling life of home. Evils came from society—why not banish it? In his home Diard found peace and respect; he reigned there. She felt herself strong to accept the trying task of making him happy,—he, a man dissatisfied with himself. Her energy increased with the difficulties of life; she had all the secret heroism necessary to her position; religion inspired her with those desires which support the angel appointed to protect a Christian soul—occult poesy, allegorical image of our two natures!

Diard abandoned his projects, closed his house to the world, and lived in his home. But here he found another reef. The poor soldier had one of those eccentric souls which need perpetual motion. Diard was one of the men who are instinctively compelled to start again the moment they arrive, and whose vital object seems to be to come and go incessantly, like the wheels mentioned in Holy Writ. Perhaps he felt the need of flying from himself. Without wearying of Juana, without blaming Juana, his passion for her, rendered tranquil by time, allowed his natural character to assert itself. Henceforth his days of gloom were more frequent, and he often gave way to southern excitement. The more virtuous a woman is and the more irreproachable, the more a man likes to find fault with her, if only to assert by that act his legal superiority. But if by chance she seems really imposing to him, he feels the need of foisting faults upon her. After that, between man and wife, trifles increase and grow till they swell to Alps.

But Juana, patient and without pride, gentle and without that bitterness which women know so well how to cast into their submission, left Diard no chance for planned ill-humour. Besides, she was one of those noble creatures to whom it is impossible to speak disrespectfully; her glance, in which her life, saintly and pure, shone out, had the weight of a fascination. Diard, embarrassed at first, then annoyed, ended by feeling that such high virtue was a yoke upon him. The goodness of his wife gave him no violent emotions, and violent emotions were what he wanted. What myriads of scenes are played in the depths of his souls, beneath the cold exterior of lives that are, apparently, commonplace! Among these dramas, lasting each but a short time, though they influence life so powerfully and are frequently the forerunners of the great misfortune doomed to fall on so many marriages, it is difficult to choose an example. There was a scene, however, which particularly marked the moment when in the life of this husband and wife estrangement began. Perhaps it may also serve to explain the finale of this narrative.

Juana had two children, happily for her, two sons. The first was born seven months after her marriage. He was called Juan, and he strongly resembled his mother. The second was born about two years after her arrival in Paris. The latter resembled both Diard and Juana, but more particularly Diard. His name was Francisque. For the last five years Francisque had been the object of Juana's most tender and watchful care. The mother was constantly occupied with that child; to him her prettiest caresses; to him the toys, but to him, especially, the penetrating mother-looks. Juana had watched him from his cradle; she had studied his cries, his motions; she endeavoured to discern his nature that she might educate him wisely. It seemed at times as if she had but that one child. Diard, seeing that the eldest, Juan, was in a way neglected, took him under his own protection; and without inquiring even of himself whether the boy was the fruit of that ephemeral love to which he owed his wife, he made him his Benjamin.

Of all the sentiments transmitted to her through the blood of her grandmothers which consumed her, Madame Diard accepted one alone,—maternal love. But she loved her children doubly: first with the noble violence of which her mother the Marana had given her the example; secondly, with grace and purity, in the spirit of those social virtues the practice of which was the glory of her life and her inward recompense. The secret thought, the conscience of her motherhood, which gave to the Marana's life its stamp of untaught poesy, was to Juana an acknowledged life, an open consolation at all hours. Her mother had been virtuous as other women are criminal,—in secret; she had stolen a fancied happiness, she had never really tasted it. But Juana, unhappy in her virtue as her mother was unhappy in her vice, could enjoy at all moments the ineffable delights which her mother had so craved and could not have. To her, as to her mother, maternity comprised all earthly sentiments. Each, from differing causes, had no other comfort in their misery. Juana's maternal love may have been the strongest because, deprived of all other affections, she put the joys she lacked into the one joy of her children; and there are noble passions that resemble vice; the more they are satisfied the more they increase. Mothers and gamblers are alike insatiable.

When Juana saw the generous pardon laid silently on the head of Juan by Diard's fatherly affection, she was much moved, and from the day when the husband and wife changed parts she felt for him the true and deep interest she had hitherto shown to him as a matter of duty only. If that man had been more consistent in his life; if he had not destroyed by fitful inconstancy and restlessness the forces of a true though excitable sensibility, Juana would doubtless have loved him in the end. Unfortunately, he was a type of those southern natures which are keen in perceptions they cannot follow out; capable of great things over-night, and incapable the next morning; often the victim of their own virtues, and often lucky through their worst passions; admirable men in some respects, when their good qualities are kept to a steady energy by some outward bond. For two years after his retreat from active life Diard was held captive in his home by the softest chains. He lived, almost in spite of himself, under the influence of his wife, who made herself gay and amusing to cheer him, who used the resources of feminine genius to attract and seduce him to a love of virtue, but whose ability and cleverness did not go so far as to simulate love.

At this time all Paris was talking of the affair of a captain in the army who in a paroxysm of libertine jealousy had killed a woman. Diard, on coming home to dinner, told his wife that the officer was dead. He had killed himself to avoid the dishonour of a trial and the shame of death upon the scaffold. Juana did not see at first the logic of such conduct, and her husband was obliged to explain to her the fine jurisprudence of French law, which does not prosecute the dead.

"But, papa, didn't you tell us the other day that the king could pardon?" asked Francisque.

"The king can give nothing but life," said Juan, half scornfully.

Diard and Juana, the spectators of this little scene, were differently affected by it. The glance, moist with joy, which his wife cast upon her eldest child was a fatal revelation to the husband of the secrets of a heart hitherto impenetrable. That eldest child was all Juana; Juana comprehended him; she was sure of his heart, his future; she adored him, but her ardent love was a secret between herself, her child, and God. Juan instinctively enjoyed the seeming indifference of his mother in presence of his father and brother, for she pressed him to her heart when alone. Francisque was Diard, and Juana's incessant care and watchfulness betrayed her desire to correct in the son the vices of the father and to encourage his better qualities. Juana, unaware that her glance had said too much and that her husband had rightly interpreted it, took Francisque in her lap and gave him, in a gentle voice still trembling with the pleasure that Juan's answer had brought her, a lesson upon honour, simplified to his childish intelligence.

"That boy's character requires care," said Diard.

"Yes," she replied simply.

"How about Juan?"

Madame Diard, struck by the tone in which the words were uttered, looked at her husband.

"Juan was born perfect," he added.

Then he sat down gloomily, and reflected. Presently, as his wife continued silent, he added:—

"You love one of *your* children better than the other."

"You know that," she said.

"No," said Diard, "I did not know until now which of them you preferred."

"But neither of them have ever given me a moment's uneasiness," she answered quickly.

"But one of them gives you greater joys," he said, more quickly still.

"I never counted them," she said.

"How false you women are!" cried Diard. "Will you dare to say that Juan is not the child of your heart?"

"If that were so," she said, with dignity, "do you think it a misfortune?"

"You have never loved me. If you had chosen, I would have conquered worlds for your sake. You know all that I have struggled to do in life, supported by the hope of pleasing you. Ah! if you had only loved me!"

"A woman who loves," said Juana, "likes to live in solitude, far from the world, and that is what we are doing."

"I know, Juana, that *you* are never in the wrong."

The words were said bitterly, and cast, for the rest of their lives together, a coldness between them.

On the morrow of that fatal day Diard went back to his old companions and found distractions for his mind in play. Unfortunately, he won much money, and continued playing. Little by little, he returned to the dissipated life he had formerly lived. Soon he ceased even to dine in his own home.

Some months went by in the enjoyment of this new independence; he was determined to preserve it, and in order to do so he separated himself from his wife, giving her the large apartments and lodging himself in the entresol. By the end of the year Diard and Juana only saw each other in the morning at breakfast.

Like all gamblers, he had his alternations of loss and gain. Not wishing to cut into the capital of his fortune, he felt the necessity of withdrawing from his wife the management of their income; and the day came when he took from her all she had hitherto freely disposed of for the household benefit, giving her instead a monthly stipend. The conversation they had on this subject was the last of their married intercourse. The silence that fell between them was a true divorce; Juana comprehended that from henceforth she was only a mother, and she was glad, not seeking for the causes of this evil. For such an event is a great evil. Children are conjointly one with husband and wife in the home, and the life of her husband could not be a source of grief and injury to Juana only.

As for Diard, now emancipated, he speedily grew accustomed to win and lose enormous sums. A fine player and a heavy player, he soon became celebrated for his style of playing. The social consideration he had been unable to win under the Empire, he acquired under the Restoration by the rolling of his gold on the green cloth and by his talent for all games that were in vogue. Ambassadors, bankers, persons with newly-acquired large fortunes, and all those men who, having sucked life to the dregs, turn to gambling for its feverish joys, admired Diard at their clubs,—seldom in their own houses,—and they all gambled with him. He became the fashion. Two or three times during the winter he gave a fete as a matter of social pride in return for the civilities he received. At such times Juana once more caught a glimpse of the world of balls, festivities, luxury, and lights; but for her it was a sort of tax imposed upon the comfort of her solitude. She, the queen of these solemnities, appeared like a being fallen from some other planet. Her simplicity, which nothing had corrupted, her beautiful virginity of soul, which her peaceful life restored to her, her beauty and her true modesty, won her sincere homage. But observing how few women ever entered her salons, she came to understand that though her husband was following, without communicating its nature to her, a new line of conduct, he had gained nothing actually in the world's esteem.

Diard was not always lucky; far from it. In three years he had dissipated three fourths of his fortune, but his passion for play gave him the energy to continue it. He was intimate with a number of men, more particularly with the *roués* of the Bourse, men who, since the revolution, have set up the principle that robbery done on a large scale is only a *smirch* to the reputation,—transferring thus to financial matters the loose principles of love in the eighteenth century. Diard now became a sort of business man, and concerned himself in several of those affairs which are called *shady* in the slang of the law-courts. He practised the decent thievery by which so many men, cleverly masked, or hidden in the recesses of the political world, make their fortunes,—thievery which, if done in the streets by the light of an oil lamp, would see a poor devil to the galleys, but, under gilded ceilings and by the light of candelabra, is sanctioned. Diard brought up, monopolized, and sold sugars; he sold offices; he had the glory of inventing the "man of straw" for lucrative posts which it was necessary to keep in his own hands for a short time; he bought votes, receiving, on one occasion, so much per cent on the purchase of fifteen parliamentary votes which all passed on one division from the benches of the Left to the benches of the Right. Such actions are no longer crimes or thefts,—they are called governing, developing industry, becoming a financial power. Diard was placed by public opinion on the bench of infamy where many an able man was already seated. On that bench is the aristocracy of evil. It is the upper Chamber of scoundrels of high life. Diard was, therefore, not a mere commonplace gambler who is seen to be a blackguard, and ends by begging. That style of gambler is no longer seen in society of a certain topographical height. In these days bold scoundrels die brilliantly in the chariot of vice with the trappings of luxury. Diard, at least, did not buy his remorse at a low price; he made himself one of these privileged men. Having studied the machinery of government and learned all the secrets and the passions of the men in power, he was able to maintain himself in the fiery furnace into which he had sprung.

Madame Diard knew nothing of her husband's infernal life. Glad of his abandonment, she felt no curiosity about him, and all her hours were occupied. She devoted what money she had to the education of her children, wishing to make men of them, and giving them straightforward reasons, without, however, taking the bloom from their young imaginations. Through them alone came her interests and her emotions; consequently, she suffered no longer from her blemished life. Her children were to her what they are to many mothers for a long period of time,—a sort of renewal of their own existence. Diard was now an accidental circumstance, not a participator in her life, and since he had ceased to be the father and the head of the family, Juana felt bound to him by no tie other than that imposed by conventional laws. Nevertheless, she brought up her children to the highest respect for paternal authority, however imaginary it was for them. In this she was greatly seconded by her husband's continual absence. If he had been much in the home Diard would have neutralized his wife's efforts. The boys had too much intelligence and shrewdness not to have judged their father; and to judge a father is moral parricide.

In the long run, however, Juana's indifference to her husband wore itself away; it even changed to a species of fear. She understood at last how the conduct of a father might long weigh on the future of her children, and her motherly solicitude brought her many, though incomplete, revelations of the truth. From day to day the dread of some unknown but inevitable evil in the shadow of which she lived became more and more keen and terrible. Therefore, during the rare moments when Diard and Juana met she would cast upon his hollow face, wan from nights of gambling and furrowed by emotions, a piercing look, the penetration of which made Diard shudder. At such times the assumed gaiety of her husband alarmed Juana more than his gloomiest expressions of anxiety when, by chance, he forgot that assumption of joy. Diard feared his wife as a criminal fears the executioner. In him, Juana saw her children's shame; and in her Diard dreaded a calm vengeance, the judgment of that serene brow, an arm raised, a weapon ready.

After fifteen years of marriage Diard found himself without resources. He owed three hundred thousand *francs* and he could scarcely muster one hundred thousand. The house, his only visible possession, was mortgaged to its fullest selling value. A few days more, and the sort of prestige with which opulence had invested him would vanish. Not a hand would be offered, not a purse would be open to him. Unless some favourable event occurred he would fall into a slough of contempt, deeper perhaps than he deserved, precisely because he had mounted to a height he could not maintain. At this juncture he happened to hear that a number of strangers of distinction, diplomats and others, were assembled at the watering-places in the Pyrenees, where they gambled for enormous sums, and were doubtless well supplied with money.

He determined to go at once to the Pyrenees; but he would not leave his wife in Paris, lest some importunate creditor might reveal to her the secret of his horrible position. He therefore took her and the two children with him, refusing to allow her to take the tutor and scarcely permitting her to take a maid. His tone was curt and imperious; he seemed to have recovered some energy. This sudden journey, the cause of which escaped her penetration, alarmed Juana secretly. Her husband made it gaily. Obliged to occupy the same carriage, he showed himself day by day more attentive to the children and more amiable to their mother. Nevertheless, each day brought Juana dark presentiments, the presentiments of mothers who tremble without apparent reason, but who are seldom mistaken when they tremble thus. For them the veil of the future seems thinner than for others.

At Bordeaux, Diard hired in a quiet street a quiet little house, neatly furnished, and in it he established his wife. The house was at the corner of two streets, and had a garden. Joined to the neighbouring house on one side only, it was open to view and accessible on the other three sides. Diard paid the rent in advance, and left Juana barely enough money for the necessary expenses of three months, a sum not exceeding a thousand *francs*. Madame Diard made no observation on this unusual meanness. When her husband told her that he was going to the watering-places and that she would stay at Bordeaux, Juana offered no difficulty, and at once formed a plan to teach the children Spanish and Italian, and to make them read the two masterpieces of the two languages. She was glad to lead a retired life, simply and naturally economical. To spare herself the troubles of material life, she arranged with a *traiteur* the day after Diard's departure to send in their meals. Her maid then sufficed for the service of the house, and she thus found herself without money, but her wants all provided for until her husband's return. Her pleasures consisted in taking walks with the children. She was then thirty-three years old. Her beauty, greatly developed, was in all its lustre. Therefore as soon as she appeared, much talk was made in Bordeaux about the beautiful Spanish stranger. At the first advances made to her Juana ceased to walk abroad, and confined herself wholly to her own large garden.

Diard at first made a fortune at the baths. In two months he won three hundred thousand dollars, but it never occurred to him to send any money to his wife; he kept it all, expecting to make some great stroke of fortune on a vast stake. Towards the end of the second month the Marquis de Montefiore appeared at the same baths. The marquis was at this time celebrated for his wealth, his handsome face, his fortunate marriage with an Englishwoman, and more especially for his love of play. Diard, his former companion, encountered him, and desired to add his spoils to those of others. A gambler with four hundred thousand *francs* in hand is always in a position to do as he pleases. Diard, confident in his luck, renewed acquaintance with Montefiore. The latter received him very coldly, but nevertheless they played together, and Diard lost every penny that he possessed, and more.

"My dear Montefiore," said the ex-quartermaster, after making a tour of the salon, "I owe you a hundred thousand *francs*; but my money is in Bordeaux, where I have left my wife."

Diard had the money in bank-bills in his pocket; but with the self-possession and rapid bird's-eye view of a man accustomed to catch at all resources, he still hoped to recover himself by some one of the endless caprices of play. Montefiore had already mentioned his intention of visiting Bordeaux. Had he paid his debt on the spot, Diard would have been left without the power to take his revenge; a revenge at cards often exceeds the amount of all preceding losses. But these burning expectations depended on the marquis's reply.

"Wait, my dear fellow," said Montefiore, "and we will go together to Bordeaux. In all conscience, I am rich enough today not to wish to take the money of an old comrade."

Three days later Diard and Montefiore were in Bordeaux at a gambling table. Diard, having won enough to pay his hundred thousand *francs*, went on until he had lost two hundred thousand more on his word. He was gay as a man who swam in gold. Eleven o'clock sounded; the night was superb. Montefiore may have felt, like Diard, a desire to breathe the open air and recover from such emotions in a walk. The latter proposed to the marquis to come home with him to take a cup of tea and get his money.

"But Madame Diard?" said Montefiore.

"Bah!" exclaimed the husband.

They went down-stairs; but before taking his hat Diard entered the dining-room of the establishment and asked for a glass of water. While it was being brought, he walked up and down the room, and was able, without being noticed, to pick up one of those small sharp-pointed steel knives with pearl handles which are used for cutting fruit at dessert.

"Where do you live?" said Montefiore, in the courtyard, "for I want to send a carriage there to fetch me."

Diard told him the exact address.

"You see," said Montefiore, in a low voice, taking Diard's arm, "that as long as I am with you I have nothing to fear; but if I came home alone and a scoundrel were to follow me, I should be profitable to kill."

"Have you much with you?"

"No, not much," said the wary Italian, "only my winnings. But they would make a pretty fortune for a beggar and turn him into an honest man for the rest of his life."

Diard led the marquis along a lonely street where he remembered to have seen a house, the door of which was at the end of an avenue of trees with high and gloomy walls on either side of it. When they reached this spot he coolly invited the marquis to precede him; but as if the latter understood him he preferred to keep at his side. Then, no sooner were they fairly in the avenue, then Diard, with the agility of a tiger, tripped up the marquis with a kick behind the knees, and putting a foot on his neck stabbed him again and again to the heart till the blade of the knife broke in it. Then he searched Montefiore's pockets, took his wallet, money, everything. But though he had taken the Italian unawares, and had done the deed with lucid mind and the quickness of a pickpocket, Montefiore had time to cry "Murder!

Help!" in a shrill and piercing voice which was fit to rouse every sleeper in the neighbourhood. His last sighs were given in those horrible shrieks.

Diard was not aware that at the moment when they entered the avenue a crowd just issuing from a theatre was passing at the upper end of the street. The cries of the dying man reached them, though Diard did his best to stifle the noise by setting his foot firmly on Montefiore's neck. The crowd began to run towards the avenue, the high walls of which appeared to echo back the cries, directing them to the very spot where the crime was committed. The sound of their coming steps seemed to beat on Diard's brain. But not losing his head as yet, the murderer left the avenue and came boldly into the street, walking very gently, like a spectator who sees the inutility of trying to give help. He even turned round once or twice to judge of the distance between himself and the crowd, and he saw them rushing up the avenue, with the exception of one man, who, with a natural sense of caution, began to watch Diard.

"There he is! there he is!" cried the people, who had entered the avenue as soon as they saw Montefiore stretched out near the door of the empty house.

As soon as that clamour rose, Diard, feeling himself well in the advance, began to run or rather to fly, with the vigour of a lion and the bounds of a deer. At the other end of the street he saw, or fancied he saw, a mass of persons, and he dashed down a cross street to avoid them. But already every window was open, and heads were thrust forth right and left, while from every door came shouts and gleams of light. Diard kept on, going straight before him, through the lights and the noise; and his legs were so actively agile that he soon left the tumult behind him, though without being able to escape some eyes which took in the extent of his course more rapidly than he could cover it. Inhabitants, soldiers, gendarmes, every one, seemed afoot in the twinkling of an eye. Some men awoke the commissaries of police, others stayed by the body to guard it. The pursuit kept on in the direction of the fugitive, who dragged it after him like the flame of a conflagration.

Diard, as he ran, had all the sensations of a dream when he heard a whole city howling, running, panting after him. Nevertheless, he kept his ideas and his presence of mind. Presently he reached the wall of the garden of his house. The place was perfectly silent, and he thought he had foiled his pursuers, though a distant murmur of the tumult came to his ears like the roaring of the sea. He dipped some water from a brook and drank it. Then, observing a pile of stones on the road, he hid his treasure in it; obeying one of those vague thoughts which come to criminals at a moment when the faculty to judge their actions under all bearings deserts them, and they think to establish their innocence by want of proof of their guilt.

That done, he endeavoured to assume a placid countenance; he even tried to smile as he rapped softly on the door of his house, hoping that no one saw him. He raised his eyes, and through the outer blinds of one window came a gleam of light from his wife's room. Then, in the midst of his trouble, visions of her gentle life, spent with her children, beat upon his brain with the force of a hammer. The maid opened the door, which Diard hastily closed behind him with a kick. For a moment he breathed freely; then, noticing that he was bathed in perspiration, he sent the servant back to Juana and stayed in the darkness of the passage, where he wiped his face with his handkerchief and put his clothes in order, like a dandy about to pay a visit to a pretty woman. After that he walked into a track of the moonlight to examine his hands. A quiver of joy passed over him as he saw that no blood stains were on them; the haemorrhage from his victim's body was no doubt inward.

But all this took time. When at last he mounted the stairs to Juana's room he was calm and collected, and able to reflect on his position, which resolved itself into two ideas: to leave the house, and get to the wharves. He did not *think* these ideas, he *saw* them written in fiery letters on the darkness. Once at the wharves he could hide all day, return at night for his treasure, then conceal himself, like a rat, in the hold of some vessel and escape without any one suspecting his whereabouts. But to do all this, money, gold, was his first necessity,—and he did not possess one penny.

The maid brought a light to show him up.

"Felicie," he said, "don't you hear a noise in the street, shouts, cries? Go and see what it means, and come and tell me."

His wife, in her white dressing-gown, was sitting at a table, reading aloud to Francisque and Juan from a Spanish Cervantes, while the boys followed her pronunciation of the words from the text. They all three stopped and looked at Diard, who stood in the doorway with his hands in his pockets; overcome, perhaps, by finding himself in this calm scene, so softly lighted, so beautiful with the faces of his wife and children. It was a living picture of the Virgin between her son and John.

"Juana, I have something to say to you."

301

"What has happened?" she asked, instantly perceiving from the livid paleness of her husband that the misfortune she had daily expected was upon them.

"Oh, nothing; but I want to speak to you—to you, alone."

And he glanced at his sons.

"My dears, go to your room, and go to bed," said Juana; "say your prayers without me."

The boys left the room in silence, with the incurious obedience of well-trained children.

"My dear Juana," said Diard, in a coaxing voice, "I left you with very little money, and I regret it now. Listen to me; since I relieved you of the care of our income by giving you an allowance, have you not, like other women, laid something by?"

"No," replied Juana, "I have nothing. In making that allowance you did not reckon the costs of the children's education. I don't say that to reproach you, my friend, only to explain my want of money. All that you gave me went to pay masters and—"

"Enough!" cried Diard, violently. "Thunder of heaven! every instant is precious! Where are your jewels?"

"You know very well I have never worn any."

"Then there's not a *sou* to be had here!" cried Diard, frantically.

"Why do you shout in that way?" she asked.

"Juana," he replied, "I have killed a man."

Juana sprang to the door of her children's room and closed it; then she returned.

"Your sons must hear nothing," she said. "With whom have you fought?"

"Montefiore," he replied.

"Ah!" she said with a sigh, "the only man you had the right to kill."

"There were many reasons why he should die by my hand. But I can't lose time—Money, money! for God's sake, money! I may be pursued. We did not fight. I—I killed him."

"Killed him!" she cried, "how?"

"Why, as one kills anything. He stole my whole fortune and I took it back, that's all. Juana, now that everything is quiet you must go down to that heap of stones—you know the heap by the garden wall—and get that money, since you haven't any in the house."

"The money that you stole?" said Juana.

"What does that matter to you? Have you any money to give me? I tell you I must get away. They are on my traces."

"Who?"

"The people, the police."

Juana left the room, but returned immediately.

"Here," she said, holding out to him at arm's length a jewel, "that is Dona Lagounia's cross. There are four rubies in it, of great value, I have been told. Take it and go—go!"

"Felicie hasn't come back," he cried, with a sudden thought. "Can she have been arrested?"

Juana laid the cross on the table, and sprang to the windows that looked on the street. There she saw, in the moonlight, a file of soldiers posting themselves in deepest silence along the wall of the house. She turned, affecting to be calm, and said to her husband:—

"You have not a minute to lose; you must escape through the garden. Here is the key of the little gate."

As a precaution she turned to the other windows, looking on the garden. In the shadow of the trees she saw the gleam of the silver lace on the hats of a body of gendarmes; and she heard the distant mutterings of a crowd of persons whom sentinels were holding back at the end of the streets up which curiosity had drawn them. Diard had, in truth, been seen to enter his house by persons at their windows, and on their information and that of the frightened maid-servant, who was arrested, the troops and the people had blocked the two streets which led to the house. A dozen gendarmes, returning from the theatre, had climbed the walls of the garden, and guarded all exit in that direction.

"Monsieur," said Juana, "you cannot escape. The whole town is here."

Diard ran from window to window with the useless activity of a captive bird striking against the panes to escape. Juana stood silent and thoughtful.

"Juana, dear Juana, help me! give me, for pity's sake, some advice."

"Yes," said Juana, "I will; and I will save you."

"Ah! you are always my good angel."

Juana left the room and returned immediately, holding out to Diard, with averted head, one of his own pistols. Diard did not take it. Juana heard the entrance of the soldiers into the courtyard, where they laid down the body of the murdered man to confront the assassin with the sight of it. She turned round and saw Diard white and livid. The man was nearly fainting, and tried to sit down.

"Your children implore you," she said, putting the pistol beneath his hand.

"But—my good Juana, my little Juana, do you think—Juana! is it so pressing?—I want to kiss you."

The gendarmes were mounting the staircase. Juana grasped the pistol, aimed it at Diard, holding him, in spite of his cries, by the throat; then she blew his brains out and flung the weapon on the ground.

At that instant the door was opened violently. The public prosecutor, followed by an examining judge, a doctor, a sheriff, and a posse of gendarmes, all the representatives, in short, of human justice, entered the room.

"What do you want?" asked Juana.

"Is that Monsieur Diard?" said the prosecutor, pointing to the dead body bent double on the floor.

"Yes, monsieur."

"Your gown is covered with blood, *madame.*"

"Do you not see why?" replied Juana.

She went to the little table and sat down, taking up the volume of Cervantes; she was pale, with a nervous agitation which she nevertheless controlled, keeping it wholly inward.

"Leave the room," said the prosecutor to the gendarmes.

Then he signed to the examining judge and the doctor to remain.

"Madame, under the circumstances, we can only congratulate you on the death of your husband," he said. "At least he has died as a soldier should, whatever crime his passions may have led him to commit. His act renders negatory that of justice. But however we may desire to spare you at such a moment, the law requires that we should make an exact report of all violent deaths. You will permit us to do our duty?"

"May I go and change my dress?" she asked, laying down the volume.

"Yes, *madame*; but you must bring it back to us. The doctor may need it."

"It would be too painful for *madame* to see me operate," said the doctor, understanding the suspicions of the prosecutor. "Messieurs," he added, "I hope you will allow her to remain in the next room."

The magistrates approved the request of the merciful physician, and Felicie was permitted to attend her mistress. The judge and the prosecutor talked together in a low voice. Officers of the law are very unfortunate in being forced to suspect all, and to imagine evil everywhere. By dint of supposing wicked intentions, and of comprehending them, in order to reach the truth hidden under so many contradictory actions, it is impossible that the exercise of their dreadful functions should not, in the long run, dry up at their source the generous emotions they are constrained to repress. If the sensibilities of the surgeon who probes into the mysteries of the human body end by growing callous, what becomes of those of the judge who is incessantly compelled to search the inner folds of the soul? Martyrs to their mission, magistrates are all their lives in mourning for their lost illusions; crime weighs no less heavily on them than on the criminal. An old man seated on the bench is venerable, but a young judge makes a thoughtful person shudder. The examining judge in this case was young, and he felt obliged to say to the public prosecutor,—

"Do you think that woman was her husband's accomplice? Ought we to take her into custody? Is it best to question her?"

The prosecutor replied, with a careless shrug of his shoulders,—

"Montefiore and Diard were two well-known scoundrels. The maid evidently knew nothing of the crime. Better let the thing rest there."

The doctor performed the autopsy, and dictated his report to the sheriff. Suddenly he stopped, and hastily entered the next room.

"Madame—" he said.

Juana, who had removed her bloody gown, came towards him.

"It was you," he whispered, stooping to her ear, "who killed your husband."

"Yes, *monsieur*," she replied.

The doctor returned and continued his dictation as follows,—

"And, from the above assemblage of facts, it appears evident that the said Diard killed himself voluntarily and by his own hand."

"Have you finished?" he said to the sheriff after a pause.

"Yes," replied the writer.

The doctor signed the report. Juana, who had followed him into the room, gave him one glance, repressing with difficulty the tears which for an instant rose into her eyes and moistened them.

"Messieurs," she said to the public prosecutor and the judge, "I am a stranger here, and a Spaniard. I am ignorant of the laws, and I know no one in Bordeaux. I ask of you one kindness: enable me to obtain a passport for Spain."

"One moment!" cried the examining judge. "Madame, what has become of the money stolen from the Marquis de Montefiore?"

"Monsieur Diard," she replied, "said something to me vaguely about a heap of stones, under which he must have hidden it."

"Where?"

"In the street."

The two magistrates looked at each other. Juana made a noble gesture and motioned to the doctor.

"Monsieur," she said in his ear, "can I be suspected of some infamous action? I! The pile of stones must be close to the wall of my garden. Go yourself, I implore you. Look, search, find that money."

The doctor went out, taking with him the examining judge, and together they found Montefiore's treasure.

Within two days Juana had sold her cross to pay the costs of a journey. On her way with her two children to take the diligence which would carry her to the frontiers of Spain, she heard herself being called in the street. Her dying mother was being carried to a hospital, and through the curtains of her litter she had seen her daughter. Juana made the bearers enter a *porte-cochere* that was near them, and there the last interview between the mother and the daughter took place. Though the two spoke to each other in a low voice, Juan heard these parting words,—

"Mother, die in peace; I have suffered for you all."

An Episode Under
the Terror

Dedication

To Monsieur Guyonnet-Merville.

Is it not a necessity to explain to a public curious to know everything,
how I came to be sufficiently learned in the law to carry on the business of my little world? And in so doing, am I not bound to put on
record the memory of the amiable and intelligent man who, meeting
the Scribe (another clerk-amateur) at a ball, said, "Just give the office a
turn; there is work for you there, I assure you"? But do you need this
public testimony to feel assured of the affection of the writer?

De Balzac

An Episode Under the Terror

On the 22nd of January, 1793, towards eight o'clock in the evening, an old lady came down the steep street that comes to an end opposite the Church of Saint Laurent in the Faubourg Saint Martin. It had snowed so heavily all day long that the lady's footsteps were scarcely audible; the streets were deserted, and a feeling of dread, not unnatural amid the silence, was further increased by the whole extent of the Terror beneath which France was groaning in those days; what was more, the old lady so far had met no one by the way. Her sight had long been failing, so that the few foot passengers dispersed like shadows in the distance over the wide thoroughfare through the *faubourg*, were quite invisible to her by the light of the lanterns.

She had passed the end of the Rue des Morts, when she fancied that she could hear the firm, heavy tread of a man walking behind her. Then it seemed to her that she had heard that sound before, and dismayed by the idea of being followed, she tried to walk faster toward a brightly lit shop window, in the hope of verifying the suspicions which had taken hold of her mind.

So soon as she stood in the shaft of light that streamed out across the road, she turned her head suddenly, and caught sight of a human figure looming through the fog. The dim vision was enough for her. For one moment she reeled beneath an overpowering weight of dread, for she could not doubt any longer that the man had followed her the whole way from her own door; then the desire to escape from the spy gave her strength. Unable to think clearly, she walked twice as fast as before, as if it were possible to escape from a man who of course could move much faster; and for some minutes she fled on, till, reaching a pastry-cook's shop, she entered and sank rather than sat down upon a chair by the counter.

A young woman busy with embroidery looked up from her work

at the rattling of the door-latch, and looked out through the square window-panes. She seemed to recognize the old-fashioned violet silk mantle, for she went at once to a drawer as if in search of something put aside for the newcomer. Not only did this movement and the expression of the woman's face show a very evident desire to be rid as soon as possible of an unwelcome visitor, but she even permitted herself an impatient exclamation when the drawer proved to be empty. Without looking at the lady, she hurried from her desk into the back shop and called to her husband, who appeared at once.

"Wherever have you put?—" she began mysteriously, glancing at the customer by way of finishing her question.

The pastry-cook could only see the old lady's head-dress, a huge black silk bonnet with knots of violet ribbon round it, but he looked at his wife as if to say, "Did you think I should leave such a thing as that lying about in your drawer?" and then vanished.

The old lady kept so still and silent that the shopkeeper's wife was surprised. She went back to her, and on a nearer view a sudden impulse of pity, blended perhaps with curiosity, got the better of her. The old lady's face was naturally pale; she looked as though she secretly practised austerities; but it was easy to see that she was paler than usual from recent agitation of some kind. Her head-dress was so arranged as to almost hide hair that was white, no doubt with age, for there was not a trace of powder on the collar of her dress. The extreme plainness of her dress lent an air of austerity to her face, and her features were proud and grave. The manners and habits of people of condition were so different from those of other classes in former times that a noble was easily known, and the shopkeeper's wife felt persuaded that her customer was a *ci-devant*, and that she had been about the Court.

"Madame," she began with involuntary respect, forgetting that the title was proscribed.

But the old lady made no answer. She was staring fixedly at the shop windows as though some dreadful thing had taken shape against the panes. The pastry-cook came back at that moment, and drew the lady from her musings, by holding out a little cardboard box wrapped in blue paper.

"What is the matter, *citoyenne?*" he asked.

"Nothing, nothing, my friends," she answered, in a gentle voice. She looked up at the man as she spoke, as if to thank him by a glance; but she saw the red cap on his head, and a cry broke from her. "Ah! *You* have betrayed me!"

The man and his young wife replied by an indignant gesture, that brought the colour to the old lady's face; perhaps she felt relief, perhaps she blushed for her suspicions.

"Forgive me!" she said, with a childlike sweetness in her tones. Then, drawing a gold *louis* from her pocket, she held it out to the pastry-cook. "That is the price agreed upon," she added.

There is a kind of want that is felt instinctively by those who know want. The man and his wife looked at one another, then at the elderly woman before them, and read the same thoughts in each other's eyes. That bit of gold was so plainly the last. Her hands shook a little as she held it out, looking at it sadly but ungrudgingly, as one who knows the full extent of the sacrifice. Hunger and penury had carved lines as easy to read in her face as the traces of asceticism and fear. There were vestiges of bygone splendour in her clothes. She was dressed in threadbare silk, a neat but well-worn mantle, and daintily mended lace,—in the rags of former grandeur, in short. The shopkeeper and his wife, drawn two ways by pity and self-interest, began by lulling their consciences with words.

"You seem very poorly, *citoyenne*—"

"Perhaps *madame* might like to take something," the wife broke in.

"We have some very nice broth," added the pastry-cook.

"And it is so cold," continued his wife; "perhaps you have caught a chill, *madame*, on your way here. But you can rest and warm yourself a bit."

"We are not so black as the devil!" cried the man.

The kindly intention in the words and tones of the charitable couple won the old lady's confidence. She said that a strange man had been following her, and she was afraid to go home alone.

"Is that all!" returned he of the red bonnet; "wait for me, *citoyenne*."

He handed the gold coin to his wife, and then went out to put on his National Guard's uniform, impelled thereto by the idea of making some adequate return for the money; an idea that sometimes slips into a tradesman's head when he has been prodigiously overpaid for goods of no great value. He took up his cap, buckled on his sabre, and came out in full dress. But his wife had had time to reflect, and reflection, as not unfrequently happens, closed the hand that kindly intentions had opened. Feeling frightened and uneasy lest her husband might be drawn into something unpleasant, she tried to catch at the skirt of his coat, to hold him back, but he, good soul, obeying his charitable first thought, brought out his offer to see the lady home, before his wife could stop him.

"The man of whom the *citoyenne* is afraid is still prowling about the shop, it seems," she said sharply.

"I am afraid so," said the lady innocently.

"How if it is a spy? . . . a plot? . . . Don't go. And take the box away from her—"

The words whispered in the pastry-cook's ear cooled his hot fit of courage down to zero.

"Oh! I will just go out and say a word or two. I will rid you of him soon enough," he exclaimed, as he bounced out of the shop.

The old lady meanwhile, passive as a child and almost dazed, sat down on her chair again. But the honest pastry-cook came back directly. A countenance red enough to begin with, and further flushed by the bake-house fire, was suddenly blanched; such terror perturbed him that he reeled as he walked, and stared about him like a drunken man.

"Miserable aristocrat! Do you want to have our heads cut off?" he shouted furiously. "You just take to your heels and never show yourself here again. Don't come to me for materials for your plots."

He tried, as he spoke, to take away the little box which she had slipped into one of her pockets. But at the touch of a profane hand on her clothes, the stranger recovered youth and activity for a moment, preferring to face the dangers of the street with no protector save God, to the loss of the thing she had just paid for. She sprang to the door, flung it open, and disappeared, leaving the husband and wife dumfounded and quaking with fright.

Once outside in the street, she started away at a quick walk; but her strength soon failed her. She heard the sound of the snow crunching under a heavy step, and knew that the pitiless spy was on her track. She was obliged to stop. He stopped likewise. From sheer terror, or lack of intelligence, she did not dare to speak or to look at him. She went slowly on; the man slackened his pace and fell behind so that he could still keep her in sight. He might have been her very shadow.

Nine o'clock struck as the silent man and woman passed again by the Church of Saint Laurent. It is in the nature of things that calm must succeed to violent agitation, even in the weakest soul; for if feeling is infinite, our capacity to feel is limited. So, as the stranger lady met with no harm from her supposed persecutor, she tried to look upon him as an unknown friend anxious to protect her. She thought of all the circumstances in which the stranger had appeared, and put them together, as if to find some ground for this comforting theory, and felt inclined to credit him with good intentions rather than bad.

Forgetting the fright that he had given the pastry-cook, she walked on with a firmer step through the upper end of the Faubourg Saint Martin; and another half-hour's walk brought her to a house at the corner where the road to the Barriere de Pantin turns off from the main thoroughfare. Even at this day, the place is one of the least frequented parts of Paris. The north wind sweeps over the Buttes-Chaumont and Belleville, and whistles through the houses (the Hovels rather), scattered over an almost uninhabited low-lying waste, Where the fences are heaps of earth and bones. It was a desolate-looking place, a fitting refuge for despair and misery.

The sight of it appeared to make an impression upon the relentless pursuer of a poor creature so daring as to walk alone at night through the silent streets. He stood in thought, and seemed by his attitude to hesitate. She could see him dimly now, under the street lamp that sent a faint, flickering light through the fog. Fear gave her eyes. She saw, or thought she saw, something sinister about the stranger's features. Her old terrors awoke; she took advantage of a kind of hesitation on his part, slipped through the shadows to the door of the solitary house, pressed a spring, and vanished swiftly as a phantom.

For awhile the stranger stood motionless, gazing up at the house. It was in some sort a type of the wretched dwellings in the suburb; a tumble-down hovel, built of rough stones, daubed over with a coat of yellowish stucco, and so riven with great cracks that there seemed to be danger lest the slightest puff of wind might blow it down. The roof, covered with brown moss-grown tiles, had given way in several places, and looked as though it might break down altogether under the weight of the snow. The frames of the three windows on each story were rotten with damp and warped by the sun; evidently the cold must find its way inside. The house standing thus quite by itself looked like some old tower that Time had forgotten to destroy. A faint light shone from the attic windows pierced at irregular distances in the roof; otherwise the whole building was in total darkness.

Meanwhile the old lady climbed not without difficulty up the rough, clumsily built staircase, with a rope by way of a hand-rail. At the door of the lodging in the attic she stopped and tapped mysteriously; an old man brought forward a chair for her. She dropped into it at once.

"Hide! hide!" she exclaimed, looking up at him. "Seldom as we leave the house, everything that we do is known, and every step is watched—"

"What is it now?" asked another elderly woman, sitting by the fire.

"The man that has been prowling about the house yesterday and today, followed me tonight—"

At those words all three dwellers in the wretched den looked in each other's faces and did not try to dissimulate the profound dread that they felt. The old priest was the least overcome, probably because he ran the greatest danger. If a brave man is weighed down by great calamities or the yoke of persecution, he begins, as it were, by making the sacrifice of himself; and thereafter every day of his life becomes one more victory snatched from fate. But from the way in which the women looked at him it was easy to see that their intense anxiety was on his account.

"Why should our faith in God fail us, my sisters?" he said, in low but fervent tones. "We sang His praises through the shrieks of murderers and their victims at the Carmelites. If it was His will that I should come alive out of that butchery, it was, no doubt, because I was reserved for some fate which I am bound to endure without murmuring. God will protect His own; He can do with them according to His will. It is for you, not for me that we must think."

"No," answered one of the women. "What is our life compared to a priest's life?"

"Once outside the Abbaye de Chelles, I look upon myself as dead," added the nun who had not left the house, while the Sister that had just returned held out the little box to the priest.

"Here are the wafers . . . but I can hear some one coming up the stairs."

At this, the three began to listen. The sound ceased.

"Do not be alarmed if somebody tries to come in," said the priest. "Somebody on whom we could depend was to make all necessary arrangements for crossing the frontier. He is to come for the letters that I have written to the Duc de Langeais and the Marquis de Beauseant, asking them to find some way of taking you out of this dreadful country, and away from the death or the misery that waits for you here."

"But are you not going to follow us?" the nuns cried under their breath, almost despairingly.

"My post is here where the sufferers are," the priest said simply, and the women said no more, but looked at their guest in reverent admiration. He turned to the nun with the wafers.

"Sister Marthe," he said, "the messenger will say *Fiat Voluntas* in answer to the word *Hosanna*."

"There is some one on the stairs!" cried the other nun, opening a hiding-place contrived in the roof.

This time it was easy to hear, amid the deepest silence, a sound echoing up the staircase; it was a man's tread on the steps covered with dried lumps of mud. With some difficulty the priest slipped into a kind of cupboard, and the nun flung some clothes over him.

"You can shut the door, Sister Agathe," he said in a muffled voice.

He was scarcely hidden before three raps sounded on the door. The holy women looked into each other's eyes for counsel, and dared not say a single word.

They seemed both to be about sixty years of age. They had lived out of the world for forty years, and had grown so accustomed to the life of the convent that they could scarcely imagine any other. To them, as to plants kept in a hot-house, a change of air meant death. And so, when the grating was broken down one morning, they knew with a shudder that they were free. The effect produced by the Revolution upon their simple souls is easy to imagine; it produced a temporary imbecility not natural to them. They could not bring the ideas learned in the convent into harmony with life and its difficulties; they could not even understand their own position. They were like children whom mothers have always cared for, deserted by their maternal providence. And as a child cries, they betook themselves to prayer. Now, in the presence of imminent danger, they were mute and passive, knowing no defence save Christian resignation.

The man at the door, taking silence for consent, presented himself, and the women shuddered. This was the prowler that had been making inquiries about them for some time past. But they looked at him with frightened curiosity, much as shy children stare silently at a stranger; and neither of them moved.

The newcomer was a tall, burly man. Nothing in his behaviour, bearing, or expression suggested malignity as, following the example set by the nuns, he stood motionless, while his eyes travelled round the room.

Two straw mats laid upon planks did duty as beds. On the one table, placed in the middle of the room, stood a brass candlestick, several plates, three knives, and a round loaf. A small fire burned in the grate. A few bits of wood in a heap in a corner bore further witness to the poverty of the recluses. You had only to look at the coating of paint on the walls to discover the bad condition of the roof, and the ceiling was a perfect network of brown stains made by rain-water. A relic, saved no doubt from the wreck of the Abbaye de Chelles, stood like an ornament on the chimney-piece. Three chairs, two boxes, and a rickety chest of drawers completed the list of the furniture, but a door beside the fireplace suggested an inner room beyond.

The brief inventory was soon made by the personage introduced into their midst under such terrible auspices. It was with a compassionate expression that he turned to the two women; he looked benevolently at them, and seemed, at least, as much embarrassed as they. But the strange silence did not last long, for presently the stranger began to understand. He saw how inexperienced, how helpless (mentally speaking), the two poor creatures were, and he tried to speak gently.

"I am far from coming as an enemy, *citoyennes*—" he began. Then he suddenly broke off and went on, "Sisters, if anything should happen to you, believe me, I shall have no share in it. I have come to ask a favour of you."

Still the women were silent.

"If I am annoying you—if—if I am intruding, speak freely, and I will go; but you must understand that I am entirely at your service; that if I can do anything for you, you need not fear to make use of me. I, and I only, perhaps, am above the law, since there is no King now."

There was such a ring of sincerity in the words that Sister Agathe hastily pointed to a chair as if to bid their guest be seated. Sister Agathe came of the house of Langeais; her manner seemed to indicate that once she had been familiar with brilliant scenes, and had breathed the air of courts. The stranger seemed half pleased, half distressed when he understood her invitation; he waited to sit down until the women were seated.

"You are giving shelter to a reverend father who refused to take the oath, and escaped the massacres at the Carmelites by a miracle—"

"*Hosanna!*" Sister Agathe exclaimed eagerly, interrupting the stranger, while she watched him with curious eyes.

"That is not the name, I think," he said.

"But, *monsieur*," Sister Marthe broke in quickly, "we have no priest here, and—"

"In that case you should be more careful and on your guard," he answered gently, stretching out his hand for a breviary that lay on the table. "I do not think that you know Latin, and—"

He stopped; for, at the sight of the great emotion in the faces of the two poor nuns, he was afraid that he had gone too far. They were trembling, and the tears stood in their eyes.

"Do not fear," he said frankly. "I know your names and the name of your guest. Three days ago I heard of your distress and devotion to the venerable Abbe de—"

"Hush!" Sister Agathe cried, in the simplicity of her heart, as she laid her finger on her lips.

"You see, Sisters, that if I had conceived the horrible idea of betraying you, I could have given you up already, more than once—"

At the words the priest came out of his hiding-place and stood in their midst.

"I cannot believe, *monsieur*, that you can be one of our persecutors," he said, addressing the stranger, "and I trust you. What do you want with me?"

The priest's holy confidence, the nobleness expressed in every line in his face, would have disarmed a murderer. For a moment the mysterious stranger, who had brought an element of excitement into lives of misery and resignation, gazed at the little group; then he turned to the priest and said, as if making a confidence, "Father, I came to beg you to celebrate a mass for the repose of the soul of—of—of an august personage whose body will never rest in consecrated earth—"

Involuntarily the *abbe* shivered. As yet, neither of the Sisters understood of whom the stranger was speaking; they sat with their heads stretched out and faces turned towards the speaker, curiosity in their whole attitude. The priest meanwhile, was scrutinizing the stranger; there was no mistaking the anxiety in the man's face, the ardent entreaty in his eyes.

"Very well," returned the *abbe*. "Come back at midnight. I shall be ready to celebrate the only funeral service that it is in our power to offer in expiation of the crime of which you speak."

A quiver ran through the stranger, but a sweet yet sober satisfaction seemed to prevail over a hidden anguish. He took his leave respectfully, and the three generous souls felt his unspoken gratitude.

Two hours later, he came back and tapped at the garret door. Mademoiselle de Beauseant showed the way into the second room of their humble lodging. Everything had been made ready. The Sisters had moved the old chest of drawers between the two chimneys, and covered its quaint outlines over with a splendid altar cloth of green watered silk.

The bare walls looked all the barer, because the one thing that hung there was the great ivory and ebony crucifix, which of necessity attracted the eyes. Four slender little altar candles, which the Sisters had contrived to fasten into their places with sealing-wax, gave a faint, pale light, almost absorbed by the walls; the rest of the room lay well-nigh in the dark. But the dim brightness, concentrated upon the holy things, looked like a ray from Heaven shining down upon the unadorned shrine. The floor was reeking with damp. An icy wind swept in through the chinks here and there, in a roof that rose sharply on either side, after the fashion of attic roofs. Nothing could be less imposing; yet perhaps, too, nothing could be more solemn than this mournful ceremony. A silence so deep that they could have heard the faintest sound of a voice on the Route d'Allemagne, invested the night-piece with a kind of sombre majesty; while the grandeur of the service—all the grander for the strong contrast with the poor surroundings—produced a feeling of reverent awe.

The Sisters kneeling on each side of the altar, regardless of the deadly chill from the wet brick floor, were engaged in prayer, while the priest, arrayed in pontifical vestments, brought out a golden chalice set with gems; doubtless one of the sacred vessels saved from the pillage of the Abbaye de Chelles. Beside a ciborium, the gift of royal munificence, the wine and water for the holy sacrifice of the mass stood ready in two glasses such as could scarcely be found in the meanest tavern. For want of a missal, the priest had laid his breviary on the altar, and a common earthenware plate was set for the washing of hands that were pure and undefiled with blood. It was all so infinitely great, yet so little, poverty-stricken yet noble, a mingling of sacred and profane.

The stranger came forward reverently to kneel between the two nuns. But the priest had tied crape round the chalice of the crucifix, having no other way of marking the mass as a funeral service; it was as if God himself had been in mourning. The man suddenly noticed this, and the sight appeared to call up some overwhelming memory, for great drops of sweat stood out on his broad forehead.

Then the four silent actors in the scene looked mysteriously at one another; and their souls in emulation seemed to stir and communicate the thoughts within them until all were melted into one feeling of awe and pity. It seemed to them that the royal martyr whose remains had been consumed with quicklime, had been called up by their yearning and now stood, a shadow in their midst, in all the majesty of a king. They were celebrating an anniversary service for the dead whose body lay elsewhere. Under the disjointed laths and tiles, four Christians were holding a funeral service without a coffin, and putting up prayers to God for the soul of a King of France. No devotion could be purer than this. It was a wonderful act of faith achieved without an afterthought. Surely in the sight of God it was like the cup of cold water which counterbalances the loftiest virtues. The prayers put up by two feeble nuns and a priest represented the whole Monarchy, and possibly at the same time, the Revolution found expression in the stranger, for the remorse in his face was so great that it was impossible not to think that he was fulfilling the vows of a boundless repentance.

When the priest came to the Latin words, *Introibo ad altare Dei*, a sudden divine inspiration flashed upon him; he looked at the three kneeling figures, the representatives of Christian France, and said instead, as though to blot out the poverty of the garret, "We are about to enter the Sanctuary of God!"

These words, uttered with thrilling earnestness, struck reverent awe into the nuns and the stranger. Under the vaulted roof of St. Peter's at Rome, God would not have revealed Himself in greater majesty than here for the eyes of the Christians in that poor refuge; so true is it that all intermediaries between God and the soul of man are superfluous, and all the grandeur of God proceeds from Himself alone.

The stranger's fervour was sincere. One emotion blended the prayers of the four servants of God and the King in a single supplication. The holy words rang like the music of heaven through the silence. At one moment, tears gathered in the stranger's eyes. This was during the *Pater Noster*; for the priest added a petition in Latin, and his audience doubtless understood him when he said: "*Et remitte scelus regicidis sicut Ludovicus eis remisit semetipse*"—forgive the regicides as Louis himself forgave them.

The Sisters saw two great tears trace a channel down the stranger's manly checks and fall to the floor. Then the office for the dead was recited; the *Domine salvum fac regem* chanted in an undertone that went to the hearts of the faithful Royalists, for they thought how the child-King for whom they were praying was even then a captive in the hands of his enemies; and a shudder ran through the stranger, as he thought that a new crime might be committed, and that he could not choose but take his part in it.

The service came to an end. The priest made a sign to the sisters, and they withdrew. As soon as he was left alone with the stranger, he went towards him with a grave, gentle face, and said in fatherly tones:

"My son, if your hands are stained with the blood of the royal martyr, confide in me. There is no sin that may not be blotted out in the sight of God by penitence as sincere and touching as yours appears to be."

At the first words the man started with terror, in spite of himself. Then he recovered composure, and looked quietly at the astonished priest.

"Father," he said, and the other could not miss the tremor in his voice, "no one is more guiltless than I of the blood shed—"

319

"I am bound to believe you," said the priest. He paused a moment, and again he scrutinized his penitent. But, persisting in the idea that the man before him was one of the members of the Convention, one of the voters who betrayed an inviolable and anointed head to save their own, he began again gravely:

"Remember, my son, that it is not enough to have taken no active part in the great crime; that fact does not absolve you. The men who might have defended the King and left their swords in their scabbards, will have a very heavy account to render to the King of Heaven—Ah! yes," he added, with an eloquent shake of the head, "heavy indeed!—for by doing nothing they became accomplices in the awful wickedness—"

"But do you think that an indirect participation will be punished?" the stranger asked with a bewildered look. "There is the private soldier commanded to fall into line—is he actually responsible?"

The priest hesitated. The stranger was glad; he had put the Royalist precisian in a dilemma, between the dogma of passive obedience on the one hand (for the upholders of the Monarchy maintained that obedience was the first principle of military law), and the equally important dogma which turns respect for the person of a King into a matter of religion. In the priest's indecision he was eager to see a favourable solution of the doubts which seemed to torment him. To prevent too prolonged reflection on the part of the reverend Jansenist, he added:

"I should blush to offer remuneration of any kind for the funeral service which you have just performed for the repose of the King's soul and the relief of my conscience. The only possible return for something of inestimable value is an offering likewise beyond price. Will you deign, *monsieur*, to take my gift of a holy relic? A day will perhaps come when you will understand its value."

As he spoke the stranger held out a box; it was very small and exceedingly light. The priest took it mechanically, as it were, so astonished was he by the man's solemn words, the tones of his voice, and the reverence with which he held out the gift.

The two men went back together into the first room. The Sisters were waiting for them.

"This house that you are living in belongs to Mucius Scaevola, the plasterer on the first floor," he said. "He is well known in the Section for his patriotism, but in reality he is an adherent of the Bourbons. He used to be a huntsman in the service of his Highness the Prince de Conti, and he owes everything to him. So long as you stay in the

320

house, you are safer here than anywhere else in France. Do not go out. Pious souls will minister to your necessities, and you can wait in safety for better times. Next year, on the 21st of January,"—he could not hide an involuntary shudder as he spoke,—"next year, if you are still in this dreary refuge, I will come back again to celebrate the expiatory mass with you—"

He broke off, bowed to the three, who answered not a word, gave a last look at the garret with its signs of poverty, and vanished.

Such an adventure possessed all the interest of a romance in the lives of the innocent nuns. So, as soon as the venerable *abbe* told them the story of the mysterious gift, it was placed upon the table, and by the feeble light of the tallow dip an indescribable curiosity appeared in the three anxious faces. Mademoiselle de Langeais opened the box, and found a very fine lawn handkerchief, soiled with sweat; darker stains appeared as they unfolded it.

"That is blood!" exclaimed the priest.

"It is marked with a royal crown!" cried Sister Agathe.

The women, aghast, allowed the precious relic to fall. For their simple souls the mystery that hung about the stranger grew inexplicable; as for the priest, from that day forth he did not even try to understand it.

Before very long the prisoners knew that, in spite of the Terror, some powerful hand was extended over them. It began when they received firewood and provisions; and next the Sisters knew that a woman had lent counsel to their protector, for linen was sent to them, and clothes in which they could leave the house without causing remark upon the aristocrat's dress that they had been forced to wear. After awhile Mucius Scaevola gave them two civic cards; and often tidings necessary for the priest's safety came to them in roundabout ways. Warnings and advice reached them so opportunely that they could only have been sent by some person in the possession of state secrets. And, at a time when famine threatened Paris, invisible hands brought rations of "white bread" for the proscribed women in the wretched garret. Still they fancied that Citizen Mucius Scaevola was only the mysterious instrument of a kindness always ingenious, and no less intelligent.

The noble ladies in the garret could no longer doubt that their protector was the stranger of the expiatory mass on the night of the 22nd of January, 1793; and a kind of cult of him sprung up among them. Their one hope was in him; they lived through him. They added special petitions for him to their prayers; night and morning the pious souls prayed for his happiness, his prosperity, his safety; entreating God to remove all snares far from his path, to deliver him from his enemies, to grant him a long and peaceful life. And with this daily renewed gratitude, as it may be called, there blended a feeling of curiosity which grew more lively day by day. They talked over the circumstances of his first sudden appearance, their conjectures were endless; the stranger had conferred one more benefit upon them by diverting their minds. Again, and again, they said, when he next came to see them as he promised, to celebrate the sad anniversary of the death of Louis XVI., he could not escape their friendship.

The night so impatiently awaited came at last. At midnight the old wooden staircase echoed with the stranger's heavy footsteps. They had made the best of their room for his coming; the altar was ready, and this time the door stood open, and the two Sisters were out at the stair head, eager to light the way. Mademoiselle de Langeais even came down a few steps, to meet their benefactor the sooner.

"Come," she said, with a quaver in the affectionate tones, "come in; we are expecting you."

He raised his face, gave her a dark look, and made no answer. The sister felt as if an icy mantle had fallen over her, and said no more. At the sight of him, the glow of gratitude and curiosity died away in their hearts. Perhaps he was not so cold, not so taciturn, not so stern as he seemed to them, for in their highly wrought mood they were ready to pour out their feeling of friendship. But the three poor prisoners understood that he wished to be a stranger to them; and submitted. The priest fancied that he saw a smile on the man's lips as he saw their preparations for his visit, but it was at once repressed. He heard mass, said his prayer, and then disappeared, declining, with a few polite words, Mademoiselle de Langeais' invitation to partake of the little collation made ready for him.

After the 9th Thermidor, the Sisters and the Abbe de Marolles could go about Paris without the least danger. The first time that the *abbe* went out he walked to a perfumer's shop at the sign of *The Queen of Roses*, kept by the Citizen Ragon and his wife, court perfumers. The Ragons had been faithful adherents of the Royalist cause; it was through their means that the Vendean leaders kept up a correspondence with the Princes and the Royalist Committee in Paris. The *abbe*, in the ordinary dress of the time, was standing on the threshold of the shop—which stood between Saint Roch and the Rue des Frondeurs—when he saw that the Rue Saint Honore was filled with a crowd and he could not go out.

"What is the matter?" he asked Madame Ragon.

"Nothing," she said; "it is only the tumbrel cart and the execution-er going to the Place Louis XV. Ah! we used to see it often enough last year; but today, four days after the anniversary of the twenty-first of January, one does not feel sorry to see the ghastly procession."

"Why not?" asked the *abbe*. "That is not said like a Christian."

"Eh! but it is the execution of Robespierre's accomplices. They defended themselves as long as they could, but now it is their turn to go where they sent so many innocent people."

The crowd poured by like a flood. The *abbe*, yielding to an impulse of curiosity, looked up above the heads, and there in the tumbrel stood the man who had heard mass in the garret three days ago.

"Who is it?" he asked; "who is the man with—"

"That is the headsman," answered M. Ragon, calling the execu-tioner—the *executeur des hautes oeuvres*—by the name he had borne under the Monarchy.

"Oh! my dear, my dear! M. l'Abbe is dying!" cried out old Mad-ame Ragon. She caught up a flask of vinegar, and tried to restore the old priest to consciousness.

"He must have given me the handkerchief that the King used to wipe his brow on the way to his martyrdom," murmured he. " . . . Poor man! . . . There was a heart in the steel blade, when none was found in all France . . . "

The perfumers thought that the poor *abbe* was raving.

The Napoleon
of the People

'The Napoleon of the People' was originally published in chapter 3 of *Le Medicin de Campagne* (*The Country Doctor*), it is a story told to a group of French peasants by Goguelat, the village postman, who had served under Napoleon in an infantry regiment.

The Napoleon of the People

Napoleon, my friends, was born, you know, in Corsica. That's a French island, but it's warmed by the sun of Italy, and everything's as hot there as if it were a furnace. It's a place, too, where the people kill one another, from father to son, generation after generation, for nothing at all; that is, for no reason in particular except that it's their way.

Well, to begin with the most wonderful part of the story, it so happened that on the very day when Napoleon was born, his mother dreamed that the world was on fire. She was a shrewd, clever woman, as well as the prettiest woman of her time; and when she had this dream, she thought she'd save her son from the dangers of life by dedicating him to God. And, indeed, that was a prophetic dream of hers! So she asked God to protect the boy, and promised that when he grew up he should re-establish God's holy religion, which had then been overthrown. That was the agreement they made; and although it seems strange such things have happened. It's sure and certain, anyhow, that only a man who had an agreement with God could pass through the enemy's lines, and move about in showers of bullets and grape-shot, as Napoleon did. They swept us away like flies, but his head they never touched at all. I had a proof of that—I myself, in particular—at Eylau, where the Emperor went up on a little hill to see how things were going. I can remember, to this day, exactly how he looked as he took out his field glass, watched the battle for a minute, and finally said: "It's all right! Everything is going well." Then, just as he was coming back, an ambitious chap in a plumed hat, who was always following him around, and who bothered him, they said, even at his meals, thought he'd play smart by going up on the very same hill; but he had hardly taken the Emperor's place when—*batz!*—away he went, plume and all!

Now follow me closely, and tell me whether what you are going to hear was natural.

Napoleon, you know, had promised that he'd keep his agreement with God to himself. That's the reason why his companions and even his particular friends—men like Duroc, Bessières, and Lannes, who were strong as bars of steel, but whom he moulded to suit his purposes—all fell, like nuts from a shaken tree, while he himself was never even hurt.

But that's not the only proof that he was the child of God and was expressly created to be the father of soldiers. Did anybody ever see him a lieutenant? Or a captain? Never! He was commander-in-chief from the start. When he didn't look more than twenty-four years of age he was already an old general—ever since the taking of Toulon, where he first began to show the rest of them that they didn't know anything about the handling of cannon.

Well, soon after that, down comes this stripling to us as general-in-chief of the Army of Italy—an army that hadn't any ammunition, or bread, or shoes, or coats; a wretched army—naked as a worm. "Now, boys!" he said, "here we are, all together. I want you to get it fixed in your heads that in fifteen days more you're going to be conquerors. You're going to have new clothes, good leggings, the best of shoes, and a warm overcoat for every man; but in order to get these things you'll have to march to Milan, where they are." So we marched. We were only thirty thousand bare-footed tramps, and we were going against eighty thousand crack German soldiers—fine, well equipped men; but Napoleon, who was only Bonaparte then, breathed a spirit of—I don't know what—into us, and on we marched, night and day. We hit the enemy at Montenotte, thrashed 'em at Rivoli, Lodi, Arcola, and Millesimo, and stuck to 'em wherever they went. A soldier soon gets to like being a conqueror; and Napoleon wheeled around those German generals, and pelted away at 'em, until they didn't know where to hide long enough to get a little rest. With fifteen hundred Frenchmen, whom he made to appear a great host (that's a way he had), he'd sometimes surround ten thousand men and gather 'em all in at a single scoop. Then we'd take their cannon, their money, their ammunition, and everything they had that was worth carrying away. As for the others, we chucked 'em into the water, walloped 'em on the mountains, snapped 'em up in the air, devoured 'em on the ground, and beat 'em everywhere. So at last our troops were in fine feather—especially as Napoleon, who had a clever wit, made friends with the inhabitants of the country by telling them that we had come to set them free; and then, of course, they gave us quarters and took the best of care of us. And it was not only the men: the women took care of us too, which showed their good judgment!

Well, it finally ended in this way: in Ventose, 1796,—which was the same time of year that our March is now,—we were penned up in one corner of the marmot country: but at the end of the first campaign, lo and behold! we were masters of Italy, just as Napoleon had predicted. And in the month of March following—that is, in two campaigns, which we fought in a single year—he brought us in sight of Vienna. It was just a clean sweep. We had eaten up three different armies in succession, and had wiped out four Austrian generals; one of them—a white-haired old chap—was burned alive at Mantua like a rat in a straw mattress. We had conquered peace, and kings were begging, on their knees, for mercy. Could a man have done all that alone? Never! He had the help of God; that's certain! He divided himself up like the five loaves of bread in the Gospel; he planned battles at night and directed them in the daytime: he was seen by the sentries going here and there at all hours, and he never ate or slept. When the soldiers saw all these wonderful things, they adopted him as their father.

But the people at the head of the government over there in Paris, who were looking on, said to themselves: "This schemer, who seems to have the watchword of Heaven, is quite capable of laying his hands on France. We'd better turn him loose in Asia or America. Then maybe he'll be satisfied for a while." So it was written that he should do just what Jesus Christ did—go to Egypt. You see how in this he resembled the Son of God. But there's more to come.

He gathered together all his old fire-eaters—the fellows that he had put the spirit of the Devil into—and said to them: "Boys! They've given us Egypt to chew on—to keep us quiet for a while; but we'll swallow Egypt in one time and two movements—just as we did Italy. All you private soldiers shall be princes, with lands of your own. Forward!"

"Forward, boys!" shouted the sergeants.

So we marched to Toulon, on our way to Egypt. As soon as the English heard of it, they sent out all their ships of war to catch us; but when we embarked, Napoleon said to us: "The English will never see us; and it is only proper for you to know now that your general has a star in the sky which will henceforth guide and protect us."

As 't was said, so 't was done. On our way across the sea we took Malta (just as one would pick an orange in passing) to quench Napoleon's thirst for victory; because he was a man who wanted to be doing something all the time.

And so at last we came to Egypt; and then the orders were different. The Egyptians, you know, are people who, from the beginning of the world, have had giants to rule over them, and armies like innumerable ants. Their country is a land of *genii* and crocodiles, and of pyramids as big as our mountains, where they put the bodies of their dead kings to keep them fresh—a thing that seems to please them all around. Of course you can't deal with such people as you would with others. So when we landed, the Little Corporal said to us: "Boys! The country that you are going to conquer worships a lot of gods that must be respected. Frenchmen should keep on good terms with everybody, and fight people without hurting their feelings. So let everything alone at first, and by and by we'll get all there is."

Now there was a prediction among the Egyptians down there that Napoleon would come; and the name they had for him was Kebir Bonaberdis, which means, in their lingo, "The Sultan strikes fire." They were as much afraid of him as they were of the Devil; so the Grand Turk, Asia, and Africa resorted to magic, and sent against us a demon named Mody (the Mahdi), who was supposed to have come down from the heaven on a white horse. This horse was incombustible to bullets, and so was the Mody, and the two of 'em lived on weather and air. There are people who have seen 'em; but I haven't any reason, myself, to say positively that the things told about 'em were true. Anyhow, they were the great powers in Arabia; and the Mamelukes wanted to make the Egyptian soldiers think that the Mody could keep them from being killed in battle, and that he was an angel sent down from heaven to fight Napoleon and get back Solomon's seal—a part of their equipment which they pretended to believe our general had stolen. But we made 'em laugh on the wrong side of their mouths, in spite of their Mody!

They thought Napoleon could command the genii, and that he had power to go from one place to another in an instant, like a bird; and, indeed, it's a fact that he was everywhere. But how did they know that he had an agreement with God? Was it natural that they should get such an idea as that?

It so happened, finally, that he carried off one of their queens—a woman beautiful as the sunshine. He tried, at first, to buy her, and offered to give for her all his treasure, and a lot of diamonds as big as pigeons' eggs; but although the Mameluke to whom she particularly belonged had several others, he wouldn't agree to the bargain; so Napoleon had to carry her off. Of course, when things came to such a pass as that, they couldn't be settled without a lot of fighting; and if there weren't blows enough to satisfy all, it wasn't anybody's fault. We formed in battle line at Alexandria, at Gizeh, and in front of the Pyramids. We marched in hot sunshine and through deep sand, where some got so bedazzled that they saw water which they couldn't drink, and shade that made them sweat; but we generally chewed up the Mamelukes, and all the rest gave in when they heard Napoleon's voice.

He took possession of Upper and Lower Egypt, Arabia, and the capitals of kingdoms that perished long ago, where there were thousands of statues of all the evil things in creation, especially lizards—a thundering big country, where one could get acres of land for as little as he pleased.

Well, while Napoleon was attending to his business inland, where he intended to do some splendid things, the English, who were always trying to make us trouble, burned his fleet at Aboukir. But our general, who had the respect of the East and the West, who had been called "my son" by the Pope, and "my dear father" by the cousin of Mahomet, resolved to punish England, and to capture the Indies, in payment for his lost fleet. He was just going to take us across the Red Sea into Asia—a country where there were lots of diamonds, plenty of gold with which to pay his soldiers, and palaces that could be used for *etapes*—when the Mody made an arrangement with the Plague, and sent it down to put an end to our victories. Then it was, Halt, all! And everybody marched off to that parade from which you don't come back on your feet. Dying soldiers couldn't take Saint Jean d'Acre, although they forced an entrance three times with noble and stubborn courage. The Plague was too strong for us; and it wasn't any use to say "Please don't!" to the Plague. Everybody was sick except Napoleon. He looked fresh as a rose, and the whole army saw him drinking in pestilence without being hurt a bit. How was that? Do you call that natural?

Well, the Mamelukes, who knew that we were all in ambulances, thought they'd bar our way; but they couldn't play that sort of game with Napoleon. He turned to his old fire-eaters—the fellows with the toughest hides—and said: "Go clear the road for me." Junot, who was his devoted friend and a number one soldier, took not more than a thousand men, and slashed right through the army of the pasha which had had the impudence to get in our way. Then we went back to Cairo, where we had our headquarters.

And now for another part of the story. While Napoleon was away France was letting herself be ruined by those government scallywags in Paris, who were keeping back the soldiers' pay, withholding their linen and their clothes, and even letting them starve. They wanted the soldiers to lay down the law to the universe, and that's all they

331

cared for. They were just a lot of idiots jabbering for amusement instead of putting their own hands into the dough. So our armies were beaten and we couldn't defend our frontiers. *The man* was no longer there. I say "the man" because that's what they called him; but it was absurd to say that he was merely a man, when he had a star of his own with all its belongings. It was the rest of us who were merely men. At the battle of Aboukir, with a single division and with a loss of only three hundred men, he whipped the great army of the Turks, and hustled more than half of them into the sea—*r-r-rah*—like that! But it was his last thunderclap in Egypt; because when he heard, soon afterward, what was happening in France, he made up his mind to go back there. "I am the saviour of France," he said, "and I must go to her aid." The army didn't know what he intended to do. If they had known, they would have kept him in Egypt by force and made him Emperor of the East.

When he had gone, we all felt very blue; because he had been the joy of our lives. He left the command to Kléber—a great lout of a fellow who soon afterward lost the number of his mess. An Egyptian assassinated him. They put the murderer to death by making him sit on a bayonet; that's their way, down there, of guillotining a man. But he suffered so much that one of our soldiers felt sorry for him and offered him his water-gourd. The criminal took a drink, and then gave up the ghost with the greatest pleasure.

But we didn't waste much time over trifles like that.

Napoleon sailed from Egypt in a cockle-shell of a boat called Fortune. He passed right under the noses of the English, who were blockading the coast with ships of the line, frigates, and every sort of craft that could carry sail, and in the twinkling of an eye he was in France; because he had the ability to cross the sea as if with a single stride. Was that natural? Bah! The very minute he reached Fréjus, he had his foot, so to speak, in Paris. There, of course, everybody worships him. But the first thing he does is to summon the government. "What have you been doing with my children the soldiers?" he said to the lawyers. "You are nothing but a lot of poll-parrots, who fool the people with your gabble, and feather your own nests at the expense of France. It is not right; and I speak in the name of all who are dissatisfied."

They thought, at first, that they could get rid of him by talking him to death; but it didn't work. He shut 'em up in the very barrack where they did their talking, and those who didn't jump out of the windows he enrolled in his suite, where they soon became mute as fish and pliable as a tobacco-pouch. This coup made him consul; and as he wasn't one to doubt the Supreme Being who had kept good faith with him, he hastened to fulfil his own promise by restoring the churches and re-establishing religion; whereupon the bells all rang out in his honour and in honour of the good God.

Everybody then was satisfied: first, the priests, because they were protected from persecution; second, the merchants, because they could do business without fearing the "we-grab-it-all" of the law; and finally the nobles, because the people were forbidden to put them to death, as they had formerly had the unfortunate habit of doing.

But Napoleon still had his enemies to clear away, and he was not a man to drop asleep over his porringer. His eye took in the whole world—as if it were no bigger than a soldier's head. The first thing he did was to turn up in Italy—as suddenly as if he had poked his head through a window; and one look from him was enough. The Austrians were swallowed up at Marengo as gudgeons are swallowed by a whale. Then the French *victory* sang a song of triumph that all the world could hear, and it was enough.

"We won't play any more!" declared the Germans.

"Nor we either," said the others.

Sum total: Europe is cowed; England knuckles down; and there is universal peace, with all the kings and people pretending to embrace one another.

It was then that Napoleon established the Legion of Honour; and a fine thing it was, too. In a speech that he made before the whole army at Boulogne he said: "In France everybody is brave; so the civilian who does a noble deed shall be the brother of the soldier, and they shall stand together under the flag of honour." Then we who had been down in Egypt came home and found everything changed. When Napoleon left us he was only a general; but in no time at all he had become Emperor. France had given herself to him as a pretty girl gives herself to a lancer.

Well, when everything had been settled to everybody's satisfaction, there was a religious ceremony such as had never before been seen under the canopy of heaven. The Pope and all his cardinals, in their robes of scarlet and gold, came across the Alps to anoint him with holy oil, and he was crowned Emperor, in the presence of the army and the people, with great applause and clapping of hands.

But there is one thing that it would not be fair not to tell you; and that is about the *Red Man*. While Napoleon was still in Egypt, in a desert not far from Syria, the Red Man appeared to him on the mountain of Moses (Sinai), and said to him, "It's all right!" Then again, at Marengo, on the evening of victory, the same Red Man appeared to him a second time, and said: "You shall see the world at your feet: you shall be Emperor of France; King of Italy; master of Holland; sovereign of Spain, Portugal, and the Illyrian provinces; protector of Germany; saviour of Poland; first eagle of the Legion of Honour—everything!"

This Red Man, you see, was his own idea; and was a sort of messenger whom he used, many people said, as a means of communication with his star. I've never believed that, myself, but that there was a Red Man is a real fact. Napoleon himself spoke of him, and said that he lived up under the roof in the palace of the Tuileries, and that he often used to make his appearance in times of trouble. On the evening of his coronation Napoleon saw him for the third time, and they consulted together about a lot of things.

After that the Emperor went to Milan, where he was crowned King of Italy; and then began a regular triumph for us soldiers. Every man who knew how to read and write became an officer; it rained dukedoms; pensions were distributed with both hands; there were fortunes for the general staff which didn't cost France a penny; and even common soldiers received annuities with their crosses of the Legion of Honour—I get mine to this day. In short, the armies of France were taken care of in a way that had never before been seen.

But the Emperor, who knew that he was the emperor not only of the soldiers but of all, remembered the bourgeois, and built wonderful monuments for them, to suit their own taste, in places that had been as bare before as the palm of your hand. Suppose you were coming from Spain, for example, and going through France to Berlin. You would pass under sculptured triumphal arches on which you'd see the common soldiers carved just as beautifully as the generals.

In two or three years, and without taxing you people at all, Napoleon filled his vaults with gold; created bridges, palaces, roads, schools, festivals, laws, harbours, ships; and spent millions and millions of money—so much, in fact, that if he'd taken the notion, they say, he might have paved all France with five-*franc* pieces.

Finally, when he was comfortably seated on his throne, he was so thoroughly the master of everything that Europe waited for his permission before it even dared to sneeze. Then, as he had four brothers and three sisters, he said to us in familiar talk, as if in the order of the day: "Boys! Is it right that the relatives of your Emperor should have to beg their bread? No! I want them to shine, just as I do. A kingdom must be conquered, therefore, for every one of them; so that France may be master of all; so that the soldiers of the Guard may make the world tremble; so that France may spit wherever she likes; and so that all nations may say to her,—as it is written on my coins,—'God protects you.'"

"All right!" says the army. "We'll fish up kingdoms for you with the bayonet."

We couldn't back out, you know; and if he had taken it into his head to conquer the moon, we should have had to get ready, pack our knapsacks, and climb up. Fortunately, he didn't have any such intention.

The kings, who were very comfortable on their thrones, naturally didn't want to get off to make room for his relatives; so they had to be dragged off by the ears. Forward!

We marched and marched, and everything began to shake again. Ah, how he did wear out men and shoes in those days! He struck such tremendous blows with us that if we had been other than Frenchmen we should all have been used up. But Frenchmen are born philosophers, and they know that a little sooner or a little later they must die. So we used to die without a word, because we had the pleasure of seeing the Emperor do this with the geographies. [Here the old soldier nimbly drew a circle with his foot on the floor of the barn.]

"There!" he would say, "that shall be a kingdom!" And it was a kingdom. Ah, that was a great time! Colonels became generals while you were looking at them; generals became marshals, and marshals became kings. There's one of those kings still left, to remind Europe of that time; but he is a Gascon, and has betrayed France in order to keep his crown. He doesn't blush for the shame of it, either; because crowns, you understand, are made of gold! Finally, even sappers, if they knew how to read, became nobles all the same. I myself have seen in Paris eleven kings and a crowd of princes, surrounding Napoleon like rays of the sun. Every soldier had a chance to see how a throne fitted him, if he was worthy of it, and when a corporal of the Guard passed by he was an object of curiosity; because all had a share in the glory of the victories, which were perfectly well known to everybody through the bulletins.

And what a lot of battles there were! Austerlitz, where the army manoeuvered as if on parade; Eylau, where the Russians were drowned in a lake as if Napoleon had blown them in with a single puff; Wagram, where we fought three days without flinching. In short, there were as many battles as there are saints in the calendar. And it was proved then that Napoleon had in his scabbard the real sword of God. He felt regard for his soldiers, too, and treated them just as if they were his children, always taking pains to find out if they were well supplied with shoes, linen, overcoats, bread, and cartridges. But he kept up his dignity as sovereign all the same; because to reign was his business. However, that didn't make any difference. A sergeant, or even a common soldier, could say to him "Emperor," just as you sometimes say "my dear fellow" to me. He was one that you could argue with, if necessary; he slept on the snow with the rest of us; and, in short, he appeared almost like any other man. But when the grape-shot were kicking up the dust at his very feet, I have seen him going about coolly,—no more disturbed by them than you are at this minute,—looking through his field-glass now and then, and attending all the time to his business. Of course that made the rest of us as calm and serene as John the Baptist. I don't know how he managed it, but when he spoke to us, his words put fire into our hearts; and in order to show him that we really were his children, and not the kind of men to shrink from danger, we used to march right up to great blackguards of cannon which bellowed and vomited balls without so much as saying "Look out!" Even dying men had the nerve to raise their heads and salute him with the cry of "Long live the Emperor!" Was that natural? Would they have done that for a mere man?

Well, when he had settled all his folks comfortably, the Empress Josephine—who was a good woman all the same—was so fixed that she couldn't give him any family, and he had to leave her. He loved her quite a little, too; but for reasons of state he had to have children. When the kings of Europe heard of this trouble, they came to blows over the question who should give him a wife. He finally married, they told us, an Austrian woman. She was a daughter of Caesar's—a man of ancient times who is much talked about, not only in our country, where they say he made everything, but in Europe. It's true, anyhow, that I have myself been on the Danube, and have seen there the remains of a bridge that this man Caesar built. It appears that he was a relative of Napoleon's in Rome, and that's why the Emperor had a right to take the inheritance there for his son.

Well, after his marriage, when there was a holiday for the whole world, and when he let the people off ten years' taxes (which were collected all the same, because the tax-gatherers didn't pay any attention to what he said), his wife had a little boy who was King of Rome. That was a thing which had never been seen on earth before—a child born king while his father was still living. A balloon was sent up in Paris to carry the news to Rome, and it made the whole distance in a single day. Now will any of you tell me that that was natural? Never! It had been so written on high.

Well, next comes the Emperor of Russia. He had once been Napoleon's friend; but he got angry because our Emperor didn't marry a Russian woman. So he backs up our enemies the English. Napoleon had long intended to pay his respects to those English ducks in their own nests, but something had always happened to prevent, and it was now high time to make an end of them. So he finally got angry himself, and said to us: "Soldiers! You have been masters of all the capitals of Europe except Moscow, which is the ally of England. In order to conquer London, as well as the Indies, which belong to London, I find it necessary to go to Moscow."

Well, there assembled then the greatest army that ever tramped in gaiters over the world; and the Emperor had them so curiously well lined up that he reviewed a million men in a single day.

"*Hourra!*" shout the Russians. And there they were—those animals of Cossacks who are forever running away, and the whole Russian nation, all complete! It was country against country—a general mix-up, where everybody had to look out for himself. As the Red Man had said to Napoleon, "It's Asia against Europe."

"All right!" replied the Emperor, "I'll take care." And then came fawning on Napoleon all the kings of Europe,—Austria, Prussia, Bavaria, Saxony, Poland, Italy,—all flattering us and going along with us. It was splendid! The French eagles never cooed as they did on parade then, when they were held high above all the flags of Europe. The Poles couldn't contain themselves for joy, because the Emperor intended to set them up again as a nation—and for that reason the French and the Poles have been like brothers ever since.

"Russia shall be ours!" cried the army.

We crossed the frontier,—the whole lot of us,—and marched, and marched, and marched. No Russians! At last we found the rascals, camping on the bank of the Moscow River. That's where I got my cross; and I take leave to say that it was the damnedest of battles! Napoleon himself was worried, because the Red Man had appeared again and had said to him, "My son, you are going too fast; you will run short of men, and your friends will betray you." Thereupon the Emperor proposed peace; but before the treaty was signed he said to us, "Let's give those Russians a drubbing!"

"All right!" said the army.

"Forward!" shout the sergeants.

My clothes were going to pieces and my shoes were all worn out from tramping over the bad roads out there, but I said to myself, "Never mind; since this is the last of the rumpus, I'll make 'em give me a bellyful!"

337

We were drawn up near the edge of the great ravine—in the front seats! The signal was given, and seven hundred pieces of artillery began a conversation that was enough to bring the blood from your ears. Well, to do justice to one's enemies, I must admit that the Russians let themselves be killed like Frenchmen. They wouldn't give way, and we couldn't advance.

"Forward!" shouted our officers. "Here comes the Emperor!" And there he was, passing at a gallop, and motioning to us that it was very important to capture the redoubt. He put new life into us, and on we ran. I was the first to reach the ravine. Ah! *Mon Dieu!* How the colonels are falling, and the lieutenants, and the soldiers! But never mind! There'll be all the more shoes for those who haven't any, and epaulets for the ambitious fellows who know how to read.

At last the cry of "Victory!" rang all along the line; but—would you believe it?—there were twenty-five thousand Frenchmen lying on the ground! A trifle eh? Well, such a thing had never been seen before. It was a regular harvest field after the reaping; only instead of stalks of grain there were bodies of men. That sobered the rest of us. But the Emperor soon came along, and when we formed a circle around him, he praised us and cheered us up (he could be very amiable when he liked), and made us feel quite contented, even although we were as hungry as wolves. Then he distributed crosses of honour among us, saluted the dead, and said, "On to Moscow!"

"All right! To Moscow!" replied the army.

And then what did the Russians do but burn their city! It made a six-mile bonfire which blazed for two days. The buildings fell like slates, and there was a rain of melted iron and lead which was simply horrible! Indeed, that fire was the lightning from the dark cloud of our misfortunes. The Emperor said: "There's enough of this. If we stay here, none of my soldiers will ever get out." But we waited a little to cool off and to refresh our carcasses; because we were really played out. We carried away a golden cross that was on the Kremlin, and every soldier had a small fortune.

On our way back, winter came upon us, a month earlier than usual,—a thing that those stupid scientific men have never properly explained,—and the cold caught us. Then there was no more army; do you understand? No army, no generals, no sergeants even! After that it was a reign of misery and hunger—a reign where we were all equal. We thought of nothing except of seeing France again. Nobody stooped to pick up his gun, or his money, if he happened to drop them; and every one went straight on, arms at will, caring nothing for

338

glory. The weather was so bad that Napoleon could no longer see his star—the sky was hidden. Poor man! It made him sick at heart to see his eagles flying away from victory. It was a crushing blow to him.

Well, then came the Beresina. And now, my friends, I may say to you, on my honour and by everything sacred, that never,—no, never since man lived on earth—has there been such a mixed up hodgepodge of army, wagons, and artillery, in the midst of such snows, and under such a pitiless sky! It was so cold that if you touched the barrel of your gun you burned your hand.

It was there that Gondrin—who is now present with us—behaved so well. He is the only one now living of the pontooners who went down into the water that day and built the bridge on which we crossed the river. The Russians still had some respect for the Grand Army, on account of its past victories; but it was Gondrin and the pontooners who saved us, and [pointing at Gondrin, who was looking at him with the fixed attention peculiar to the deaf] Gondrin is a finished soldier and a soldier of honour, who is worthy of your highest esteem.

I saw the Emperor that day, standing motionless near the bridge, and never feeling the cold at all. Was that natural, do you think? He was watching the destruction of his treasure, his friends, his old Egyptian soldiers. It was the end of everything. Women, wagons, cannon—all were being destroyed, demolished, ruined, wrecked! A few of the bravest guarded the eagles; because the eagles, you understand, stood for France, for you, for the civil and military honour that had to be kept unstained and that was not to be humbled by the cold.

We hardly ever got warm except near the Emperor. When he was in danger, we all ran to him—although we were so nearly frozen that we would not have held out a hand to our dearest friend. They say that he used to weep at night over his poor family of soldiers. Nobody but he and Frenchmen could ever have pulled out of there. We did pull out, but it was with loss—terrible loss. Our allies ate up all of our provisions, and then began the treachery which the Red Man had foretold.

The blatherskites in Paris, who had kept quiet since the formation of the Imperial Guard, thought that the Guard had finally perished. So they got up a conspiracy and hoodwinked the Prefect of Police into an attempt to overthrow the Emperor. He heard of this and it worried him. When he left us he said: "Goodbye, boys. Guard the posts. I will come back to you."

After he had gone, things went from bad to worse. The generals lost their heads; and the marshals quarrelled with one another and did all sorts of foolish things, as was natural. Napoleon, who was good to everybody, had fed them on gold until they had become as fat as pigs, and they didn't want to do any more marching. This led to trouble, because many of them remained idle in forts behind the army that was driving us back to France, and didn't even try to relieve us by attacking the enemy in the rear.

The Emperor finally returned, bringing with him a lot of splendid recruits whom he had drilled into regular war-dogs, ready to set their teeth into anything. He brought also a bourgeois guard of honour, a fine troop, which melted away in battle like butter on a hot gridiron. In spite of the bold front that we put on, everything went against us; although the army performed feats of wonderful courage. Then came regular battles of mountains—nations against nations—at Dresden, Lützen, and Bautzen. Don't you ever forget that time, because it was then that Frenchmen showed how wonderfully heroic they could be. A good grenadier, in those days, seldom lasted more than six months. We always won, of course; but there in our rear were the English, stirring up the nations to take sides against us. But we fought our way through this pack of nations at last. Wherever Napoleon showed himself, we rushed; and whenever, on land or sea, he said, "I wish to pass," we passed.

We finally got back to France; and many a poor foot-soldier was braced up by the air of his native country, notwithstanding the hard times we had. As for myself, in particular, I may say that it renewed my life.

It then became a question of defending the fatherland—our fair France—against all Europe. They didn't like our laying down the law to the Russians, and our driving them back across their borders, so that they couldn't devour us, as is the custom of the North. Those Northern peoples are very greedy for the South, or at least that's what I've heard many generals say. Then Napoleon saw arrayed against him his own father-in-law, his friends whom he had made kings, and all the scoundrels whom he had put on thrones. Finally, in pursuance of orders from high quarters, even Frenchmen, and allies in our own ranks, turned against us; as at the battle of Leipsic. Common soldiers wouldn't have been mean enough to do that! Men who called themselves princes broke their word three times a day.

Well, then came the invasion. Wherever Napoleon showed his lion face the enemy retreated; and he worked more miracles in defending France than he had shown in conquering Italy, the East, Spain, Europe, and Russia. He wanted to bury all the invaders in France, and thus teach them to respect the country; so he let them come close to Paris, in order to swallow 'em all at a gulp and rise to the height of his genius in a battle greater than all the others—a regular mother of battles! But those cowardly Parisians were so afraid for their wretched skins and their miserable shops that they opened the gates of the city. Then the good times ended and the *ragusades* began. They fooled the Empress and hung white flags out of the palace windows. Finally the very generals whom Napoleon had taken for his best friends deserted him and went over to the Bourbons—of whom nobody had ever before heard. Then he bade us goodbye at Fontainebleau.

"Soldiers!"

I can hear him, even now. We were all crying like regular babies, and the eagles and flags were lowered as if at a funeral. And it was a funeral—the funeral of the Empire. His old soldiers, once so hale and spruce, were little more than skeletons. Standing on the portico of his palace, he said to us:

"Comrades! We have been beaten through treachery; but we shall all see one another again in heaven, the country of the brave. Protect my child, whom I entrust to you. Long live Napoleon II!"

Like Jesus Christ before his last agony, he believed himself deserted by God and his star; and in order that no one see him conquered, it was his intention to die; but, although he took poison enough to kill a whole regiment, it never hurt him at all—another proof, you see, that he was more than a man: he found himself immortal. As he felt sure of his business after that, and knew that he was to be Emperor always, he went to a certain island for a while, to study the natures of those people in Paris, who did not fail, of course, to do stupid things without end.

While he was standing guard down there, the Chinese and those animals on the coast of Africa—Moors and others, who are not at all easy to get along with—were so sure that he was something more than man that they respected his tent, and said that to touch it would be to offend God. So he reigned over the whole world, although those other fellows had sent him out of France.

Well, then, after a while he embarked again in the very same nutshell of a boat that he had left Egypt in, passed right under the bows of the English vessels, and set foot once more in France. France acknowledged him; the sacred cuckoo flew from spire to spire; and all the people cried, "Long live the Emperor!"

In this vicinity the enthusiasm for the Wonder of the Ages was most hearty. Dauphiny behaved well; and it pleased me particularly to know that our own people here wept for joy when they saw again his grey coat.

On the 1st of March Napoleon landed, with two hundred men, to conquer the kingdom of France and Navarre; and on the 20th of the same month that kingdom became the French Empire. On that day *the man* was in Paris. He had made a clean sweep—had re-conquered his dear France, and had brought all his old soldiers together again by saying only three words: "Here I am." It was the greatest miracle God had ever worked. Did ever a man, before him, take an empire by merely showing his hat? They thought that France was crushed, did they? Not a bit of it! At sight of the Eagle a national army sprang up, and we all marched to Waterloo. There the Guard perished, as if stricken down at a single blow. Napoleon, in despair, threw himself three times, at the head of his troops, on the enemy's cannon, without being able to find death. The battle was lost.

That evening the Emperor called his old soldiers together, and, on the field wet with our blood, burned his eagles and his flags. The poor eagles, who had always been victorious, who had cried "Forward!" in all our battles, and who had flown over all Europe, were saved from the disgrace of falling into the hands of their enemies. All the treasure of England couldn't buy the tail of one of them. They were no more!

The rest of the story is well known to everybody. The Red Man went over to the Bourbons, like the scoundrel that he is; France was crushed; and the old soldiers, who were no longer of any account, were deprived of their dues and sent back to their homes, in order that their places might be given to a lot of nobles who couldn't even march—it was pitiful to see them try! Then Napoleon was seized, through treachery, and the English nailed him to a rock, ten thousand feet above the earth, on a desert island in the great ocean. There he must stay until the Red Man, for the good of France, gives him back his power. It is said by some that he is dead. Oh, yes! Dead! That shows how little they know him! They only tell that lie to cheat the people and keep peace in their shanty of a government. The truth of the matter is that his friends have left him there in the desert to fulfil a prophecy that was made about him—for I have forgotten to tell you that the name Napoleon really means "Lion of the Desert."

This that I have told you is gospel truth; and all the other things that you hear about the Emperor are foolish stories with no human likeliness. Because, you see, God never gave to any other man born of woman the power to write his name in red across the whole world— and the world will remember him forever. Long live Napoleon, the father of the soldiers and the people!

THE JENA CAMPAIGN: 1806 *by F. N. Maude*—The Twin Battles of Jena & Auerstadt Between Napoleon's French and the Prussian Army.

PRIVATE O'NEIL *by Charles O'Neil*—The recollections of an Irish Rogue of H. M. 28th Regt.—The Slashers— during the Peninsula & Waterloo campaigns of the Napoleonic wars.

ROYAL HIGHLANDER *by James Anton*—A soldier of H.M 42nd (Royal) Highlanders during the Peninsular, South of France & Waterloo Campaigns of the Napoleonic Wars.

CAPTAIN BLAZE *by Elzéar Blaze*—Elzéar Blaze recounts his life and experiences in Napoleon's army in a well written, articulate and companionable style.

LEJEUNE VOLUME 1 *by Louis-François Lejeune*—The Napoleonic Wars through the Experiences of an Officer on Berthier's Staff.

LEJEUNE VOLUME 2 *by Louis-François Lejeune*—The Napoleonic Wars through the Experiences of an Officer on Berthier's Staff.

FUSILIER COOPER *by John S. Cooper*—Experiences in the 7th (Royal) Fusiliers During the Peninsular Campaign of the Napoleonic Wars and the American Campaign to New Orleans.

CAPTAIN COIGNET *by Jean-Roch Coignet*—A Soldier of Napoleon's Imperial Guard from the Italian Campaign to Russia and Waterloo.

FIGHTING NAPOLEON'S EMPIRE *by Joseph Anderson*—The Campaigns of a British Infantryman in Italy, Egypt, the Peninsular & the West Indies During the Napoleonic Wars.

CHASSEUR BARRES *by Jean-Baptiste Barres*—The experiences of a French Infantryman of the Imperial Guard at Austerlitz, Jena, Eylau, Friedland, in the Peninsular, Lutzen, Bautzen, Zinnwald and Hanau during the Napoleonic Wars.

MARINES TO 95TH (RIFLES) *by Thomas Fernyhough*—The military experiences of Robert Fernyhough during the Napoleonic Wars.

HUSSAR ROCCA *by Albert Jean Michel de Rocca*—A French cavalry officer's experiences of the Napoleonic Wars and his views on the Peninsular Campaigns against the Spanish, British And Guerilla Armies.

SERGEANT BOURGOGNE *by Adrien Bourgogne*—With Napoleon's Imperial Guard in the Russian Campaign and on the Retreat from Moscow 1812 - 13.

LEONAUR

ALSO FROM LEONAUR
AVAILABLE IN SOFTCOVER OR HARDCOVER WITH DUST JACKET

LIGHT BOB by *Robert Blakeney*—The experiences of a young officer in H.M 28th & 36th regiments of the British Infantry during the Peninsular Campaign of the Napoleonic Wars 1804 - 1814.

NAPOLEON'S RUSSIAN CAMPAIGN by *Philippe Henri de Segur*—The Invasion, Battles and Retreat by an Aide-de-Camp on the Emperor's Staff

SWORDS OF HONOUR by *Henry Newbolt & Stanley L. Wood*—The Careers of Six Outstanding Officers from the Napoleonic Wars, the Wars for India and the American Civil War. Illustrated.

HUSSAR IN WINTER by *Alexander Gordon*—A British Cavalry Officer during the retreat to Corunna in the Peninsular campaign of the Napoleonic Wars.

THE LIFE OF THE REAL BRIGADIER GERARD VOLUME 1 THE YOUNG HUSSAR 1782 - 1807 by *Jean-Baptiste De Marbot*—A French Cavalryman Of the Napoleonic Wars at Marengo, Austerlitz, Jena, Eylau & Friedland.

THE LIFE OF THE REAL BRIGADIER GERARD VOLUME 2 IMPERIAL AIDE-DE-CAMP 1807 - 1811 by *Jean-Baptiste De Marbot*—A French Cavalryman of the Napoleonic Wars at Saragossa, Landshut, Eckmuhl, Ratisbon, Aspern-Essling, Wagram, Busaco & Torres Vedras.

THE LIFE OF THE REAL BRIGADIER GERARD VOLUME 3 COLONEL OF CHASSEURS 1811 - 1815 by *Jean-Baptiste De Marbot*—A French Cavalryman in the retreat from Moscow, Lutzen, Bautzen, Katzbach, Leipzig, Hanau & Waterloo.

RIFLEMAN COSTELLO by *Edward Costello*—The adventures of a soldier of the 95th (Rifles) in the Peninsular & Waterloo Campaigns of the Napoleonic wars.

WITH THE LIGHT DIVISION by *John H. Cooke*—The Experiences of an Officer of the 43rd Light Infantry in the Peninsula and South of France During the Napoleonic Wars.

COLBORNE: A SINGULAR TALENT FOR WAR by *John Colborne*—The Napoleonic Wars Career of One of Wellington's Most Highly Valued Officers in Egypt, Holland, Italy, the Peninsula and at Waterloo.

A VOICE FROM WATERLOO by *Edward Cotton*—The Personal Experiences of a British Cavalryman Who Became a Battlefield Guide and Authority on the Campaign of 1815.

LEONAUR

ALSO FROM LEONAUR
AVAILABLE IN SOFTCOVER OR HARDCOVER WITH DUST JACKET

CAPTAIN OF THE 95th (Rifles) *by Jonathan Leach*—An officer of Wellington's Sharpshooters during the Peninsular, South of France and Waterloo Campaigns of the Napoleonic Wars.

BUGLER AND OFFICER OF THE RIFLES *by William Green & Harry Smith* With the 95th (Rifles) during the Peninsular & Waterloo Campaigns of the Napoleonic Wars

BAYONETS, BUGLES AND BONNETS *by James 'Thomas' Todd*—Experiences of hard soldiering with the 71st Foot - the Highland Light Infantry - through many battles of the Napoleonic wars including the Peninsular & Waterloo Campaigns

THE ADVENTURES OF A LIGHT DRAGOON *by George Farmer & G.R. Gleig*—A cavalryman during the Peninsular & Waterloo Campaigns, in captivity & at the siege of Bhurtpore, India

THE COMPLEAT RIFLEMAN HARRIS *by Benjamin Harris as told to & transcribed by Captain Henry Curling*—The adventures of a soldier of the 95th (Rifles) during the Peninsular Campaign of the Napoleonic Wars

WITH WELLINGTON'S LIGHT CAVALRY *by William Tomkinson*—The Experiences of an officer of the 16th Light Dragoons in the Peninsular and Waterloo campaigns of the Napoleonic Wars.

SURTEES OF THE RIFLES *by William Surtees*—A Soldier of the 95th (Rifles) in the Peninsular campaign of the Napoleonic Wars.

ENSIGN BELL IN THE PENINSULAR WAR *by George Bell*—The Experiences of a young British Soldier of the 34th Regiment 'The Cumberland Gentlemen' in the Napoleonic wars.

WITH THE LIGHT DIVISION *by John H. Cooke*—The Experiences of an Officer of the 43rd Light Infantry in the Peninsula and South of France During the Napoleonic Wars

NAPOLEON'S IMPERIAL GUARD: FROM MARENGO TO WATERLOO by *J. T. Headley*—This is the story of Napoleon's Imperial Guard from the bearskin caps of the grenadiers to the flamboyance of their mounted chasseurs, their principal characters and the men who commanded them.

BATTLES & SIEGES OF THE PENINSULAR WAR by *W. H. Fitchett*—Corunna, Busaco, Albuera, Ciudad Rodrigo, Badajos, Salamanca, San Sebastian & Others